JOSEPHINE COX

~

Lovers and Liars

HarperCollins*Publishers*

HarperCollins*Publishers*
77–85 Fulham Palace Road,
Hammersmith, London W6 8JB

www.harpercollins.co.uk

This paperback edition 2004

First published in Great Britain by
HarperCollins*Publishers* 2004

Typeset in New Baskerville by
Rowland Phototypesetting Ltd, Bury St Edmunds, Suffolk

Printed and bound in Great Britain by
Clays Ltd, St Ives plc

This book was written during a time in my life when I needed friends and family like never before, and thankfully you were there for me, as always.

Every day is difficult and I dare say it will be that way for a long time yet and maybe it will never get easier, but it is comforting to know that so many of you, my loyal friends and readers, have included Ken and me in your thoughts and prayers.

I want to thank my family from the bottom of my heart. Warm, wonderful people I am privileged to belong to, it would take a book to mention each and every one of you, but you know how very much I love you all, and always have. We're there for each other when it matters and, God willing, always will be. What would I do without you, eh?

Among the many old and new friends who were there for me, I include those at my present publishers, HarperCollins, and my previous publishers, Headline. And those of you at Gillon Aitken. Thank you so much for caring.

I want also to say how touched and moved I am

by all of the wonderful letters I have received from you, the readers. They arrived in their thousands, and though I have managed to answer most of them in order, I am still replying to a bundle every day.

My gratitude and thanks to every one of you. You have all helped me more than you could ever realise.

For those of you who write and tell me how you have not been fortunate enough to have the support of family in your time of need, please look on me as someone you can talk to, whenever you feel the need.

God bless. Take care,

Josephine

CONTENTS

Lovers and Liars

PART ONE

~

June, 1902

The Girl

CHAPTER ONE

IT WAS THE most glorious summer's day, but even as the sun warmed her face and the sound of birdsong thrilled her ears, Emily Ramsden's young heart trembled with fear as she hurried stealthily from the house.

He was in there. He must not suspect what she was up to, or her life would not be worth living.

Running across the yard, she was oblivious to the sharp mounds of dried mud and rough hoggin that sliced open the soles of her bare feet. She was desperate to get as far from the farmhouse as possible, away from prying eyes and into the upper reaches of the old hayloft. From there, she would know if anyone approached. He hasn't caught me yet, she thought defiantly. He won't catch me today, neither!

Something was about to happen, but as yet she didn't know what. All she had been told was, 'Be at the usual place, at the usual time, and there might be cause to celebrate.'

Excitement raced through her. She could hardly wait. In fact, she was far too early, so she had time enough to waste.

Overnight there had been a torrent of rain, still evident in the many puddles and flooded potholes along the walkways of Potts End Farm. Though the sun was already beginning to dry them up, there were still places where the squelchy earth pushed up and squeezed between her toes, creating long, thin sausages like her mammy made. It was uncomfortable and messy, but it didn't matter. She would run down to the brook later, and wash her feet in the fresh, cool water.

With that in mind, she happily gathered the hem of her long skirt and splashed her way through.

Yet in the midst of her excitement the fear was never far away. *He* was never far away.

Nearing the barn, she felt a deep sense of relief. Soon, she would be safe.

Safe! She groaned inwardly. Not so long ago she'd felt safe all the time. But ever since *he* had arrived, their lives had changed for the worse – until it seemed she and her mammy and dear old Grandad would never be safe again.

'I won't let him ruin everything!' the girl muttered to herself. 'Especially not today.' Her heart almost burst with pride at the thought of her lover. 'Today is *our* day . . . mine and John's.'

Yet even as she drew pleasure from the sights and

sounds around her, she had no way of knowing that this day would prove to be the worst day of her life.

~

Emily Ramsden was such a pretty little thing. Small and slim, with thick plaits of sun-kissed brown hair and warm, smiling eyes the colour of nutmeg, she had a loving nature and a gentle heart.

At only sixteen years of age, a girl trembling on the brink of womanhood, she worked as hard on the family farm as did any of the hired labour, and through her generosity and honest demeanour, she had earned the respect and affection of men and women alike.

Yet there was one man in particular who yearned for more than a friendly word or an innocent smile. This was a man without compassion or decency. Just lately, his avaricious eyes were following her every move, his cravings growing stronger every passing day.

Now, just as she reached the clearing in front of the barn, she heard the kitchen door being flung open. When his angry voice called out, her heart sank like a lead weight. How had he known? She had been as quiet as a mouse, and still he must have heard her leaving the house.

Quickly, before he could see her, she dodged behind the huge pile of newly-chopped logs, her heart beating so fast she was certain he must hear it. Whatever happened, he mustn't find her! These days, ever since he had rescued Potts End Farm financially, her Uncle Clem ruled their lives with an almost insane passion, and though it was against her nature, Emily had learned to hate him with that same passion.

'*Emily!*' his familiar voice boomed out. '*You'd best not be skiving again, or you'll feel the crack o' my belt across yer bare arse!*' In that same instant, Emily recognised the ominous whistle of his thin leather belt as it sliced through the air. She knew that sound as well as her own heartbeat, for all too often, she had felt the sting of his belt across the back of her legs.

Stealing into the barn, she softly closed the door and instantly felt more at ease in the twilight of that great dark place.

'YER BUGGER, WHERE ARE YER?' His voice shook with rage. 'WHAT THE DEVIL ARE YOU UP TO, YER LITTLE BITCH?'

Emily pressed herself against the cobwebby wall and, for what seemed an age, she hardly dared breathe. To comfort herself, she clutched the locket John had given her on her sixteenth birthday, and which she wore hidden beneath her pinafore. Within lay a lock of his hair. It was so romantic! She loved to feel that a part of him was so close to a part of her.

When, a moment later, the barn door inched open, she thought she would die of fright. *He was coming into the barn and there was no other way out!*

She almost laughed aloud when her mammy's voice called out, 'Clem! Clem, get back to the house. There's somebody here to see you.'

Outside, in the yard, Clem Jackson swung round to face the older woman, who was hurrying towards him. 'What the devil d'yer want?'

Aggie Ramsden was a weathered version of Emily, but with blue eyes and a tiredness about her that told its own tale.

The likeness to her daughter was uncanny, for she had the same confident way of standing, the small, straight nose, full mouth, and that peculiar air of defiance in the face of hardship. Taller than Emily, she had a slight stoop at the shoulders, and though she was only in her thirty-fourth year, her long, dark brown hair was already streaked with grey. Tied tightly back, it made her look severe, when in fact she was a kindly soul at heart.

'Didn't you hear what I said?' she repeated. 'There's somebody to see you.'

'What?' His mind was still on the girl. 'Yon Emily's gone missing again, the little besom!'

'Oh, for God's sake, why don't you leave the lass alone?' Weariness marbled her voice.

'And why don't *you* bugger off.' There was the sound of that belt again, threatening, vicious – like himself. With the toe of his heavy work boot, he lashed out at the barn door, which slammed shut. 'What d'yer mean by fetching me from my work, woman!'

'Hmh! You should be glad I took the trouble,' Aggie retaliated. 'I've left my own work to come and find you. Besides, you wouldn't have been pleased if I'd sent him away without telling you.'

For what seemed an age, he regarded her through daggers of resentment. He recalled how his sister had once been a real beauty, but that was a long time ago. 'I thought I told you to bugger off.'

'An' I told *you* . . . there's somebody as wants to see you.' Her voice was flat and uncaring. Her spirit seemed broken, when before it was bright and alive.

'Aye well, happen I don't want to see *them,* 'ave yer thought o' *that*?'

'I don't get paid to think. I'm just passing on a message, and I've got better things to do than run errands on your account.'

'You'd best watch yer tongue, woman! Anyway, what are all these "things" yer 'ave to do? You're two o' the bloody same, you and your skiving daughter . . . allus trying to dodge whatever work comes along.'

'We both do our share and well you know it.'

'Not so's you'd bloody notice!'

He had a way of sneering that fired her anger like nothing else, but after six months of his tyrannical rule, she had learned to keep her anger under control, or suffer the consequences.

Yet now, when he belittled Emily's role in the running of this small farm, she had to put him right. 'My lass works hard and long on this place. She puts in as much time as anybody else and gets no thanks for it neither! As for me, I tend to the house and them as live in it, including yourself. On top of that, I do what I can when I'm needed outside. In fact, me and my lass are *both* capable of turning our hands to anything. *And* we do. Which is more than I can say for some.'

His features hardened. 'An' what the devil is *that* supposed to mean?'

'It means whatever you want it to mean.' Pride and anger swelled her voice. 'Since we lost her daddy, me and my lass have worked as a team. And I don't mind saying . . . we're a damned good team at that!'

Laughing, he mimicked her words. 'Yer didn't "lose" her daddy. He just ran off, like the coward he was!'

Returning his probing stare she observed the red leathery face and small, milky-grey eyes. Clem Jackson was a bully of the worst kind, as big and evil as the bulls he had thought to breed here on the farm. Though he was her own brother, Aggie had never really liked him. In fact, he had never been like a brother to her, and never would be.

What was more, she wouldn't want it. All she wanted was for him to be gone from this place and leave them in peace.

'Michael Ramsden is no coward!' she said hotly.

'Well, o' course *you'd* say that, but you'd be wrong, 'cause he's a coward all right, he's yeller through and through.'

Drawing herself to her full height, Aggie momentarily lost her fear of him. 'Mark my words, Clem Jackson, Michael will be back, and when he is, you'll be gone from here like a cat with a scalded tail. What! You'll be sent down the road so fast you won't have time to look back!'

Leaning forward she dared to taunt him. 'I can tell you one thing an' all,' she said. 'I for one won't be sorry, and neither will the lass.'

'You'd best watch yer tongue,' he cautioned her, trembling with rage. 'You know what happened the last time yer 'ad the gall to stand up to me!'

She remembered all right, and her courage wavered. 'I just want you to know that my man is no coward.'

'Rubbish! What kinda husband and father runs off an' leaves his family to the wolves?'

'I already told you – he had a breakdown of sorts. We'd had a real hard winter.' She remembered it only too well. 'It came on suddenly and with such a fierceness there was little could be done in time. The sheep froze on the hillside before we could get them to shelter. And if that weren't enough to contend with, the summer before had been a drought. We suffered our worst-ever crop when we could least afford it.'

Clem burst out, 'His old man had handed the farm to him on a plate – but that weren't good enough, were it? Oh no. He were a farmer, for Gawd's sake! He were allus carping on about what a hard life it were – so why didn't he either learn to take it in his stride, or give it up altogether? I'll tell yer why: it's 'cause he were too much of a coward to leave, an' too damned useless to stay.'

'You know that's not true.' His sister's anger faded beneath a measure of sadness. 'Like his dad afore him, he gave his life to the land. It's just that everything came at once . . . one bad thing after another. Like a nightmare, it was.'

She swallowed the emotion that threatened to overwhelm her. 'His poor mother was tekken by the consumption, and you know what happened after that.' At the time it had seemed as though the nightmare would never end. 'It were the last straw,' she recalled. 'It were *that* which pushed him over the edge.'

Clem stared at her downturned face and sorry eyes, and said without pity, 'Lost yer babby, too, didn't yer, eh?'

Seeing as how he was angling for a fight, his sister remained silent, but still he goaded her. 'Two week early and not enough strength to kick itself out, eh? Well, if it were *that* much of a weakling – just like its father – happen it were best it didn't survive. I mean, what use is a puny little thing like that? It would be no good at all on a farm, would it, eh? And when all's said an' done, the old woman were nowt but a nuisance. Huh! If yer ask me, yer were well shut o' the pair of 'em!'

When at his spiteful jibe she lifted her hand to strike him, he grabbed her fist, raised it high in the air and held it there, in an iron-tight grasp that had her wincing with pain.

'You're treading on dangerous ground, lady!' His jowls trembled with rage. 'I can see I'll have to teach yer a lesson or two afore you know yer place in the scheme o' things!'

Suddenly, as was his unpredictable way, he was smiling again, his feigned sigh ending in a soft, cruel laugh. 'Oh, I know all about that lad as yer lost . . . "born two week early an' hardly drew a single breath". I know it all, word for bloody word! Christ! I've been told about it so many times by that daft old bugger inside, it's beginning to turn my guts over. I swear, if he tells me once more, I might wrap my hand round his scraggy old throat and squeeze the life out of him.'

'You'll not lay a hand on him!' Now she would not be silenced. 'Thomas Isaac is a sick old man. Touch him and you'll have me to deal with!'

Chuckling like a maniac, he entreated her, 'Just listen to yersel'.' He cackled. 'By! You'll 'ave me shivering in me shoes next.' He touched her on the shoulder, not surprised when she shrank from him. 'Oh, you'd rather be touched by that cowardly husband o' yourn, is that it?'

Without replying, she turned away, but he came after her, laughing and taunting, driving her crazy. 'Oh, I forgot! You don't like me calling him a coward, do yer, eh? But that's what he is, all right. A shameful bloody coward! He cleared off an' left yer to face it all on yer own. An' yet you still have feelings for him. Mind, if I were you, I'd be praying he never again sets foot in Salmesbury again, never mind on this land. Or if he did, I'd be waiting for him with a loaded shotgun an' no mistake.'

She shook her head. 'Well, thank God you're not me. The truth is, I pray every night for Michael to come home, and when he does, I'll be waiting for him with open arms.'

'Then yer a bigger fool than I took yer for!'

She merely shrugged her shoulders. 'Like I said, it was one thing after another. When his mammy was took ill, he was already battling with debt. Then what with the babby an' all . . . It was just too much. We'd waited all those years for a brother or sister for our Emily.' Tears filled her eyes. 'Michael fell to pieces – as any man might have done in the same circumstances.'

'Not *me*!' he said boastfully. 'I'm not the kinda man to turn tail and run.'

'That's because life has never tried you hard enough.'

This time he grabbed her by the hair, making her cry out. 'What are you saying . . . bitch!'

She looked at him with a measure of pity that turned his insides over. 'Hurt me if you like, Clem, but I won't have it that my Michael is a coward.'

'Hmh! Then like I say, yer a bigger bloody fool than I took yer for.' Thrusting her aside, he sneered: 'All the same, it's as well I were on hand to help you out with a bob or two, or you'd have lost this place – and serve yer bloody well right!'

Having gone to him cap in hand was her greatest regret. 'If I could turn back the clock, I would never have come to you,' she informed him quietly.

'Well, yer did. An' it were me as paid off all the debts, an' never you forget that.' Spitting on the ground he reminded her, 'With the old fella too useless to put one foot afore the other, an' folks knocking at your door for their money or your blood, you were in a sorry mess. All yer need to remember is that your husband left *me* to pick up the pieces, and that's what I did. An' for that, yer should be grateful, you *and* that daughter o' yourn!'

At his words, Emily shivered behind the barn door.

Surveying the land about him, Clem grinned with satisfaction. 'I've saved all o' this, and now it's as good as mine! Matter o' fact, if I wanted, I could throw the three of youse out on the streets right now.' He took a step forward, his eyes glaring, his face contorted in triumph. 'I might even do that!' he threatened. 'Yes, happen I'd be better off getting rid of the bloody lot o' you. There's allus cheap labour about to help me run this place.' He gave her a push. 'Go on. Get outta my sight!'

As she turned to leave, she thought it time to remind him of something he appeared to have forgotten. 'This farm isn't yours, and it never will be.'

'It might be . . . if I decide to call in what's owed me.'

'I already told you: somehow or another we'll pay you back. It's just a matter of time.'

'Aye well, time and tide waits for no man, an' I'll not wait for ever to collect my money.' Taking a long, laborious breath he finished, 'Until I get back what I've paid out, with profit, this farm is as good as mine – an' as far as I'm concerned, that mcks mc thc mastcr round 'crc.'

'Enjoy it then, while you can,' she retorted, 'because I mean to pay you back at the first opportunity, and I will, or my name's not Aggie Ramsden.'

'Give it up, woman. Yer a dreamer.' Though he didn't much care for the look in her eyes nor the determination in her voice. However, he had the upper hand at the moment and there was nothing she could do. He knew it and she knew it, however defiant she might pretend to be.

'You've not a brass farthing to yer name, none

of yer! It's *my* money as keeps this place up and running. If I took a mind to move on, you'd sink without trace.' For good measure, he gave her a vicious dig in the ribs that made her gasp with surprise and pain. 'Like it or not, yer all dancing to my tune. It might serve yer well to keep that in mind.'

She didn't argue. But she looked at him ... *looked through him* ... wishing with all her heart that it might have been different.

He could almost read her thoughts. 'You want me gone from 'ere so bad yer can taste it, can't yer?' he muttered curiously.

When she gave no answer, he took great pleasure in informing her: 'Well, yer can want on, 'cause I'll not be going nowhere!' He smiled, a nasty little smile she had come to know only too well. 'I mean, a man would be mad to leave such a nice, cosy set-up, wouldn't he, eh?'

She looked at him for what seemed an age, during which his smile faded and a look of hardness fired his eyes. 'Got summat else to say, 'ave yer ... sister dear?'

To his consternation, she continued to observe him, wondering how this man who seemed like a stranger to her could ever have been her kith and kin. 'I'd best go.' She turned from him.

'Oh, aye, that's right!' his taunting voice followed her. 'You'd best hurry away to tend to them "things" you reckon are so pressing!'

His laughter grated on her, but she wasn't about to rise to any more of his taunts. Too often she had experienced his rage at first-hand, and she knew only too well what monstrous things he was capable of.

Then there was the other, shocking thing. He hadn't mentioned it yet, but he would. When it suited his purpose.

If only she could get rid of him once and for all, she wouldn't even hesitate. But there was no way that she could see. At least, not without her being hanged for it.

His voice shattered her thoughts. 'Who is it then?'

'What!' Startled, she looked up.

'Wake up, woman! Yer said there were somebody to see me. Who is it?'

'You'll know when you get there, won't you?'

With that she flounced off, leaving him cursing and grumbling as he stomped back to the farmhouse. 'Bloody women!' He spat on the ground in disgust. 'The lot of 'em want shooting.'

～

Through the crack in the barn wall, Emily saw them leave; first her mammy, then him, that great bulk of a man, striding along as though he owned the place. 'Good riddance to you!' she muttered, though her face shone with love as she followed the homely figure of her dear mammy. Her heart ached. Given the chance, she would do anything to protect her.

When at last they were gone, the girl breathed a sigh of relief. So as to not trip over it, she gathered up the hem of her long skirt, and went at a run towards the ladder at the far end of the barn.

Unable to trust him, she frequently glanced back.

When Clem first arrived, after her daddy deserted them, she had tried hard to like him, for her mother's sake. But she couldn't. He was not the sort of man you could take to, and how he came to be her mother's brother she would never know, for Aggie was a kind, gentle soul – though she did have a fierce temper when put out.

Clambering up the ladder, Emily pulled herself into the hayloft and made for the far corner. Here, she reached up on tiptoe, her arm stretching into the roof, where the two great wooden rafters joined together. The small brown notebook clutched tightly to her chest, soon she was seated cross-legged in the hay, her eyes closed and her heart beating fast with excitement.

In her mind's eye she could see every word written there, all her secret thoughts: the sorrow she had suffered when her Granny Clare had sickened from consumption and died, nearly breaking her grandad's heart; the wrenching sobs she and her family had wept at the tragic loss of her darling baby brother. Some tears trickled down her rosy cheeks as she remembered little Michael, so pale and still, wrapped in her own baby shawl that couldn't warm him ... Then her tears dried as bitter resentment took their place – hatred for the man who soon after had invaded their lives. She had written about her love for her mammy, and her grandad, and prayed for her daddy, wherever he was.

In fact, all her life as it was, had been entered in the pages of that little book.

More recently she had confided of her growing love for John; of her hopes for the future, and even a little prayer that Clem would go away and everything would be all right again, just like it used to be.

After a while, she laid the notebook on her lap and gingerly eased it open. She needed to reread the last entry – to make sure she had not been dreaming.

Suddenly, a small, shuffling sound startled her. What was that!

With fear licking at her insides, she laid the book face down and shrank into the background. Was there somebody else here? she thought worriedly. Did someone come in just now?

A ray of early-morning sunshine crept in from the one window high up in the barn, and shone down on the page. A gentle wind blew against the old barn-walls, which creaked and groaned as if alive. And she heard the faint splash of a coal-barge wending its way along the nearby canal.

She glanced about, satisfying herself that there was no one there. 'You're beginning to imagine things,' she told herself, but then was it any wonder, if her nerves were on edge?

Pushing aside her two plaits, Emily roved her gaze over the previous day's entry and began to read it aloud.

CHAPTER TWO

INSIDE THE FARMHOUSE, Thomas Isaac Ramsden waited for his daughter-in-law. He heard her come in through the back door, then a few minutes later he was relieved to see her enter the living room. 'Here you are then, Dad.' Aggie set the tray down on his lap. 'There's a nice cuppa tea in your favourite mug, and one of my raisin biscuits. You sit and enjoy that, while I go an' hang out the washing.'

While she spoke she smiled down on him, the love shining in her blue eyes. 'Later on, we'll go for a gentle walk if you like?' she offered. 'It's a beautiful day outside. The fresh air will do us both good.'

He nodded. 'I can't go far, lass,' he reminded her. 'Me old legs aren't what they used to be.' He carefully lifted his Coronation mug, which showed the new King, Edward VII, in his full-bearded glory, and took a grateful sup of the hot brew.

'It's all right, Dad,' Aggie said. 'We'll just go as far as the orchard and back.'

He nodded appreciatively. 'Happen once we're there we can sit awhile on the bench.' He took another long slurp of his tea.

'That'll be nice,' she agreed. 'Let's do that then, shall we?'

'Happen I can smoke me pipe?'

She smiled. 'You allus do. To tell you the truth, Dad, I'll be glad of a sit-down.' She gave a low sigh. 'Whatever we turn our hand to, me and Emily allus seem to be in a rush these days. There's too much work, and not enough time to get it all done.' Not so long ago, life had been so much easier, she thought. Her husband had still been here, and their new baby was growing in her womb. Potts End had been a joyful place then.

Lost in his own thoughts, Thomas merely nodded. 'Where *is* Emily?'

'Gone off by herself somewheres. You know what the lass is like – up at first light to do her chores, then away across the fields.'

'She'll be back though, won't she?' His eyes dimmed over. 'She *will* be back?'

'O' course she will. Whatever meks you say a thing like that?'

'Michael never came back, did he?' He paused, then: 'I miss him.'

'We all miss him, Dad.' Aggie's voice dropped to a whisper. 'But he'll be back.'

Cupping his ear, he asked worriedly, 'What's that you say, lass?'

She gave him her cheeriest smile. 'I said . . . *Michael will be back.* You'll see . . . some bright day, in the not too distant future, he'll walk through that door and we'll all be together again.'

On her words he looked up and smiled. It was a sad smile. Though he didn't want to dash her hopes, he believed there was little chance of his son ever coming home. His heart ached for Clare, and he lifted the mug to his lips again.

Aggie read his thoughts and a pang of loneliness stabbed her heart. 'Will you be all right if I go outside now?' she asked.

'O' course I will.' He looked surprised. 'I'm not in me second childhood yet, you know!'

She laughed at that. 'Don't I know it!' Humouring him, she wagged a finger. 'By! I've yet to see the day when anybody can get one over on you!'

The old man pointed to his half-eaten biscuit. 'I don't suppose there's another one o' them going, is there? Or mebbe even a couple?'

Prompted by an impulse of affection, she kissed the top of his head. 'Oh, I dare say there might be a couple more hiding in the larder.'

He gave her a little push. 'Go on then!' He grinned, a wide, uplifting grin that showed his surprisingly even teeth, of which he was very proud. 'A poor old man could starve afore he got any attention round 'ere.'

'Give over!' She feigned shock. 'You get more attention than anybody and well you know it, you old devil.'

'Mebbe. But it's another biscuit I'm wanting . . . that's if you've a mind to fetch me one?'

Straightening up, she sighed, 'If it's a biscuit you're wanting, then it's a biscuit you'll get.' With that she marched off, only to pause at the door and look back on him.

Her heart was full to overflowing as she took stock of that dear old man, his head bent as he lost himself in private thoughts of days gone by. She and her father-in-law had a special kind of relationship, and she was grateful to have him in her life.

Thomas Isaac had no idea she was taking stock of him. He was thinking of his home and his life, and his heart was warmed. Once a big strong farm-hand, he had worked his way up, and put money by, until one proud day, he could buy his own little farm. Potts End wasn't big by anyone else's standards, but it had been his, lock, stock and barrel, until he had signed it over to Michael and Aggie, and he had good reason to be proud of his achievement. Nowadays, he was too old and tired to pick up a spade, but there were other con-solations in life, such as the smell of dew on the morning air, the special excitements of haymaking and harvest, and the sun coming up over the hills. And most of all, the sight of Emily running towards the cottage after one of her long ramblings. Although he missed his wife, Clare, a bonny lass until the consumption took her, he thanked God he had these two wonderful women in his life, Aggie and Emily, for they meant the whole world to him.

He thought back on his youth and smiled inwardly. He'd been a bit of a lad in his day, but had few regrets – except o' course, it would be good to roll up his sleeves and bend his back to his work, but it wasn't to be.

From the doorway, Aggie's thoughts were much the same. She had known Thomas Isaac as a big strong man, and had seen his body become frail and slow. But though his strength was broken, his spirit was not. He still had an eye for the women and a sprightly story to tell. He had a good head of iron-grey hair, and the pale eyes carried a sparkle that could light up a room when he turned on the charm.

Lately though, since all their trials and tribulations, the sparkle had grown dim.

Like her daughter, Aggie cherished the ground the old fella walked on.

'Are you still there?' Looking up, he caught her observing him. 'I'm still waiting on that biscuit.'

'Coming right up, Dad,' she promised, and hurried away.

Behind her the old man leaned back in his chair and shook his head. 'You've a lot to answer for, son,' he murmured. 'When you took off, you left a pack o' trouble for these lovely lasses, and no mistake!'

Through the scullery window Aggie saw her brother, Clem, and her heart sank. He was emerging from the outhouse, his huge black dog, Badger, skulking at his side; there was a look of murder on his face, and a shotgun slung over his shoulder. God Almighty, what was he up to now?

She went into the larder and, taking half a dozen biscuits from the tin, she placed them on a saucer and carried them in to the old man. 'If you want any more, just give me a shout,' she told him.

Instead of acknowledging the biscuits, Thomas jolted her by declaring in a worried voice, 'There's bound to be trouble, mark my words.'

She stooped to answer, her voice low but clear. 'Why should there be trouble?'

He pointed to the window, where a young man could be seen pacing back and forth. 'That's young John Hanley, ain't it?'

Following his gaze, she too saw John pacing back and forth, growing increasingly agitated. 'He's waiting to speak with Clem,' she informed the old fella. 'I've just been to fetch him.'

'What does the lad want wi' that surly bugger?'

She also had been a little curious when John turned up at the doorstep earlier. 'He wouldn't say,' she shrugged. 'Happen he's after more work.

He's already finished that job our Michael started him on.' She gave a cheeky wink. 'He's done a grand job an' all. After eight months o' breaking his back, he's made both them wagons as good as new ... they're completely rebuilt from the bottom up, so they are. The hay-trailer is stronger than ever, the ladders are safe to climb since he replaced all the rotting rungs, and he's repaired so much o' the fencing.' She paused, before going on quietly, 'All the jobs Michael would have done, if only he'd been himself.'

'Well, young John seems to know what he's doing.' The old fella's feelings were too raw to get caught up in that kind of discussion. 'The lad may not be the fastest worker in the world but, by God, he's thorough – I'll not deny that.'

'Yes, but all those smaller jobs are finished now,' Aggie said. 'And I dare say he'll be keen to get started on the old barn, just like Michael planned. It'll be a secure job for him as well.' She peered out of the window towards the dilapidated barn. 'By! There has to be at least a year's work there. Aye, that's what he'll be after, right enough ... a steady run o' work right through to next spring.'

'Look, lass, yer mustn't forget who's holding the purse-strings,' the old fella cautioned. 'That miserable brother o' yourn won't part with a penny more than he has to. I mean, he only paid the lad for all his work 'cause he'd only just got here and wanted to mek a suitable impression.'

Aggie knew that but, 'It won't matter either way, if he doesn't have John back to repair the barn,' she remarked warily. 'I imagine the lad can get work wherever he wants.' She knew he had a good reputation. 'They say as how he can turn a hand to anything.'

Thomas Isaac looked up. 'Between you an' me, lass, I reckon young John is after summat other than work.'

'What's on your mind then?'

He frowned. 'If yer ask me, there's summat going on,' he ventured knowingly.

'Oh? And what might *that* be then?'

He looked her in the eye. 'Yer know very well,' he tutted.

And it was true – she did. These past weeks she had been meaning to speak with Emily about the growing friendship between her and John, only work had got in the way. 'You're not to worry,' she told the old fella. 'Our Emily's a sensible lass.'

'She's missing her da.'

'What's that got to do with it?' Fear, and a measure of anger rippled through her. 'We're *all* missing him. It doesn't mean to say we'll throw caution to the winds.'

'Emily's just a lass. She'll be looking for someone to talk to . . . someone near her own age.'

'I know that, Dad, and I'm sure that's all the two of 'em will be doing – talking to each other. They're just friends, after all.'

He took a deep breath. 'Happen!' That was all he had to say on the matter. But he could *think*, and what he thought was this: there was trouble brewing. He could feel it in his tired old bones.

~

Outside, Clem rounded the farmhouse and, coming face to face with the young man, demanded to know his business.

Though needfully respectful, John Hanley was not afraid of this bully. It showed in his confident stance, and in the way he spoke, quietly determined. 'I came to have a talk with you, sir,' he replied, 'if you could spare me a few minutes?'

'Oh! So you've come to 'ave a talk with me, 'ave yer?' The older man regarded the other with derision, and a certain amount of envy. He saw the lean, strong frame of this capable young man, and he was reminded of his own shortcomings. The eyes, too, seemed to hold a man whether he wanted to look into them or not; deepest blue and fired with confidence, they were mesmerising.

'It won't take long, sir.' While Clem took stock of him, John did the same of the older man.

He had no liking for Clem Jackson. Nor did he respect him, but he owed this bully a certain address, for it was Clem Jackson who appeared to have taken charge of things round here, including Emily. And it was Emily he had come about this morning.

Stamping his two feet, the older man impatiently shifted himself. 'Get on with it then, damn yer!' he instructed roughly. 'Spit it out! I'm a busy man. I've no time to wait on such as you!'

Taking a deep breath, John said, 'I've come to ask if you will allow me and Emily to walk out together?'

'*Yer what!*' Growing redder in the face, Clem screamed at him, 'Yer devious little bastard! You'd best get from my front door, afore I blow you to bloody Kingdom Come!' Beside him, Badger's hackles were raised, and he growled low in his throat.

Raising the shotgun, Clem aimed it at John's throat, his one eye trained down the barrel and his finger trembling on the trigger. 'I'll count to ten, and if yer not well away by then, yer'll not be leaving on yer own two feet, I can promise yer *that*!'

With his heart beating fifteen to the dozen, John stood his ground. 'We're just friends, sir,' he said quietly. 'There's nothing untoward between us. Only, I am very fond of her, and I know she's fond of me, because she's said so. But it's all right and proper, sir. I respect Emily too much to harm her in any way.'

At any minute, this madman might pull the trigger, or that hound might fly at his throat, but John felt compelled to say his piece. He and Emily had these strong feelings: in truth, they were growing to love each other in a way that only a man and woman could love. Now, it was time to put it all on a proper footing.

'All we want is for the two of us to spend more time together ... out in the open, without any shame.'

Oh dear Lord. John knew he was saying all the right things, only they seemed to be coming out all wrong. 'Look, sir, I didn't come here to cause trouble, and you mustn't blame Emily. She doesn't even know I'm here. I just wanted us to be together and not to be hiding like we do. And for that, we need your permission.' He paused, at a loss. 'I hope you'll consider what I'm saying?'

He had been expecting the shotgun to ring out any minute. Instead it was suddenly swung high in the air and when it came down on his temple, he hardly felt the pain, although he stumbled backwards and fell down – and felt the wet, sticky blood trickling across his face.

As he crumpled to the ground, he received a second blow. Time and again the heavy butt of the shotgun rained down, dulling his senses and his thinking, until he knew that if he didn't get up now, he would never get up again. But each time he made the effort, he was knocked back by another blow, or a kick of the older man's heavy boot. Somewhere in his distant mind he could hear Jackson yelling obscenities, but the voice came from so far away, and his every bone jolted with the force of the beating.

Inside the farmhouse, Aggie had seen what was happening, and she ran to the door. As she flung it open, she saw with horror how John had scrambled back on his feet and was launching himself at Clem, his eyes blinded by the blood that was pouring down his head and face. 'NO!' Careering forward she tried to come between the two men but was driven back. 'Stay out of it!' she was told. 'Unless you want some an' all?'

But Aggie would not be stopped. Throwing herself between them, she screamed: 'Leave him be! For God's sake, Clem . . . you're killing the lad!'

'Out – of – my – way!' With one mighty shove, Clem sent her sprawling to the ground. In a minute she was on her knees, her two arms round the young man, and her face upturned.

'Kill him, and you'll have to kill me too,' she said, her eyes filled with hatred.

His answer was to reach out and drag her away, but she crawled back, fiercely protecting John with her own body. 'I mean it, Clem. I won't let you do it.'

'I'll do what I see fit. Get outta the bloody way!'

'*NO!*' She tried appealing to any sense of decency he might still have. 'He's just a boy!' she cried. 'Shame on you, hitting him with your gun . . . that's a coward's way!'

When at that moment John tried feebly to get

up, she pressed the full weight of her body against his. 'No!' she hissed. 'Stay down, John. *Please!* Stay down!' She knew if he got up, it might be the last thing he ever did.

Eager to finish what he had started, Clem took a step forward. 'LET HIM UP!' Suddenly the muzzle of the shotgun was jammed into her side. 'Let him up, or I swear to God I'll finish the pair of you!'

'No!' Aggie knew, from the mad look in his eyes, that he meant every word. And still she wouldn't budge. At the back of her mind she hoped and prayed that somewhere in that warped mind, he had a shred of compassion.

Instead he gave her a vicious kick that sent her flying. She coiled up, whimpering from the pain.

Enraged, John struggled to his feet and, staggering towards the older man, managed to send him backwards, but he was weak and hurt, and it was only a matter of seconds before he himself was at the receiving end again. Bloodied and dazed by the punishment he had taken, he found himself sprawled on the ground, with the shotgun pushed tight against his throat. 'Yer pack a sizeable punch, an' yer a hard man to put down, I'll give yer that!' Clem grudgingly admitted. 'But it'll do yer no good.'

Puffing and panting from John's determined attack, he gave a harsh, mocking laugh. 'Happen I shoulda took yer on, man to man. But I ain't got time for all that. Not when it's so much easier just to pull the trigger.'

The deadly click of the trigger-hammer being drawn back echoed against Aggie's scream. 'NO, CLEM . . . FOR PITY'S SAKE, NO!'

They didn't see the old man as he sneaked out of the house. It was only when he was directly behind Clem that Aggie spotted him and her heart fell. Dear God! If Clem turned, her father-in-law wouldn't stand a chance.

Thankfully, Clem was far too intent on training his eye on John, so that when he did hear a movement behind him and felt the cold sharp end of the shotgun thrust into his neck, it was too late. 'You ain't the only one who knows how to use one o' these!' Thomas Isaac chuckled. 'I expect you thought I were too old and past it to shift outta my rocking-chair?'

Shocked and frightened, Clem began to plead. 'Now then, Grandad, don't do anything silly. Put the gun down.'

But the old fella had no intention of doing that, as he told Clem in no uncertain terms. 'I can't see yer hammer that young man into the ground, without doing summat about it.' He slowly raised the shotgun, until it was level with Clem's forehead. 'Happen I should just blow yer ugly 'ead off, right now.'

Fearing for his life, Clem stretched his arms up. 'All right, all right! What d'yer want from me?'

'I want you to leave the lad alone!'

Searching for a way out of a bad situation, Clem appealed to him. 'Open yer eyes, man! Can't yer see the young scoundrel's got a yearning for the girl? That's what he's 'ere for . . . to ask if the pair of 'em can couple up. Is that what yer want for yer granddaughter . . . to be tekken advantage of by this young thug?'

Thomas pursed his lips in thought. 'I don't reckon John has any such thing in mind, but even if 'e *did* want to see our Emily, then I'd say that was for her mammy to deal with, wouldn't yer agree?'

'If yer say so.' It galled him to kow-tow to the old man.

'I *do* say so.' Thomas saw how Aggie was helping John to his feet. 'Ain't that right, Aggie, lass?' he asked pointedly. 'Anything to do with our Emily is first and foremost *your* business?'

She nodded. 'Leave it now, Dad. It's all right.' She feared he might well have taken on more than he could handle. 'I'm sure Clem knows the score, now you've spelled it out.'

She considered asking him to go back inside but it would have been of no use. From somewhere – she didn't know where – her father-in-law had gathered enough strength and courage to come out and fight for his loved ones – and what right had she to interfere? No right at all, she decided, with a little burst of pride.

All the same, just now she had seen Clem eyeing the old fella with a cunning look on his face. And it worried her. One way or another, she needed to get them all back inside and out of harm's way. 'Come on now, Dad,' she urged. 'Give me a hand to get John inside, will you?'

Unfortunately her little ploy came too late, for just then, while her father-in-law was observing young John's sorry plight, Clem made a sudden move that took everyone by surprise. With the cry of a madman, he lunged forward to wrench the shotgun out of the old fella's hands. 'Yer never learn, do yer?' he snarled. 'I should empty this barrel into yer dozy skull.'

Proud and defiant, the old man looked him in the eye. 'You don't frighten me,' he declared. 'I've had more experience of bullies in my life than you'll ever know, and they're allus brought down, somehow or another.'

Clem laughed aloud at his show of defiance. 'Hmh! So, yer reckon you can bring me down, do yer?' With a poke of his finger in Thomas's bony ribs he jeered, 'An' how do yer plan to do that, might I ask?'

The old farmer shook his head. 'I don't know yet,' he answered, 'but I'll find a way in time. Right now, you've got the upper hand – but it won't allus be like that.'

'Really?' Leaning forward with his face almost touching that of the old fella's, the younger man demanded, 'Got some money tucked away, 'ave yer? Managc without me, can yer?'

'I wish to Gawd I had got money behind me!' the old man replied harshly. 'You'd soon be on yer way, an' no mistake!'

Clem merely laughed. 'All show and gab, that's what you are. Go on! Get outta my road!' With a hefty push he sent Thomas Isaac toppling backwards, into the wall. 'As for you . . . !' Grabbing Aggie by the arm, he wrenched it up behind her back, making her almost faint with the pain.

Blood pouring from his wounds, the injured youth took a step forward as if to go for Clem yet again. 'Take your hands off her!' His mouth was so swollen he could hardly spit out the words.

'Or what?' Clem jabbed at him with the shotgun. 'Look at yer!' he jibed. 'By! Yer can hardly bloody stand.'

'I can stand up to you any day.' Squaring up, John clenched his fists. 'Come on. I'm ready when you are!'

'I would stop while the going's good,' Clem warned him angrily. 'I haven't got time for games.' Turning his attention to Aggie, he ordered her to, 'Get that old fool inside, and stay outta my sight, the pair of youse.' Jerking a thumb to John, he suggested fiercely, 'I'll deal with this young thug!'

Aggie was in a dilemma. She couldn't let go of

the old fella, who by now was growing heavy and limp in her arms, and she feared for John, who was in a bad way. 'You heard what Dad said,' she answered with a warning. 'If it's to do with our Emily, then it's for *me* to deal with it.' Beckoning John she told him, 'Come inside, lad. I need to see what damage is done.'

John shook his head. 'There's no need,' he answered. 'I'm all right. Look, you'd best do as he says . . . take Mr Ramsden inside.' The last thing he had wanted was to cause trouble for Emily's family.

Aggie hesitated, but then Clem said meaningfully: 'You've got a choice, woman. Yer can watch me use the shotgun on this young bugger, or you can go inside, while I try and talk some sense into 'im.' He kept a wary eye on John. 'It's up to you,' he told her. 'Either way don't bother me.'

Aggie looked at John, who gave her a smile and a nod. 'Go on,' he urged. 'Go inside.' He gestured at Thomas. 'He's all done in.'

Clem appeared to have calmed down somewhat, so Aggie had little choice, because now the old man was beginning to shiver, and so was she. The ordeal of facing up to Clem had taken its toll.

'Come on, Dad,' she said kindly, letting him lean on her. 'You've had enough excitement for one day.'

Hoping things would settle down now, she guided him inside.

~

Once they were gone, Clem turned on John, though he deliberately kept his distance. '*You want the girl, don't yer?*' His voice was little more than a whisper, with a certain inference that riled the younger man. 'Want 'er real bad, don't yer?'

John knew well enough what he was implying and answered him with a rush of disgust. 'Not in the way *you* mean.'

'Oh, an' what way is that?'

'Whatever you might think, I would never take advantage of Emily,' John said proudly. 'I mean to wed her – if she'll have me.'

Clem took a step forward, the anger reddening his face. '*I'll* tell yer what you'll do, you young pup! You'll stay away from my niece. In fact, you'll get as far away from 'er as you can, an' never show yer face round these parts again.'

John shook his head. 'I'm not going anywhere. Like I said, I mean to wed her one day.'

'So you'll defy me, is that it?'

'You can do your worst, Mr Jackson, but I'll never leave her!'

For a time they regarded each other, the air heavy with hatred. When next Clem spoke, it was to dash all John's hopes into the ground.

'What if I decided not to punish you, after all?'

he asked cunningly. 'What if I decided it were *the girl* that's bad – and not you at all? By! A young harlot like that would need some discipline, wouldn't yer say?'

As he watched the horror unfold on John's face, he chewed the fleshy part of his bottom lip, like an animal devouring its prey. And all the while observing John, with a sense of delight that he could hardly conceal. 'Yer wouldn't like that, I'll be bound, but there'd be nowt yer could do about it.'

'I could rip your heart out . . . that's what I could do!' Stumbling forward, John realised he was in no fit state to do anything at that minute, but he wouldn't let this bully beat him. He couldn't let Emily be hurt. 'You touch one hair on her head, and I swear to God, I'll kill you.'

The dog bared its teeth at him and growled.

Clem merely took a step back. 'You're not going to kill anybody!' he snapped. 'But if yer think anything of the girl, you'll get as far away from this place as you can, and as quick as yer can! Because if yer don't, it'll be Emily that suffers, I can promise yer that.'

With a flick of his wrist he had John by the throat and the gun pushed into his belly. 'I could do for yer right now,' he whispered, 'but there's no need. I can see now how I might have got it all wrong, and that it really were the girl that led you on.' He gave a little sideways turn and spat on the ground. 'Yon Emily's no more than a little slut – I can see that now. She needs teaching a lesson, that's what!'

He gave a sly wink. 'If you were to sling yer hook and clear off from round these parts, I dare say she would realise her mistake and be the good girl she allus was.' His face darkened. 'But if yer insist on staying, I reckon she'll just go on being bad. An' then – well, I'd have no option but to give her a good hiding.'

Struggling to free himself, John was frantic.

'The thing is,' Clem took pleasure from seeing the boy cornered, 'I can do whatever I want. Like the old man said, it's *me* that's got the upper hand round this place, and it's me that will 'ave to keep order, if yer know what I mean?'

'You hurt her, and it'll be the last thing you do.'

'Oh, I *will* hurt her! I'll have to, won't I – unless you do as I ask. Look now, if you really are fond of the girl, you'll sling yer hook an' never come back. Do that, an' the girl will be safe. But if yer defy me, then like I say, it won't be *you* as suffers. It'll be *her.* An' even if by some unlikely chance you get to me afterwards – well, by then it'll be too late, won't it?' Grinning wickedly, he let his next words sink in. 'Because I'll 'ave got to our Emily first.'

'You bastard!'

'Oh, I'll not deny it.' Clem paused, before going on in a low, trembling whisper. 'You're right – I am a bastard. Of the worst kind.' His eyes hardened until they shone like marbles. 'It might pay yer to remember that.'

With that he turned away and strode into the distance, Badger trotting at his side, leaving John to reflect on his words. And the more John thought on them, the more afraid he was – for Emily.

Because now he knew without a shadow of doubt that Clem Jackson was capable of anything, even murder.

~

Down at the brook, Emily had no idea of the horrible scenes happening up at the farm. All she knew was that John had arranged to meet her here at their usual place, and now here she was, patiently waiting for him, her heart leaping at every sound and her face flushed with anticipation.

Time and again she had wandered along the water's edge, her eyes trained on the top field. She knew from their meetings in the past, it was the track he would take. Never once had he been late, not even when he had to put in extra work. He always got through it in time to be there when he promised.

Today, though, he was already late, she thought anxiously. And what did he have to tell her that was so urgent?

When they spoke last night, and he told her he would have some good news for her today, there had been a sparkle in his eye, making her think that he was going to see her mammy, and maybe ask if it was all right for him and Emily to start courting. She smiled at that. 'A surprise' – that's all he would say, so now she would have to wait and see what it was.

Waiting wasn't so hard though, she told herself. Not if she knew for certain he would be there.

Sitting cross-legged on the bank, with the sound of the brook playing over the boulders, she felt so content. This was a beautiful place, where the two of them had sat many a time over the past six months or so, talking and laughing, putting the world to rights. Making plans, dreaming dreams, and every passing minute, learning to love each other. John had been at Potts End Farm for just on eight months now, living with his Aunt Lizzie in a cottage over the rise in Salmesbury. Nearly twenty years old, the lad had been just a good friend to Thomas's granddaughter for a few weeks, chatting to her while he worked on the wagons, and occasionally helping her with the animals when his own chores were done. From being good mates, the two of them had discovered love, and by now, each knew they were made for the other.

While she waited for John, Emily watched the late spring lambs at play and smiled. God's world was a wonderful place, she thought.

Just then, a fat little lamb came to her side, curious as to what she was doing there. She ran her hands along its woolly shoulders. 'My! You get bigger every time I see you.' She laughed when it skipped off to find its mother. 'Look at you . . . tapping your mammy for milk, and you're almost as big as she is, poor thing.' She watched with pleasure as the lamb nuzzled under the ewe's belly, its tail wagging and its mouth locked onto its mammy's long red teat, while the noise of its sucking echoed in that quiet morning air.

Emily loved it here. The bottom field was the furthest from the house and the prettiest of all. With the ragged hedges of dog roses and other wild flowers spilling their colour across the skyline, and the soft ripple of water as it meandered along, she thought this must be as close to Paradise as anybody could get.

Here in this idyllic place, alone or with John, she could sit and think, and wonder, and hope that one day her Uncle Clem would leave and their world would be happy again.

For now though, as the lambs skipped about her, she held out her arms and embracing the smallest of the flock, she gazed into its big dark eyes. The love in her heart spilled over. 'His name is John,' she whispered into its woolly ear. 'We like each other a lot, and one day, maybe we'll get married.' Her face flushed a bashful pink. 'Oh, I don't mean he's told me that's what he wants, but I can feel it,' she said to the wriggling creature. 'At least, I *hope* he wants to marry me, because

I don't think I'll ever want to marry anybody else.'

A sudden awareness filled her young heart. 'I really do love him,' she confided. 'I must do, because when we're together I'm so happy, I don't even let Clem upset me. Then, when we're apart, I feel so lonely.' She looked to the top field. 'He'll be here any minute. Isn't that wonderful!'

Giving the lamb a final hug, she took a leisurely stroll along the water's edge. Her thoughts lingered with John, and the possibility of spending the rest of her life with him. It was a daring, wonderful thought, and it brought a smile to her face. I wonder what he's got to tell me? she asked herself for the twentieth time.

Once again, she trained her gaze on the top field. Still no sign of him, but it didn't matter. There was time enough before she had to be back. Besides, if she had to, she would wait for him for ever.

Filled with the energy of youth, she began to run, gently at first, her bare feet feeling every bump and curve of the land. Soon though, urged on by a rush of exhilaration, she was running like the wind, her hair loose and lifted by the breeze, and her strong legs covering the ground with surprising speed. Caught up in her own private joy, she didn't notice the locket fly from around her neck and lose itself in a patch of sweet-scented clover.

Laughing out loud, on she ran, along the brook's edge, then through the cool water and back again.

Thrilled to see the lambs leaping after her, she led them up and down, but they stopped at the stream's edge and, in spite of her cajoling, would not enter the water. So she played the game and took great delight in their company. She ran and splashed and ran again, up the field and down with the lambs in pursuit. Until at last she fell in a heap, exhausted and happy, certain that today was special.

Because John had some important news to tell her.

~

Lying there, spreadeagled on the grass, her face uplifted to the sun and her heart pounding, Emily had never felt so alive. 'I love him!' she shouted to the elements. 'I LOVE HIM!' Her smile deepened and her laughter was a joyful sound that echoed across the fields.

She felt free out here; free to say what was in her heart. Free to be herself and not be afraid.

It was a wonderful feeling.

CHAPTER THREE

MAKING HIS WAY slowly and painfully to the brook, John looked towards that special place where he and Emily had arranged to meet. His sorry eyes scoured the area, but he couldn't see her, and a small wave of relief surged through him. Though he had longed to see her, he had not wanted Emily to look on him the way he was now; nor was he ready to tell her what was on his mind. He needed time to think. He had decisions to make, and above all else, whatever the cost, he had to do what was right for Emily. Nothing else was important. Nothing else mattered.

Right now, though, he had to clean himself up, so with that in mind he headed for that part of the brook where the water tumbled down from the hillside. Here there was a deep pool where he could immerse himself in the cool, soothing waters, and put his mind to what lay ahead.

Afterwards, he would speak with his Aunt Lizzie. She was the wisest person he knew. All his life, whenever he had been troubled, she had been there to guide him. Like Emily, she was kind and giving, with a way that put a man's heart at peace.

Determined now, he pushed on, his mind alive with thoughts of Emily.

There were things she had to know, and other, more worrying things that she must never find out, such as Jackson's determined threat to 'punish' her unless John left the area for good. But how could he go? How could he leave her behind? Dear God! It didn't bear thinking about.

On the other hand, how could he stay, when that maniac had promised to harm her? And even though he was ready to guard and protect her with his life, how could he stop Jackson from carrying out his threat?

Balancing against a tree, he slowly shed his outer garments. His best shirt was torn and bloody; every part of his body hurt abominably. He knew he was lucky to be alive, and that by nightfall he would probably be in agony, once a lot of the shock had worn off. As he reached the water and slid into its cold, shocking depths, he considered the options open to him. He could defy Jackson and stay, which would mean risking Emily's well-being. Or he could go, and live a life of loneliness without her. And what of Emily? He had seen the love in her eyes, and it warmed his heart. But she would get over him, and in time maybe he, too, would learn to live without her. Oh, but it was a sorry prospect, and one he would rather not face.

There were other options, he reminded himself. He could do away with Jackson – an 'accident' maybe, one dark night, across the far fields where the man often walked. If he planned it carefully, no one would ever know it was him.

He mentally shook himself. God Almighty! He was talking *murder!* If he was found out, he'd be hanged and Emily would be on her own just the same. Even worse, she would have to live with the shame and horror of what he had done. And what about Lizzie? She and Emily were the two people he loved most in the whole world. How could he do such a terrible thing to them?

Suddenly the full horror of what he was considering hit him like a hammer blow. No! Murder was not an option.

He wondered whether Aggie might allow him and Emily to get wed? But he already knew the answer to that. 'Emily is far too young,' she would say. 'You haven't known each other long enough to know your own minds.' And Emily's grandfather would agree with that wholeheartedly. The whole idea of marriage would be thrown out of the window. In fact, the mere mention of it might result in him being forbidden to see Emily again, until she was older.

What if he were to warn Aggie of the threat Jackson had made to her daughter? They could take it in turns to watch him. But no, that wouldn't work either. Aggie already had more than enough on her hands. Besides, even with the two of them on guard, they couldn't watch Jackson twenty-four hours a day. He was a devious, evil creature, and if he set out to do something, he was bound to do it. That was the nature of the man.

The authorities then? Another bad idea, because even if he went to the police and told them of Jackson's threat to Emily, Clem was such a clever liar, he was bound to come out on top.

While he washed away some of the physical hurt, John's mind was frantically searching for guidance. Maybe he could go back to Jackson and try to reason with him? But the man had no reasoning powers in him. Should he fight him, then? In a fair fight, he might be able to bring him to his knees . . . send him on his way. He reminded himself that Jackson was like no ordinary man. He would simply crawl away like some injured wild animal, to lick his wounds and bide his time. Then he'd be back, more dangerous and determined than ever.

After a while, chilled through and beginning to shiver, John climbed out and stood in the sun; it was good to feel the warmth on his bruised ribcage and back. But there was no warmth in his soul, for he was torn in so many ways. Time and again he had to remind himself: it was Emily he had to think of. Not himself. Not that maniac. *Only Emily.* But what to do?

With his whole body shivering uncontrollably, he fumbled on his clothes and began to walk home. He could think of nothing except his Emily. Even if she was aware of the danger, she would still want him to stay – he was as sure of that as he was sure of his love for her. She had such spirit.

He smiled. That was just one of the facets of her nature that made him love her so. Then, sighing, his heart once more heavy, he made his way home.

~

Taking full advantage of the morning sunshine, Lizzie Hanley was busy pegging out the washing. A small round person in her latter years, she was a quick, familiar figure. With bright green eyes, homely face and a halo of silver hair, she took great pleasure from the ordinary things that brightened her day: the trill of a blackbird overhead, the bees' contented buzz as they gathered nectar, and the feel of a mischievous breeze as it tugged at stray hairs in her bun and tickled her face with them.

Just then, a long-eared hare on the skyline stood up on its hindquarters to stare at her. She stared back . . . only for a moment, and then it was gone. She smiled. This was her place. This was her life. And she was grateful for it.

Having used two pegs to hang out her long

red-flannel nightgown, she promptly wedged another two in her mouth while she bent to the
wicker-basket and lifted a damp sheet from the
pile of freshly laundered items there.

Immersed in her task, she didn't realise John
was approaching. Always a happy soul, she sang
to herself – a strange, muffled melody as it filtered
through the two wooden pegs clenched in her
teeth.

It was only when she heard a sound behind her
that she swung round to see him standing there,
his face swollen and bruised, and the wet shirt on
his back clinging to him like a second skin. 'Good
Lord!' Dropping the sheet to the ground, she spat
out the pegs and took hold of him. 'What in God's
name happened to you?' Without waiting for an
answer she propelled him inside, with John pro-
testing all the way, 'I'm all right, Auntie. Don't
fuss.'

But fuss she did, because it was her way. Moreover, she could see he'd been badly hurt, and
knowing him, she suspected he was in more pain
than he would ever admit.

Inside the pretty thatched cottage, John sat by
the fire-range, his thoughts still with Emily. He
had searched for an answer and now he knew what
must be done.

'Who've you been fighting?' Returning with a
bowl of hot water and a cloth, Lizzie set them
down on the table, together with arnica and

some strips of clean soft cotton from an old sheet.

Seeming not to have heard her, and disturbed by his own thoughts, John stood up and moved to the window, from where he looked out on the garden; it was such a pretty garden, with a winding gravel-path flanked by blossom of all kinds, and all of it lovingly tended by his Aunt Lizzie's hand.

She came to stand by his side. 'When a man's been fighting,' she said softly, 'it's usually over some woman or other.' She tugged at his shirt-sleeve. 'You'd best get outta these wet things.'

'You're right.' He turned. 'You might as well know ... I've had a bit of a set-to with Clem Jackson.'

The old woman nodded grimly. 'Aye, I thought as much.' She gestured to the injuries on his neck and temple. 'He didn't do those with his fists neither, did he?'

'I'd best get out of these wet clothes, like you said.'

Lizzie barred his way. 'Was it because of the lass?'

John nodded.

She sighed knowingly. 'I've seen it coming. You and the lass, making up to each other like a pair o' young doves. Oh yes, I've seen trouble brewing for some weeks now.' She looked up at him. 'Aw, look now! You're both too young to be getting serious.'

'I love her.' His voice dropped to the merest whisper. 'I always will.'

Again she gestured to his wounds. 'Looks to me like you've been warned off.'

He gave a little smile. 'You could say that.'

'Does young Emily know you've been beaten because of her?'

'Not yet.' He limped back to the chair, but he didn't sit. Instead he leaned against the arm. 'But I'm sure she'll be told soon enough.'

'This is not good, son.' Though she was his aunt and not his mother, Lizzie had called him 'son' from the first day he was given into her care at the age of five. He had made her life a happy one, but now she was deeply worried. She wagged a podgy finger. 'Happen the two of you had better stay away from each other for the time being?'

John appreciated her concern, but this was something he had to deal with in his own way. 'Leave it to me, Lizzie,' he said. 'You know I'll do the right thing by her.'

The old dear was penitent. 'Oh lad, I didn't mean to interfere, and o' course I know you'll do the right thing ... but it's got me worried, what with Clem Jackson calling the tune at that house, and now you coming home in this state. There's things here that I don't much care for ... *bad* things! Just you be careful. That's all I'm saying.'

'You're not to worry.' Laying his two hands on

her shoulders, he promised, 'Like I say, I'll deal with it.'

And for the moment, as he climbed the narrow stairway to his room, she had to be content with that.

~

Concerned that she might have missed him, and wondering if she'd made a mistake about the time or the place, Emily made her way home.

Aggie saw her coming. 'Where've you been, lass?' That was always her first question whenever Emily returned from her wanderings. 'I've been worried about you.'

Emily glanced at the mantelpiece clock, surprised to see she'd been away for almost two hours. 'I've been down by the brook,' she said reassuringly. 'I didn't realise I was gone so long.'

Aggie wondered whether she should tell her about John being here, and how Clem had beaten him with the butt of his gun. Deciding there was really no way out of it, she went straight in. 'Lass, I want to ask you something, and I need you to tell me the truth.' She smiled. 'But then you allus do.'

Going to the larder, she took down two china beakers and a jug of home-made sarsaparilla covered with a muslin and bead cloth to keep away the flies. She half-filled the beakers with a measure of the dark brown liquid, and handing one of them to Emily, she urged, 'Sit down for a minute, lass.' She pointed to the rocking-chair by the window, where she herself had been sitting only a few minutes since. At the same time she drew up another chair close by. 'We need to talk, you an' me.'

Emily did as she was told, and when she was seated, she asked curiously, 'What's wrong?' She only had to look at her mammy's face to realise there was trouble of some kind, and it didn't take long for her to realise it must have something to do with Clem Jackson. If ever there was any trouble round here, you could depend on *him* being at the centre of it.

Seating herself opposite, Aggie looked her daughter in the eye. 'It's about you and John,' she said quietly. 'It seems you've been keeping me in the dark, and because of it, Clem's got his back up. And now, this very morning while you've been away, there's been a right set-to. I'm sorry, lass, but I'm none too pleased.' She gave the girl her sternest stare. 'Happen none of this would have come about if you'd been open with me from the start!' Though she adored Emily, she didn't take kindly to her keeping secrets from her.

Emily was taken by surprise. 'What do you mean, trouble?' she asked worriedly. 'What kind of trouble?'

'The worst kind. Even Grandad got himself involved.' When Emily opened her mouth to ask after the old man, Aggie put up a staying hand. 'It's all right,' she assured her. 'The silly old fool didn't get hurt, thank God, but it could have been very different.'

'I'm sorry, Mam.' Emily knew she should have confided in her, but she hadn't known herself how serious were her feelings for John. Not until last night, when he took her in his arms and made her feel like the most important person in the whole wide world. 'I didn't mean to keep anything from you.'

Brushing aside her apology, Aggie needed to know: 'How far has it gone with you and John?'

Emily was embarrassed by her mother's question.

'Well, child? Answer me. You and John – how far has it gone atween you?'

'We haven't done anything wrong, if that's what you mean!'

'So, what *are* your feelings? I need to know.'

Emily blushed bright pink. 'I think I love him, Mammy.' She allowed herself a shy little smile. 'I want to be with him all the time, and when we're apart, I feel so lonely.' Pausing to remember how it was whenever she was with John, Emily admitted, 'I've never felt like this before.'

If Aggie had been concerned before, she was even more so now, for she had seen the look in Emily's eyes, and it gave her a jolt. She had long thought of her daughter as just a lass, but now she knew that the 'lass' was fast becoming a woman, with all the complications that went with it. So, she loved young John, did she? Or she *thought* she did. In her opinion, Emily was still far too young to be getting serious like that, and she said so in no uncertain terms.

While Emily listened with horror, Aggie told her about John and Clem, and how the two of them had fought like tigers. 'John stood up to him, I'll give him that. By! He took such a beating . . . but he kept coming back for more. Look, lass, I want you and John to stop seeing each other,' she finished. 'Afore there's murder done.'

Her words fell on deaf ears, however, because Emily was already out of the door and running like the wind, over the fields towards the rise, to the cottage – and John.

~

On his way back to the barn, Clem Jackson glanced up to see Emily fleeing across the fields. 'She's probably heard how I trounced that young feller-me-lad,' he grinned. 'It's wild she is!' He chuckled. 'A wild beauty that needs a bit o' taming.' He had long fancied himself as the one to do the 'taming'. These past months, the girl had seemed to blossom. He spent hours just watching her. It gave him such secret pleasure.

Climbing the ladder to the hayloft, he dumped his bag of tools and began to examine the faulty winding mechanism that winched heavy sacks of potatoes and other items up to the door at the top of the barn. He threw a bit of the chain up to lie out of the way on the crossbeams, and as he did so, a small notebook fell into the hay at his feet.

'Hello, what have we here?' Clem said aloud, and picked it up.

The initial pages were merely the innocent jottings of a young girl, telling of her joy in this place, then the dismay after her daddy went away, and the arrival of her mother's brother, Clem Jackson. She spoke of the way their lives had changed with the death of her granny, and her stillborn brother, and how she prayed every day that Clem would go away and they might find some peace from him.

There were many entries about John, and how they enjoyed each other's company. *I like him a lot*, she had written. *I think he likes me too.* Girlish things. Simple and lovely. But there was little here to fire Jackson's imagination.

Until he came across the latest entry.

'By! This is a real eye-opener an' no mistake!' he declared, the slaver dripping from his mouth as he read aloud to himself:

'Last night, John and I held each other. It was so good. He told me he loved me, and I said I felt the same way. Something wonderful happened then. He kissed me, not like a friend,

but like a lover. I knew that he wanted more, and so did I. But I was afraid, yet oh so excited. I had such powerful feelings, I couldn't stop trembling.

He touched my breast . . . it was a strange and beautiful feeling and I didn't want him to stop. But he did, and when I asked him why, he said he didn't know, except we shouldn't go so far. At least not yet. He didn't want to spoil me, or hurt me. He thought it was best if we courted for a while, and then we would both see how we felt.

I know he was right. In fact, I felt ashamed at my own part in it, because I must have led him on. It's just that I do love him so. I know that now. Even if it takes years, it's John I want.

If Uncle Clem knew we had been so forward, he would go mad. I know he would put all the blame on John, but I was as bad. Nothing happened though. John stopped it before we got carried away, and in a way I'm glad he did.

Clem says John is only after what he can get and that he has no respect for me. But now I know he's wrong, and besides, I don't care what my uncle says. He will never stop me from loving John. He makes me feel different – alive – like I've never felt before.

When he held me close last night, when he touched me, it made me shiver inside. We'll do

like he says, though. We'll court for a while,
then one day we'll marry, and I'll be his wife.
John, and his children: that's all I want, and
I'll be happy for ever.'

Lizzie was the first to see Emily running towards the cottage. 'The lass is here!' she called up to John, who was in his bedroom pacing the floor, deep in thought. 'Best get yersel' downstairs.'

When a moment later he emerged to see Emily coming down the lane, his first impulse was to go to her, but Lizzie reached out to restrain him.

'Listen to me, son,' she persuaded softly. 'When my brother Petey was lost in the mine disaster, getting on for fifteen year ago now, and your mammy pined herself away soon after, you and me had nobody else but each other. I promised my sister-in-law I'd do my best to raise you as she and Petey would have done. I've loved you and cared for you, and you've been like my own son, and I thank God for every minute.'

'I know that,' he answered, and hugged her. 'You've been like a mother to me, and I'll always be grateful for that. But this time you can't help me. I'm a man now, Auntie, and this is something I have to deal with myself.'

Though Emily was opening the garden gate by now, and he was aching to go to her, the urgency in his aunt's voice made him pause.

'In all these years I've never asked you to do anything against your nature,' she said. 'But I'm asking you now, and you have to listen, son . . . for your own good, and for the good o' that dear lass.'

Tears filled her eyes. 'Let things happen gradual between the two of youse. Don't be too hasty and do something you'll regret. You're both so young – you've got all the time in the world.'

'Don't worry.' Gently gripping her plump shoulders, he said, 'Trust me. You know I'll do what's right by her.'

As he went out to meet Emily, Lizzie watched them fold into each other's arms, and her heart sank. 'By! It's a bad bugger who's took over Potts End,' she murmured. 'I don't know what'll become of the two of youse, but he'll not let you have any peace, I'm sure o' that!'

Her sorry gaze followed the couple as they walked away, towards the fells, where the canal rose and dipped through the lock-gates, and the skylarks sang their cheery song overhead.

It's a lonely old world for such as me, Lizzie sighed. She recalled her own young love many years ago, and the rush of nostalgia brought a smarting of tears to her pretty green eyes.

~

Down by the canal, Emily chided John for having gone to see Clem. 'If you'd told me what you meant to do, I'd never have let you go,' she said. She was horrified by John's injuries.

Drawing her down to sit next to him on the bank, John slid his arm about her shoulders. 'I just wanted for you and me to have our courtship put out in the open,' he explained. 'I didn't want us hiding round corners and being afraid at every footstep.'

She looked up, an appreciative smile on her face. 'I know,' she said, 'but you can't reason with a man like that.'

He studied her now; those intense nutmeg-brown eyes and that innocent smile. Today, her hair was free from its plaits and tumbled silkily onto her shoulders. His heart turned somersaults. 'Emily?'

She looked up. 'Yes?'

'There's something I have to tell you.'

Sitting round she looked him full in the face. 'You'd best tell me then.'

Shifting uncomfortably he began, 'Do you want us to get married one day?'

Her eyes opened with astonishment. 'You *know* I do!'

'That's what I want too, sweetheart.' Cupping her pretty face in the palms of his hands he studied her every feature. 'Look, I've been thinking – about you and me, and our future. When we do get married, I want us to have the best wedding, one we'll remember for the rest of our lives.'

'That's not important.' Putting her finger to his poor split lips, she told him, 'All I want is to be your wife. All the fancy trimmings won't make any difference.'

'I know that. But there are other things that do matter. I need to make you a home, and give you nice things, and later when we have children, we won't want them to go without. You know what I'm saying, don't you, sweetheart?'

'I'm not sure.' She shook her head, the beginnings of doubt creeping into her heart.

'The truth is,' he went on, 'I have no savings, and precious few prospects.'

'No! You have your work – every wagon round these parts has been either repaired by you, or built from scratch. You're well respected hereabouts. Folk always call on you whenever they need a roof fixed, or other jobs done. There's all sorts you turn your hand to.'

'I won't deny that, but it still makes me just a handyman. That won't build us a house, or provide enough to give our children the best of everything.'

Emily would have none of it. 'We'll manage,' she protested. 'When the time comes, we'll have a bit put by. We'll be fine, you'll see.'

Realising he was in danger of losing the argument, and putting her in more danger than she could ever imagine, he said firmly, 'I've made a decision.'

She didn't answer, for somewhere deep inside she feared what he was about to say. 'You're going away, aren't you?' Her heart sank like a dead weight inside her.

He nodded. 'There's a big world out there, and a chance for me to make something of myself. I won't be away too long – a year or two, that's all. We're young enough to spare that time, and when I come back, I'll have made enough money to get us everything you deserve.' He paused; the pain in her eyes as she looked at him was strangling his heart. In a choked voice, he promised her he would come back, and when he did, it would be to make her his wife.

'But I don't need a big wedding,' she said tearfully. 'I only need you.'

'Do you want rid of your uncle?'

Wiping her eyes she shook her head. 'Him! *He*'ll never go,' she said bitterly.

Her answer gave an edge to his argument. 'I'll *make* him go!' he promised. 'When I've got enough money to clear your mammy's debts, I'll be back, and we'll be rid of him once and for all.'

She smiled through her tears. 'Would you do that for us?'

'You know I would.'

She thought how wonderful it would be if her uncle was gone, and for a brief moment her heart was lifted by his promise. But then she imagined what her life would be like without John, and it seemed unbearable. 'Don't go,' she pleaded.

Common-sense crumbled when, suddenly, he was filled with a compulsion to take her away. *'Come with me, Emily!'*

Thrilled, she drew away from him, her eyes alight with excitement. 'Yes!' She laughed out loud. 'Oh *yes*, John. Take me with you and I'll get work. I'll help you make your fortune!' Like John, she had momentarily forgotten harsh reality.

In the heat of the moment, John wondered why he had not thought of it before. The solution was staring him in the face! Of course! If he couldn't keep Jackson away from Emily, the next thing was to remove her out of harm's way.

Besides, the idea of himself and Emily travelling life's highway to make their fortune was wonderful. Later, they would come back and free her mammy and grandad from Jackson's clutches. Potts End Farm would be returned to them, and life would be as it was before Clem came to taint it.

When, in that instant, common-sense prevailed and realisation dawned, a painful silence fell between them. It was broken by Emily's quiet voice. 'I can't go with you.' She raised her tearful gaze. 'I have to stay and help Mammy. She could never manage on her own. Then there's Grandad.' She made a gesture of helplessness. 'They need me.'

He nodded. 'I know. I'm sorry, Emily. I wasn't

thinking.' He held her hand and said reflectively, 'Maybe Lizzie was right.'

'What do you mean?'

He recalled his conversation with his aunt. 'She said we were too young, and I've just proved her right.' He was mortified. 'The idea of you coming with me just took away my thinking.'

'Don't go, John,' she murmured. 'Please! Don't go.'

'I have to.' Her pain was his.

Taking her by the arms, he drew her up, and for a time they stood together, he with his arms about her, and Emily nestled against him. Each could hear the other's heart beating, as if they shared just one between them. They didn't speak. All that needed saying had already been said.

With a suddenness that startled him, she wrenched away. 'If you go, I'll hate you!' she cried, and when he reached out to console her, she turned and ran.

With his emotions torn in so many ways, all he could do was let her go. That dearly loved, familiar figure, running like the very wind, her hair flying in the breeze, and her feet bare as the day she was born. This was how he would remember her. This was the image he would carry with him, until he came back to claim her, one day when he had the means to free that troubled family.

Lowering his gaze for a moment, he wished with all his being that it could have been different. 'I have to go,' he said helplessly. '*He* gave me no choice.'

~

Sobbing uncontrollably, Emily fled to the barn and up the ladder to that secret place where she often came to write her deepest thoughts into her little book. Seeking comfort, she reached for her locket – and found it gone. Dear Lord! Horrified, Emily recalled her two wild journeys across the fields – the first in happy expectation of a rendezvous, the second a panicked dash to her lover's aid. The locket must have come adrift from its chain then, and be lost on the farm or in Potts End Lane. She'd never find it again.

Sinking to her knees, her face in her hands, she gave vent to her grief.

She didn't hear the soft crunch of footsteps as the man stepped towards her across the strewn hay. Nor was she aware that he stood for a full minute staring down on her, licking his lips and remembering what he had read in that book of hers. And now she was here, and his need of her was like a red-hot iron in his gut.

When in a minute he was on her, she fell backwards, helpless and terrified as he tore at her clothes. The instinct for survival gave her the will to fight, but she was no match for his bull-like strength.

'For God's sake, Uncle Clem – *leave me be*!'

But he didn't leave her.

Instead, he slid his hand over her mouth to stop her screams. 'We can't 'ave yer mammy come a-running now, can we, eh?' he panted.

In the shocking minutes that followed, he took her innocence, and coveted every part of her. And try as she could, she was helpless to stop him.

When it was over, and she was slumped to the floor, degraded and broken, he pointed down at her as he buttoned up his flies. 'One word o' this to anybody – *anybody*, mind – and I'll set fire to the house . . . with all three of you buggers inside.' He laughed, a dark, evil sound that sent ripples of terror through her every nerve-ending. 'One dark night when yer think yer all safe, that's when I'll come a-prowling. Yer know I'd do it an' all, don't yer, eh?' When she didn't answer, he gave her a kick. 'DON'T YER?'

Nodding, she kept her gaze to the wall.

'There's a good lass.' He grinned with pleasure and cast one more lingering look at her naked thighs, smeared with a mixture of her blood and his seed.

Quickly now, he scurried to the ladder and began his descent. 'Yer a woman now,' he gloated. 'What's more, it took a *man* to mek yer blossom! Not some young whippersnapper who doesn't know what day it is!' He grinned and called up,

'Pretend it were him, if yer like. That don't bother me none. In fact, it might suit me all the way.'

A moment later he was gone, and she was alone; her young life ruined, and her hopes for the future torn apart.

~

Some short distance away, John paused to look back on his journey down Potts End Lane and out of Emily's life. 'I'll keep my promise,' he vowed, his gaze trained on the farmhouse where Emily lived. 'However long it takes, I'll be back, my love. And *nothing* will ever part us again.'

PART TWO

~

December, 1904

Consequences

CHAPTER FOUR

EMILY WAS AT the kitchen window, showing her daughter the newly-fallen layer of snow. 'It's Christmas Day tomorrow,' she told the bairn. 'Last year it rained all day, but look there!' Excitedly she held the infant higher so she could see. 'Your very first white Christmas!' Last year had been wet and bitter, with never a sign of snow.

Made curious by the delicate manner in which the robin tripped across the snow's surface to leave its tiny prints there, Emily did not notice the laden milk-cart approaching.

But now, as the infant began squealing and struggling to get out of her arms, Emily looked up. 'What's wrong, eh?' Following the direction of little Cathleen's gaze, she saw him over the hedge: Danny Williams, the local milkman, his familiar head and shoulders bobbing up and down with the movement of the cart-horse as it plodded its way through the snow. 'It's Danny!' Emily laughed out loud. 'You saw him coming down the lane – that's why you're so excited!'

At that very minute the mantelpiece clock struck eight. 'Right on time,' she said. 'I should have known.'

Having recently returned from three years away fighting in the Transvaal, Danny had left the Army to take over the milk-round from his retired widower father. The Williamses were a popular family hereabouts, and when Danny had collected milk from neighbouring farms, he always dropped in for a cuppa at Potts End. He and the horse both enjoyed the break. Dedicated and reliable, he was never known to be late.

'Hmh!' Emily smiled into her daughter's eyes. 'I do believe you'd rather see Danny than have a white Christmas.' Nuzzling the infant's mop of dark hair, she wasn't surprised to see the joy in those bright blue eyes as they caught sight of Danny in his lofty seat. 'Always pleased to see him, aren't you, sweetheart?' she asked, and the child's spontaneous bubble of laughter was enough of an answer.

Over this past year, since Danny Williams had returned from South Africa, he and Emily's child Cathleen had struck up a warm friendship. At first, Emily had been wary, but Danny's natural humour and honest nature soon allayed her fears and won her over.

'You'd best get down, while I put the kettle

on.' Lowering the child to the floor, she turned towards the range. 'He'll be wanting his cup of tea.'

'Aye, an' he'll be wanting a muffin too, I'll be bound.' That was Aggie, having entered the kitchen from the adjoining room. 'You see to the child,' she suggested, 'while I mek us all a brew.'

Tugging at her skirts, little Cathleen let her mammy know she wanted to go outside. 'I can't let you go out just yet,' Emily chided. 'We don't want you squashed under the wheels of the cart now, do we, eh?' The very thought sent shivers of horror through her.

Holding the child close, Emily took a moment to observe her. Cathleen was a year and nine months old now, and every minute spent with her was pure joy. It seemed astonishing to her that this darling little girl, with her laughing blue eyes and shock of dark hair, had been conceived out of fear and hatred.

At first, after a hard and painful birth, it had been impossible for Emily to accept her. For weeks afterwards, Emily had turned her back on the newborn, leaving Aggie to nurse, bath and cuddle the child. And that dear woman never complained. 'You'll tek to the bairn when you're good and ready,' she declared. 'You see if you don't!'

She was right because, little by little, Emily had come to realise that the child, like herself, carried no blame for what had happened. The miracle to

Emily was that neither in physical appearance or nature, did Cathleen show any trait of the man who had forced himself on her mother.

Since that dreadful day, and for some reason known only to himself, Clem Jackson had kept his distance. That much at least Emily was grateful for. But if she had hated him before, she now loathed him with a vengeance.

There had been many times during the days and months following the rape when she had yearned for someone to confide in: her mother, her grandfather maybe. Even John, if he'd been here. Deep down though, she knew she could never tell anyone. Clem had threatened all manner of retribution if she so much as mentioned his name in the same breath as the child. And so, fearful of the consequences for her family, Emily had suffered the worst ordeal of her young life, without recourse to the comfort of being able to tell someone the truth of what had really happened.

At the pubs where he drank with his cronies, in his evil way, Clem had spread the word that John Hanley was the one who had got his niece pregnant, and soon it was common knowledge. Emily for her part neither confirmed nor denied it. Instead she kept her own counsel. The time would come when the truth could be told, she promised herself. When John came home, they would put the record straight together. That was what she believed, with all her heart. And yet, after two years and more without word or sight of him, she had no choice but to believe that John had deserted her.

Lizzie Hanley had taken umbrage at the rumours and no longer had any dealings with Potts End. Too proud to beg for news of John, Emily threw herself into her work, and made the child and her family her life.

The hatred and fear of Clem Jackson were always alive in her. But she was ever thankful that there was no sign of his character in little Cathleen; only a strong, brave heart filled with love and the joy of living, and a natural kindness that endeared the tiny girl to all who met her.

Inevitably, Emily grew to love and adore her – as did her grandad and Aggie, who quite naturally believed the child to be John Hanley's. Never in her wildest nightmares did Aggie suspect that Cathleen's father was her own brother, Clem. Since the tragic stillbirth of her son, and the disappearance of her husband, Aggie now took life as it came, and refused to overreact to something as natural as pregnancy, within or without a marriage ceremony. Children were gifts from God, to be cherished – that was her view, and she cared nothing for the opinion of others.

'Danny!' Cathleen's small voice swept away Emily's troublesome thoughts.

'All right, sweetheart.' Clutching the child to

her, Emily looked out to return Danny's friendly wave.

The two of them followed his progress up the lane. Because of the recent snowfall, the wheels made no sound on the ground, though the dozen or so milk-churns on the cart rattled and clanged as the horse picked his docile way towards the gate.

When at last both horse and cart came to rest, that great old cob straightaway began pawing the ground with his hoof. The smell of hay from the back made his stomach rumble. 'Behave yourself now!' Danny leaped down, his boots skidding in the soft snow. 'Hang on, me ol' darlin',' he told the horse. 'You'll get your breakfast, never fear.'

Unhooking a haybag from beneath the cart, he strapped it round the horse's ears, whereupon that great gentle animal dipped his nose into the bag and began contentedly munching. He had earned his breakfast and meant to enjoy it.

By the time Danny tapped on the back door, Aggie was ready with a fresh brew of strong tea, and a plate full of home-made muffins. 'The tea's mashed!' she said, beckoning him to the kitchen table. 'Get that hot tea down you, son,' she urged Danny as they all took their places. 'By! You look frozen to the bone.'

'Nay, I'm used to it,' Danny assured her. 'Mind you, it feels like there's a bad night in the making. I noticed the hedges are beginning to stiffen with cold. Come dark there'll be ice on the lanes, you can count on it.'

Aggie chided him, 'And there's you with only a thin jacket and muffler to keep out the cold. It's time you got yourself a warm overcoat, my boy!'

'Ever since Africa, I can't stand to be smothered,' came Danny's reply. 'As long as I keep working, I'll be fine, so I will.'

Holding out his arms, he spoke to the child. 'Is there a cuddle and a kiss to go with my tea and muffins?' His gaze fell on Emily. In his heart it was her he wanted; her and the child both, for he had come to love them dearly these past months.

Releasing the child, Emily watched her go to him. She saw the affection in his kind grey eyes, and the way his ready smile enveloped Cathleen as they cuddled close. 'Now this was worth waiting for,' he joked. 'Tea, muffins, and a pretty girl's arms round my neck – what more could a man ask for?' Again, his gaze fell on Emily, and knowing what was on his mind, she looked away.

Lately there had been warm stirrings in her heart for him and, for so many reasons, this frightened her.

For the next twenty minutes or so, they chatted about this and that: Danny told them how glad he was to be back in Salmesbury, and how he had never been certain he would enjoy the milk-round, but that now he was loving every minute. 'We've got plenty of customers and they're all a pleasure to serve. Besides, I reckon I'm privileged to be working in these beautiful surroundings. You get to appreciate your home patch, when you've been overseas for so long.'

Aggie had often wondered and she asked him now: 'How does your father feel about you taking over the reins, so to speak?'

Danny laughed. 'Oh, it's still Father who holds the reins, I can assure you of that! There are days when I can't do a single thing right. He's always one step behind me – "do this, do that" . . . I never seem to please the old bugger.' He chuckled. 'All the same, he's one of the best. They broke the mould when they made Bobby Williams.'

The love he had for his father was evident in the manner in which he referred to him, and the joy in his face whenever he mentioned his name.

Aggie spoke candidly about work on the farm. 'It seems to get harder with every passing year,' she groaned. 'We can't afford any hired help at the moment, and what with Dad's rheumatism, and Emily having to tend the bairn, we can't seem to keep on top of everything.' She gave her daughter a warm smile. 'Mind you, my Emily works every minute she can, bless her heart, and she never complains. In fact, I don't know what I'd do without her.'

'It's easier at this time of year, though – no crops or harvest to gather in?' Danny knew all about the countryside and farming.

Aggie had to agree, but, 'Winter *is* easier, yes. But as you well know, there are always things to do in preparation for the coming spring . . . animals to be tended and repairs done – as well as other jobs that need seeing to afore the season changes.'

Emily had her own opinions about that, and she aired them with a frown. 'If certain people didn't clear off whenever the fancy took them, there would be *three* pairs of hands to the pump, instead of two!' They all knew who she was referring to.

'If you ask me, the place is much happier when he's not around anyway!' Aggie put in. She had come to hate her brother with a passion that shamed her. Potts End Farm hadn't been the same since his arrival. A shadow hung over them all.

Not for the first time, Danny offered his help. 'I'm sure I can spare an hour or two each day to give you a hand,' he volunteered. 'I could take the weight off both your shoulders, if only you'd let me.'

Fearing the trouble that might cause, Emily intervened. 'It's not that we aren't grateful, Danny,' she started, 'because we are. It's just that,' glancing towards the door, she lowered her voice, 'it might not be appreciated in other quarters, if you see what I mean.'

'I understand exactly what you're saying,' he

answered softly, 'but where's the man himself, any-way?' He'd expected to see Clem somewhere here-abouts. 'Usually he's in the field, checking them bulls of his, but there was nary a sign of him this morning.'

Terrified of the two great bulls that Clem had brought to the farm, Aggie confessed, 'I'd feel a whole lot better if he was to take them back where he got them from. I believe he earns money from 'em but he never discusses the fees he charges for them to cover the cows. It makes my blood run cold to think little Cathleen could wander into that field at any time.'

Emily assured her that would not happen. 'We always keep well away from there,' she promised. 'The very sight of those huge beasts puts the fear of God in me.'

Danny was afraid for them all. 'Mind you keep well away,' he cautioned. 'I've seen lesser bulls go on the rampage and leave a trail of destruction in their wake, and them bulls out there are two of the biggest I've ever clapped eyes on.' He shook his head. 'Out and out killers, that's what they are. Keep as far away as you can.' The very thought of any of these three lovely women being hurt was like a knife to his heart.

For a time, they continued to talk about more pleasant things, such as the coming Christmas celebrations. 'I'm sure Mother wouldn't mind if you and your father joined us for Christmas dinner?' Emily couldn't stand for the two Williamses to be alone on Christmas Day. Danny was an only child, and poor Mr Williams would be facing his first Christmas without his wife.

'Well, of course I don't mind!' Aggie was quick to assure them. 'In fact, I was about to ask him the very same thing.' Turning to Danny she said, 'Do you think you could persuade your father to trust my cooking?'

'Well, it's got to be better than mine!' he joked.

Emily was thrilled. 'He'll be company for Grandad too.' She didn't voice her more private thoughts, that having Danny here on Christmas Day would be a pleasant thing for them all. 'Cathleen would be glad to have you here as well,' she finished lamely.

'I hope *you'll* be pleased too,' he remarked softly, and when she blushed to the roots of her light brown hair, both Danny and Aggie couldn't help but notice.

Suddenly, though, Emily's mind was filled with thoughts of John, and when the emotion became too much, she picked Cathleen up and excused herself. 'I'll be outside if you want me,' she told Aggie.

In a moment she and the child were dressed against the winter cold. In another moment they were gone, and for Danny the room seemed terribly empty.

'She's a bit on edge lately,' Aggie explained.

'Every day she waits to hear from John, and every day she's disappointed. It's been over two years now, and there's not been a single letter. It meks me hoppin' mad to see what she's going through, poor lass.'

Danny couldn't understand it. 'All I can say is, he must be mad. To have somebody like Emily waiting for you is every man's dream.'

'The child too.' Aggie knew it had become common knowledge that John was Cathleen's father. 'Though, as far as I'm aware, he doesn't yet know of his daughter's existence.'

Danny would have given anything for the child to be his. 'Wouldn't his Aunt Lizzie have let him know – about the child, I mean?'

Aggie let her thoughts dwell on that for a while. 'Happen she has. Happen she hasn't,' she said at length. 'As far as I can tell, Lizzie's not one for the writing. She's the first to admit she's a poor scholar, bless her heart.'

'It all seems a rare mess an' no mistake,' Danny said reflectively. 'She still wants him though, doesn't she?' Danny had waited in the wings long enough and lately wanted so much to declare his love for Emily. 'I mean, she wouldn't consider any-one else, would she?'

Aggie shrugged. 'That's not for me to say. If I were you, I'd be patient a while longer. But don't give up,' she advised knowingly. 'I've seen how she smiles more when you're around.'

'Do you think so?' Now it was Danny's turn to smile. 'Well, I never!'

When the teapot was empty and the muffins all gone, Danny thanked her. 'I'll be off to my work again now,' he declared, and put his muffler back on.

Emily saw him from the bottom fence; she and little Cathleen had been watching the birds feed on the lard thrown out by Aggie earlier. There had been a clear space under the shelter of the barn-roof where the snow had not yet penetrated. It seemed all the birds in the air had swooped down on that one tiny spot, and were excitedly jostling for the juicy niblets.

'Danny's going,' she said as the child pointed to the birds, her face a wreath of joy at their antics. 'We'd best go and see him off, eh?'

With Cathleen in her arms, she made her way to the cart. 'Away now, are you?' she asked.

'Wish I didn't have to,' he said. 'I'd be more than content to stay here with you and the bairn, but I've got a living to earn.'

'We'll see you tomorrow though, won't we?' As soon as the words left her lips, Emily felt compelled to shift her meaning. 'I mean . . . you will be able to persuade your father to come along, won't you?'

'Oh, I see!' he teased her openly. 'So you'll not want me if I have to come along all on my own?'

'Oh no!' Now she really was embarrassed. 'I

didn't mean that, only it would be good for him and Gramps to get together and talk about old times, don't you think?'

As the child opened her arms to go to Danny, Emily let her loose. In spite of her deeper love for John, it always did her heart good to see the honest love between Danny and her child.

With one strong arm, Danny held Cathleen on the rim of the cart. 'When you're bigger and your mammy allows me, I'll take you off on my rounds – what d'you think to that, eh?' He laughed out loud when the child gave him a wide, happy grin. 'Oh, so you'd like that, would you?'

'I'm sure she would,' Emily remarked, 'but that's a long way off yet, so don't get her hopes up.' There were times when she felt she had to curb the growing bond between these two, and other times when she thanked the Good Lord for it.

Lifting the child once more into his arms, and content to let her entwine the strands of his hair round her tiny fingers, he asked Emily in a sincere voice, 'Do you want to know what I think?'

Momentarily lost in thoughts of John, and how she would explain Cathleen to him, Emily was jolted back to the present. 'Sorry, Danny,' she apologised. 'I was miles away.'

'I can see that,' he remarked softly. 'I was just asking if you wanted to know what I really thought?' He had no doubt but that she had been 'miles away' with John Hanley, but he made no mention of it. Instead he went on, in the same steady voice, 'Just now you asked what I thought about the two old fellas getting together to talk about past times. And I'm trying to tell you that there are other things on *my* mind at the minute.'

'What kind of things?' She knew that he had special feelings for her. At first it had been a worry, but lately she had come to see him for the true friend he was, and had come to rely on that friendship; every minute he was here, she honestly enjoyed his company.

Right now though, she suspected he was about to try and deepen their friendship into something else – something she wasn't ready for and probably never would be. Suddenly, she was on the defensive. 'Please, Danny . . . not now, eh?'

'All right, my beauty.' He loved her too much to go against her wishes. 'But I think you already know that it would make me the happiest man on God's earth if you'd agree to be my wife. You could have whichever home you wanted . . . I'm not short of a bob or two.' His gaze shifted to the child. 'I could give this darling lass a name and a father . . . if only you'd let me?'

When instead of answering she cast her gaze down, he felt mortified. Taking her by the hand he apologised. 'Aw look, I'm sorry . . . opening my big mouth yet again. I know I should keep my feelings to myself, but it's so hard sometimes.'

Emily looked up. 'I understand,' she conceded. 'But you know how it is. I'm John's woman. I can't change that, nor would I want to.' Hard words but they needed saying.

He gave a sad little nod. Then his smile warmed her heart. 'Forgive me, eh? Don't have me shot if now and again I take the liberty of reminding you that I'm always here, if you ever need me.'

'I know, Danny, and I'm very lucky to have a friend like you. You're a lovely man, but instead of wasting your time on me, you should be looking for someone who is free to give you all the love you deserve.'

Danny's gaze softened. 'Don't you understand?' he murmured, taking a step forward. 'As long as I live, I can never look in any other direction. The truth is, my beauty, if I can't have you, then I want no one.'

Emily was cut to the core. 'No, Danny! Please don't talk like that. You were made for family life – for children and such. I don't want to be the one who deprives you of that.'

For a long moment he looked at her, at that pretty face and those quiet brown eyes now scarred with sadness, and he couldn't bear it. 'Whatever decision I make, it'll be my decision and no one else's. You remember that, and remember this too. Other than you, there is no woman on God's earth I want, nor ever will.'

Choking with emotion, Emily reached up and

with the greatest tenderness stroked his face. 'I'd give anything to love you as you deserve,' she said, 'but I've already given my heart away. I'm so sorry, Danny. Really I am.'

'Ah, it's me that should be sorry!' Grabbing her hand he pressed it to his heart. 'Do you forgive me?'

She didn't hesitate. 'There's nothing to forgive,' she said.

With a quick smile and cheeky wink, he confessed, 'I can't say I don't wish you would change your mind, but I promise I'll try and keep my feelings to myself from now on.' Making the sign of the cross over his heart, he looked a sorry sinner. 'Cross my heart, and may all the milk turn sour if I'm lying!'

At the sight of his eyes rolling heavenward and that naughty, twinkling smile, Emily burst out laughing. 'You're a devil, Danny Williams, so you are!'

'Well now, will ye look at that!' Hugging the child into his chest, he swung her round. 'We made your mammy laugh. Isn't that something, eh?' Plonking a quick kiss on Cathleen's forehead, he handed her back to Emily. 'I'd best get on, or I'll have my father breathing down my neck when I get home!'

With one easy movement, he swung himself onto the cart. The great churns were stacked behind him. From the foot of the cart Emily watched him stow the nosebag and pick up the reins. It was a privilege to have him about, she thought, and these days, with no word from John, she desperately needed someone to talk to. Danny was a kind-hearted, honest sort of a bloke, and she respected him enormously. Up to now though, that was as far as her feelings went.

Danny, though, had fallen for her straight away, ever since he'd returned to the village. Twice he had asked her to wed him, and twice she'd refused. All along she had been honest with him. She didn't love him, she explained, and never could, not in the way she loved John.

But little Cathleen loved him, and sometimes, in the dark of night when sleep eluded her, Emily would look at her darling child and the doubts would creep in yet again. Should she put the child first and give her a proper daddy who would love and care for her? Should she give up on John, who now seemed to have given up on her? Was she being unfair to her mammy by denying Danny the chance to be a son-in-law to her, and a father to Cathleen? Right from the start, Aggie had taken to Danny. And it was painfully obvious that little Cathleen adored that good man. What's more, her daughter would probably love to have a younger brother or sister.

Sometimes, Emily believed she was being selfish in putting her own feelings before those of her loved ones. And yet, how could she give herself in marriage to someone she didn't love in that way? So many questions. So many doubts, haunting her through the long, sleepless nights.

But then, when morning came the questions faded beneath her steadfast love for John.

She couldn't deny she had grown fond of Danny, and it pained her to keep rejecting him, but what choice had she? In her deepest heart she had always believed John would come back. She believed it now, and would go on believing it, until all hope was gone.

Right now, there were three men in her life: her old grandfather, who had bad days and good days, but was always a kind and loving man; then there was Clem Jackson, whose presence was like a dark blanket over the sun. If only he'd go! No one wanted him here at Potts End.

And then there was Danny! A gem of a man, wasted in his affection for her, but nothing she could say would make him see that.

'Some of this milk came from old Daisy at Glebe House Farm,' he was telling the wide-eyed Cathleen. 'Up at four every morning she is, waiting first in line, bellowing her head off, to have her bursting udders emptied into this here churn.' Wiping the tip of his finger round the rim of the churn he sucked on it and rolled his eyes. 'A gift from the heavens, that's what it is!' he sighed.

Winking at Emily, he leaned towards the child, his voice a magical whisper. 'It's what all the stars in the sky are made of. That's what makes 'em twinkle so bright.'

His eyes grew wider with amazement. 'Do you know, I wouldn't be surprised if all the little children in the world were made with Daisy's milk. That's why *their* pretty little eyes twinkle and shine. Daisy mixed the magic into her milk and when the Good Lord made the children, He gave them each a little sip.'

Lowering his voice he shifted his gaze to Emily. 'He must have given some to your mammy too, because whenever I'm near her, all sorts o' wonderful magic begins to happen.'

For the briefest of minutes, there was an awkward pause between them. Emily didn't know quite what to do or say, and Danny longed to take her in his arms and kiss her until she came to love him the way he loved her.

But then he realised he had almost spoiled the moment, so returning his attention to the child, he pointed to the little pools of spilt milk on the floor of the cart. 'Will ye look at that! You know what that means, don't you, eh? Well, I'll tell ye. It means the cat will have it, and give it to the kittens, and that's why the kittens are able to see in the dark. I bet you didn't know that, eh? I bet you didn't know it was Daisy's magic milk that made all the cats see in the dark?'

Emily laughed. 'Give over, Danny Williams! What should we do with you, eh?'

As his gaze fell on her upturned face, he was about to say, 'Marry me, that's what you should do with me.' Instead, he laughed with her. 'It's true!' he protested. 'Daisy herself told me – and she's never lied to me before.'

Now, as he poured a small measure of milk into the palm of his hand and gave it to a stray cat who had grown wise to his daily treat, the tiniest of smiles lifted the corners of Emily's mouth. There was no denying he brought a measure of sunshine and joy into their lives, she thought. With that mop of wavy dark hair and those laughing grey eyes he had such charm and sincerity, and a way that instantly endeared him to both animals and children alike.

In fact, throughout the village of Salmesbury she knew of no one who had a bad word to say about him. There were plenty of lasses who fancied him, though.

Suddenly, Danny hopped down from his seat. 'I've yet to pass the time o' day with your old gramps,' he reminded Emily. 'That's if your mammy doesn't mind?'

'I'm sure that'll be fine.' Emily was glad he wasn't rushing away, though time was wasting and she would soon have to get on with her own work. There were so many chores still to be done, it left little time for socialising. 'He's always glad to see you,' she said. 'You leave him chuckling every time, and we're all grateful for that.'

He gave her a sideways glance. 'The village clown, that's me.'

Emily was horrified, and put him straight at once. 'You're nothing of the sort! You're a warm, intelligent man who's full of the joys of life, and somehow you always manage to make a person feel good.' Smiling up at him, she told him from the heart, 'It's a real gift you have, Danny. And you seem to be the only one who doesn't realise it.'

When he smiled back, it was a free and easy smile that spoke volumes. 'So, there's hope for me yet, is there?' His words carried a mixed message and Emily was quick to pick up on it. So, instead of answering, she hastened her steps and got to the farmhouse door before him.

His voice followed her. 'So there's *no* hope – is that what you're saying? Aw, you're a wicked woman, Emily Ramsden, a wicked, *wicked* woman!' He feigned desperation. 'Aw, come on now. Give us a kiss and we'll say no more.'

Suppressing her laughter, Emily rushed inside, and almost fell in the sitting-room door.

'Good God, lass!' On her knees, Aggie had been cleaning out the fire-grate, and as she looked up, the small shovelful of cinders tumbled to the hearth. 'Whatever's the matter?' By now, Emily had dropped the child on the sofa and was heartily chuckling. 'What's tickling you, eh?'

Composing herself, Emily explained. 'Danny's

behind me. He wants to see Gramps before he leaves.'

Aggie smiled knowingly. 'Oh, I understand. And I suppose he's been weaving his magic on you and the bairn, has he?'

'You could say that,' Emily answered. 'Sometimes I wonder if he's not mad as a hatter.'

'Oh aye, lass, he *is* mad,' her mother agreed. 'Mad on you and the bairn, that's what.'

Afraid she and her mammy were about to get into a deeper conversation, Emily changed the subject. 'Is it all right then, if I take him up to see Gramps?'

'That is, if it's no trouble.' Danny came to the doorway.

'It's no trouble at all, and well you know it,' Aggie chided. 'What! Tom Isaac would never forgive me if I let you leave without seeing him.' Pointing a blackened hand towards the stairs she told Emily, 'Go on then, lass. Take him up, and take the child with yer. Your grandad's been asking after her.'

While Aggie continued with cleaning out the grate, Emily climbed the narrow winding stairs to the upper part of the farmhouse. Behind her came Danny, who insisted on carrying little Cathleen, who all the way entwined his hair round her tiny finger, until he feared she'd soon have it out by the roots. But he didn't mind. In fact it gave him a comforting, fatherly feeling.

The old fellow must have heard them tramping up the stairs because when they entered his room, he was already struggling to sit up. 'Easy now, Gramps!' Rushing forward, Emily helped him get comfortable. 'How's that?' Plumping up the bolster, she made sure his back was properly supported. 'Comfortable, are you?' Aggie had lit a fire in the little grate earlier, and the small bedroom was warm.

'Stop fussing, woman!' Visibly thinner, his face deeper-lined by the passage of time, Thomas still had fire in his eyes and a sharp tongue when needed. But now as he spoke to the child, his eyes softened and his arms opened to take her. 'An' what 'ave you been up to, young 'un?' he asked with a crinkled smile. 'Been out there feeding the birds, 'ave yer?'

Danny put the child into his arms, where she sat for a while, looking up at the old man and chuckling at whatever he said, even though she didn't really understand half of it.

A few moments later when he seemed to tire, Emily gently collected Cathleen into her arms. 'You and Danny have a chat,' she suggested, 'while I go and make you a brew.' She knew how much he loved to be alone with Danny, when the two of them would talk about things only men appreciated.

'Aye, go on then, lass,' he replied. 'An' see if Aggie's got any o' that bread-puddin left an' all.'

He licked his lips. 'By! Your mammy meks the best bread puddin in the whole world!' He pointed to Danny. 'While you're at it, lass, you'd best fetch your young man a helping an' all.'

Being referred to as Emily's 'young man' put a smile on Danny's face, but Emily made a mental note to correct her grandad's thinking once Danny was gone.

'I wouldn't say no to another cuppa, but I'm full o' those tasty muffins,' Danny said politely, rubbing his tummy appreciatively.

With Emily out the door, Danny told the old fella, 'That was wicked of you.' He wagged a finger. 'You know very well I'm not her young man.'

Thomas gave a sly little chuckle. 'Mebbe not. But you'd like to be, wouldn't you, eh?'

'You know I would,' Danny told him.

'And have you asked her?'

'I have. Time and again, on my knees, on my feet, and even once with my face covered in Cathleen's chocolate.'

'So what did she say?'

'What she always says.'

'I see.' The old man nodded knowingly. 'She's still hankering after John Hanley, is that it?'

'She loves him, that's why.' Danny envied John that kind of love, especially when he'd been away so long and in his opinion didn't deserve such loyalty.

The same thoughts invaded the old fellow's

mind. 'Where the devil is that young scoundrel, that's what I'd like to know!'

Danny could see how the old man was in danger of getting too excited. 'That's not for us to know, and not for me to comment on,' he said guardedly.

The old man didn't agree. 'Ah, well now, that's where you're wrong!' he declared. 'That young bugger will get the length o' my tongue if he ever does come back, I can tell you! What kind of a man is it that gets a young girl with child, then goes off to Gawd knows where and never a word in over two years.' His voice shook with anger. 'Like my own cowardly son, he's run for his life, that's what he's done. By! They'd neither of 'em best come back to these parts in a hurry, because they'll 'ave me to deal with, I can tell yer!'

'Take it easy, Tom.' Afraid he was working himself up to fever pitch, Danny changed the subject. 'I'll tell you what though,' he said, 'I reckon you'd give anybody a run for their money, eh? What!' Clamping a hand over the old man's now clenched fist, he feigned admiration. 'You've a fist like a hammer. They tell me you were a bit of a fighter in your time, is that right?'

'Oh, aye!' Tom's proud old eyes were alight with memories. 'They said I were one o' the best street-fighters around. It got so they couldn't get any man to stand against me. It were a shame, but once the police got on our trail, we had to move into 'fficial premises. After that it all got too organised like. Above board and proper, if yer know what I mean? All Queensberry rules and regulations.' He shook his head woefully. 'It were never the same after that.'

Danny knew the story well. 'I've heard it from my da time and again,' he revealed. 'He loves to talk about it; raw fighting in the back alleys and such. "Skin and blood up the walls and bits o' flesh under the feet," that's how he puts it. Then how it changed when the authorities took over. Mind you, according to him, there was corruption by the bucket-load, even in higher places!'

The old man nodded enthusiastically. 'Oh aye, that's true enough. By! There were some bad buggers behind the scenes. The old way were the best though – big money changing hands at the drop of a hat; men facing up to each other on impulse, bare-backed and wound up so tight they'd fight till they dropped. I've known men go down and never come up again, and others would walk away and leave 'em there. No rules nor regulations then. No ropes nor bells. Just bare knuckles and raw courage.'

Danny chuckled. 'Men were men and to hell with all the rigmarole!'

Thomas Isaac smiled, his heart heavy with nostalgia. 'They were the good days,' he mused. 'Days when you knew who your friends were and if called on, you'd put your own life on the line for a mate.'

Danny saw the tears gathering. 'There are still

men like that,' he told him. 'Although mebbe they're not so thick on the ground.'

'Mebbe!' The anger returned. 'But there's more evil bastards than there are good 'uns!' Lowering his voice, he said vehemently, 'There's one bugger right 'ere under this roof. If I were twenty years younger, I'd do for him tomorrow, so I would!'

Danny nodded his understanding. 'I know who you mean,' he said quietly. 'But there's nothing to be gained by tormenting yourself.'

'Aye, I know that.' The old man glanced at the door again. 'By! He's a bad bugger, is that one though!'

Danny let it be known, 'I wish there was something I could do, but there isn't, more's the pity.'

As always, the old man had the answer. 'Marry the lass, then it'll gi' you the right to be rid of him.'

Danny shook his head. 'I can't marry her against her will, Tom, and well you know it.' One way or another he believed he'd got the full picture of what was happening here at the farm. 'And even if Emily did agree to marry me, it isn't as simple as all that, is it?'

The old man knew that was only too true. 'Happen not,' he conceded. 'The truth is, that bastard's got us tied up every which way.'

'Don't lose heart, though,' Danny counselled. 'Folks like him will always come undone in the end. Be patient. It'll all come right, you'll see.'

Every time he and the old man were alone together, the matter of Clem Jackson came up. It was a torture to the old man, and apart from offering money, Danny couldn't see how he might interfere where his offer of help had already been rejected.

The old man seemed to read Danny's mind. 'If you and our Emily were wed, it would put a spoke in his wheel. You could find out things. You'd have a certain right, d'yer see?'

With a careful choice of words, Danny had to stop it right there. 'We're not wed, Grandad, and, unfortunately, not likely to be. So it might be best if we don't get down that road. Let's leave it at that, eh?'

~

In fact, they had little choice, because now Emily was back, with a tray containing a dish of cold bread pudding and two mugs of tea. 'I hope you are ready for this, Gramps,' she said, her quick smile lighting up the room. 'Mam's given you a helping and a half, although she says it's a funny sort of a breakfast.' She set the tray down before making good her escape. 'Mam's baking and Cathleen's asleep. I've got a pile of washing bubbling in the copper, so I'd best be off.' With that she was across the room and out the door.

'I'll pop in and see you before I leave!' Danny called out, and from somewhere down the stairs came a muffled reply.

'Ask her while she's up to her armpits in soap-suds,' the old man suggested with a wink.

'You won't give up, will you?' Danny laughed. And neither will I, he thought.

Because, as sure as day followed night, he would keep asking Emily to be his wife, until in the end she had to agree.

Ten minutes later, feeling all the better for this break, Danny called in on Emily as he had promised.

The girl was not up to her armpits in soapsuds, as the old man had predicted. Instead she had already lifted the clothes out of the copper boiler with the wooden tongs and was in the middle of rinsing them in the big sink. The small stone outhouse was thick with steam erupting from the copper, and Emily's face was bright pink from the heat.

'Here, let me do that!' Dodging the many clothes-lines stretched criss-cross from one end of the outhouse to the other, Danny made his way through to her.

As Emily fought to wring out a huge bedsheet, he took hold of it and without effort fed it through the mangle and then folded it and draped it over the line. He looked at the growing mountain of damp clothes on the wooden drainer. 'Do you want me to stay and help?' he asked hopefully.

She thanked him, but, 'You get off now and finish your rounds,' she suggested graciously. 'I've almost done here.'

He hid his disappointment. 'These bedsheets weigh a ton when they're wet,' he remarked.

Knowing he would linger all day if she encouraged him, Emily was adamant. 'I'm used to it,' she said. 'If I had help, I'd lose the routine and it would only take longer in the end, if you know what I mean?'

Grudgingly, but with a ready grin, he bade her goodbye. 'I'll see you tomorrow then?'

'I'll look forward to it,' she said. And that was the truth.

Coming to the door of the outhouse, she waved him away. You're persistent, I'll give you that, she thought kindly. Somewhere, there's a woman who would give her right arm to be your wife. I'm sorry, Danny, but it's not me. Without even being aware that she'd been thinking it, the words fell out. 'More's the pity.'

A little surprised and bewildered, she made her way back into the outhouse, where she threw herself into the task in hand. It had been an odd thing to say, she mused. As though to shut it out, she filled her mind with thoughts of John. And, as always, the love for him was overwhelming.

∼

An hour later, Emily had finished. With all the washing hanging limp and bedraggled over the lines, she made her way to the shed where she collected an armful of kindling.

That done she returned to the outhouse, where she made a bed of newspaper in the fire-grate; on top of that she laid the wood in a kind of pyramid. Next, taking a match from the mantelpiece, she set light to the paper.

When that was all flaring and crackling, she took the smallest pieces of coal from the bucket and built another pyramid over the first. On her knees, she stretched a sheet of paper over the fireplace to encourage the flames, then watched and waited until the whole lot was burning and glowing; the heat tickling her face and making her warm.

'That'll soon dry it out,' she murmured, clambering to her knees.

Replacing the screen in front of the fire, she made her way out, carefully dodging and ducking the damp clothes as she went.

Inside the scullery, Aggie had a brew of tea waiting for her. 'All done, are you, lass?' Taking off her long goffered apron and wearily lowering herself into the fireside-chair, Aggie laid back and closed her eyes. 'Me back's fit to break in two,' she groaned. 'I swear, there's enough work in this farmhouse to keep an army on their toes! I'll have to get the dinner going in an hour or so. It'll be a simple meal, seeing as it's Christmas Day tomorrow. I've got some cold beef and pickled onion with mashed potato, and tapioca wi' bottled gooseberries for afters. What d'you reckon to that, lass?'

Settling in the chair opposite, her tea clutched in her fist, Emily said, 'It sounds lovely, Mam. Cathleen still asleep, is she?'

'The bairn hasn't moved a muscle since you went out,' Aggie answered, opening one eye. 'Looks like Danny's worn her out.'

Emily laughed. 'He's worn me out an' all.'

Detecting the underlying seriousness of Emily's remark, Aggie asked pointedly, 'Been on at you to wed him again, has he?'

'He means well,' Emily said. 'And I dare say he would move heaven and earth to make me and Cathleen happy . . .'

'But?'

Emily knew all the old arguments. 'But what?'

Aggie answered exactly the way Emily had expected. 'But your heart's out there with John Hanley. I expect that's what you told Danny?'

'Yes, but he already knows it.'

'I see.' As ever, Aggie read the situation well. She also knew that in the end, someone was bound to get hurt.

For a few minutes, the two women sat lost in thought, quietly listening to the fire roaring. The tassels on the chenille runner that covered the mantelshelf danced in the heat, and light reflected off the glass dome of the clock and the framed picture of Queen Victoria that Clare Ramsden had bought on a visit to Blackpool in 1885.

After a while, Aggie asked, 'How long are you prepared to wait, lass?'

Emily had been so deep in thought she hadn't heard the full question. 'Wait for what?'

'For John to come home?'

'I wish I knew, Mam.' Emily had asked herself that same question time and again, and still she wasn't sure. 'As long as it takes, I suppose.'

'And how long is that?' Aggie was concerned about her daughter's wellbeing. She had seen her growing lonelier and quieter, and it cut her to the quick. 'Are you thinking weeks, months . . .' her eyebrows went up at the prospect. 'Or do you mean to wait for years – is that it?' Part of her acknowledged her own pain at Michael's abandonment. She and Emily were made of the same strong clay: they could manage without their men, but that didn't mean it was easy. And Emily was still young – she should be wed to someone who loved her and who could give her another bairn as company for Cathleen.

'I don't know,' Emily admitted. 'All I do know is that I love him with all my heart. When John left, he said he'd be back. I promised him I'd wait. And I will keep that promise.'

Aggie pressed the point. 'And will you wait until

little Cathleen is two or three? Or will you wait until she starts playing with other children from the village – children who know what it's like to have a daddy at home. And when she starts asking where *her* daddy is, have you got an answer ready, my girl? Tell me that.'

Now as Emily glanced up her eyes were moist with tears. 'I know what you're trying to say, Mam, and I understand,' she said brokenly. 'I've been thinking of little Cathleen too, and the older she gets the more I worry. But I can't marry Danny. As much as I like and respect him, and as much as I know he would look after us, I can't bring myself to marry him, not when I still love John. I keep hoping that John is safe and well: I can't stop thinking about him, Mam. He's on my mind the whole time, night and day.'

Wiping a tear, she finished, 'Besides, Danny deserves better than that.'

Aggie said nothing. Instead she sipped at her tea and wondered what would become of them all.

Emily was grateful for the lull in the conversation. Only time would tell whether John would return, and if he didn't do so soon, she would have to decide what to do. But it wouldn't be easy, she knew that.

The child's waking cries shook them out of their reverie. But when the infant's cries lapsed into a string of happy gobbledy-gook, Emily lingered a moment. 'I've a good mind to go and see Lizzie,' she revealed. 'You never know. She might have word of John.'

Aggie warned her, 'Well, I hope the old bugger makes you more welcome than she did last time!' she declared. 'What! She wound you up so much you wouldn't speak for a whole hour.'

Emily remembered. 'She was a bit . . . difficult, that's all.'

'Hmh!' Aggie sat up. 'Cantankerous, more like! Heaven knows what's the matter wi' her. Ever since her John went away she's been as sour as a rhubarb pie without a morsel o' sugar.'

'She's getting old, poor thing.' Emily had a soft spot for Lizzie. 'She suffers a lot from pain in her joints.'

Aggie had little sympathy. 'She's too proud – won't let anybody help her. You heard Danny say how he found her climbing a ladder to mend that hole in the thatch the other week. When he offered to do it for her, she told him to sod off – said that she wasn't yet ready for the knacker's yard!' She wagged a finger. 'If you ask me, you'll do well to steer clear of the old battle-axe.'

Emily was not deterred. 'Why are you so hard on her, Mam? That's not like you at all! Didn't she used to be your friend?'

Aggie blushed with shame. 'Aye well, happen I might be a bit hard on her, but she's been hard on you, and I don't tek kindly to that.'

There were times when Emily had the same stubborn streak in her as Aggie. 'I still intend going,' she decided. 'I'm gonna pluck up my courage. I need to know if she's heard from John.'

'Even if she has, what meks you think she'll tell *you*?'

Emily was already at the door. 'Why shouldn't she tell me?'

Just then the child began crying again. '*That's* why!' Gesturing towards the stairway, Aggie reminded her, 'Lizzie refuses to believe the child is John's. She thinks you've been up to no good with some other man, and that you're trying to blame her nephew.' She chuckled. 'Mother hen protecting her chick, that's what she is. My God! The way you feel about John, who else's child could it be? The whole world knows it's his, yet that old besom won't have it no way!'

Rolling her eyes to heaven she finished angrily, 'It'll be a damned good thing when he does come back. *Then* she'll know well enough!'

Emily remained silent, but was grateful when her mother did not notice the guilt and shame in her face. 'I'd best be off now, Mam.' Rushing off upstairs, she felt the tears smarting her eyes. She hated herself for deceiving her mammy. But the truth about little Cathleen's beginnings was far more hurtful and damaging. She dreaded John's reaction; for the hundredth time, she recalled that awful summer day, of such hope and happiness, ending in a darkness that had engulfed her for many a long month. Would he understand?

~

A short time later, well wrapped up and carrying the child in a shawl-sling, Emily began the walk across the fields to Lizzie's pretty cottage.

On the way she stopped several times to put the child down; she held her hand and encouraged her to walk. But though Cathleen's sturdy little legs stumbled a clear path through the snowy grass, they soon tired, and it wasn't long before Emily had to carry her again. 'You're taking advantage of my good nature,' she teased her breathlessly. 'I reckon it should be you carrying me!'

Just as Aggie had feared, Lizzie was not exactly pleased to see her. 'What is it you want from me?' Holding the door open just so far, she peered at Emily through suspicious eyes. 'I've not heard from him, if that's what yer after.'

Emily reasoned with her. 'I don't want us to be enemies, Lizzie. Please may I come inside?'

'What for?'

'To talk, that's all.'

The woman scowled. 'We've nowt to talk about.'

Sensing a weakening, Emily persisted. 'Please, Lizzie. I've carried little Cathleen nearly all the way here, and my arms are aching. Besides, we're both thirsty.'

Glancing from one to the other, Lizzie saw how the child was smiling at her, and it touched her troubled old heart. 'All right, but only for a minute. Yer can have a rest and a drink, then I'll thank you to leave.' She opened the door wider. 'Either come in or stay out. It's too damned cold to be standing here all day with the door wide open!'

With a muttered apology, Emily darted inside. She waited until the other woman shut the door. 'Go on!' Gesturing for Emily to go ahead, Lizzie told her, 'You've been here with John often enough to know the way by now.'

Feeling uncomfortable under Lizzie's scowl, Emily led the way to the back-parlour.

Lizzie followed her in. 'Sit yersel' down,' she ordered. 'Now then, what does the infant want to drink?' She gave a grudging look at the beautiful little girl, and deliberately closed her heart against any feelings of warmth.

'A drop of milk would suit fine,' Emily answered as she sat down in the big squashy chair by the fire. 'Thanks, Lizzie.'

'And I expect you'll be wanting a cuppa tea, will yer?'

Emily nodded appreciatively. 'Yes, I'd love one. If that's all right?'

The old woman grunted. 'I wouldn't be asking if it weren't!' With that she disappeared into the scullery, only to return a few minutes later with a mug of milk for the child, and a drop of lukewarm tea for Emily. 'It's only been made a few minutes,' she explained, 'but it's warm enough to thaw your bones.'

Emily took a sip from the teacup. It was all she could do not to grimace, for the tea was like dishwater. 'It's fine, thanks, Lizzie,' she lied handsomely.

'Fine or not, it'll have to do!' retorted the woman. 'I don't intend mekking a fresh pot just yet.' Pointing an accusing finger at Emily's feet, she tutted, 'Look at the state of your feet! By! They must be frozen.' Emily's two ankles were bright pink. 'Good God, lass! Have yer no decent shoes to yer name?'

Instinctively pulling her thick skirt over her feet to hide them, Emily told her, 'I don't seem to feel the cold, and besides, I didn't walk through the snow just now. I came along by the hedges. I've got a pair of boots at home but I can't stand to wear them. I thought you knew that?'

'Hmh!' Scowling her disapproval, Lizzie told her, 'I might know it, but that don't mean to say I think it's right.' Waving her hand in a gesture of impatience, she reminded Emily, 'You said you were thirsty. So drink up and be off with yer. I've other things to do than sit here wasting time with the likes of you.'

Emily had to say it. 'Why have you turned against me, Lizzie?'

'You know why!'

'Is it because of John?'

The woman glared at her. 'It's not so much because of John, as what you've told folks.' She shifted her gaze to the child. 'John's been branded with being the father of this little 'un.' Now as she stared Emily in the eye, her gaze hardened. 'It's a lie and well you know it. John would never have got you with child and then run off. He thought too much of you to do that!'

Emily defended herself. 'I was not the one to spread that rumour.'

'Huh! Well, somebody did, because it's common knowledge now.'

'Lizzie, can I ask a question?'

'Yer can ask if yer like, but I might not answer.'

'Have you heard from John lately?'

The old woman shook her head. 'Not that it's any of your business, but no, I haven't.'

Emily's heart sank. 'I haven't heard a single word since he's been gone.'

'Huh! I'm not surprised. He's probably heard you've given yourself to some other man and tried to lay the blame at his door. I wouldn't be at all surprised if he never sets foot in these parts again, thanks to you!'

Emily was cut deep by what Lizzie had said. 'I never gave myself to anyone!' she protested. 'It's John I love. There's never been anyone else for me, and never will be.'

'Liar!'

Emily shook her head. 'No, Lizzie. It's true. John has always been the only one.'

'So, yer still claiming the child is John's, are yer?' By now Lizzie was on her feet and staring down at Emily with quick, accusing eyes.

Emily stood up. 'No, Lizzie, I'm not claiming that.'

'Oh, so now you're saying the child is *not* John's? By! Your story changes by the minute.'

'Please. Listen to me.' Emily confessed to as much as she dared. 'I'm telling you now. Little Cathleen is not John's, and I never said she was. I want you to believe that.'

But Lizzie was past listening. 'I'm not about to believe anything you say, young lady. Besides, I thought I asked you to leave?'

Emily had things to get off her chest before she left. 'I swear to you, Lizzie, John has always been the only man I love, and he still is. But if he doesn't want me, I'll understand and accept it.'

'Will yer now?' In spite of her harsh retort, Lizzie was moved by the sincerity in Emily's voice, and when the tears welled up in the girl's eyes, she was half-inclined to believe her. But there was still the question. 'If, as you say and I know, the child is *not* John's, then whose child is she?'

For one mad moment it was on the tip of Emily's tongue to blurt out the awful truth, about how her uncle had attacked her in the barn and got her with child. But then she thought of her mother and grandfather and the consequences of her words. And she could not take the risk of the truth leaking out. 'I'm sorry, Lizzie. I can't tell you,' she finished lamely.

The other woman's moment of compassion melted away in the heat of anger. 'No, o' course yer can't!' Stepping back, she flung open the door. 'Yer can't tell me, because it's too shameful. But I know well enough what happened! While John were away yer went with some man – that's the sorry truth, ain't it? And now yer too ashamed to give up his name, or to admit that you could hardly wait until my John's back were turned afore yer went behind the cowsheds with somebody else. And now yer come here and tell me that John is the only man you ever want.' Disgust trembled in her voice. 'You're a disgrace, that's what you are.'

Emily tried to calm her. 'But it's true, Lizzie. And I need John now, more than you could ever know.'

The other woman laughed out loud. 'Well, o' course you do! You need him to raise another man's child – a child that belongs to Danny Williams, I shouldn't wonder. God knows he's at the farm often enough, hanging about, trailing after yer like a dog on a lead. Oh, don't think it ain't been noticed! And now you've had your little fling, you've got your sights set higher than a milkman. You need a father for the child, some fool to take care of you, and I dare say you reckon our John will come home a rich man. Well, I'm on to you, lady! And I will not let my John take the blame for what some other man's done. You're a shameful little hussy, and John is best rid of yer.'

She took a step forward. 'If you've come to find comfort here, I can tell yer now, you'll get none! So be off with yer, and yer bastard child, afore I tek it on meself to throw you out!'

Sensing the troubled atmosphere, and frightened by the woman's anger, little Cathleen began to wail.

Shocked to the core by Lizzie's vicious outburst, and especially shaken by her belief that Danny was Cathleen's father, Emily picked up the crying toddler, wrapped her in the shawl, and took her leave.

In the circumstances, it was all she could do.

~

As Emily and the child disappeared over the snow-covered brow of the hill, Lizzie moved away from the window and for a time just stood there, her head bowed into her hands and her whole body shaking.

A moment later, she had dropped into the chair and was sobbing aloud. It had been a bad thing she'd done in throwing mother and child out into the cold like that. Such harsh behaviour went against her nature.

But as far as she could tell, Emily had given her no choice.

CHAPTER FIVE

STRIDING ALONG THE ship's deck, John made a handsome figure. Taller than when he had first joined the Merchant Navy, he had filled out to become a man of substance. His dark hair was longer; his skin browned by the changing of seasons in the two years and more that he had travelled the high seas. Now, back in Liverpool docks, with money in his pocket and a considerable sum put by, he showed a confidence that had grown with every pay-packet.

'Where might you be off to, looking so full of yourself?' Leaning over the railings, the fat, bearded Captain puffed on his pipe and gave John a wink. 'From the look on your face, I'd say there was a woman involved somewhere along the way?' He gave another, cheekier wink. 'Is she worth it? That's what you need to ask yourself.'

John's rich blue eyes lit up. 'Oh, she's worth it all right, sir,' he answered happily. 'And I can't wait to see her again.' To hold Emily in his arms

and to see her face when he showed her the cache
of hard-earned money that would rid her of Clem
Jackson forever – it was all he had dreamed of
these past two years and more. A shadow crossed
his mind as he wondered why he had never
received any replies to his letters; he shivered, and
it disappeared.

'Well, I for one am sorry to see you go, young
fella, and that's a fact. You're a better worker than
most, and you don't cause trouble. That's the kind
of a man I like on my ship.'

John thanked him. 'I'm not a natural sailor,'
he admitted. 'I prefer the solid earth beneath my
feet.'

'Maybe you do, son. But the earth can give way
beneath your feet as well as any ship. You take it
from me.' The Captain had lived a long time and
learned many things that made him thankful
to live out his life in the middle of the oceans.
'Besides, on board a ship you come to know your
enemies. I can't say the same for the big wide
world, where you never know who's creeping up
on you – or from which direction.'

'I dare say you're right.' During his time aboard,
John had come to like and respect this old tar.
'But I'm willing to take my chances.'

'Hmh! She really *must* be worth it then.'

'She is.'

'Best o' luck then, son.'

'Thank you, sir, and the same to you.' Eager

now to be gone, John bade the Captain goodbye. 'I'd best be on my way. I've a considerable journey to make yet.' That particular journey was long overdue, and he was desperately impatient to see Emily.

Sucking on his old pipe, the Captain joked, 'A few days with your little woman, and you'll be ready for off again.'

John shook his head. 'Sorry, but I'll be staying put this time round.'

The Captain pondered on that. 'Oh, but that's what they all say, and they always come back, for one reason or another.' He gave another of his cheeky winks. 'I've an idea you'll be coming with us next time round. And don't forget, I always like to turn around inside a month, so I hope to be away by the first week in April. I'd like to take you with me. What d'you say?'

'Nothing doing, Captain,' John assured him. 'You see, I've a wedding to go to.'

'A wedding, eh? Still, I'm sure she wouldn't mind seeing you off for a while, especially if I up your wages?'

John thanked him, but, 'No offence, sir, but I wouldn't care if I never saw a ship's deck again. I'm happiest with my two feet on dry land, the rabbits in my sights, and the sound of birdsong in my ears.'

The Captain laughed. 'A country lad at heart, more's the pity.'

Smiling up at him, John doffed his seaman's cap, which he then threw into the air, laughing aloud as it splashed into the sea. 'Thanks for everything,' he called, quickening his steps. 'Fair weather and good luck to you and your ship.'

Behind him, the Captain waved. 'We'll still be here if you change your mind!' he called. But John was already out of earshot, running like the wind along the quayside and his heart tapping out a dance inside his chest. 'I'm home, Emily!' he murmured. 'I've come back for you. Just like I promised.'

First stop was the quayside barber's for a shave. After that a visit to the local tailor's for a new set of clothes.

'My shoes will have to do,' John told the lanky assistant, 'but I'll need everything else from top to bottom.' He didn't intend going back to Emily looking like some tramp off the streets. 'I don't want to be spending all my savings on clothes,' he warned, 'but I'll not be wanting rubbish neither.'

The assistant gave him a thin smile. 'Follow me, sir. I'll have you fixed up in no time at all.' He led John to the back shelves, where a multitude of shirts, collars and cravats were all arranged in neat piles. 'You'll not find better anywhere,' he declared with pride. 'What size are you, sir?'

He then swept his arm to encompass another wall where hung a selection of jackets in every size and shape. 'Try them on,' he suggested. 'You're bound to find one to fit. The mirror is there, on the wall.' Pointing to the four large drawers beneath the shelves, he added, 'I shall find whatever else you need in those drawers there.'

With that he produced his measuring tape with a flourish and gazed critically at John's garments.

It wasn't long before John was holding a parcel, neatly wrapped in brown paper and tied with string, knotted into a helpful little handle so he could carry it easily. He paid with a large, white £5 note and left the shop with a spring in his step.

Next stop was the local inn, for a well-earned drink to cool his throat, and a bath to take away the smell of the last couple of weeks at sea.

'Will you be wanting one towel or two?' The landlord of the Sailor's Rest Hotel was of the same ilk as the old captain; ruddy of feature and round of belly, with a pipe in his mouth and a full beard just like the King's.

'How big are your towels?'

The landlord looked him over, thinking what a fine body of a man he was. 'Big enough, I reckon.'

'In that case one should do,' John replied heartily.

Reaching under the counter, the landlord drew out a towel and suggested, 'Take a look, pal. You'll maybe want two after all.' It was extra money in his own pocket.

Opening out the folded towel, John scrutinised it. Albeit hard and scratchy, it was a fair size, and he said so.

'And you needn't be examining it for lice!' the landlord advised. 'But if you do find one, that'll be an extra tuppence.' At that the other drinkers in the hotel bar laughed and chuckled, before sinking their teeth into their jugs of ale.

'I'll take the bath now if you don't mind,' John said. 'It's a long way from Liverpool to Blackburn, and I'll not be wasting no time here if I can help it.'

'Got a sweetheart waiting, have you?' This was a small voice from the end of the bar; its owner a shrunken little man with big watery eyes, and a smile like a mischievous leprechaun.

As John looked to see who was speaking, the little man shuffled to his side. 'Can't wait to see your Emily, eh?'

Delighted to see him, John slid an arm round the old fellow. 'Hello, Archie!' He and this kind old man had spent many an hour talking during that last trip. 'You old rascal. I looked for you aboard, and couldn't catch sight of you no-how. And here you are, propping up the nearest bar. I should have known this is where you'd be.'

'You'll have a drink with me afore you go, won't you, son?' Archie's eyes clouded over. 'Being as this is my last trip.'

Knowing how upset he was at not sailing away

again, John didn't have the heart to refuse. 'I'll be glad to,' he answered. Beckoning the landlord, he ordered, 'A pint jug for my mate here . . . and a half-jug for me.' The last thing he wanted was to be smelling of ale when he met up with Emily.

The landlord set about the order. 'Will you be wanting soap?'

'What?' John had momentarily forgotten the gist of their previous conversation.

'I said, will you be wanting soap? For your bath?' He placed the two jugs of ale within John's reach.

Collecting the drinks and holding them in his fists, John was astonished at such a question. 'O' course I will! How can I wash without soap?'

'Oh, you'd be surprised at how many folks do,' came the answer.

'Well, I'll have the soap if you please.' Turning to Archie, he suggested, 'We'll sit at the table over there. It'll be easier to talk if we're away from the bar.'

It was a mystery to him why folks always wanted to linger round the bar when there were perfectly comfortable tables and chairs to be got. But sometimes a man needed to stay upright, near to companions, and close to the booze. Once or twice, when they'd docked at some foreign port to offload the cargo, he himself had been in that same situation – lost and lonely, and in need of something to help spirit him home, across those endless waters to Salmesbury, Potts End Farm – and his beloved Emily.

'Will you be wanting a full bar, or half a bar?' The landlord's voice cut across his thoughts.

John was bemused. 'Half a bar of what exactly?'

'Soap, o' course!'

'Oh, I think half a bar should do it.'

'And will you be wanting your water hot, cold or lukewarm?'

'Well, I'll not want it cold, that's for sure, and I'll not want it to be scalding the skin off my back, so I'll have it just above lukewarm, if that's all right with you.' He thought the landlord to be either a bit dim, or cunning as a fox. 'And how much is all this gonna cost me?'

'All depends.'

'On what?'

'Whether you want a full bath o' water, or half a bath full?'

Growing frustrated, John set the jugs of ale on the bar. 'Look, I'm not a difficult man. All I want is a full-sized towel, half a bar of soap and a bath of water, not scalding and not ice-cold. So, how much will that run me?'

'And will that be a bath half-full, or a bath filled to the brim?'

'A bath filled three-quarters,' John answered with a little rise of laughter. 'If it's half-filled, I'll not get a proper wash, will I? And if it's filled to the brim, half the water will spill out the minute I set foot in it.'

To his consternation, the landlord went carefully through his list again. 'Right. I reckon that's done it.' He put down his pencil. 'It'll be ready inside o' twenty minutes.'

'You still haven't said what it'll cost me.'

'Let me see now.' Once more he consulted his list, muttering all the while, until he raised his head. 'That'll be sixpence halfpenny.'

'What's the halfpenny for?' John asked, highly amused.

The landlord gave a wink. 'For the girl who fills the bath, o' course.' Leaning forward he whispered, 'For another tuppence, she'll wash your back, *if* you know what I mean?' His bushy eyebrows went up like two pheasants let loose.

John's answer was short and sweet. 'I'll manage to wash my own back, thank you. Just get it all ready inside of twenty minutes, will you? I've an itch to be on my way soon as ever.'

As he and Archie crossed the room to their table, John was not surprised to hear a shout from the landlord. 'That'll be another halfpenny!'

John swung round. 'What for?'

'Well, if you're gonna wash your own back, you'll be needing a scrubbing brush – unless you've an arm long enough to reach your backside?'

When John was lost for words, he promptly wrote it down on his list.

'He's a crafty old bugger is that one!' Grateful to sit down, Archie dropped himself into the hard, wooden chair. His feet were aching, and these days he found it hard to stand for too long at a time.

John placed his jug of ale before him. 'Get that down you,' he said, 'before he charges us another sixpence for the use of the jugs.' At which they both laughed out loud.

'I was hoping you'd show up here.' During their time at sea, Archie had found a real friend in John. 'I'd have been disappointed to miss you.'

'Me too, Archie. I'm glad we found each other before I left these parts for good.'

'You haven't changed your mind then, about that one more trip?'

'Never!' Seated astride the chair, John assured him with passion, 'I've sailed my last voyage, and thankful for it.'

'You there!' The landlord's voice sailed across the room. 'You'll be wanting a comb for your hair. I could do that for tuppence?'

Reaching into his jacket pocket, John withdrew the comb he'd bought in some foreign port. 'Got my own, thanks.' He held it high for the landlord to see. 'This one only cost me a halfpenny in the marketplace.'

'Oh, please yourself!' The landlord scowled as he put away his list.

Archie chuckled. 'The cost of a good bath goes up an' up, though I've not had one in months, and don't care to. Besides, I've seen enough of water to last me a lifetime.'

John saw the disappointment in the old man's face. 'You'll miss it though, won't you, Archie?'

'What's that you say?' Archie cupped a hand to his ear. Some days he could hear a whisper from twenty yards away. Other days, he couldn't even hear his own thinking.

'The sea!' John leaned forward, emphasising his words. 'You'll miss being at sea, won't you?'

Understanding flooded the old man's face. 'Oh.' He nodded. 'I will that,' he confessed. 'But you understand, I can't do the job any more.' He gave an almighty sigh. 'Me legs won't go as fast as I want, and me back's more bent and crooked with every trip.' He glanced out the window at the merchant ships and the many different sails billowing in the March breezes; a great sadness came over his heart. 'I must admit I would have liked to go on, but it's not easy being ship's cook. You need to be strong and able, and this last trip I wasn't up to the job at all.'

Spreading out his hands, he told John, 'See that, son? My fingers are as crooked as twigs off a tree. I drop things all the time now. I can't seem to get a grip on anything proper. I forget things too, like not ordering enough flour on the last trip, so's the men had short rations of bread. How long will it be before I forget to order the food altogether, tell me that? And though the men didn't rile me about the bread, what would they say if they didn't have their bellies filled morning and night, eh?'

John had to admit, 'They'd not take kindly to it, that's for sure.'

A third voice interrupted, 'Like as not they'd throw you over the side.'

Turning towards the voice, John and Archie looked at the fellow seated at the next table; a sad-looking, unkempt individual with long, straggly brown hair and beard, it was instantly clear he hadn't shaved or bathed in weeks. They saw how he wolfed down the remains of his ale as though his thirst was strangling him. 'Been at sea yourself, have you?' Archie asked.

'I don't think there's anywhere I *haven't* been,' the fellow answered. 'But I do know that a cook who can't deliver a meal to the crew won't be welcome on any ship that I know of.'

With that he got up from his seat and struggled drunkenly to the bar.

John followed him with a curious gaze. Poor devil, he looked like he'd been through the mill. Yet there was something familiar about him ... He shook his head. The strange feeling lingered, and then Archie was talking again, drawing his thoughts back to the conversation between them.

'So, you see, shipmate, I ain't got much choice, have I?'

John nodded in agreement. 'So, what will you do with yourself?'

'Oh, I dare say I'll sleep well at night, and wander about the quayside during the daylight hours. I was born and bred in Liverpool, so I know most o' these seafaring folks. I expect I'll find a bit o' work here and there.'

At that moment, raised voices were heard from the bar, and Archie said with a grin, 'It seems our friend's had more than enough ale, and now the landlord wants shut of him.'

Archie was right. With a good measure of ale inside him, the fellow who'd been sitting next to them was loudly explaining to the landlord, 'I've money to pay for it. Look!' Emptying a shower of farthings, ha'pennies and threepenny bits all over the counter, he showed he had the wherewithal for a couple more pints at least.

The landlord pushed the coins back irritably. 'Put your money away. Look at yourself, man! You can hardly stand up!'

When the man leaned over the bar, the landlord thought he was in for a spell of trouble, so he was taken aback when suddenly the sad-eyed fellow asked him, his voice breaking with emotion, 'Would you take me for a coward?'

'Maybe.' The landlord could see he was at his

wits' end. 'Maybe not. We're all cowards sometimes, one way or another.'

The man looked him straight in the eye. 'Well,
I'm the worst kind of all.'

'Oh, aye? An' what kind is that then?'

The man smiled back, the sorriest smile the
landlord had seen in all his years behind that bar.
'What kind would you call a man who runs out
on his family?'

The landlord thought of his own shortcomings
and gave a sheepish grin. 'I reckon we've all done
that in our time.'

The younger man wagged a finger. 'Ah, but you
see, I ran out on the finest daughter in the world,
and her mammy too . . . the best wife a man could
have.' He gave a soul-destroying sigh. 'My poor
Aggie, God forgive me! I left her with my poorly
father, and debts she could never pay in a hundred
years. So, tell me! What kind of coward does that
make me, eh?'

The landlord's answer was to draw him a jug of
ale and, planting it in front of him, he instructed,
'This is your last one in this establishment. So,
come on! Sup up, and be on your way. I've enough
of my own troubles to worry about yours!' But he
said it in a kind way, and refused any payment.

The sad-eyed man nodded. 'Thank you, sir.' He
took a sip, and then another and, as always, the
more he sank into his ale, the further away his
troubles receded.

Archie too, was sipping his ale, lost in thought, when suddenly John's voice intruded. 'Have you got a place to stay?'

'Not yet, but I'll get fixed up soon enough.' Archie tapped his jacket pocket. 'I've enough to pay for a room and feed myself for a few weeks. Meantime, as I said, I'll soon be running errands and suchlike to keep the roof over my head.' He gave a sort of smile. 'I'll need to earn a wage, so's I can come and sit in here and watch the world go by.'

Underneath the little man's bravado, there was a sense of fear, and John was concerned about him. 'I'll stay with you if you like, until you're fixed up with a room.'

Archie was horrified. 'You will not!' Wagging a finger he argued, 'You'll finish your drink, then you'll get yourself off to that lovely girl of yours.' Realising there were those nearby who were listening to their conversation, he lowered his voice to a whisper. 'I'm grateful for your concern, but I've been on my own since I was a lad in short breeches. I'm more than capable of looking after meself.'

John was mortified to have offended him. 'I'm sorry,' he apologised, 'only I thought you might need a friend.'

Archie thanked him again, but, 'It's Emily that needs you now,' he said kindly.

John's face lit up. 'Oh Archie! I can't wait till I see her again!'

'Well, o' course you can't. What! She's all you've talked about these past two years. "Emily this" . . . "Emily that". Day and night, until I feel I know her as well as you do.'

Something was still worrying John. 'Why didn't she reply to my letters, Archie?' he burst out. 'I wrote all those letters and every time we got to a port, I took them to be posted home. But I never got any reply.'

The old man knew this had been on John's mind for some time, and yet again, he tried to explain it away the best he could. 'How many letters did you write to your Auntie Lizzie?'

John did a mental calculation. 'One a month . . . same number as I wrote to Emily.'

'And how many replies got through to you?'

Reaching into his pocket, John took out a crumpled envelope. 'Just the one.' He had read that letter time and again, until the folds were almost worn through, and the words hardly visible any more.

Archie waved a crooked finger. 'There you go then! It's just like I told you. Some of them foreign post offices take your money and don't give a bugger for your letter. Like as not they'll tear it up and drop it into the ocean. It's often the truth that a letter never gets to its destination. And even if it's put on a ship to be brought home, who's to say it ever gets to the right address? What! I've known men send hundreds and never a one reached home. It happens, that's all. And there isn't a damned thing you can do about it.'

'I expect you're right, Archie.' Taking a deep sigh, John blew it out with the words, 'I hope that's all it is. I hope she hasn't found somebody else to take my place.'

Archie wouldn't hear of it, and besides, 'Didn't you say your aunt told you in that there letter, how soon after you'd gone, Emily was so lonely for you, she wouldn't hardly leave the farm?'

John recalled every word, but, 'This was got to me in the first month of me being away. I've not heard a word since.'

'Aw, stop your worrying.' Archie took a swig of his ale and, wiping the froth from his mouth, he promised John, 'She'll be there, waiting for you. You needn't worry about that.'

Encouraged by his pal's assurances, John put the worries to the back of his mind. 'I'm going home, matey,' he said. 'I'm going home to my Emily, and I'm never leaving her side again.'

Raising his jug of ale, Archie bade John do the same. He gave a toast. 'To Emily, and yourself. May you live long and be happy together.'

John had another toast. 'To yourself, Archie. That you find contentment in your new life back ashore.'

They drank to that, and soon Archie took his leave. 'Got to see a man about a room, then it's off to find work of a kind,' he said. 'You take care of yourself, son. You've already given me your aunt's address, so as soon as I'm settled, I'll write to you.' A big grin lifted his features. 'This letter won't have oceans to cross, so you should get it all right.'

John watched him leave, and when the loneliness flooded over him, he strode across the room to the bar, where he took instructions from the landlord, paid his way, and was soon shown to the back parlour, where his 'lukewarm' bath was ready and waiting.

Some time later, he emerged refreshed, smartly dressed in his new clothes, and ready for his journey. With a lighter heart, he bade the landlord goodbye and headed for the door.

The sooner he was out of the Sailor's Rest and on his way home, the better.

CHAPTER SIX

'I T'S NO USE you arguing with me,' Thomas Isaac insisted. 'I haven't been out of this room in weeks, and now I'm feeling stronger, I intend being downstairs to see that little lass blow out her birthday candles.' His homely old face withered into a crooked smile. 'Two year old – I can't believe it!'

Aggie sighed. 'That's how quickly life passes us by,' she said philosophically. 'She were born March 1903, now it's suddenly 1905. Two year old today ... twelve year old tomorrow. Afore you know it, our Cathleen'll be a woman with a husband and childer of her own, Lord help us!'

The old fella lapsed into a mood of nostalgia. 'I just hope the same Good Lord lets me live to see the day.'

Aggie rolled her eyes to the ceiling. 'Aw, give over, Dad. You'll not get round me that way. I know you too well to let you bamboozle me into feeling sorry for you.' She gave him a knowing wink. 'So you might as well stop trying.'

He looked shocked. 'I don't know what yer talking about, woman!'

'Oh, yes you do,' Aggie retaliated. 'You're badgering me to get you downstairs, even after the doctor has given strict instructions that after this last chest cold o' yourn, you're to stay in bed, well wrapped up and with a roaring fire in the grate.' She was pleased to see that the fire had got a good hold, with the flames already leaping up the chimney. Even in March, when the sun began to struggle through, these farmhouse bedrooms were awfully cold.

'You make me out to be a tyrant.' The old man's querulous voice brought her attention back to him.

'That's what you are,' she teased. 'And when you can't find a good argument as to why I should let you get out of your sickbed and risk catching pneumonia, you then start on about the Good Lord, and how you pray He might let you live to see little Cathleen have childer of her own. Playing on my sympathies, so you are – making out you're hard done by. Same as you allus do.'

He groaned. 'Yer a fierce woman, Aggie Ramsden. A poor old fella like meself don't know how to take yer from one minute to the next.'

'There you go again!' Aggie cried. 'Calling yourself a poor old fella, when we all know you're as crafty as a wagonload o' monkeys!' She gave a hearty chuckle. 'But I can't blame you for wanting to see the lass blow out her two candles. Moreover, she wouldn't be happy unless you were there and neither would me or Emily.' She tried another tack to keep him in his bed. 'Mind you, we could allus fetch the child and her cake up here to you?'

'Oh no, you don't!' he retorted. 'I'm coming down. I've had enough o' lying in this damned bed.'

Aggie took a deep, invigorating breath. 'It doesn't look like I've got much choice.'

'At last!' His face lit up like a beacon. 'So you agree? I'm to be taken downstairs the first minute you get?'

'We'll see.' She knew how to play her father-in-law at his own game. It was asking for trouble to let him win too easily.

'What d'yer mean, "we'll see"?' Opening the palm of his hand, he twirled the porcelain balls on the head of his bed, until they danced and jangled like a band playing a tune. 'One way or another, I'm going down them stairs, an' that's that!'

Knowing how stubborn he could be when the mood took him, Aggie relented. 'All right, then. But the minute I see you looking peaky, I'll have you back up these stairs and into that bed afore you know it!'

'Oh, will yer now?' Giving her a cheeky wink, he laughed. 'By! It's been a long time since a woman made me an offer like that, I can tell yer.'

Aggie, too, laughed out loud. 'Behave yourself.' She craftily turned the tables on him. 'By! I wonder how I'll get on, carrying you down them stairs?' she groaned. 'I mean, you're not as fit and slim as you were. Come to think of it, you're an awkward lump. It wouldn't surprise me if I had to let go of you halfway down. Then what would we do, eh? You could break a leg or summat.'

'Tormenting me now, is it?' he said with a twinkle in his eye. 'You'll 'ave me down them stairs no trouble,' he declared. 'Wi' you on the one side and Emily on the other, I'll be safe as 'ouses.'

'Well, I certainly hope so,' she answered. 'Look, there's no need to be getting out of yer bed just yet.' Glancing at the mantelpiece clock she told him, 'It's only just gone ten past six. The child is still fast and hard asleep, bless her little heart. What's more, our Emily only put the cake in the oven an hour ago. We're not setting the birthday table until twelve o'clock, so you've time enough to get another few hours' sleep.'

But the old fella didn't like that idea at all. 'How can I sleep when I'm not tired?'

'I don't know,' Aggie replied. 'But you might as well try, 'cause you're not coming down them stairs for a while yet. And that's an end to it.' She repeated her warning in a serious voice. 'You're not to tire yourself out, Dad. And if I say you need to get back to your bed, I don't want no argument. All right?'

Ignoring her pointed question, he asked, 'Will *he* be there?'

Aggie was momentarily thrown. 'Who?'

'You know who,' he retorted. 'That ugly brother o' yourn.'

Aggie visibly bristled. 'I've no idea where Clem is,' she answered in a hard voice. 'What's more, I don't care.' She glanced at the window, her eyes glittering with hatred. 'If somebody came to the door and told me he'd had an accident and there was no hope for him, I'd throw my hat up in the air.'

'Good God!' In all the time he'd known this lovely, caring woman, he had never witnessed such loathing in her eyes. 'D'yer really hate him that much, lass?'

For a moment he thought she had not heard, because now, as she wandered to the window and stared out, her thoughts appeared to be miles away.

'Aggie?' His voice was probing but gentle.

She turned, a quizzical look on her face. 'What is it, Dad?'

He smiled. 'I asked . . . d'yer really hate him that much?'

Giving a wry little smile, she answered, 'Yes, I

hate him that much,' then added, 'more than you'll ever know.' Then, fearing she had given too much away, she strode back to the bedside. 'I asked *you* a question,' she reminded him. 'And I still haven't got an answer.'

He grimaced. 'I can't recall you asking me no question.'

'Right then,' she declared. 'I'll ask it again, and this time I'd like an answer.' Leaning forward, she stared him in the eye, the smallest of smiles on her face. 'I asked if you might be thinking of giving me trouble, should I decide you ought to be back in your bed?'

'By! Yer a persistent devil.' Taking in a long, deep breath, he blew it out through swollen cheeks. 'Go on then. I promise.'

～

Back downstairs, Emily was nowhere to be seen. 'Where is the lass?' Realising she must be outside, Aggie set about her tasks. She checked the fire and opened one window slightly to let the fumes from the burning coals disperse. She then replaced the fire-screen and going to the oven, checked the cake which was rising nicely.

When that was done, she went outside to find Emily.

The girl was in the outhouse, her sleeves rolled back, and up to her elbows in the washing tub.

'I can't seem to get these stains out,' she said, rubbing hard at a corner of the bedsheet. 'I've soaked them with a blue bag and scrubbed them with soda, and rubbed them over the wash-board until my knuckles are raw, but they just won't shift.'

Dropping the sheet back into the copper boiler, she blew away a wisp of hair. Wiping an arm over her brow, she leaned against the wall, her face glowing pink and wet from the heat. 'It's the last time I let Gramps have beef broth in his bed,' she said.

Aggie had warned her at the time. 'I told you,' she chided. 'I said not to let him hold the soup-bowl himself.'

'He threw a fit when I tried to spoon-feed him!' Emily recalled the occasion well. 'He said I had no right treating him like a babby and that he was more than capable of holding his own soup-bowl an' spoon.'

Aggie chuckled and said, imitating Thomas Isaac's voice: 'If you can't trust me to feed meself, then I'll not eat at all. In fact, yer can take the damned soup away and fetch me some milky-pobs. That's what yer give babbies, ain't it?'

Emily laughed. 'All right, don't rub it in. He caught me good and proper, but from now on, I'll be one step ahead of him, the old devil.' She couldn't help but feel for him though. 'It's his poor old fingers. Some days they're no problem at all, and other times he can't even grip the sheet to pull it up over himself.'

'Aye, lass.' Aggie felt the same compassion for her father-in-law. 'That's what comes of working out in all weathers for the best part of your life.'

Even Aggie couldn't get the stain of beef broth out of the sheet. 'Leave it to soak in saltwater,' she told Emily. 'You can have another go at it later on. We'd best get on. There's a cake to be iced and sprinkled wi' hundreds and thousands, a few cheese straws to make, sandwiches and little fancies to be got ready. Oh, and you'd best preserve your strength,' she warned. 'I promised Grandad we'd fetch him down for the occasion.'

With that in mind the two of them set off, back to the scullery and the excitement of the day.

~

Keeping his distance, Clem Jackson watched them go back into the farmhouse. 'Bloody women!' he cursed. 'I'd just as soon do away with the lot of 'em!'

Recalling how he had attacked Emily in the barn, he had no shame or guilt, but when he realised he had got her with child, he had suffered a few sleepless nights, but only because he was afraid his sister Aggie would find out, and take revenge. Given the right circumstances, she was capable enough. When the blame fell on John

Hanley, he was relieved – though up to now he had been wise enough to keep his distance from Emily.

From afar he had watched his daughter grow into a little person, and he was oddly fascinated – though he was not foolish enough to lay claim to her. He was a man who enjoyed his fun, but refused to take the consequences.

Slinging the shotgun across his shoulder, he whistled to his dog and thought, To hell with them all. The taste of John's name on his tongue was bitter. That young bugger had a lot of gall. At one point, Clem had really feared he might be getting the better of him, and that would never have done, oh no! He recalled how even when he was torn open and bleeding, John had kept coming back at him. That one was dangerous, he mused grudgingly. A man to be reckoned with.

He congratulated himself on having seen the last of John Hanley. One thing was for sure: it would make his life that much easier, now Emily had picked up with the milkman – especially as the man seemed besotted enough to take on the bastard as his own.

All in all, Clem thought he had been clever enough to turn the whole situation to his own advantage. And if ever he felt the need for another tumble in the hay with Emily, he would have no compunction about helping himself.

She would know better than to blab: if she so

much as hinted at what had gone on between them, he would make damned sure they would all suffer. She was intelligent enough to know that.

For now though, he had a 'friend' of his own in the barmaid at the Red Lion. Bold and brassy, Betty Warwick was more than capable of satisfying his carnal needs for the time being.

As he came up to the top field and his prize-bulls, he leaned on the fence, his proud gaze focused on the great beasts. 'I knew you were winners right off,' he told them. 'Another season an' you'll be the best there is. What! I'll be the envy of every breeder for miles around.'

Nodding with satisfaction he drew such a large breath his chest expanded to twice its size. With the confidence of a man who believes himself to be above the proudest beast, he bade the dog stay where he was, lest he spooked the bulls, then climbed the fence and swaggered past them.

He was not deterred by the sly, watchful look in their eyes. Nor by the reason he had got them at a low price. The cowman's son at an adjacent farm was nearly trampled to death by them. As it was, he'd been kicked in the thigh and would always walk with a limp. He'd tripped over in his haste to escape, and being a skinny lad, had just managed to roll under the fence in time, their stink in his nostrils, before he'd fainted.

'The lad was crossing the far side of the field when they came at him,' the owner had confessed.

'He was lucky they didn't kill him.' He was all for shooting them. But Clem Jackson persuaded him otherwise.

~

It was eleven-thirty the next morning when John climbed aboard the tram in Blackburn. Tanned by sea and sun, and with a jaunt to his step, he caught the attention of several women passengers. 'Now there's a good-looking young man.' The woman who whispered this was nearer sixty than fifty, and when John smiled at her she didn't know which way to look, so she turned to her friend. 'Did you see that?' she breathed. 'He's got a lovely smile, don't you think?'

Her friend was older and wiser, and the teeniest bit envious. 'Lovely smile or not, he's probably on his way to break some young woman's heart.' She'd been around long enough to know about such things.

Some way along the tram, John seated himself, paid his fare and got chatting to the conductor. 'You've made a conquest back there,' the conductor said, rolling the ticket out of his machine and handing it over. 'Them poor women are swooning all over the place.'

'I can't be seen flirting with other women,' John said with a grin. 'I don't think my future wife would like that.'

Being as the tram was almost empty, and this

route was a lonely one, the conductor sat in the seat opposite. 'Oh aye?' He was ready for a chat. 'On your way to be wed, are you?'

John nodded. 'Soonever we can arrange it,' he said proudly. 'I've been away, but now I'm back for good.'

'What's her name?'

'Emily.'

'Pretty name.'

'Pretty lady.'

'What made you leave her?'

Here, John grew cautious. 'Oh, this and that.'

The conductor guessed. 'Family problems, I expect,' he remarked knowingly. 'We all have 'em.'

John neither denied nor confirmed it. Instead he answered lightly, 'Getting wed is an expensive business.'

'So, you went away to make your fortune, is that it?'

'Summat like that.' He patted his coat pocket. 'I've enough here to make us a good life. It took over two years of being without her, but it'll all be worthwhile now. We can make a fresh start. We'll get wed and have a family, and the time spent apart will soon fade.' His heart soared with joy. 'By! I can't wait to see her.'

The conductor was realistic. 'Ah, but will she still feel the same way?'

Taken aback, John asked, 'What do you mean?'

'Well, you said yourself, you've been two year

and more apart. Folks change in that length o' time. How can you be sure she hasn't found herself another fella while you've been gone?'

John's heart sank. 'Because she wouldn't, that's all. We love each other. We've *always* loved each other.'

'Oh, aye! I'm sure.' Then, regretting his thoughtless remark, the conductor now tried to soften it. 'Tek no notice o' me,' he said. 'I wish you both all the happiness in the world.'

Pointing out of the window, he said, 'We've another couple of passengers coming on board.' And as the tram slowed to accept them, he was glad to move away. You and your big mouth! he chided himself. Trust you to put a damper on that young fella's homecoming.

Some folks had a talent of saying the wrong thing at the wrong time. Unfortunately, he was one of 'em.

~

Some short time later, having got off the tram in Salmesbury, John slung his kitbag across his back and set off across the fields towards the spinney and Potts End Farm.

The nearer he got, the harder his heart pounded. He couldn't believe that now, after their long separation, he was so close to her. It was the most wonderful feeling in the world. For too long now he had been stumbling through every minute of every day, longing to be with his darling Emily.

Memories flashed through his mind – of himself going away, of Emily's pleas for him to stay and his persuading her it had to be done if they were to spend the rest of their lives together in contentment. Then that last embrace, and the awful feeling of loneliness at leaving her. Afterwards, when she was gone from his sight, the long, empty time between, when he had waited only for the day he would be back.

His heart lifted. That day was here now, and it was the most important day of his life. He thought briefly of Clem Jackson, and his lip curled. He'd learned a lot about self-defence in the Navy, and he was more than ready to take that fat bastard on and teach him a lesson he'd never forget.

As he got to the top of the hill, he could see the curl of smoke rising from the Ramsdens' chimney. 'I'm here, my darling,' he murmured, his heart bouncing inside him. 'I'm home.'

He could barely wait to throw his arms round her and hold her tight. Thinking about it, he quickened his steps. He was so close. So tantalisingly close.

It was when he got to the spinney that he heard the laughter. Curious, he slowed his step. Some instinct kept him back, partly hidden by the overhanging branches, yet able to see down to the farm.

And what he saw was like ice-cold spray, flung in his face by an angry sea.

Not knowing what to think or how to deal with it, he stayed there, out of sight; watching the scene unfold below him, and with every minute his dream slipping away.

At first his gaze fell on Emily, and his love for her was all-consuming. With the chill March daylight glinting in her golden-brown hair and that familiar, lovely face, she was everything he remembered. And yet she was different somehow, though for the moment he could not tell why.

Curious, he followed her proud gaze. He saw the child run towards her; he saw how she opened her arms and caught that tiny bundle to her heart, her eyes alight with love – and when in that moment she shared the laughter with the child, she seemed to John to be the most beautiful, fulfilled woman on God's earth.

Slowly, when the truth began to dawn, the revelation was crippling.

For a moment, he could not think straight, though his every nerve-ending was telling him that this little girl was Emily's child. But how could that be? The conductor's words ran through his mind. 'How can you be sure she hasn't found another fella?'

Torn by what he was seeing, he could not move away.

From the corner of his eye he caught sight of

the stranger as he walked towards Emily and the child. He saw him smile and open his arms to take her from Emily; she released the child without a moment's hesitation. The man swung the child round, while Emily laughed out loud at the little one's delight.

After a while, Emily approached the man and collected the child into her arms. As she did so, the child uplifted her face for a kiss from the man. Obligingly, he cupped her tiny face in his hands to gently kiss her on the forehead. But then before he drew away, he quickly turned his head to Emily and kissed her full on the mouth.

Unable to look any longer, John turned away, his heart breaking. 'No, it can't be!' he muttered. 'It can't be!' The images of Emily, the child and the man, burned in his mind.

Summoning all the courage he had, he forced himself to look again. The couple had gone inside to the kitchen and closed the door on the chilly day. John strained to see inside. The table was set with food, and in the centre, a cake with two bright candles told him it was the child's birthday.

There were six people seated at the table: the child, Emily and her mother Aggie, the old grandad whom he knew and loved; and the two men, the younger one who had kissed both Emily and the child, and last of all an older man who looked vaguely familiar. There was no sign of Clem.

As he watched, still hidden in the spinney, the child leaned forward to blow out the candles, her small arms wrapped round Emily on one side, and the man on the other. Emily glanced at the man, and he smiled back. It was a warm, intimate smile, and it cut through John's heart like a knife through butter.

Devastated, he turned away for the last time. 'Oh, dear God.' His voice broke with emotion. The reality of what he had seen was too much to take in. Without further ado, he cut a path to Lizzie's cottage. His aunt would put him straight, he thought. She would tell him the truth.

~

When she saw him approaching over the hill, Lizzie could hardly believe her eyes. 'John? Oh my goodness, is it really you?' Peering from the bench where she had been resting after finishing her work in the yard, she recognised that familiar long stride and that mop of dark hair, and in a minute was on her feet and hurrying towards him.

When he took her in his arms she laughed and cried, and held him for what seemed an age. 'Oh lad – I thought I'd never see you again.' Wiping away the tears, she looked up at him, and her love was bright in her expressive green eyes.

'Come in!' she laughed. 'Come away on in. You're at home now, son.' With her arm entwined in his and her heart full of joy, she went inside with him. In the midst of her own happiness, she did not notice how sad and subdued he seemed.

Inside the cosy parlour, Lizzie bustled about. 'Eee, you're a sight for sore eyes, my lad. Let me cut you some fresh-baked bread and a hunk o' cheese – how does that sound? Oh, and a pint mug o' tea.'

John shook his head. 'Not just yet,' he answered gently. 'There's things I need to ask you first.' Even now after what he had seen down there in the valley, he still nurtured the smallest gleam of hope.

'We'll talk while you eat,' Lizzie said firmly. 'You must be famished.'

'Sit down, Auntie,' he begged her. 'I need to talk.'

'What about?' Suddenly, Lizzie saw how he was, and thoughts of Emily crept into her mind.

'Please.' Taking her by the hand, John sat her down. 'I need to know about Emily.'

A ripple of fear shivered through her. 'What is it you need to know?' she asked apprehensively.

For a moment he dropped his gaze, not wanting to ask, but needing to. 'Just now, I went down towards the farm.' He looked up, his eyes full of pain. 'There was a child . . .'

Lizzie groaned. This was the moment she had been dreading.

John looked her in the eye. 'Is it Emily's child?'

'Oh, lad!' She had not wanted to be the one to tell him.

John persisted, 'Is it her child, Lizzie?'

She nodded. 'I'm sorry, son. Yes, the child is Emily's.'

Anger flooded her heart. This was not the homecoming she had wanted for her beloved nephew. Emily had betrayed him, and she for one could not forgive that.

John had another question. 'Who's the father?'

Lizzie shook her head. 'You'll have to ask Emily that.'

'No, Lizzie. I'm asking *you*.'

The woman took a moment to consider her answer. 'His name's Danny Williams. You may not remember him. He's the milkman round here these days. Some time ago, his ma died, then his father fell ill and had to retire. Danny came home from soldiering agin the Boers to take the business on.'

John recalled the two men at the cottage; the young one and an older man, probably his father. Quickly describing the two men, he asked, 'Would it be them?'

Lizzie nodded. 'Aye, son. It would.'

'Are they wed – him and Emily?' The words choked in his throat as he waited anxiously for the answer. 'Have I lost her altogether?'

Lizzie fought with her conscience. She knew he loved Emily enough to take on the child Emily had conceived by another man. She did not want that for him. It wouldn't be fair, and besides, what kind of woman was Emily, if at the drop of a hat she could turn to some other man while John was away working for their future? Emily had done a bad thing. Who was to say she wouldn't do it again, even after she and John were wed?

She thought of how when she herself took John on as a little lad of five, she had vowed to always do the best for him. Up to now, she had not really been tested. But this was her trial, and she would deal with it the way she thought fit. She saw herself as his mother, just as much as if she had given birth to him herself. She loved him, more than she had ever loved anyone in her whole life.

Her mind was made up. There was no way on earth she would stand by and see him used by a woman who had already shown herself to be wanton. There could be no worthwhile future ahead with a wife like that.

His voice penetrated her thoughts. 'Auntie! I want the truth. Is Emily wed to him?'

She looked up, tears hovering but not falling. She had to do this for his sake. 'Yes, son,' she lied. 'Emily is wed to the child's father. That's how it is.'

Now, as she saw the torment in his face, she silently prayed that the Good Lord would forgive her. Yet, driven by motherly love and a need to protect him, she truly believed she had done the right thing for John. If at some time in the future, she was called on to pay for her sins, then so be it.

In that cosy little parlour, the silence thickened until the soft ticking of the clock on the mantel-piece seemed to echo the sound of their own hearts.

Each was torn by what had been said; Lizzie because she had lied against her nature, and John, because he had heard the one thing that he had never expected to hear . . . that Emily had grown tired of waiting and had wed someone else. More-over, they had a child. That had been his dream, to have her as his wife and to raise a family. Emily had been his life. And now she had given herself to someone else. No wonder she had not replied to his letters. Dear God! How quickly she had for-gotten him.

But he would never forget her, nor would he stop loving her. She was his first and last love, and that would never change, however long he might live.

Quietly, Lizzie got out of her chair, and going into the tiny scullery, she put on the kettle and proceeded to make them a pot of tea. Whenever she was tired or troubled, she always made tea: it had always soothed and comforted before. Yet this was not like before. This was John and Emily, and the end of their future – and, God help her, she was partly responsible for that.

A few minutes later she returned to find him stood by the window, his dark blue eyes staring out across the landscape, his mind deep in thought. 'Drink this, son.' She pressed the mug of hot liquid into his hands, then when he took it, she asked hopefully, 'Will you not have a bite to eat?'

He turned to look down on her. 'This can't have been easy for you,' he said. 'I'm sorry.'

She gave a bitter laugh. Sorry! If only he knew, she thought. If only he knew how she had deliberately lied. 'I'm sorry too,' she answered truthfully. 'Sorry it had to turn out this way.'

He nodded, took a gulp of his tea, and when the liquid choked in his throat, he placed the mug on the windowsill.

'Will you stay?' Lizzie was behind him.

Continuing to stare out of the window, he replied, 'Just for tonight. Then I'll be gone . . . back to the sea.' He had waited and prayed for the day to come when he would return to these parts, and Emily. But in just a few short minutes, everything he had ever wanted was snatched away. How could he stay now? It would be torture, to be so close to her, and yet so far away.

Lizzie understood. 'I had an idea you'd be going back.' Part of her wanted to plead with him to stay. Part of her knew he couldn't. And all she could think of was how she had deceived him. 'I'll need to get your bed aired,' she said. 'Meantime, son, you should try and eat. There's cheese and ham in the larder. Oh, and a deep apple pie I made first thing this morning.' How odd it seemed, to be talking about such things as ham and apple pie, when their whole world had been turned upside down.

'Maybe later,' he told her. 'Just now I think I'll go for a walk alongside the brook.' That same brook where he and Emily had walked so many times in the past. That same brook where they had confessed their love for each other.

'Aye, lad. Mebbe your appetite will be sharper by the time you get back.'

Upstairs, Lizzie threw open the bedroom window, and hanging the blankets out over the sill, she let the breeze lift and play with them. She then took the sheets and gave them a sound shaking out the window, her quiet gaze following John as he went away towards the far fields and the brook beyond.

Struck with guilt at what she had done to the young lovers, she paused in her task, eyes welling up with emotion and heart full. She stood there until he was out of sight. Then she stood a moment longer, before returning to the bed. Taking hold of the two handles on the mattress, she hoisted it up and then heaved it over, after which her back ached and her arms felt as though they had been wrenched out of their sockets.

Waiting a minute to recover her breath, she went back to the window, where she collected the bedding and threw it over the iron bedframe at the foot of the bed.

That done, she set about making a fire in the tiny grate. The kindling and coal were always kept in a bucket by the pretty tiled hearth.

When the fire was flaring she sat beside it for what seemed an age. Then she made up the bed, tucking in the sheets and tweaking the counterpane until all was smooth and tidy. She laid the big bolster across the top, and placed a sprig of dried lavender on it, to make the linen smell sweet.

Closing the window, she scoured the countryside for a sight of John. But he was nowhere to be seen. *Don't go back there*, she willed him silently. *Stay away from her, son. She'll only bring you heartache.*

~

John avoided Potts End. Instead he kept on walking, across the fields and on towards the canal, where for a time he sat with his back to a tree, watching the barges chug up and down the waterway. His emotions were in turmoil, and yet there was a strange calm about him. Images dipped in and out of his mind. Images of the child, and the man, and the joy on Emily's face.

She seemed so happy, he thought. And wasn't that what he had always wanted – for his Emily to be happy?

A kind of rage came over him. Clenching his fist he slammed it into the tree-trunk. He didn't feel the splinters driving through his flesh. Yet he felt a pain of another kind. The kind of deep-down pain that would stay with him for the rest of his life.

After a time, when the darkness thickened, he made his way back.

Walking along by the brook, he lingered there awhile, listening to the tumble of water over the boulders and thinking of Emily. He remembered how it had been. How young and excited they were, and how deeply in love. But it was different now. Emily was a married woman, with a child, and because of it, he had no part in her life any more.

It was a shocking and agonising thing, but he could not change that kind of situation. Nor would he want to, not after seeing her so happy. Even now her laughter echoed in his mind. Emily's laughter, his pain. Danny Williams's gain, his loss. Life was a cruel master, he thought.

It was almost pitch dark when he got back to the cottage. 'You had me worried.' Lizzie was waiting anxiously for him. 'Are you all right, son?'

'I'm fine,' he lied, 'but I shouldn't have worried you like that. I'm sorry. I just lost track of time.'

When she saw his fist, bloodied and torn, she insisted on tending it, and while he sat she talked, about everything but Emily. 'When me old bones let me, I intend digging over that hard area at the bottom of the garden,' she declared. 'Y'see, I've a mind to extend the vegetable patch.'

John didn't comment. It was just small talk. What good was small talk, when his whole life had just fallen apart around him? But he smiled and nodded, and Lizzie seemed content enough at that.

After a while, when the hand was washed and treated and she had out-talked herself, Lizzie gave a sigh. 'I'm off to my bed now,' she said. 'I reckon you should do the same, son.'

He looked so tired, she thought. 'In the morning, I'll wake you to the smell of crispy bacon curling in the pan, and some of my fresh-laid eggs – oh, and did you know I bought another two chickens? O' course, I can't eat all the eggs meself, but I earn an extra bob or two selling them at market.' She chuckled. 'I've a good life here, in Salmesbury,' she said. 'To tell you the truth, son, there's nowhere else in the world I want to be.'

With his arm round her shoulders, John kissed her good night. 'You're a good woman, and I love you,' he said fondly. 'If there's ever anything you need, I'll always be there for you.'

'I know that,' she said. 'And I hope I'll always be there for you.'

That night, when Lizzie was fast asleep in her bed, John went outside and, taking the spade and fork from the lean-to shed, he rolled up his sleeves and set about digging over the small patch of ground at the foot of Lizzie's garden. He soon got into the rhythm of digging, then breaking up and forking over the soil, chucking weeds onto the compost heap.

When that was done and the last spadeful of earth had been turned over, he stood back and surveyed it. Satisfied, he returned to the house and after washing off the dirt and tidying himself up, he dug in his kitbag for paper and pencil.

A few moments later, seated at the table, with the glow of lamplight illuminating the page, he began the first of his letters:

Dearest Lizzie,

You've been the best mother anyone could have. It hurts me to leave you like this, but I have a feeling you will understand. You have always understood me, better than anyone.

The news of Emily has shaken me to my roots, as you must know. I came back here to marry her, but sadly, it wasn't to be.

I'm leaving you this money. It is part of the sum I had put aside for our wedding, and to resolve other matters which would make life easier for Emily and her family. But she has made her choice, and there is nothing I can do about that.

Use the money wisely. Don't overwork yourself, and stay well. I know now you will never leave this place, and who could blame you? If all had been well with me and Emily, I too would never want to live anywhere else.

I'm enclosing a letter for Emily. It's just to wish her well, that's all. I ask that you might please take it to her. But you must not let her know that I was here, or that I have learned she has a husband and child. I ask you that for a reason.

All my love. I will keep in touch, so please don't worry.

Your loving nephew,
John

Because of its content, his letter to Emily was shorter. Rather than make her feel guilty, he took the blame on himself.

When it was written, he went to the dresser-drawer, where he knew Lizzie kept envelopes and such. From here, he took one small envelope, folded Emily's letter inside Lizzie's, and enclosed them both in the envelope. He then propped it in front of the mantelpiece-clock, laid the wad of money beside it, and with one last, fond glance upwards, towards Lizzie's bedroom, he took his kitbag and left.

All his instincts wanted to take him by way of Potts End Farm. He knew how Emily would already be out of her bed and working at some task or other. He had visions of going to her and begging her to leave the husband she had taken and come away with him. It was a shameful thing, he thought, and the idea was soon thrust away. 'She isn't yours any more,' he told himself, his gaze wandering towards the spinney.

All the same, leaving her behind was the hardest thing he had ever done.

~

In the morning when Lizzie woke, she knew instinctively that he had gone. 'John?' she called down the stairs. There was no answer, so she called louder. 'JOHN!'

Throwing a robe over her nightdress, she hurried downstairs. The minute she entered the room, she saw the letter. Oh, dear Lord. He'd gone! Her heart fell. But he'd be back, she knew he would. Though whether that would be a good thing or a bad one, she couldn't tell.

The wad of money shocked her. By! What did he have to go and do that for? She quickly read the note and was enlightened. 'I'll not spend it wisely,' she said aloud, ' 'cause I'll not spend it at all. One o' these fine days, son, you'll be looking to wed some young woman or other, and when that day comes, the money will be here waiting for you.'

She thought of her situation and of how she had always managed to earn a living selling her produce and pies at the market. A proud woman, she had never taken a helping hand from anyone, and she wasn't about to start now, even if that hand belonged to the person she loved most in the whole world.

Crossing to the kitchen range, she took a loose stone from the wall to reveal a clever hidey-hole. From here she drew out a small square baccy tin. Inside was a small hand-stitched drawstring bag containing a number of guineas.

She counted the coins for the umpteenth time. Five whole guineas! Not bad for an old woman, was it? Mind, it had taken hard work and thrift to build up such a cache over the years. The wad of notes was far more money than she could ever save in her lifetime, and she instinctively glanced about before placing the wad into the drawstring bag. She then returned the baccy tin to the hole in the wall, replaced the stone and pushed a saucepan up against it.

~

Later that afternoon, Lizzie put on her best shawl and hat, and made her way across the fields and down through the spinney to Potts End Farm. Just as she had expected, Emily was to be found in the wash-house. 'I've heard from John,' Lizzie said abruptly, standing in the door. 'He sent this for you.'

Holding out the letter, she was made to feel guilty when Emily ran across the room, her face alight. 'Oh, Lizzie!' Wiping her hands on her apron, she took the letter in hands that had begun to shake. 'What does he say? Is he coming home? *Is* he?' The words tumbled out as she unfolded the letter.

But when the young woman read her lover's message, her tears of joy turned to sobs of despair:

> *Dear Emily,*
>
> *Forgive me for what I'm about to tell you. I won't be coming home, or getting wed as we planned.*
>
> *I never meant for it to happen, but I've found a new love.*
>
> *I had to write to you straight away, for I don't want you wasting your life in waiting for me.*
>
> *I hope you'll find someone who will love and cherish you as you deserve; because although it wasn't meant for you and me to be together, you are a very special and lovely person, Emily.*
>
> *Please forgive me,*
> *John*

Now, as Emily looked up, her face crumpled with shock and pain, Lizzie was stricken with a terrible remorse. 'Aw, lass.' Going over to the girl, she put a comforting arm round her heaving shoulders. 'I'm so sorry.' And she was. But she couldn't confess why; not to Emily nor to anyone else.

Even now, she could not deny in her own heart how she truly believed the parting would be best for both of them in the long run.

She comforted Emily as best she could, but it was of little consolation to the girl, who felt as though her life had come to an end. 'How can I live without ever seeing him again?' she asked brokenly. 'How can I be without him, when I love him with all my heart?'

Unable to provide the answers, Lizzie left some short time later. As she climbed the brow of the hill, she thought she could still hear the sound of Emily's sobbing, carried on the breeze.

'God help me!' Lizzie murmured. But it was for the best that Emily should wed the father of her child. For the best, that John was not fettered by another man's responsibility.

And not forgetting the child itself, wasn't it for the best that Cathleen should be brought up in the family security of her own father and mother?

Suddenly, when the breeze became wild, cutting across the hills like a banshee, Lizzie tightened her shawl and quickened her steps.

'I did right!' she told the wind. 'I'm sorry for the pain I caused, but it was the right thing to do.' A woman of high principles, Lizzie believed that mistakes had to be paid for, and that was Emily's punishment.

As for John, he had done nothing wrong as far as she could see, so it was only right that he should make a new life without encumbrances not of his making.

As far as Lizzie was concerned, that was how she saw it, and if there was any blame to be apportioned in this deceitful business, it lay fair and square with young Emily.

~

Behind her, Emily was wracked with loneliness. 'Why didn't you come back for me, John?' she sobbed. 'How could you fall out of love with me so easily?'

Seated in the train and travelling further away from her with every minute, John was asking the very same question of Emily.

However long he lived, and whichever way his life turned, he was certain of only one thing.

He would never love anyone as he loved his Emily.

PART THREE

~

March, 1905

Apart

CHAPTER SEVEN

'It's a pound a week if you're wanting bed, breakfast and a meal after work. An' it won't be the kind of meal you choose neither,' she warned. 'It'll be what I've been able to get cheap over the butcher's counter.'

The round-faced woman with the pot belly and wild iron-grey hair had been opening her house near the Liverpool docks to strangers these past twenty years. In all that time, not once had she encountered such a good-looking and civilised fella as the one who stood on her doorstep now. 'If you're only wanting bed and breakfast,' she went on, 'that'll cost you just eight shilling.'

Smiling broadly, she showed the most frightening set of naturally large white teeth. 'I reckon I could put your washing in for that price an' all,' she observed. 'And that's only because you look more particular than the usual ragamuffin types who come looking to set foot over this doorstep.

What! I would no more put their shirts in with my laundry than I would eat tripe and jam on the same plate.'

John liked her straight off. She was down-to-earth, with no fancies nor frills, and she spoke her mind – which left a man in no doubt as to where he stood. 'It would be bed, breakfast and a meal after work,' he informed her.

'That'll cost yer a pound a week then – how's that?' And when he nodded, she said briskly, 'Right then, young fella-me-lad! We seem to know where we stand with each other.' Just now when she wagged a finger with that certain no-nonsense twinkle in her eye, she put him in mind of his Aunt Lizzie. But that was where the likeness ended. Where Lizzie was small and neat, albeit plump, this kindly soul was large and spreading. Where Lizzie's feet were dainty and narrow, this one's feet were the size of canal barges.

Also, he had never seen traces of Lizzie snuff-taking, while there was a distinct brown 'tash drawn between the landlady's nostrils. Moreover, the thick powdery smell of snuff permeated the air.

As if to confirm his observations, she now took a small shiny tin from her pocket. 'So, will you be wanting to see the rooms? I've got two available; one at the front, one at the back.' Taking the lid from the tin, she dipped finger and thumb into the brown granules and lifting out a generous helping, proceeded to ram it up each nostril in turn, sniffing and coughing as it went.

'I'd be thankful for either,' John answered gratefully. 'I've spent hours wandering the streets, looking for good lodgings and a clean bed.'

'Hmh!' Observing him again, she wondered why a presentable young man like himself might have been wandering the streets. But she didn't ask. In her experience it was always wisest to keep to your own business. 'You'll find a clean bed and good lodgings here,' she answered, 'so, if you want to follow me, I'll show you the two rooms.'

Flicking the brown dust from her blouse, she replaced the lid on the tin, and the tin into her pocket.

'I've got rules and regulations,' she warned. 'I don't mind you entertaining a ladyfriend, but there'll be no goings-on after nine p.m. All strangers and visitors must be out o' the door by then. What's more, there'll be no card-playing, or loud talking, and I don't take kindly to things being pinned to the doors . . . if you know what I mean?'

John recalled the many postcards he had seen pinned up inside the ship; saucy pictures of women winking, or smiling suggestively, and there had been some baring more than their smile. 'I understand,' he said with the merest of smiles, and his answer seemed to satisfy her well enough.

Puffing and panting as she led him up the narrow stairway, she declared sternly, 'I run a decent house and am proud of it!'

'I'm sure you do, Mrs . . . Miss . . . ?' Not having been enlightened as to her name, he lamely finished the sentence.

Pausing to glance back at him, she imparted the information. 'The name's Harriet Witherington.' Her expression hardened. 'And it's *Miss* Harriet Witherington, *if* you don't mind.'

That said, she reached the top of the stairs, where she paused again to catch her breath. 'These blessed stairs will be the finish of me!' she groaned, quickly setting off again.

'Go on in, young man.' Having covered the short distance along the landing, she threw open a bedroom door. 'This one is at the front of the house. You'll get a clear sight of the docks from here, but you'll get the noise too.' She tutted loudly. 'Drunken sailors and streetwomen . . . touting and fighting at all hours of the night. I warn you now – you'll get little sleep in this room.'

Thinking her too honest for her own good, John followed her inside. The room was spacious enough, with a bed, wardrobe and manly chest-of-drawers. In keeping with its owner, there was a strong, sensible air about the place. Curtains were serviceable rather than pretty; the bedcover was plain and well worn, but spotlessly clean, and the bowl with its matching jug on the washstand was almost large enough to bathe in.

'Look out of the window,' she instructed, 'and you'll see what I mean.'

Intrigued, John looked out.

Just as she had promised, there was a clear view of the docks. In fact, some of the ships seemed so close you might think they would sail right into the room. At this time of the morning, there was much coming and going, with every sound melting one into the other. Curious, he opened the window and at once, the volume of life going on rose like a crescendo to fill his ears. Surprised, he quickly closed the window.

'Well, what d'you think?' Her voice rose above the medley of distant noise.

'I'd like to see the other before I make up my mind,' John decided.

'Right then, young man! Follow me.'

Gathering her skirts, she lumbered along the landing until coming to the second room. Here she stopped and flinging open the door invited him inside. 'See what you make o' that.'

As in the first room, the dry smell of snuff tickled his nostrils, though he did wonder whether that was because Harriet was near him wherever he went. Either way he wasn't too bothered by it. On board ship you had to endure many different smells; in their spare time, some sailors took comfort from chewing or smoking a wad of pungent baccy, or from drinking a drop of rum, and there were others who, like Harriet here, preferred a pinch of snuff.

'I've a feeling this room will suit you better.' Harriet's voice boomed in his ear.

'Maybe.' As yet, John had not taken stock of it. When he did, he found it to be much smaller, and somehow not quite so homely as the other. Furnished much as the first room, it was definitely a far quieter place.

On going to the window, he saw how it overlooked the back of a huge warehouse. 'I'm sure this is much more suitable,' Harriet told him. 'The doors to the warehouse are at the other side, and all you'll ever hear are a few bangs and noises, and the clip-clop of horses as they trot over the cobbles. All in all though, I would say there's nothing to break your sleep, or disturb you in any way.'

John thought about that, and felt unsettled all the same. 'I prefer the other room,' he told her. 'I'm used to noise and besides, I reckon I'll get a deal of comfort from all the comings and goings.' He moved away from the window. 'I wouldn't be content in all this quiet. No, not content at all.'

'Right! So now you'll want to see the bathroom.' With John in tow the big woman sailed out of the room, down the stairs and across the yard. In the outhouse she proudly gestured to her newly appointed bathroom. 'This was the old washhouse,' she explained, 'but being as I don't intend to spend what's left of my life slaving over a hot tub, I now send all my washing to the laundry. This place seemed a waste of good space, so I got the workmen to fit it out as a bathroom. The only drawback is you might need to wrap up warm as you come in and out, especially in the winter months.' She shivered. 'Coming out of a hot tub and being thrust straight out in all weathers could cause a body to catch his death of cold.'

In her abrupt fashion, she led him out. 'Well, what d'you think?'

John was impressed and told her so. 'At home I've always been used to washing at the kitchen sink, or having a dip in the brook. A bathroom will be a luxury.'

'The other lodgers don't use it much,' she revealed with a disapproving shake of her head. 'Like as not, most times you'll have it all to yourself.'

So, it was settled.

John paid his rent a week in advance, and was soon seated in Harriet's kitchen enjoying a large cup of tea, and an even larger teacake. 'Bought from the baker's first thing,' she told him proudly. 'I never bake if I can help it. God only knows, I've more than enough to do without all that.'

John was astonished. 'You don't bake? You send your washing to the laundry? By! You're well organised, I'll say that for you.'

'Oh, I am that,' she declared proudly. 'What's

more, I have a little man round once a month to wash my windows, and a little woman once a week to polish the furniture, change the beds and beat all the rugs in the house.'

She was very content with her leisurely life. 'I saw my mother work her fingers to the bone to fetch up my six brothers and sisters. When they were old enough they left home one by one, and never contacted her again. Two weeks after the last one left, my father decided he was off as well.' As she spoke, her fists clenched and unclenched. 'Soon after he'd gone, my mother keeled over in the street and that was the end of her.'

Tears of anger filled her eyes. 'I long ago disowned my immediate family. After what happened to that good woman, I swore I would never be tied by man nor child, and from that day to this I've never regretted it.'

John was sorry for the upset she had suffered and, to her surprise and gratitude, he told her so.

'As far as I'm concerned, I'm best on my own,' she went on, calmer now. 'I've no responsibilities. I've got my own business, which pays for all the help I get, and nobody to answer to . . .'

While she chatted on, seemingly oblivious to his presence, John supped his tea and let his thoughts drift back to Emily. It was barely forty-eight hours since he had left her behind, and since arriving here he had walked the streets, not knowing or caring where he was. Some blind instinct had brought him back to Liverpool, although he had now decided against going back to sea. *Oh, Emily . . .* he yearned for her.

It was hard to understand that she could just stop loving him, especially when they had spoken at great length of their feelings for each other and their plans for a future life together. He truly believed she had been as sincere as himself. And now, seeing her like that, so idyllically happy with her new man, and the two of them blessed with a beautiful daughter, was soul-destroying.

It all seemed so final. And however much he might want to change what had happened, he realised there was nothing he could do but accept the situation.

Emily had stopped loving him. That was painfully clear.

In the early hours, after arriving back in Liverpool, wandering the streets and trying to fathom out where it had all gone wrong, he had slowly begun to think more clearly, and what he thought was this.

As far as he could see, he had two choices. He could either throw himself into the murky waters of the River Mersey and end it all, or he could be grateful that Emily had found happiness, and forge ahead to do the best with what Fate handed him.

In the end there was no choice at all.

Whether he liked it or not, however much it

weighed on his heart, he had to make a new life without her.

He had money in his pocket, and plans to make. *Tomorrow he would look for his old friend, Archie.*

So, with that in mind he climbed the stairs to his bedroom, though he knew he would not sleep.

How could he, with Emily so strong in his mind?

~

Woken by the delicious aroma of bacon, John climbed sleepily out of bed. He had slept like a log, oblivious to any of the noises outside. His first thought was Emily; his second was the hard-earned money that would forge his future without her. Although he had left a substantial sum with Lizzie, he had taken enough to see him through, for a while at least.

Always aware of thieves and opportunists, John had wisely taken precautions against someone stealing his money while he slept. He was sure that his landlady was vigilant in her choice of lodgers, but you never could tell. He'd locked his door too, mind . . .

Going straight to the window, he took hold of the curtain and, drawing it aside, checked that his wad of money was still securely rolled into the hem. Archie himself had relayed the trick of hiding valuables in the curtain. 'A thief will turn furniture upside down and tear your mattress from end to end, but he'll hardly ever examine the curtains.' That was his advice and John had never forgotten it.

Having checked that it was secure, John decided to leave it there while he had his wash at the basin. The smell of that warm, crisping bacon was playing tunes on his stomach.

Stripping to the waist, John filled the bowl with cold water from the jug and began to wash and shave. The generous layer of carbolic felt good and invigorating on his skin, and the swill of water afterwards made his skin tingle and shiver. It was a good feeling.

At the dresser, where he had unpacked his kit-bag, he shook out a clean singlet and soft collarless shirt, which he quickly buttoned on. That done, he was soon ready for a hearty breakfast.

As always, when he went out of the door, locking it behind him, it was Emily who kept him company. She filled his heart and mind as he went down the stairs, and she was beside him as he entered the breakfast-room.

'Good morning, young man!' Harriet waved a knife towards the one empty table. 'Sit yourself down and I'll have your breakfast in front of you before you know it.' With that she ambled away.

As John made himself comfortable at the tiny table, the other two lodgers gave him the once-over. 'Morning!' The man who spoke was middle-aged, bald, and bore the hangdog look of someone weighed down with worries.

Judging by the smart clothes and the newspaper laid out before him, John thought he might be a salesman or a clerk. 'Morning,' he replied with a nod of his head and a smile. 'The landlady seems a good sort, don't you think?' The smile soon faded when the man looked away without another word.

'You're right. She *is* a good sort.' That was the frail, elderly woman by the window. 'I've lodged in this house for almost two years off and on, and never a cross word.' She was buttering a slice of toast while peering at it through her lorgnettes; her hands, he noticed, were clad in old-fashioned lace mittens.

John gave her a friendly nod. 'Really?' He wondered what she meant by the remark that she had lodged in the house 'for almost two years off and on', and thought maybe she was a relative of Harriet's, who liked to pay a visit from time to time. Her scent of lavender and camphor made him think of his Aunt Lizzie.

There was no chance to carry on any conversation, because the woman then took her leave, shortly followed by the man. A moment later, Harriet returned with his breakfast. 'I wasn't sure of what you liked best,' she told him, 'so I gave you a measure of everything. What you don't want, you can leave. I won't mind a bit.'

Setting the plate on the table she watched his mouth open in astonishment. 'My God!' The plate was piled high with fried tomatoes, four rashers of bacon, three sausages, two eggs, a generous helping of fried potatoes, and two plump rings of black-pudding. 'You must think I need fattening up!'

'That's because you do!' she retorted. 'You sailors are all alike. Surviving on meagre rations at sea, and afraid to spend your money on good food when you come ashore.'

John took up his knife and fork. 'How did you know I was a sailor?'

'Hmh!' Placing her two hands on her chubby hips, she gave him a knowing smile. 'It didn't take much. I knew it the minute I clapped eyes on you. Your kitbag, for one. You were browned from the sea-air for another. And you looked like you needed a good meal inside you. What! I've seen more fat on a dried-up chicken-bone.' She gave him a curious look. 'I suppose you'll be going back to sea soonever you've spent your hard-earned money?'

Digging the prongs of his fork into a juicy sausage, John took a bite; the sausage melted in his mouth, leaving behind all manner of sensational tastes. 'That's the best sausage I've ever tasted,' he told her, his mouth full.

'Ah well, that's because I make them myself,' she revealed. 'Best cut of young pork, minced with a mangling of apple and a mix of my own spices, churned to perfection, then cooked on a wire tray over the pan.' She lowered her voice. 'I cooked some for the butcher once and he's been after me for the recipe ever since. He won't get it though. It was my mother's.'

John thought there was a deeper side to this woman than she ever let on. 'I thought you said you didn't bake if you could help it?'

'And I don't. Baking and cooking are not the same thing, young man.'

John was curious. 'Oh, and how's that then?'

Harriet explained the best she could. 'Baking is kneading over a bowl for hours on end. It's making bread and pies and such, and rolling out pastry until your back aches. Or it's beating cake mixtures until your hand is ready to drop off. Y'see, cooking is quicker, not so laborious. In fact, it's a pleasure.'

John laughed. 'Well, I never. I always thought they were one and the same.'

She too gave a hearty laugh. 'And now you know different, don't you? Oh, and you still haven't answered my question.'

John took another bite of the sausage, allowing the meat to ooze its juices onto his taste-buds. He gave a sigh of satisfaction. 'What question was that?'

'I asked if you would be going back to sea?'

'No, I won't be going back . . . ever.'

'Why not?'

'It's a long story.'

'I've got the time if you have.'

'I don't think so.' Shaking his head, John cut a slice of the egg. 'Do I get a drink with this breakfast?' He wasn't in the mood for talking about Emily, not even to this likeable soul.

Harriet was mortified. 'A mug o' tea for you and a drop of the old stuff for me,' she said. 'I'll sit alongside you while you eat your breakfast, and you can tell me all about your troubles.' No sooner said than done, she was off and, in a minute, had the kettle whistling on the stove.

John didn't know whether to wolf down his breakfast and leave, or enjoy it at leisure while confiding his 'troubles' in Harriet.

He didn't have much time to ponder, because now she was back and seated opposite, a large mug of tea steaming in front of his plate, and a glass of what looked like wine in her hand. 'What do I call you?' she asked. 'You must have a name.'

'The name's John,' he answered. 'John Hanley.'

'Go on then, John Hanley,' she urged. 'Talk away. There's only the two of us here now, and don't you worry, because whatever you have to say won't go beyond these four walls. It's a rule of mine, never to pass on what's told me in confidence.'

For some reason John trusted her. This was surprising to him, as he had only just met her. As a rule, he was wary of strangers but somehow she had a way about her that made him think of Lizzie.

So he opened his heart to her. He told her

about Emily, and the plans they had made. He gave a short account of Clem Jackson, and how that monster of a man had the Ramsden family by the throat. He outlined how he and Emily had spoken at length, about their love and their future, and how he had decided that the only solution for them all was for him to go where he could make money. Afterwards they would be rid of Clem Jackson, and he and Emily would wed and raise a family. 'But she didn't wait,' he said sadly. 'She married some other man. They have a child – a lovely daughter.'

Harriet had listened intently, and now she had a question. 'When you saw her there, did you think she seemed happy?'

John thought of Emily, of how she was laughing. He saw the light in her eyes and recalled how she and the man seemed to share such joy in the child, and each other. 'Yes,' he answered quietly. 'She seemed happy enough.'

Harriet could see his pain, and now as she spoke, it was with a tenderness that belied her clumsy frame and hitherto brusque manner. 'For what it's worth,' she told him, 'I think you must put her behind you and start again. It seems that someone else came along with the means of giving her the contentment she needed. Be glad for her. That's all you can do.'

John knew she was right and thanked her. 'I can try,' he said. 'But I'll never forget her.'

She gave a knowing smile. 'Of course you won't,' she said. 'That first love is the one you remember for the rest of your life.'

John was surprised at the softness in her voice, and when he looked at her as he did now, he was taken aback to see a lone tear run down her homely face. Realising he had seen it, she quickly brushed it away and was her usual brisk self again. 'Right! Must get on.' In a minute she was out of her chair and heading for the kitchen.

A moment later John followed her. She was standing at the pot-sink with her back to him. 'I wanted to ask you something . . .' he began.

When in that moment she turned round, he saw her puffy eyes and the hurried way in which she thrust the handkerchief into her pinny pocket, and he was sorry to have intruded. 'It doesn't matter,' he apologised. 'It can wait.'

As he turned to leave, she called him back. 'If it could wait, you wouldn't have come to the kitchen after me,' she chided. 'What is it you want to ask?'

John told her about Archie. 'He's been a good friend,' he explained. 'His seafaring life is over, and now he has nothing to fall back on. The last time we parted, he told me he was looking for digs. He didn't have much money, and he wouldn't let me help. I've a feeling he has need of me, and the trouble is, I don't know where to look for him.'

Harriet considered the matter for a moment before telling John, 'If he did find a place to stay, you'll have to try every lodging-house in Liverpool until you find him. On the other hand, if he didn't find one to suit his purse or person, you might try the inns hereabouts; it's likely you'll find him drowning his sorrows. If that fails, you'll need to look under the railway arches. That's where some unfortunate folks lay their heads when they don't find a home for whatever reason.'

John had an inkling of hope. 'When I find him, and if he isn't yet fixed up, is it possible you could arrange a bed for him here? I've got the money to pay, and it would only be for a few nights, until we get him a regular place. Is the back room still unoccupied?'

Reluctantly, Harriet had to refuse. 'I only have the three bedrooms, and Miss Hamilton came yesterday and took the last, so no, I'm sorry, I can't do it.'

As John thanked her and made to leave, she had an idea. 'If it was only for two or three nights at the most, I dare say I could put a camp-bed in with you. It would be a squash and I couldn't allow it for more than three nights.' She paused. 'I don't mind telling you, I'm not happy about the idea. It's not a big room at the best of times, and it would be a terrible nuisance cleaning around all that clutter . . .'

Sensing she was about to change her mind,

John gave her a hug. 'Archie may have already found himself a bed,' he pointed out, 'but if he needs to share my room, I promise it won't be for longer than three nights, and with me alongside, we can double the efforts to find him a place of his own.'

Swayed and delighted by John's impulsive hug, Harriet relented. But she had terms, and she stated them now. 'I'll want an extra shilling a day for use of the cot, and cleaning and such, and that will cover his breakfast as well. I'll also need to give him the once-over before I agree altogether,' she warned. 'As you know, I'm particular as to who stays in my house.'

John thanked her again. 'I hope I find him, and that if I do, he's in good spirits,' he told her. 'He's not a young man any more.'

~

For the next four hours, John tramped the streets and back alleys of Liverpool. He searched every inn along the dockside, his first call being at the Sailor's Rest, where he had last seen Archie.

'I've not seen him since the two of you sat at that there table.' The same big, hairy landlord pointed to the table where John and Archie had sat talking. 'Hey! If you're in need of another bath, I'll soon have one at the ready . . .'

Disappointed, John thanked him and left to continue his search.

The answer was the same at every inn, and now, two sore feet and a heavy heart later, this was the last. 'Sorry, matey.' The landlord shook his head. 'Can't recall nobody of that description.'

Before he left, John asked the same of this landlord that he'd asked of all the others. 'If he does come in, tell him John Hanley's looking for him, and say I'll keep looking till I find him.' He didn't give his address; revealing too much about yourself was never a wise thing. He had learned that along the way.

Next stop was the railway arches.

Going from the docklands, he crossed a network of narrow streets and, following the run of the railway-track, headed off towards the arches. What he saw there was a sobering reminder to John of the desperation that dogged the lives of so many in this big city. There were vagabonds huddled under sacks, ragged boys raiding middens for food, scowling, devious characters lurking at every corner, and stray dogs roaming. The stench of urine and booze hung over every back alley.

Hoping against hope that his friend Archie would be found safe and well, John intensified his search.

When he had checked every nook and cranny, he sat dejected on the doorstep of a narrow house. He couldn't think where he should look next, for he had already looked everywhere in the vicinity. Besides, he suspected Archie would never wander far away from the docks. Man and boy, he had always lived hereabouts.

Suddenly, from somewhere close by, he heard a woman screeching abuse: 'And don't come back, you filthy, lying old git! Not unless you want the dogs tearing at your arse. Go on! Bugger off with you!'

The tirade was followed by the slam of a door, then the sound of a man in desperate voice. 'You've got it all wrong, Sadie! I really have got property abroad. Anybody will tell you the same. When you and me get wed, I'll take you there. SADIE! Let me in.' There came the sound of a boot against wood. 'Oh, sod you then! You're not the only woman to be had, not by a long chalk. You'll be the sorry one. You see if I'm not right, you miserable old cow!'

Now, as the little man turned, it was to see John standing there, legs akimbo and a smile across his face. 'Shame on you, Archie,' he tutted with a shake of his head. 'I knew you had a reputation with women, but I'd have thought you were past all that by now?'

It took a moment for the little man to realise who it was, and when it dawned on him, he gave a loud whoop and a holler and threw his cap in the air. 'JOHN! Well, I never!' With his wispy hair stood on end, and a broad grin from ear to ear, he more than ever resembled a leprechaun. 'I'm blowed if it's not my old shipmate. Oh, but am I glad to see a familiar face!'

Eagerly flinging his arms round John he almost had the two of them unbalanced. 'What's brought you back, son? Oh, look now, this calls for a drink, only I'm spent out. That bloody Sadie – took me for every penny, she did, then threw me out on the streets like some old baggage. What d'you think to that, eh?'

John thought it served him right and said so. Soon, though, he had a comforting arm round his old mate, and was marching him off to the nearest public-house. 'I knew you'd be up to no good,' he chided. 'Chasing women, causing trouble and dossing anywhere you could lay your head.'

Having now reached the pub on the corner, he threw open the door and propelled Archie inside. 'I've found you a bed for a night or two. Just until we get you settled elsewhere.'

Archie was intrigued. 'But what's brought you back all of a sudden? What's happened to your wedding plans and the little woman, eh? Tell me that.' The old sailor had a feeling that John's homecoming had not gone well, and his heart sank. 'Has it all gone wrong, son?' he asked sorrowfully. 'Did it not turn out the way you planned, is that it?'

'You might say that,' John conceded. 'But look, I'll tell you all about it in a minute.'

Once they were seated, each with a jug of ale,

John explained what had happened between himself and Emily. 'So there you have it, Archie,' he finished quietly. 'Everything we planned – marriage, a family of our own . . . it's all gone.' Even now he found it so hard to comprehend.

Archie knew how badly his young friend had taken it, and he gave his best advice. 'The way I see it, son, is this,' he said. 'Your woman has found what she wants and it doesn't appear to be you. Now there's one or two things you can do. You can go back to her now and plead with her to leave the husband she's taken in your place. If she agrees to that, you have to ask yourself if you could ever trust her again. Moreover, you'll be taking on another man's child, and all the aggravation that goes with it, because I dare say he won't take it lying down.'

John had already considered all that. 'If I thought Emily could still love me, I'd take on the world if she asked,' he confessed. 'Only I saw her there, with him and the child.' It was like a moving picture in his mind; the mature Emily, so beautiful, so happy with her family. 'She was like someone I never knew before.'

'Ah, that's it, y'see, son.' Archie had known many women in his time. 'Women are changeable creatures. It's in their nature – they can't help it. And it's not surprising how, in the space of time you've been away, your Emily has grown from a girl to a woman.'

'You're right.' John had been astonished at the change in Emily. 'She's more beautiful than I remembered, especially when she took the child into her arms. It was a lovely thing to see.'

Cutting through John's bitter-sweet smile when he spoke of her, Archie reminded him, 'The truth is, she's chosen another man over you, and that's hard to accept. It's your pride, son. A man's pride is easily dented.'

John gave a wistful smile. 'Pride has nothing to do with it,' he murmured. 'You can't know how it was between us; nobody can. Emily may have turned from me to another, but I still love and want her. I always will.'

'Then I pity you.' Archie had never seen a man so devoted.

Taking a gulp of his ale, John asked, 'Go on then, Archie. What was the other thing?'

After half a jug of ale, Archie's memory was not what it used to be. 'What other thing?'

'You said there were two things I could do.'

Archie's brain limped into action. 'Oh yes. Well, it's simple enough, I should have thought.'

Urging him on, John asked, 'In what way?'

'Your woman chose another man over you; they got wed and now she has a family she loves, and from what you told me, she seemed more than happy enough with her lot. Is that correct?'

John confirmed it was so.

'So now, you're within your rights to do the same.'

'And what exactly would you have me do then, Archie?'

'Cut loose, man! Why! You could choose any woman that took your fancy. Lord knows, you're a good catch for any of 'em. You're a fine figure of a man – fit and strong – and you've money in your pocket.'

John laughed, but it was a sound without mirth. 'I've no mind to do any such thing.'

'Then you're a fool!'

'Aye, and I'll stay a fool.' The idea of any other woman taking Emily's place was unthinkable.

'Then listen to me and listen good, son.' Leaning forward, Archie spoke in a stern voice and with the merest scowl on his face. 'No man should martyr himself for a woman who turns her back on him. If she has a husband and child, then there's no going back that I can see. She's made her bed and you'll do well to let her get on with it. You've a life to live, and every minute spent brooding over her is a minute wasted. If you can't see that now, you soon will.'

Something about the old sailor's manner, a kind of rage, made John think he must have suffered a similar experience. 'Is that what you did, Archie?' he asked curiously. 'Did the same thing happen to you that happened to me?'

For a long moment Archie stared into his ale. 'It might have,' he admitted. But he would not be drawn further on the subject. 'All I'm saying is, if you brood after one woman for the rest of your life, you might as well not *have* a life.'

The two of them drank in silence, their thoughts going back to their own lives and recalling how it was before, and each of them knowing it would never be like that again. It was a sobering thought, and the more they thought the more they drank.

Yet they had their wits about them, and even now, though he wished it was any other way, John was musing over a plan that would take them forward. 'What was your real trade?' he asked of Archie. 'Before you went as a cook on the ships?'

With a mischievous little smile, Archie held high his jug of ale. 'Delivering *this* on a horse and cart,' he revealed. 'Thirty years and more, I drove for Thwaites's Brewery . . . delivered all over the North, from when I was little more than a lad, right up to the day before I signed my name to be a sailor.'

Quietly pleased with Archie's answer, John had more questions. 'So you know how to handle a horse and cart?'

Archie stuck out his little chest. 'I was the lead driver – that should tell you how good I was.' He chuckled. 'All done up in my breeches and red jacket, there wasn't a finer sight to be seen.' Giving a wink, he revealed, 'I had my fair share of women then, I can tell you.'

John could well believe it. 'So, you know the North well, do you?'

'I do, son, yes – better than any man.'

'And who made the wagons?'

Archie had to think hard on that one, but by and by he had the answer. 'A family firm by the name of Armitage,' he said. 'The father owned a sawmill and the two sons made the wagons in a yard alongside. As I recall, each was run as a separate business.' He cocked his head as he told John, 'I were told the father passed on some years back, and the sons took over the timber business. But they can't still be going, 'cause they'd be as old as I am now. Unless o' course they too had sons and the tradition got carried on.'

John could see everything falling into place. 'Where was it situated, this timber business?'

'About four miles away, more in the country-side. The business lies alongside the Leeds and Liverpool canal – it's easier y'see, for transporting and delivering the timber on the barges.' Now it was Archie's turn to be curious. 'You're asking a lot o' questions. What's all this about?'

John had not wanted to reveal his idea until he had made some more enquiries and could be sure what he was getting into, but now that Archie was asking, he decided to outline his plans for the two of them.

'You recall I told you how I earned my living by repairing and building wagons, hay-carts and such . . . not in a big way, mind you, but I know a wheel from an axle and I had sufficient customers to bring in a fair enough wage.' His voice fell to a whisper. 'It was more than enough, until Emily and I got serious about the future.'

'I see.' Turning the idea over in his mind, Archie swallowed the dregs of his ale. 'And how do you mean to go about starting such a business?' he asked. 'It won't be easy. And I'm only saying that because I know there are enough well-established firms who supply all the wagons around these parts. What makes you think you can find an opening? And if you do find it, how could you secure enough customers to keep you going?'

John had already thought about that. 'Back home there were some who said I was the best. Any cart or wagon I made or repaired, outlasted all the ones brought in from the big towns. I took a pride in what I did, Archie. I built and repaired everything the way I'd want it myself . . . strong and lasting, with the stamp of quality.'

'Ah yes, but folks don't want to pay for that.' Archie had been around long enough to know the score. 'Build it fast and sell it cheap, never mind quality.'

'But that's false economy,' John argued. 'There must be sharp-minded folks who'd rather pay a few guineas more for something that will last twice as long. My thinking is this – if there's nobody building strong, quality wagons, the customers hereabouts might be glad of somebody like myself.'

He looked at Archie, his face determined. 'I can tell there's a place for me here,' he declared. 'Soonever I've introduced you to Harriet, I want you to take me to this yard you were talking about. I'd like to see how the land lies . . . get my bearings, so to speak.'

Archie's eyes lit up at the mention of a woman's name. 'Who's this Harriet then?'

'She's the landlady at my lodgings.'

'Bit of all right, is she?' Archie said eagerly, though whether that was the prospect of meeting Harriet, or the effects of too much ale, John couldn't tell. 'And she's agreed to put me up, has she?'

John confirmed it. 'You'll have a camp-bed in my room, and it'll be for no more than three nights, that's the deal.'

'Hmh! That's not much help, if you don't mind me saying. When the three nights are up, where am I supposed to go from there?'

Now, when John stood up, Archie followed suit. 'We'll have to see, won't we?' he answered. 'First, let's get you settled, then we'll head off to the timberyard. It won't be dark for a few hours yet.'

'And what will you do when we get there?'

John hadn't thought that far ahead. 'Oh, I don't know,' he said lamely. 'Mebbe I'll offer my skills and a deal of money to buy in as a partner.'

Archie laughed at his bare-faced cheek. 'What if they don't want a partner?'

'Then I'll set up on my own.'

Archie was impressed. 'You've got big ideas, I'll say that for you.'

Taking him by the elbow, John chided, 'Seems to me, you're slightly tipsy.' He observed how Archie was gently swaying from side to side. 'I can tell you now, Harriet won't like that.'

'Then she's not my sort o' woman and that's a fact!'

'Mebbe, but I reckon a bite to eat is in order before we see her.' He led Archie to the door. 'There's a little tearoom round the corner,' he said. 'We'll spend a few minutes in there before we make for the lodgings.'

Moaning and complaining, Archie followed him. 'If your landlady is one o' them miserable types that doesn't like a man to be merry, I'm not sure I want to lodge there at all!'

John laughed. 'I can't deny she has a forceful side to her, but she's agreed to let you stay, and that's good enough for me. So, get a move on, and stop complaining, or I might decide to leave you where I found you.'

The threat didn't worry Archie, for he knew that was the last thing John would ever contemplate.

~

An hour later, with Archie more sober and milder of mood, John presented him to Harriet. 'This is my old shipmate Archie,' he said. 'A more amiable man you'll never meet.'

While Archie took stock of this big, awkward woman with her straight face and large, unattractive hands, Harriet also observed Archie, who nervously glanced away under her scrutiny.

She walked round him a few times, sniffing at him like a dog might sniff at a bone. And when she was done, she stood before him, hands on hips and her eyes boring into his. 'You stink!'

'I do not!' Archie glared back. 'I'm a particular man and always have been.'

'Hmh! Not particular enough, from where I stand.' She took another sniff at him and wrinkled her nose. 'If you ask me, you've been keeping company with the dogs on the street, or women of a certain reputation. Either way you stink to high heaven and I'll have no argument on the matter.'

When John gave Archie a warning glance, the old man took the hint. 'All right, so mebbe I do pong a bit. It's hardly surprising, is it, when I've been forced to sleep rough. But you've shown a kind heart to a poor old fellow, and I'm ever so grateful for that.' He congratulated himself on being able to charm the birds from the trees. The trouble was, he hadn't come across a woman like Harriet before; more was the pity.

'Three nights!' she declared. 'But first, you go into the bathroom and strip off your clothes. You throw the clothes outside the door, and while you're scrubbing the dirt off yourself, I'll get the dirt off your clothes. I usually send everything to the laundry, but this is an emergency!'

Archie treated the idea with utter contempt. 'If you think I'm handing my clothes over to you, you've got another think coming, missus! Moreover, if you're expecting me to climb into a bath, you can keep your lodgings, 'cause I'm not interested.'

Harriet took him at his word. 'Fair enough,' she said. 'You can leave the same way you came in. I can't say it was a pleasure meeting you.'

Smartly turning, she was about to go out of the door when John called her back. 'He'll do as you say,' he promised, and looking at Archie with a warning glare, he instructed, 'You'll hand over your clothes and you'll take a bath, even if I have to scrub your worthless back myself. Isn't that so, Archie?'

The old chap remained sullen.

John gave him a shove. 'I said *isn't that so*, Archie?'

With great reluctance, he nodded.

Harriet tutted and John urged his old mate, 'So, tell the lady, Archie.'

Snorting with disgust, Archie glared back at John, and in the meekest of voices told Harriet,

'All right, missus. I'll do as you say.' His voice hardened. 'But I want you to know, I'm not happy about it.'

Harriet allowed herself a wry little smile. 'I'm not concerned about you being happy,' she replied. 'I'm only concerned to be rid of the stink you've brought in with you.'

When she was gone from the room, Archie gave John a piece of his mind. 'If I'd known what a tyrant she was, I'd have thought twice about coming here. Wanting the shirt off my back; demanding I get a bath. What next, that's what I'd like to know!'

Amused by the confrontation between Archie and the landlady, John told him it was no use his moaning. 'Think of it this way,' he suggested mischievously. 'Once she catches sight of your manly figure, why, she'll be like putty in your hands.'

Archie chuckled at that. 'I'm not so sure I like that idea,' he said. 'I mean, yon Harriet's not the best-looking woman I've ever seen, I can tell you that for nothing.'

Half an hour later, Archie was shoved into the bathroom. 'Throw your clothes out,' Harriet told him. 'I'll be here waiting.'

Under protest, Archie did as he was told. 'Mind you take care of them,' he warned. 'They cost money.'

Hiding behind the door he stripped off his

clothes and slung them out. 'And don't put no sweet-smelling stuff on them neither. I don't fancy walking about stinking like a ponce!'

'It's better than walking about stinking like a polecat!' Grabbing the clothes with a pair of tongs before he could snatch them back, Harriet placed them in a straw basket held at arm's length. 'Make sure you use the carbolic *and* the razor,' she reminded him. 'And don't come out of there pretending to have had a bath, because I'll soon know. I've been about too long to be taken in.'

Archie slammed shut the door. 'You're right about that,' he grumbled to himself. 'Old battle-axe!'

Tiptoeing across the cold floor, he kept on grumbling. 'You're some kind o' witch, that's what you are!' Stubbing his toe on an uneven slabstone, he swore under his breath. 'Stealing my clothes, dumping me in a tub of water and ordering me about. It's not as if I even know her. God help me, I only ever clapped eyes on the woman five minutes since!'

He dipped his toe in the warm water, shivered and took it out again. Stooping over, he gingerly ran his fingers through the water and straightening up, gave a little smile. 'It's not bad,' he said. 'Not bad at all,' and he climbed inside and lay back blissfully. In fact, it had been so long, he'd forgotten the pleasant, silky feel of warm water against his skin.

In the washroom, Harriet took Archie's clothes out of the tub. They were so clean and colourful, where before they were dark and grubby, she could hardly believe they were the same ones she'd put in there. Tutting and complaining, she fed them through the mangle, before hanging them on the line in front of the fireplace. Tugging the shirt into place, she shook her head. 'Blue,' she declared with astonishment. 'And I'd have sworn it were grey.'

Next stop was the big chest at the back of the room. From here, she took out armfuls of clean, neatly pressed clothes. When she'd finished matching them for size with Archie's, she tucked them under her arm and made her way to the kitchen. 'It's a good job I keep a few spares,' she told John. 'Sometimes I have to confiscate the clothes in lieu of payment.'

John was seated at the table, busy making notes and drawings. 'Sorry, Harriet?' He looked up. 'I didn't hear what you said.'

'That's because you're deep in what you're up to.' Reaching her gaze forward she tried to get a glimpse of his work.

'What was it you said before?'

Harriet held up the garments. 'I've found your friend some clean clothes.' She showed him the selection. 'These should carry him over until his own clothes dry out.' There was a burgundy-coloured shirt, a pair of long-johns and a singlet, together with a jacket and trousers of similar colour to Archie's own.

'I should think he'll be very grateful,' John told her though, knowing Archie as he did, he couldn't be sure. His old friend seemed to have taken against Harriet, and as for her part, she had shown little patience with him.

Draping the clothes over the back of a chair to get warm near the fire, Harriet crossed to the larder and poured them each a glass of sarsaparilla. 'Grateful or not, he'll either wear them, or walk about naked.' She chuckled. 'From the little I've already seen, that would be a terrible sight for sore eyes.'

Before taking a hearty gulp of her drink, she opened her little tin of snuff and applied a pinch to both nostrils. Then, seating herself beside him, she peered over John's shoulder at the notebook. 'What's that you're so intent on?' she asked.

'I'm making a plan.'

'What kind of plan?'

'A business plan.'

'What kind of business?'

John explained, 'I mean to have my own timberyard and men in my employ. I plan on making wagons, you see.'

Harriet thought he was a dreamer, just like many other men who had lodged here before him. 'Dreaming and making are two very different things,' she warned.

'I'm aware of that.' John, also, knew it only too well. 'But I intend making this dream into reality.'

She admired his ambitions, but, 'Building a business takes a deal of money.' She took a long gulp of her sarsaparilla. 'Money and dedication, that's what you need. Even then, it's a long, hard struggle. More often you lose your friends along the way. Life can become very lonely. Have you thought of that?'

'I've thought of everything,' John imparted. 'As for friends, if they turn their back on you when you need them most, then they can't have been worth having in the first place, that's my thinking.'

Harriet nodded. 'That's true enough. But look, as I've just said, dreaming is one thing. Making it all happen isn't quite so easy.'

'I'm sure that's true,' John replied, 'but a man has to have a dream.' He thought about Emily. She had been his dream; his life and his future.

Harriet's voice interrupted his thoughts. 'What are all these different areas?' Pointing to the sections on his map, she listened while he explained.

'These are work areas,' he said. 'Look, this is the office, and here alongside the canal, is where the timber will be lifted from the barges and stacked in different bays. The smaller sections are where the different pieces will be made and kept ready for use – such as wheels, axles, shafts and so on. Next to that is the larger area where the wagons and carts will be constructed. And the yard outside is where they'll be lined up ready for collection.'

She smiled at that. 'You seem to have given over a large area for lining up the ready wagons. Does that mean you expect business to be brisk?'

'Without a doubt,' he answered with confidence. 'I hope we've got so many orders coming in, that I'll need to employ extra men.'

Harriet drew his attention to the long bay at the back of the building. 'And what's this meant to be?'

John followed her gaze. 'That will be the repair shop.'

Surprised by the detail he'd written into his plan, she asked pointedly, 'I suppose you have the money for this grand idea?'

'Not all of it, no.' John was honest with her. 'I saved every penny I could from my wages in the Merchant Navy, but some of that has gone. I'll have to start out small – rent a yard or barn somewhere. I'll begin by doing repairs, and take it from there.'

'And do you think there'll be an opening for that kind of thing?' she wanted to know. 'I mean, won't there already be more than enough repair shops tending the wagons on the road?'

'Well, that's something I mean to find out, but according to Archie, there's a shortage of *good* repair shops. Setting up my own shop will be the first step.'

'What then?'

'Well, I'll get talking to the customers. One by one, I hope to persuade them to let me do more than just repair. I hope to show them how I can design and build top-quality wagons and such.'

Harriet liked the sound of it all. 'And push the big boys out, is that it?'

'Something like that, yes.'

'You've got your work cut out.'

'I know that.'

'And it doesn't frighten you off?'

John shook his head, a look of defiance in his eyes. 'It only makes it all the more exciting.'

Finishing her drink, Harriet prepared to leave. 'I'd best go and see what that friend of yours is about,' she said. 'It wouldn't surprise me if he hasn't just stood in that room the whole time, shivering and shaking. In fact, it wouldn't surprise me if he's never once dipped his dirty toe in the water.'

While John bent his head to his drawing, she ambled to the door. 'I think you've got a good plan there,' she casually remarked.

'Why thank you, Harriet.' It was good to have her believe in him.

Her next throwaway remark took him aback. 'If you've need of capital to help get you started, I've got some savings tucked away. Mind you, it'll only be a loan. I'll want it back with interest!' She took out her little tin of snuff and tapped the lid.

By the time John looked up, she was gone. 'Good God!' Her words echoed in his mind. 'She offered me a loan.' He could scarcely believe it. 'Miss Harriet Witherington offered me a loan, and she hardly knows me from Adam!'

He had left himself a sizeable sum of money, after providing for Lizzie, but it wasn't enough to take him where he wanted to go. His idea had been to approach the bank and ask for a loan, though he didn't think much to his chances. But Harriet had offered him a loan just like that. It was incredible.

My God! he thought. If she really is serious, and she's talking real money, I might just take her up on it. He laughed out loud. It was possible, of course, that Harriet's idea of a loan wouldn't even buy him a set of tools. He got back to his drawing. All the same, it was kind of her to offer.

His estimation of the landlady had gone up when she offered Archie a few nights under her roof, but with this latest offer, his regard for her was tenfold. In fact, he was beginning to realise that her bark was far worse than her bite. More-over, he had a sneaking suspicion that there was more to Harriet Witherington, spinster, than she was letting on.

CHAPTER EIGHT

A COUPLE OF hours later, as the two of them clambered off the tram, Archie chortled, 'Did you see her face when I came out of the bathroom, all spruced up and dressed to the nines?' Stroking the lapels of his borrowed jacket, he looked like a man with a purpose. 'Shocked to the roots, that's what she was.'

John took stock of his old pal, and he still couldn't believe the transformation. With shining, shaven face, freshly washed hair and clean, pressed clothes, Archie looked like a new man. 'I'm not surprised she was shocked,' he commented. 'I'm still wondering if this is the same Archie I spent time with on the high seas.' There was even a spring to Archie's step that hadn't been there before. He appeared years younger, and not all that bad-looking.

Suddenly Archie was tugging at his sleeve. 'Hey! Did you see that?' he cried excitedly. 'That young woman just gave me the eye.' Waving in the direction of the departing tram, he beamed from ear to ear.

John glanced at the woman, who had seen Archie waving and had turned away, embarrassed. 'Behave yourself!' he said laughingly. 'She was looking in the shop-window.'

Archie wasn't convinced. 'She were looking at me,' he argued. 'Do you think I can't tell when a woman fancies me?'

John left it at that, because now they had reached the canal bridge, and right there in front of them on the other side, was the sawmill and buildings Archie had described – Armitage's.

'The place is falling down!' Archie was shocked. 'Look at that! The buggers have let it go to rack and ruin.'

John took a good look, and the more he saw the more pleased he was. There were four large wooden buildings, all in a row and all in a state of disrepair.

And yet, from what John could tell, the business was ongoing. In the first building, a number of men could be seen moving back and forth, some carrying tools, others pushing wagon-wheels over to a half-built wagon. Two fit, strong men were offloading timber from a barge, and overseeing it all were another two men. One was about Archie's age, the other somewhat younger, but each was well into his middle age.

'It's them!' The little fella's mouth fell open.

'Well, bugger me. I would have thought they'd have packed it in years ago, and yet here they still are, working in their father's yard and letting it fall apart all at the same time.'

John took careful stock of the two men. He had seen how smartly dressed they were, and how little attention they paid to the workmen. Instead of which, they appeared to be arguing with each other. 'They don't get on that well, do they?' he remarked.

Archie knew of them from old, for hadn't he come in and out of those same buildings while working for Thwaites's Brewery? 'They hate each other's guts,' he revealed. 'Always have.'

'And why's that?' John thought it more interesting by the minute.

'Jealousy,' Archie answered succinctly. 'It's all to do with rivalry and money. I don't know if the years have changed him for the better, but the younger of the two used to enjoy a gamble – threw money about like it was of no use to man nor mouse. As I recall, he was a lazy bugger into the bargain. One day he'd turn up at work, and then you wouldn't see him for weeks on end. The older brother nearly got to fighting with him once or twice. It got so bad the father threatened to cut the pair of them out of his will, or so I heard.'

John thought it got better and better. 'Why didn't you tell me all this before?'

'Because you never asked.'

John glanced to where the older man was wagging a finger at his brother. 'Looks to me like there's still bad blood between them.'

'You're right,' Archie agreed. 'It looks that way to me an' all.'

'Might make it easier for me to buy them out, eh?' John was already smiling at the prospect.

Archie looked at him with curiosity. 'Even with the buildings falling apart, and happen the business too for all we know, I reckon the buying of it is beyond you. What! It'd take all the money you've put by and a great deal more besides.'

'I expect it would.' John had no doubts on that score. 'But if I could raise the extra money, I reckon I might be in there with a chance. What d'you think?'

'I think you could be right. But it won't be handed to you on a plate – you can be sure o' that.'

John gave a wink. 'Slowly, slowly,' he said. 'There's always a way.'

Archie had a warning. 'Their father was a gentleman, but these two are a pair of cunning devils.'

'I reckon I'm a match for them,' John answered.

Archie didn't argue with that. 'So, what's your plan?'

John's plan was simple. 'Even though it's on its last legs, this yard is perfect for what I have in mind. I know I'll not get better. Besides, from what

I can see with my own eyes, them buildings won't be standing much longer, not without something being done, and that takes money, which they may not have.' His mind was working fast. 'I'm wondering if that younger brother isn't still wasting money by the fistful.'

The same thought had crossed Archie's mind. 'You know what they say: once a gambler, always a gambler.'

'Ah, but we can't know that for sure, can we?' John was cautious. 'I need to see how the land lies before I make my move.'

'And how d'you mean to do that?'

John had it all figured out. 'We'll go across and introduce ourselves. We're just two men looking for work, that's all they need to know for now. They won't recognise you from before, will they?'

Archie shook his head. 'No, not a chance. They never gave the likes o' me a second glance. As for now, they might set *you* on, son, but they'll not want an old lag like me.'

'You're not an old lag,' John argued. 'Now that you're all washed and smartened up, you look ten years younger.'

'Mebbe, but it doesn't alter the fact that my fingers are crooked and half-useless. You know yourself I can't hold anything of any weight before I have to put it down.'

'Aye, but they don't know that, do they?'

'Oh, but they will. First time I attempt to pick

up a piece of heavy wood, they'll know I'm next to useless.'

'You've got other talents.'

'Oh, an' what might they be then?'

'You can cook, can't you?'

'That's true, right enough. But they're not about to want no cook, are they? And besides, it's even got so's I find it difficult to hold a full pan.'

'All right. But you can use a broom, can't you?'

'I hope so,' Archie retorted. 'I should imagine anybody can use a broom.'

'So that's what you'll tell them,' John suggested. 'You're capable of using a mop, and keeping the place safe underfoot, aren't you?'

Archie cheered up. 'Oh, I should think so.'

'So there you are then, Archie. You're not as useless as you think.'

'Hmh! Useless enough, all the same.'

With Archie still moaning, they crossed the bridge and approached the yard. 'Let me do most of the talking,' John said.

'Suits me,' Archie readily agreed, but with one reservation. 'Don't talk me into doing anything too demanding,' he instructed. 'I can do mopping and cleaning, and mebbe washing down a bench or two. But that's it.'

Deciding to speak with the older brother, John led the way. Unfortunately as they drew near, there was a sharper exchange of words between the two men, resulting in the older one angrily striding away; leaving John with no choice but to address the other.

'We're looking for work,' he told him. 'I'm a carpenter, and my mate here is first class with a broom and mop.'

'You're wasting your time here.' The other man's answer was swift and clear. 'We've no need of you, so bugger off, before you get the sharp end of my boot.'

At that moment his brother returned. 'What's the problem here?'

'No problem.' The younger man bristled. 'These two were just about to leave.' He glared at John and Archie. 'You've been told. On your way . . . NOW! Before I have you thrown in the canal.'

Controlling the urge to smack him one, John retaliated. 'You can try! But more likely than not, it'll be you who ends up in the canal.'

'All right! That's enough.' Sensing a serious confrontation, the older brother stepped in. 'I'm sorry, but he's right. We would offer you work if we could, but we're fully manned. Sorry . . . can't help.'

John and Archie had no choice but to leave. 'Is there any point in coming back in a week or so?' John was bitterly disappointed.

The older man shook his head. 'I'm afraid not.'

As they walked away, Archie glanced back. 'Seems to me there's real hatred there.'

John agreed. 'It's a terrible thing when family

turns against family.' His thoughts went to Emily and her uncle, and though he was devastated at losing her, he was glad for her sake that the situation there appeared to have been resolved.

'Look at that!' Archie drew John's attention to where a barge was being offloaded. 'I'm buggered if it ain't a young lass in charge!'

John was surprised. 'It appears so.' He observed the young woman in question and saw how the men appeared to be taking instruction from her. Not yet twenty by his reckoning, with her long fair hair tied back and the hem of her dark skirt swishing around her ankles, she wore the same kind of boots that the men wore.

At that moment she turned and smiled at him. Embarrassed to be seen watching her, he returned a nod, and quickened his steps towards the bridge.

'Well, I never. She's coming after us.' Brushing his hand over his hair, Archie preened himself. 'I expect she's heard about my reputation,' he said with a naughty wink.

Her voice carried on the air. 'Wait a minute!' She caught up with them on the bridge. 'Are you looking for work?' Brown-eyed and with a quick, easy smile, the young woman was not so much pretty as homely.

'That's right. But it seems they've no need of us.' Like Archie, John felt easy in her company. 'Why? Are you offering us work?'

'It's not full-time or anything like that,' she

replied. 'Only, one of my barges is beached, and I'm losing work because of it.'

'So, how can we help?' John was surprised to learn that she was not only the owner of that barge down there, but had another somewhere else. A woman of her tender years, owning a business like this and working alongside the men – that was something he had never come across before.

She explained, 'It's my father's business, but he's laid up. There was an accident . . . a crate fell on him and injured his back. Since then I've carried on the best I can.'

'You look like you're doing a good job an' all,' Archie answered.

'Thanks.' Then, addressing herself to John, she said, 'One of the men down there heard you say you were a carpenter. Is that right?'

John nodded. 'It's right enough, yes.'

'So – will you help me out?'

'Depends on the job.'

She described what was needed. 'When the crate fell, it smashed a huge hole right through the deck of our second barge. We managed to get her ashore, but she needs major work.'

John was curious. 'And are you telling me you can't find a carpenter to take it on?'

'Oh, I can find them all right.' She scowled. 'I can find any number who'll take it on, but they think because I'm a woman they can charge me twice the going rate.' Taking a deep breath, she let it out in anger. 'Before they take advantage of me, the barge can rot where she is!'

Archie laughed. 'Fighting talk, eh?' He'd always liked a lively lass.

One swift glance from John silenced him. 'How far away is this barge?' he asked the young woman.

'She's laid up about a mile along the canal. Once she was badly holed, we had to get her out of the water a bit quick. Thank goodness there were men on hand at the time.'

'How long ago was that?'

'A year . . . eighteen months or thereabouts.'

'Can you take me there?'

Visibly relieved, she thanked him. 'I can take you right now,' she said. 'The men are just about finished offloading and I'm ready to pull out.'

As they strolled towards the barge, John introduced himself. 'I'm John Hanley,' he said, 'and this is my old friend, Archie.'

'Hey!' Archie's feathers were ruffled. 'Not so much of the old!'

The girl shook them each by the hand. 'I go by the name of Rosie Taylor,' she said. 'My father is Lonnie Taylor, of Taylor's Carriers.' Her smile was one of relief. 'If you can put that second barge back on the canal, we'll both be very grateful to you.'

Archie was curious. 'How old are you, to be taking on the responsibility of a business?'

'Older than you think.'

'And how old is that?'

'You're a cheeky devil!'

'Born like it,' he chuckled. 'So, how old?'

'You tell me.'

'Eighteen, mebbe nineteen?'

'I'm twenty-two next birthday.'

She was the same age as himself, John noted. Archie was about to ask another question, when John gave him one of his warning glances. 'Right then!' the little man finished the conversation. 'We'd best get on.'

When she ushered them into the barge, both men were impressed by the interior. 'I've been on many a ship in my time,' Archie remarked. 'This is the first occasion I've been on a barge, and I don't mind telling you, I'm amazed. I always thought they must be too narrow for a man to move about freely, but there's room aplenty.'

'People are always surprised at how roomy they are.' Rosie handed him a cup of sarsaparilla.

'Given the chance, I could laze about here all day.' Seating himself on the little green sofa, he supped contentedly at his drink.

John considered the barge to be warm and welcoming, much like Rosie herself, he thought. Moreover, with the little stove, the oblong peg-rug and comfortable furnishings, she had made it a home. 'It's a credit to you,' he said, and meant it.

In no time at all, they arrived at their destination. 'There she is.' Pointing to the rotting hull, Rosie slowed the barge.

Manoeuvring the vessel into the bank, she tied it up. 'Before you offer to repair her, you might like to take stock of the damage.'

All three disembarking, they walked along the towpath to where the barge lay, lopsided, half-hidden by the undergrowth. 'Careful now!' Rosie warned. 'The ground lies a bit swampy just here.'

They were soon up to their ankles in water and mud, with Archie complaining tetchily. 'I'll leave you two to get on with it. I'm finding my way to higher ground.'

Rosie smiled as she watched him leave. 'He's a character, isn't he?'

John chuckled. 'You could say that.'

She drew his attention to the hull. 'What do you think?'

First he crawled all over the boat. Rosie had been right when she said the hole was huge. The central timbers immediately round the hole had rotted right through and now, after months at the mercy of the elements, there were a number of other timbers in dire need of repair, and some that would have to be replaced.

John's investigation was thorough and conclusive. Apart from the huge, gaping hole and the damaged timbers, the engine was rusted and the chimney was smashed – but that was easily fixed, he thought. Then there was the difficult task of lifting the whole thing out of the bog, where it had settled deep. As far as he could see, shifting the barge would be no easy matter.

'So, is she worth repairing?' Rosie was behind him every step he took.

'She'll be good as new,' he promised. 'But this is the picture as far as I can tell. First off, you'll need to buy a whole new batch of timbers. The engine looks to be seized, and the chimney's smashed to a pulp.' There was something else too. 'I'll need a yard to work in.'

Rosie apologised. 'We don't have a yard,' she told him. 'And the only decent yards round here are owned by the Armitage brothers.' She sighed. 'You saw the feud going on between those two, so you can guess how it is. Even if Jacob Armitage talked his brother Ronnie into letting you use part of one of their buildings, the favour wouldn't come cheap.'

John wondered if he might be able to repair the barge right here on site. 'We'd be dependent on the weather, o' course, but it could be done. Mind you, we'd need to get her to higher ground.' As he spoke, he walked to the top of the mound.

Rosie walked beside him. 'I'm sure I could arrange that,' she said thoughtfully. 'But before you decide, there's something I need to tell you.' She paused, almost afraid to go on. 'You see, I haven't been completely honest with you.'

Feeling uneasy, John wanted to know, 'What is it?'

She hesitated again, before telling him in a rush, 'These past eighteen months have been awful hard without Dad in charge.'

John sympathised. 'I can understand that.'

'I've carried on the best I know how, and at last things are picking up, but even then, there isn't enough money in the pot to pay you for any work you might do.'

'I'll do the work,' he said. 'You can pay me when you're able.'

'That won't do.' She was adamant. 'My father has never owed a penny in his entire life and I wouldn't want to be the one to let him down. So, if you're interested, I have a proposition.'

With nothing much as yet to fall back on, John was more than interested. 'Go on. I'm listening.'

Rosie outlined her plan. 'If you can put the barge back on the canal, there's a chance it will double the work. And if it doubles the work, it doubles the income. The trouble is, there's only me to keep it all going, and according to the doctor, Dad may never work again.'

'I'm sorry to hear that, Rosie.' In a strange way he felt as though he'd known this young woman all his life. She was so open and easy to get along with.

Rosie continued, 'So what I propose is this. If you repair the narrowboat, and come to work alongside me, I won't pay you in money.' She wondered how he would react to what she was about to say. 'Instead, it would make more sense to offer you a partnership . . . say twenty per cent?'

John refused without hesitation. 'I can't accept that. Besides, I thought it was your father's business. What in God's name would he have to say about such a crazy idea?'

Rosie wouldn't let it go. 'It's not so crazy if you think about it.' Brushing aside his protests, she called his attention to the facts. 'Look. First of all, I'm limping along with only one barge. I can't meet all the bills, and I can't borrow because we've reached our limit with the bank, so it's a certainty that before too long I'll have to call it a day – and that would break Dad's heart. He's run this business since he was a lad. Taylor's Carriers is his pride and joy, and now he's had to entrust it to me.' Close to tears, she said quietly, 'I don't want to be the one who lets it all fall apart.'

John was deeply moved, but there were still questions to be answered. 'From what I saw back there, you were offloading a heavy cargo. If you don't mind me saying, that one job alone must have brought in a pretty penny?'

She gave a small, wry laugh. 'It's the only job I've had all week,' she confessed. 'What's more, it won't fetch a pretty penny as you put it, because the Armitage brothers know how to take advantage when somebody's drowning. The young one, Ronnie, will cut you to the bone, and when you do finally get paid, it barely returns what you've spent out in the first place!'

She persisted with her idea. 'So you see, with the other barge and you together, I know we'll get more work. Men have little respect for a woman at the helm. A man likes to deal with a man, you should know that.'

John did know that, but, 'Times are changing,' he told her.

He thought of Emily and her mother and of how, when Aggie's husband went off, she and Emily kept Potts End Farm going almost single-handed. He was so proud of Emily. He missed and loved her, and always would. His thoughts went next to his Auntie Lizzie, who had kept a home for him all the time he was growing up. She had worked in all weathers to bring in a few coppers to pay the bills. They were strong women, all of them, and he loved and respected them for it.

Rosie's voice penetrated his thoughts. 'Most of the cargo gets shifted on the order of a man, and they don't like to deal with women, unless like the brothers, they're trying to get it done on the cheap.'

John could see her point, but, 'All I know is, your father would not take kindly to you offering me a fifth of his business.'

'What if he was to agree?'

'Well now, that might be different.'

'Consider it done,' she said. 'I know Father

would be glad for me to have a man helping out, until he gets on his feet again.'

'I can only agree if the offer of a partnership is equal to the price of the work I do.'

Rosie agreed. 'Not forgetting that the barge would only lie there and rot away if you didn't get her up and running again.'

John was adamant. 'There'll be no agreement until I talk with your father,' he said. 'I'm sure I can persuade him into delaying payment rather than making me a partner of sorts.'

'I wouldn't count on it,' she warned. 'He's a stickler for doing the right thing, and the right thing would be to pay his dues in any shape or form that he was able.'

She went to shake hands on it, but John graciously refused. 'Don't worry, I'll get the barge upright and working again, but there'll be no talk of payment until I've spoken with your father.'

Wading through the tangled undergrowth, John was suddenly in the open. Before him lay a great expanse of unkempt land, and right there, in front of his eyes was a tumbledown building. 'Who owns this land?' he asked. 'That building looks to me like it's been closed up for a good while. Maybe we could get permission to use it.'

Rosie's answer was like a gift from heaven. 'My dad knows more about it than I do,' she said, 'but from what I understand, this used to be a large, productive farm, part of the estate belonging to one of the gentry hereabouts. Then it was split up and sold off in sections – all bar this one, which includes a cottage, that building, and ten acres of land.'

John was curious. 'Why wasn't it sold?'

'Because it was all left to a lady by the name of Amy Benson. She worked for years up at the local big house – Coram Manor. Had a good position there, so I'm told.'

John was thrilled by the news. 'My God! It's exactly what I need. She obviously doesn't use the barn.' His excitement grew by the minute. 'Do you think she'll sell it, or rent it out?'

Rosie shook her head. 'Oh, she's long gone. Eight years ago, maybe nine, she was taken to the Infirmary and never came back.' Pointing across the fields towards the village, she revealed, 'She's over there, poor Amy, at rest in the churchyard.'

'So who owns all of this now?'

Rosie shrugged her shoulders. 'Who knows? Some say she had a daughter out of wedlock. Some say she left it all to a niece, who wants to remain anonymous. It seems nobody knows the real truth of it – or if they do, they're not telling.'

The story had been common gossip round these parts for many years. 'I understand that Mr Leatherhead, the solicitor, hasn't been able to locate her, so maybe it was all gossip, after all.'

John was on the point of asking further questions when Archie came at the run from the brow of the hill. 'JOHN!' Racing to a halt, he bent his head, put his hands to his knees, and took a long, frantic breath.

'Easy there, old-timer,' John said gently. 'What the devil's got into you?'

'It's a cottage.' Composing himself, Archie told John: 'I've found a lovely cottage over there. It's all locked up, but I had a peek inside. Looks champion, it does. Needs a bit o' fixing, but that won't bother us. Mebbe we could set up home in it and nobody would ever know?'

John told him what Rosie had explained. 'The best way to go about it is to see the solicitor dealing with it. There might just be a way we can secure the lot – cottage, land and the building.'

'It's just what you were after.' Archie could see the sense in what John had to say. 'Right – when do we go and see him?'

Grinning from ear to ear, John slapped his two hands on Archie's shoulders. 'There's no time like the present,' he said, and turning to Rosie: 'Don't you worry. I'll have your barge as good as new in no time,' he promised. 'But like I say, she'll need shifting to higher ground, and if I have my way . . . into that there building.'

Rosie wished him well. 'When you're ready, you'll find me at the docks tomorrow morning. I've another cargo to bring back.'

A short time later, she took them by barge down the canal, dropping the two men as near to

Liverpool town centre as was possible. 'Good luck,' she called, and watched them hurry away.

Her eyes, though, were for John only. I like him! she thought, dimpling. I like him a lot.

Since her father's accident there had been no time for anything but work, and certainly no time to be looking at men. But there was something about John; a kind of sadness maybe? Or was it because he didn't seem at all interested in her in that way? Whatever it was that attracted her to him, John lingered in her mind long after he was gone from sight.

~

Searching the area, John asked passers-by where he might find the address Rosie had given. 'Turn left by the church and straight on,' one old gent informed him. 'Halfway down on your right, turn at the pawnshop, and there you are.'

Within half an hour of leaving the barge, they were standing at the foot of the steps leading up to the office. The March day had turned cold, and the light was fading fast. Archie read the plaque on the wall. '"J. T. Leatherhead, Solicitor".'

'That's the one!' John led the way up the steps. 'If things go right, Archie,' he said nervously, 'we'll be set up to start the business, and already with one customer waiting.' This was his big chance, and come what may, he would not let it slip through his fingers.

The girl at the outer desk was a sullen little thing. 'Have you an appointment?' she asked.

'No, but I have important business to discuss with your Mr Leatherhead.'

'He won't see you without an appointment.'

'Could you try him?' John urged.

'It won't do any good.'

'Please. It's urgent.'

Tutting like an old 'un, she clambered out of her chair. 'I'll try,' she grumbled, 'but I'm afraid you'll be disappointed.' With a haughty backward glance she hurried away to the rear office. 'He's a very busy man. I can assure you, he will *not* see people straight off the street.'

John and Archie waited. They could hear voices, but not what was being said. 'Let's hope he'll make the time to see us,' John said anxiously.

'Hmh!' Archie was still bristling at the girl's attitude. 'Not if *that* young madam has her way, he won't.'

A moment later the girl returned. 'Go through.' Obviously angry at having been proved wrong, she gave them a shrivelling look and dropped into her chair with a thump. 'He tells me one thing and does another. What's the use of me being here at all, that's what I'd like to know!'

'Miserable young devil!' Archie muttered as they went into the back office. 'She wants her arse smacked!'

'Ssh!' John gave him a nudge. 'Behave yourself.'

231

The office smelled of snuff, old dust and decaying paper. The window was half-covered by shelves dipping from the weight of files and documents, which caused the whole room to be dark and dingy, and as for the man himself, he was so bent on his work, he didn't even look up. 'State your business, and be quick,' he said, 'I'm a busy man.'

Mr Leatherhead was a big man, too. His considerable frame spilled over his chair, and when he spoke his jowls wobbled up and down like jelly on a plate.

'Well! What is it that's so urgent?' Looking up, he now impatiently gestured at them to sit down.

As simply and quickly as he could, John explained how they had discovered the land with the buildings and derelict cottage. 'I'd like to buy it,' he said, 'if it's up for sale.'

'Well, depending on whether you have the money or not, it seems you might be in luck, young man, because it is in fact up for sale.'

'What's the price?'

'There is no set price.'

'Why's that?'

'It's a long story, but to put it briefly, up to quite recently, I had not been able to locate the owner of this particular parcel of land. A month or so ago, however, I had instructions to put the land up for auction. There will be no reserve on price, but I expect the bidding to be high.'

Taking off his spectacles, he vigorously rubbed

his eyes, then, replacing them, he peered at them both in turn. 'There's no use you attending the auction if you haven't got the funds available. Have you access to money?'

John assured him, 'I hope I can stand alongside any man there. But I will need an idea of what it might go for.'

Mr Leatherhead shrugged. 'There's no telling in these cases,' he said. 'Oh yes, I know the whole place lies derelict. It will need a lot of work to develop it, but there are plenty of businessmen who have long registered their interest in this particular property, with its useful outbuilding, cottage, ten acres of good land – and all situated beside the waterway. There's ample potential there, as you yourself must have seen.' He looked at Archie, then spoke to John. 'Can I ask what you would use it for?'

John answered circumspectly, for it was never a good idea to show your cards this early in the game. 'The cottage for living in, and the land for working,' he said. 'So now, if you want to tell me when and where the auction will take place, we'll leave you to your paperwork.' He couldn't help but notice the piles of paper and files littered from one end of the desk to the other.

Scribbling the information on a piece of clean paper, the solicitor handed it to John. 'The proper sale sheets are not yet available, but this is really all you need to know.'

John thanked him. 'Can you at least give me an idea as to how much I'd be looking to pay?'

'Once again, I can't say for sure.' Mr Leather-head threw out his hands in frustration. 'It all depends on so many issues.'

'And what might they be?'

'How many bidders want it. How *badly* they want it. What kind of money they have in their pockets for such a heavy commitment, because once they've bought it, they'll need more capital to recover it to a workable entity.'

'So, what would somebody be prepared to pay for it, d'you think?' If he was going borrowing, he needed to know.

Lapsing into deep thought, the solicitor finally answered vaguely, 'Twenty guineas . . . to two hundred. Probably more, maybe less. Like I say, it depends on what happens on the day. Such is the nature of auctions.' That said, he would not be drawn any further. 'I shall expect to see you there then?'

He shook their hands and bade them good-bye, and when they were gone, he told his sulky clerk, 'Time-wasters. They haven't tuppence ha'-penny between them. I doubt we'll ever see *them* again.'

~

Over dinner that evening, Harriet listened to Archie and John's account with interest. 'So you mean to bid for this land and buildings, do you?' Wolfing down a huge spoonful of apple pie and custard, she munched on that while John answered.

'I'd be crazy not to,' he replied. 'It's exactly what I need to get me started. There's a place for me and Archie to live, a fair-sized building to set up as a workshop, and a useful parcel of land. First off, I'd rent the land out to bring in some sort of income, but later I'd hope to expand the business and use it myself – happen put up a couple more buildings, and a hardstanding.' Outlining his plans, he grew excited. 'With that kind of property, there's all sorts of possibilities.'

Harriet reminded him, 'Don't forget, I've money put away if you need to borrow some.'

John had been thinking about that and it worried him that he should take money from her in her later years.

'I can't let you dip into your savings,' he said firmly. 'I've every intention of making the business a success, but it could easily go the other way. It's been known to happen.' To his mind it was too much of a gamble. 'No, Harriet. Grateful though I am for your kind offer, I can't accept.'

'So where will you get the money, if not from me?'

'From the bank. Lending money is what they do. I'll make a plan of the site, and explain what

I have in mind. I've saved a tidy sum of money myself, which I'm prepared to put up as a deposit. So they should realise how serious I am.'

'All right – if that's what you want.'

'It is. But I won't forget your kindness. Thank you.'

'How much did the solicitor say it would go for?'

Before John could answer, Harriet's attention was drawn to Archie, who was slurping his tea out of his saucer. 'Stop it!' Smacking the back of his hand, she chided, 'Cats do that, not grown men. It's disgusting!'

Looking sheepish, he replaced his saucer and wiping his mouth with the cuff of his sleeve, scooped up a spoonful of apple pie. 'You're a damned good cook, missus,' he said, grinning. 'I'll say that for you. Tek it from one who knows.'

Loudly informing him that the apple pie had come from the baker's, Harriet returned to her conversation with John. 'Did he give you any idea of what the property might fetch?'

John recalled the figures mentioned. 'He thought it might go for as much as two hundred guineas, maybe more.'

'I see.' The big woman sat and pondered. 'And dare I ask how much you have already?'

John knew it to the last penny. 'I've set aside forty-one pounds and two shillings – money got from blood, sweat and tears over a period of two years and more. That's after I left a sum for my Aunt Lizzie back home.'

During the long time he'd been at sea, John had gone without, and refrained from spending needlessly. Time and again when the other crew-members went ashore to spend their money on women and booze, he stayed behind. Other times, when the ship was laid over waiting for cargo, most of the men lazed about after their work was done; or they gambled and womanised, while he took up work on the side, just so he could go back to Emily with more money in his pocket.

And what good had it done him, he thought bitterly. For over two years, in the middle of mighty oceans and on lonely foreign shores, he had dreamed of being with his Emily, and now his dream was gone and she was lost to him.

Would anything ever compensate for that? He doubted it.

'You do realise you could lose it, don't you?'

Visibly startled by the sudden interruption of his deeper thoughts, John apologised. 'I'm sorry, Harriet, I didn't hear you.'

She reiterated: 'I was just saying that if the bank turns you down, and the bidding goes over your head, you could lose out to another buyer at the auction.'

John knew it only too well. 'It's a chance I'll have to take,' he said manfully.

Harriet didn't argue. In fact, she was quite

relieved. She had made him the offer of a loan earlier, only because she had all but promised in the first place, but now that she knew a little more, she was glad he'd refused. 'I wish you the best of luck,' she said, clearing away the dinner things. 'I hope you manage to get it, and that things work out all right for you.'

For now, that was all she wanted to say on the subject.

CHAPTER NINE

T HE FOLLOWING MORNING, John decided to attend the bank alone. 'You can wait for me in the Red Lion, if you want,' he told Archie. 'It might be better if I go to the bank on my own.'

'I won't argue with that.' Archie was grateful for the chance to opt out. 'I'd much rather be downing a jug of ale, than sit like a beggar with cap in hand, in front of some jumped-up clerk.'

'It's no good me talking to a clerk,' John said. 'For something as important as this, I need to see the manager.'

Archie wished him well. 'I'll get a jug of ale in for you,' he said, before he hurried away. 'I've a feeling you'll be back before you know it; especially if the manager has a po-faced clerk like the one at the solicitor's.'

John was optimistic. 'I mean to have an answer one way or another,' he promised, and with that he headed off in the direction of the bank.

Ten minutes later he was at the counter, and

five minutes after that he was being ushered into the manager's office. A small, shrewish man with a moustache, he exclaimed in a shrill voice, 'Your luck must be in, young man! I should have been seeing somebody else, only they didn't turn up.' Obviously rattled at being let down, he informed John, 'I can spare you ten minutes.'

When he was seated at the desk, with John sat before him, he took a moment to observe John, before asking, 'Is it a new account you want to open, or are you after borrowing?'

John came straight to the point. 'It's both. I have money in my pocket to put into an account, but that will depend on whether you're prepared to back my business venture.'

The manager leaned back in his chair. 'Well, that sounds straightforward enough.' He glanced at the fold of paper in John's hands. 'Is that for me to see?'

Spreading the paper on the desk, John told him proudly, 'There are two plans here. This one's a rough sketch of the property I intend buying at auction. The other is a layout of the business I plan on starting, plus an account of the money I have and a rough guess at the money I might need to borrow. Last of all, you'll find a detailed list of the work I'm skilled at. Oh, and you might be pleased to know, I already have one customer waiting.'

As John pushed the papers towards him, the

manager leaned forward to peruse them. 'I can't promise anything, you understand?'

John's heart sank. 'I understand.' What he really understood was that he would have to fight tooth and nail to get what he wanted. But then again, nothing ever came easy, not to such as himself it didn't anyway.

~

Two hours later, John and his old shipmate returned to their lodgings, a bit the worse for drink and full of apologies as they came face to face with Harriet. 'Been celebrating, have you?' she asked, opening the door as she heard them fumbling for the key.

'Not likely.' Archie fell in the door. 'The bastard turned him down! We've been drowning our sorrows,' he added, then burped. 'Oops, sorry, missus. That snotty-nosed toff looked at John's well-laid-out plans, then turned him down flat. One customer wasn't enough to get a business off the ground, that's what he said.'

Harriet's smile disappeared. 'Is that right?' she asked John. 'He turned you down?'

Giving her a disheartened nod, John said, 'I think I'll go upstairs for a bit,' and made his way straight up to his room.

'There are other banks.' Harriet's voice followed him up the stairs.

It was Archie who answered. 'He tried them an''

all. At first he just refused to give up. He marched me down to Victoria Street, where he managed to see the lending manager, but he wouldn't help neither. Then we went on to that small bank on the corner near the docks. The manager was very nice, and he listened to what John had to say, but he wouldn't lend him a penny. None of them wanted to help. I'll tell you what though, Harriet, my old darlin'. They can't see their noses in front of their faces. What! Give our John a year or two, and he'll be earning more money than they are. The stupid bastards!'

Harriet gave him a slap on the arm. 'That's enough of the bad language!' she chided. 'Into the kitchen with you. It's a good hot cup of tea you need and no argument!' Before he could protest, she had propelled him unceremoniously into the kitchen.

'He'll not give up though,' Archie told her robustly as he supped his cup of tea. 'I know him. I know the kind of man he is, and he'll not give up. You see if I'm not right.'

Upstairs, John laid the papers out on his bed. They none of 'em wanted to help, he thought sadly – yet he knew he could do it! He knew, too, that he had found the right place. Given the chance, he'd soon have the customers queuing at the door, only the money-men couldn't see it. All they saw was a young, inexperienced sailor who thought he could set up shop against the big boys.

Well, he could – and he would! He'd show 'em. He'd be at the auction, and God willing, things just might go his way after all.

John suddenly felt more optimistic. Who knows, there might not be enough bidders there to see him off. For one thing, the site was a mess, the outbuildings were falling down and the cottage needed a deal o' work. It would take time, energy and money to put it all together, and not every-body wanted that kind of responsibility. But *he* did, and his hopes began to flicker again.

～

On the morning of the auction, Harriet waited until Archie and John had left to walk over to the site. A few minutes later, she stood at the hall-stand mirror, shifting the bonnet on her head this way then that, until she was satisfied that she looked the part. She fastened the buttons on her long coat, tied the fur tippet at her neck, and taking her big black handbag from the hallway table, let herself out of the house and went on quickening footsteps towards the town centre.

On arriving at the corner, she peered round to make sure Archie and John were not still hanging around in the neighbourhood. There was no sign of them. Good.

Harriet smiled secretly to herself as she hurried onwards. It would never do for John to know her intention. Right from the start she had seen him as a proud, but caring man, whose ambitions would take him far. It was a pity that no one else but herself had the foresight to see it.

A couple of miles away, John and Archie were walking along the canal, going around the site one last time. 'There's only two hours to go before the auction,' Archie fretted.

Seeming not to have heard, John strode ahead, making notes as he went. 'This place was meant for us,' he called back to Archie. 'It's got everything we need.'

'Don't be too downhearted if you can't secure it.' Catching up to him, the little fella could see how desperately John wanted the property, but it was clear the odds were stacked against him from the off.

'You can't know how much getting this place means to me,' John groaned. 'I'm just praying that the money I have will be enough.'

'Aw, look! Why don't you have another word with Harriet? Ask her to go with you to the auction and if it looks like it's going away from you, well, you could still borrow the money she offered.'

'No!' John wanted the conversation ended.

'Why not? Good God, man! She said herself she's got money put by. You can pay it back to her just the same as you would to a bank.'

John wouldn't hear of it. 'And why do you think she's got money put by?' he asked. 'I'll tell you why. Her savings have been scraped together over the years and kept safe for her old age, when she's no longer capable of taking in lodgers.'

Archie persisted. 'It weren't you that asked,' he argued. 'She made the offer herself.'

'All the same, I don't want her to risk all her hard-earned money so's I can buy a site and start a business that I can't be sure will be a success. If I borrow money from a bank and fail, the worst thing they can do is throw me in jail. But if I borrow money from Harriet and fail, she'd have nothing to fall back on.' John shook his head vehemently. 'No, Archie. I won't do it.'

'So you'll risk losing the site altogether?'

'I'll look elsewhere if I have to . . . at some other site that will match the money in my pocket.' Though he knew he would be hard pressed to find one as suitable as this. 'And that's an end to it.'

A short time later they caught the omnibus back to the centre of Liverpool, and what they saw at the auction-house made John's heart sink like a lead weight. 'God Almighty, Archie, I thought I might be in with a chance, but now I don't know.'

The place was heaving with would-be buyers: some in work-clothes, others in suits, and one or two shifty-looking characters smoking cigars. 'It looks like I'm up against it,' John remarked, sidling towards the front. 'Keep your wits about you, Archie, and watch my back.'

He'd heard about 'fixed' auctions before, and something about the atmosphere here gave him the distinct feeling there was more going on than met the eye.

~

In the back office, the solicitor, Mr Leatherhead, had given his instructions and Bertram Tilbrook, the auctioneer, was even now preparing to start proceedings. There was a last-minute flurry of heated words between them, with the solicitor finishing in a low, harsh whisper: 'Make sure you keep an eye on me.' He gave him a warning glance. 'I'll be right there, in your line of vision.'

'Don't worry. I know the score!' Glaring at him angrily, Tilbrook stormed past him and out through the door.

Unconcerned, Mr Leatherhead followed at a more leisurely pace.

~

Outside on the auction-room floor, people were beginning to grow restless. 'I've had my eye on that land for some time now,' one bearded lump of a man told his colleague. 'Now it's come up for sale, I don't mean to let it go.'

His colleague laughed at that. 'You'll have me to contend with, Alan,' he retorted. 'You're not the only one who can make good use of that lot. It's mostly the buildings I'm after though, so whichever one of us gets it, we could do a deal with the other. What do you say?'

Broadly smiling, the other man shook hands on it. 'Makes sense to me,' he agreed. 'You want the buildings for storage, and I want the land to farm. I've more than enough buildings of my own, so I don't see why we couldn't do a deal of sorts.'

Archie tugged at John's coat-sleeve. 'Did you hear that?' he mouthed.

Disappointed, John nodded. 'I heard.'

'So, will we go, or will we stay?' The little man had hoped the two of them would leave and spend an hour or two in the Sailor's Rest, before returning to their lodgings.

'We stay!' Straightening his shoulders and looking ahead to the auctioneer, John told Archie, 'For all we know, most of the folks here might just be dreamers like ourselves. Happen when it comes right down to it, they've got no more money in their pockets than I have.'

Archie thought on that, then he began panicking when the auctioneer banged the wooden gavel on the table. 'Right, gentlemen!' Tilbrook blew his nose and looked round the room, his glance momentarily resting on the solicitor. By now, the big man was at the back of the room, raised by the upward slope of the floor and in Tilbrook's direct line of vision. Standing shoulder to shoulder with him was the equally large, and utterly respectable, form of Miss Harriet Witherington.

From where they stood, the two of them had a clear view of the proceedings, while the only way the bidders would get sight of them, was to make a deliberate turnabout.

'We're off!' Archie could hardly contain himself. 'What happens now?' he kept asking. 'Who's bidding? Why aren't you having a go?' It was his first auction, and the excitement was unbearable.

In minutes the bids went higher than John could have foreseen. 'Thirty-two guineas!' The auctioneer was red in the face, his worried eyes shifting to the solicitor on every count. 'Thirty-four . . . it's you, sir.' His eyes searched the crowd. 'Yes? Do I have thirty-five?'

'Bid now!' Archie urged. 'Go on!' But John preferred to wait a minute longer.

At thirty-six guineas, the bidding began to slow down. Then suddenly it picked up again and two of the bidders were the men standing directly behind John. Having made the deal beforehand between themselves, they could afford to go that extra mile, and much to John's consternation, that was exactly what they did. John could hear other bids coming in, but he was distracted by the murmuring behind him. In the excitement, each man wanted to be the one in control.

The auctioneer grew nervous. 'Thirty-nine . . . I have thirty-nine guineas!' He paused. 'Forty, then! The bid stands at forty guineas.' By now the sweat was running down his face and his eyes were more on the solicitor than on the bidding clients.

Taking everyone by surprise, there was a sudden and unexpected development.

Feeling confident, the two men behind John paused to exchange a quick word; and at that moment, four things happened in quick succession: John held up his number, as did another buyer at the far side of the room; Harriet gave the solicitor a dig in the ribs, he lifted his head and the gavel went down with unusual speed. 'Sold at forty-one guineas!'

Tilbrook's voice startled the two men, who couldn't believe their ears. 'Number sixteen? Congratulations, sir,' he said to John. 'If you'll make your way to the office, please.' Then he picked up his gavel and paperwork, and stepped smartly down from his desk. 'Thank you, ladies and gentlemen, that's all for today.'

Behind him the cries went up. 'Too quick! He brought the hammer down too bloody quick! What the 'ell were Tilbrook playing at? It's a fishy business, if you ask me. Forty-one guineas for that site! It's givin' it away!'

The loudest protests went up from the two friends, who rushed after the auctioneer, furious at being cheated out of their prize. The other bidder had already stormed out.

'What the devil's going on, man? You knew we were serious bidders. You brought that damned gavel down without giving us a chance!'

Bertram Tilbrook was used to such outcries.

'You know the rules,' he said firmly. 'If you don't keep up with the bidding, you lose out.'

'But we *were* keeping up!' one of the farmers objected. 'Good God! We were the only two bidders left.'

'No, you were not!' The auctioneer felt worried enough without letting these two get the better of him. 'You stopped bidding and I thought you were out of it. Another bid came in. I gave you time to respond, and you didn't. It's no use blaming anyone but yourselves. The parcel of land is sold and that's that.'

Feeling both angry and guilty, he hurried back to his office, unwilling to meet anyone's eye. 'Damn and bugger it!' he muttered as he went. 'Damn and bugger it!'

Behind him, the two men got to blaming each other. 'If you hadn't stopped me to ask how far I was prepared to go,' one said nastily, 'we'd have got it easy!'

The other farmer gave him a shove. 'And you, Amos, should have known better than to keep pushing up the price, yer stupid bugger. You could see we were the only two after it.'

'But we weren't, were we, you blummen bastard. Thanks to *you*, somebody else sneaked in and took it from under our noses!'

Oblivious to the furore, John felt stunned by events. 'I can't believe it! I just can't believe it.' Grabbing Archie by the shoulders, he shook him so hard that the old fellow's teeth rattled in his head. 'WE DID IT!' he cried jubilantly. 'I don't know how, but by God, we did it!'

As the people poured out, they congratulated John and Archie. 'Well done, lads!' someone told John, and another chimed in with, 'Did my heart good, so it did.' They all knew the two disappointed bidders. 'They've already got more than they need,' someone else said sagely. 'It's time one of us ordinary blokes got the better o' them.'

'Did you hear that?' John felt so good he thought he'd have to dance right there and then on the spot – and much to everyone's delight, that's exactly what he did. *'One of us.'* He reminded Archie of what the man had said. 'We're one of them now,' he laughed.

'No, we ain't,' Archie answered with a grin. ' 'Cause we're landowners now.'

Taken aback by his friend's rush of arrogance, John corrected him. 'We've been lucky today, Archie. Here in Liverpool, we've found our place, and our place is amongst the workers. The hardest part is now. We may be landowners, but that's only the start. We've still got mountains to climb.'

Sobered by Archie's unthinking remark, he said quietly, 'Every man has a dream, but he can't do it by himself.' Nodding towards the last few stragglers, he said, 'They are the kind of men we need. Men who aren't afraid to work. Men who will never

251

achieve their own dream, but who like to see folks such as you and me do it for them. Do you understand what I'm saying, Archie?'

The little man nodded. 'You're right,' he said penitently. 'I should be ashamed.'

John gave him a friendly slap on the back. 'You've nothing to be ashamed about,' he said. 'In fact, you've a right to be really proud. Nobody knows better than me how you've always done your share and more. But now we've got to get busy. Firstly we've to hand over my savings and collect the deeds. Then we'll survey our little kingdom. After that, we'll go home and wash up, put on our best togs, and take ourselves off to celebrate.'

He thought of Harriet, of her generosity and her belief in him. 'If yon Harriet wants to come, we'll take her as well.' He gave Archie a cheeky wink. 'I reckon she'd be glad to come along. She's taken a real fancy to you.'

'Lord help me then!' the little man chuckled. 'I've seen prettier horses. Besides, how could I ever get my arms far enough round her to give her a hug?'

'Prettier horses, eh?' John teased him. 'And what makes you think *you're* such an oil painting?'

Archie wagged a finger at him. 'Now, now. There's no need to get all personal.' He took on a look of embarrassment. 'In fact, if the truth were told, I do believe I've developed a soft spot for the dear lady.'

252

'Oh, an' why's that, I wonder?' John retorted with a grin. 'It wouldn't be because she's something of a good cook, would it? Or is it because you've found out she's got a bob or two?'

Archie feigned indignation. 'Not at all! She's a fine lady, is our Miss Witherington . . . even if she is a better cook than myself. I mean, what do I care if she's got her own lodging-house?' He sighed longingly. 'Mind you, I've got to admit, all o' that does make her just the weeniest bit more attractive, especially to a mature man like meself, who prefers the finer things in life.'

~

At that very moment, the woman in question was upstairs in an otherwise empty office, in deep conversation with the solicitor. 'You've caused a bad atmosphere between me and the auctioneer,' Mr Leatherhead told her worriedly. 'I don't know why you couldn't have just given Hanley the land and be done with it!'

'You know very well why,' she retaliated. 'I don't want anyone finding out that the land belonged to me. Nor do I want Mr Hanley to feel beholden to me. It was best that I had no involvement in it.' She smiled. 'It all worked out well, and if for nothing else, I thank you for that much at least.'

She fastened the buttons of her coat. 'I'd best be away now,' she said. 'I don't want them getting back to the house afore I do.' A mischievous grin

lifted her face. 'I shall have to look suitably surprised and delighted when I hear the good news.'

The moment Harriet had gone, Leatherhead
hurried downstairs to the office where the auctioneer was worriedly pacing the floor. When the door
opened, Tilbrook immediately vented his anger
on the older man. 'I could lose everything if this
ever came out!' he expostulated. 'My job, and my
good name!'

'There's no danger of that.' Releasing the
catches on his Gladstone bag, the solicitor removed a bottle of best whisky. He seized two tum-
blers from the shelf and poured them both a stiff
drink. 'It all came out well in the end, with nobody
any the wiser.' Handing the other man a glass,
he urged, 'Come on, Tilbrook, drink up. Before
number sixteen rushes in here, wanting his prize.'

Swallowing his drink, Tilbrook gasped as the
liquid went down. 'In all the years I've worked at
this game, I've never been known to end a sale
before the bidding was finished.' He looked at the
older man with stricken eyes. 'Maybe we should
have called her bluff.'

Leatherhead shook his head. 'Nay. Harriet
Witherington is no fool.'

'Why didn't she show her hand before now?'

The solicitor had wondered the same.

'I can't work it out myself, and she's never confided in me on that score,' he answered. 'All I
know is, after years of living a modest life right

under our noses – and I'm quite sure she must have known that her Aunt Amy had left her that land – she came to me with proof of her identity. All her papers were in order, and she knew what had been left to her, better than I did. That were two months ago. She wanted us to sell the job-lot by auction, so she could put the money away for an easy old age. Next thing I know, she's back in my office, saying we've got to let that young pup Hanley acquire the land for a mere forty-one guineas when it's worth so much more. How could I refuse? She'd known all along that we'd been plundering her inheritance, selling off the contents of that cottage a bit at a time, and she'll not shrink from exposing us both if we should so much as hint to that young man that she's had any part in this.' Leatherhead lifted his glass and drank down the rest of his whisky.

'She's a sharp one, I know that,' Tilbrook agreed. 'Sitting tight while we dug ourselves into a deeper hole, and then coming forward just when we thought we were safe.' The auctioneer shivered. 'I'm telling you, all this is beginning to shatter my nerves.'

'Pull yourself together, man!' The solicitor poured them both another drink.

His colleague appeared not to be listening. Instead he was thinking of every way she might get at them even now. 'How can we be certain she still won't come after us? There were some fine paintings and pieces of Regency silver in storage from that cottage – and we both got a good few quid out of that.'

'Because when she insisted that I make certain the property was knocked down to that young man, she promised to look the other way over our misdemeanours.'

'Is it watertight, that's what I want to know?'

Leatherhead gave a sly little grin. 'We're both in the clear, that's all you need to know. And now I'd better be off. Here are the signed documents you'll need from Miss Witherington.' With a triumphant flourish, the solicitor withdrew the sheafs of paper from his pocket and threw them on the desk. 'Signed, sealed and delivered. And now I really must go. A very good day to you, Bertram. It's been a pleasure doing business with you!'

The fat man's laughter had only just died away when John knocked on the door. Feeling more confident after skimreading the documents, the auctioneer sat up straight, put on his best smile, and called John inside.

'I'm here for the deeds to my property.' John placed his wad of notes and coins nervously on the desk. 'You'll find it all there, every penny.'

Archie stood directly beside him, grinning from ear to ear. 'You did well, son,' he kept saying. 'You did real well.'

As for John, he was still dazed at the speed of

events, and the subsequent outcome. The site was his! He could hardly believe it, even now. It was his future; his wildest dream come true.

Yet the glory of the day was deeply marred by Emily's absence. He needed her like he had never needed her before. He wanted her so much to be by his side, to share in this day, and all the days to come.

But she was content with her new man. She had no more need of John Hanley. It was a stark and lonely realisation.

'John!' Archie dug him in the ribs. 'The gentleman's waiting for your signature.'

Emerging from his deep thoughts of Emily, John apologised.

'Sorry. I was miles away.' Leaning forward, John took the gold fountain pen from Tilbrook's outstretched hand.

'It's not surprising that you are feeling somewhat bemused,' the other man remarked condescendingly. 'You've got yourself a valuable commodity there, at a very good price. In fact, you could probably sell it on the open market right now, for a deuced good profit.'

John signed his name and returned the pen. 'Not me,' he replied decidedly. 'It's not a quick profit I'm looking for, but somewhere to build a business that I can be proud of.'

'What kind of business would that be, if you don't mind me asking?'

Here, John saw his chance. 'You might put the word out,' he suggested. 'I'm a skilled carpenter and joiner. I repair and build wagons, carts and barges. I can bend a piece of wood to any shape or form, so whatever the customer wants, I'll provide.'

The auctioneer was not impressed. 'Not my line of interest,' he said curtly. 'But I wish you well.' In fact, he couldn't care one way or the other whether John sank or swam. 'That's our business concluded.' He handed John the deeds, and held out his hand for a farewell shake. 'Good day to you.'

John swiftly reminded him of the receipt, which Tilbrook scribbled out and shoved across the desk to him.

A few moments later, with receipt and deeds safely in his possession, John led Archie out of the building. 'Another surly stuck-up bugger!' Archie thrust his hands into his pockets and began to sulk.

Smiling, John waved the deeds under his nose. 'To tell you the truth, I wouldn't care if he was the most miserable fellow on God's earth,' he joked. 'Look at me, Archie! One minute I'm standing on the site, wishing and hoping, and the next minute, I'm holding the deeds in my hot little hand.'

Archie gave him a slap on the back. 'You're right, matey! It's time to celebrate!'

John agreed, but, 'First we must make our way

back to the lodgings and tell Harriet the good news. Then I'll ask if she'd like to come out and celebrate with us. She can advise me as to where I might safely deposit the deeds.'

Archie had his own ideas about that. 'Go to one o' them banks that turned you down and shove the deeds under their noses, lad. I dare say this time they'll fall over themselves to help you.'

John didn't care much for that idea and said so. 'Once I've tidied the site and made at least one building good enough to work in, I intend starting the business and making money hand over fist. Why should I put my hard-earned profits in a bank that wouldn't give me the time o' day when I needed help?'

Archie could see the reasoning behind it. 'I never thought o' that.'

John quickened his steps. 'Harriet will advise me, I'm sure,' he said hopefully. 'After all, she's a businesswoman in her own merit.'

'So she is,' Archie agreed loyally. 'So she is.' In fact, the more he thought about it, the more Harriet went up in his estimation.

~

They were entering the alley when Archie sent up a cry. 'Look there!' Calling John's attention to the ragged figure bent over the midden, he declared angrily, 'Filthy devil! What's he up to?'

As they approached, they saw how the man was

discarding the contents of the midden, obviously looking for food because now, he snatched at a chunk of what looked like bread and rammed it in his mouth. Intent on filling his belly, the tramp didn't see how John approached him, while Archie stayed back.

'Don't eat that filth,' John said quietly. 'Go and buy yourself a decent meal.' Laying a handful of coins on the ground, he stepped away when the man stopped and stared, his mouth stuffed with blackened bread, and his eyes bulbous with fear.

'It's all right,' John assured him gently. 'I don't mean to frighten you.'

Now, as the man backed away, John held out his arms in frustration. 'I only want to help you.'

The tramp continued to study him, his face smudged with dirt and his eyes still open wide, fearful and curious – and deep in the scrutiny there flickered a glimmer of recognition.

Seeing that flicker, which he took to be fear, John said: 'Have you no work?'

Suddenly, the tramp snatched up the coins and continued to back off, inching his way down the alley, minute by minute widening the distance between himself and John.

Watching him retreat, John was curious; in that moment when the tramp stared into his face, there was a reciprocal stirring of recognition; a deep-down feeling that he knew this man from some-where. It was unnerving.

There was something about the tramp that made John want to talk with him, to find out more about him.

Now, as the man clumsily stumbled from the alley, John called after him, 'I can give you work if you want it. Do you know the derelict site by the canal? You'll find me there most days from now on.' His voice echoed off the narrow walls. 'Don't forget to come and see us. My name is Hanley. *Hanley!*'

'He's gone.' Archie came up beside him.

'Do you think he heard me?' John asked worriedly.

Archie shrugged. 'Who knows? And even if he did, who can say whether he's prepared to work? Some o' these vagabonds are too damned lazy to do anything but scrounge.'

'Did you see how he stared at me?' John was still disturbed by it.

Archie had seen, but wasn't unduly concerned. 'I expect the poor devil's mad as a hatter. Most of 'em are.'

The chance encounter played on John's mind all the way back to Harriet's lodging-house. 'I can't help feeling I know him from some-where.'

Archie had the explanation. 'Well, o' course you do!' he said. 'He's the same fella who spoke to us the other day at the Sailor's Rest Hotel.'

When John frowned, he went on: 'We were

minding our own business, having a conversation about me not being able to do my work on board ship, when he butted in, said as how the sailors would likely throw me over the side if I didn't feed 'em.' He gave a cursory glance up the alley. 'Cheeky bugger. What's it got to do with him anyway?'

John lapsed into deep thought.

'Hey!' Archie gave him a nudge. 'Have you gone deaf or what?'

John was still thinking about the tramp. 'I can't help feeling I've met him before, not at the inn, but somewhere else.'

Shrugging, Archie pointed ahead. 'We're back,' he said, 'and you can put that fella outta your mind, 'cause you don't know him from Adam. What's more, you wouldn't want to neither.'

On seeing Harriet at the door waiting to greet them, John brought the conversation to an end. 'Happen I'll have it out with him when he turns up at the site,' he remarked hopefully.

Archie laughed out loud. 'I'll bet a pound to a penny you'll not clap eyes on that one again – unless it's to see him rummaging about in middens and such. If you want my advice, you'll steer well clear. He looks a bad lot to me, straight outta prison I shouldn't wonder – else why would he be tramping the streets, when he looks fit enough to be earning a wage, tell me that, eh?'

262

Harriet called to them. 'Get a move on! Lord knows, I've been waiting long enough for you to get back! What happened at the sale? Is it good news or bad?' She opened her tin of snuff and applied a pinch to each nostril, to help hide her emotion. She knew well enough what the news was, but they didn't know that, and they never would, if she had her way.

So, when John broke the thrilling news to her, she feigned great excitement. And neither he nor Archie were any the wiser.

~

Not too far away, in the Sun public-house, Emily's estranged father was also imparting news, but of a different nature. 'I've just seen a ghost,' he told those who would listen. 'Fair shook me up, it has.' Fumbling in his pocket for one of John's coins, he handed it to the landlord.

'I'm not surprised,' the landlord replied with a wink at his other customer. 'If you will keep roaming the streets at twilight, you'll see all manner o' ghosts. That's when they come looking for your kind.'

'That's right enough!' the other customer remarked. 'You wouldn't catch *me* out after midnight, I don't mind telling you. That's when the witches and werewolves go on the prowl. I've heard tell how some of your kind get snatched off the streets, never to be seen again.' His voice dropped to a whisper and his eyes grew wider with every word. 'Vampires, too. They're never far away, or so I'm told.'

For a minute the tramp wasn't sure whether to believe him or not; until he saw the smile and a wink pass between him and the landlord. He grinned at them through his unkempt beard. 'Go on with you! I'm not that easily taken in.'

'It's your own fault,' the landlord laughed. 'You left yourself wide open for a joshing, with your talk of seeing ghosts and such!'

Throwing another coin on the counter, the tramp ordered a refill of ale. 'I didn't mean that kind of ghost,' he explained. 'I meant a ghost from the past . . . some man I recognised.' Taking the ale, he swigged it back. Seeing John had given him a real turn.

The landlord saw how shaken up he was and said as much. 'From the way you're trembling, I'd say it was somebody you owe money to.'

Michael glared at him. 'Well, you'd be wrong!' he said, growing more confident with every gulp of the potent brew. 'If you must know, it was a young man who lived not far from my farm.'

Seeing the other men look from one to the other with disbelieving expressions, he told them. 'Oh, aye! There's more to me than what you see in front of you.'

'If you've got a farm, what the blazes are you doing wandering the streets round the docks?'

That was another customer, a slight fellow with a drooping moustache.

'Because I choose to, that's why!' When the memories came flooding back – of his father, and of Aggie and Emily, he saw again what he had lost. 'I couldn't stay, d'yer see?' he muttered as though to himself. 'I weren't strong enough.'

'Why was that then?' The landlord took up a cloth and began to wipe the counter.

'My family . . . the farm. They were my life.' Michael recalled the pleasure of bringing in crops and gathering the harvest. There was no greater feeling in the world than labouring under the sun, stripped to the waist with the sun on your back and God's green and plentiful land stretched out before you. 'I expect you think I couldn't work if I tried,' he accused the two men, 'but I've worked my fingers to the bone on that place, and never regretted a single minute of it.'

'So why did you leave it?' The landlord was cynical. He'd heard it all before, from vagabonds and dreamers, who lied through their teeth every time they opened their mouths. He observed Michael, with his filthy beard and grubby clothes, and wondered why this one should be any different.

'Things just got on top of me.'

Michael mentally relived the events that had combined to bring him to his knees: the bad seasons and failing harvests, the inevitable debts that piled up out of his control, the awful worry of it all, leading to sleepless nights and a kind of madness by day. Then his mother's passing – the burial of his stillborn son . . . his eyes filled with tears.

'I thought I were man enough to deal with it all,' he said in a choked voice. 'Only I weren't, or I wouldn't be here talking to you, would I?'

The slight fellow with the tash regarded him with suspicion. 'Under all that dirt and grime, you look able enough to work,' he observed. 'It might do you the world o' good if you turned your hand to a day's honest labouring. Make a bit o' money. Get yourself cleaned up and find decent lodgings. You never know, you might eventually find it in yourself to go home and put things right.'

Michael angrily dismissed his suggestion. 'What would you know?' he growled. 'You weren't there! You know nothing.'

'Well, I know what I see, and that's enough!' The big man felt no sympathy for him. 'As far as I can tell, you've no damned right to feel sorry for yourself,' he snapped. 'Wasting your miserable life roaming the back streets, grubbing for food and talking of what you've lost, when there are good, hardworking men who would give their right arm to own a farm and have a loving family.'

Michael did not like the picture the other man was painting. 'Like I said . . . you know nothing.'

'Look at yourself!' the fellow went on heed-lessly. 'You're a disgrace. You smell o' dog-piss and midden rubbish, and here you are, telling us you've got a farm an' family to keep you warm, and you expect such as us to feel sorry for you!'

Narrowing his eyes, he gave Michael a sus-picious look. 'Or are you lying? Mebbe you don't have a farm, or even a family, come to that. Mebbe you're just a dreamer like the rest of us.'

'I'm no liar! I worked the farm alongside my father. And I do have a family, just like I said.' Michael lowered his gaze. 'The best family a man could ever have.' Shame engulfed him.

'Oh, you do, do you?' The slight fellow's eyes glittered with hatred. 'Well, aren't you the lucky one, eh?' Prodding Michael in the chest he said threateningly, 'Well, I'm not so lucky, more's the pity. I've got no family, y'see? There's no farm neither. I eat, sleep and exist in a back room in some dingy lodging-house. Some days, I'm lucky to earn a crust by sweeping the streets, clearing away the muck that you and your kind leave behind. But I'll tell you this much, my friend! I can walk down the street holding my head up high, 'cause I don't beg nor steal from nobody!'

Momentarily silenced by the other man's out-burst, Michael quickly downed the dregs of his ale, and called for another.

'You've had enough!' Stirred by the slight fellow's brave words, the landlord took the jug away. 'What's more, I don't like the look of you, so I'll thank you to leave.'

Seeing how the situation was worsening, Michael didn't argue. Instead, he bade them good day and made his way out.

He walked awhile, then sat down on the bench outside the marketplace and began to wonder what it would be like to 'go home and put things right', like the fellow suggested.

'I'm not ready to go home,' he murmured. Made uneasy by the idea of walking back into Potts End, having to face the suffering his leaving must have caused, his courage left him altogether. One day he'd go back and ask Aggie for her forgiveness, but not yet.

Getting up from the seat, he began his aimless wanderings again. Yet in the turmoil of his mind he had not forgotten the incident in the alley. He recalled John's kindness, and the words he had shouted after him. He found himself repeating them now. '"The derelict site by the canal. You'll find me there most days".'

He paused, the merest whisper of a smile lighting his face. John Hanley, he thought with a tut. Whoever would have thought it, eh? And the burning question: Did *he* recognise *me*, I wonder?

Michael thought of all the places he'd been to all over Liverpool, and suddenly realised which site John had meant. In fact, many a time he had rested his weary bones in that old outbuilding.

As he moved on, John's generous offer continued to haunt him. Now, when he was sinking so low he could hardly recognise himself, it was something to think about. But did he really want to see John in such close quarters?

Salmesbury was a small place, where everyone knew almost everyone else. John must be aware of his desertion of family and responsibilities. But then, as he recalled, John Hanley had been sweet on his Emily. So what was he doing here in Liverpool?

Thinking of Emily, his beloved daughter, with her sunny smile, her cheeky plaits and her love of life, Michael fell against the wall and began to weep. Afterwards, when the pain was eased, he squared his shoulders and walked on.

Suddenly he was overwhelmed with a need for his family.

But there was a way to go yet.

PART FOUR

~

June, 1907

Ghosts

CHAPTER TEN

Waking with a start, Emily scrambled out of bed.

Quickly putting on her robe, she went on tiptoe to the door and let herself out onto the landing, where she stood for a time, her ear cocked for the sound she was sure had woken her. Was it Grandad, having one of his bad dreams? She glanced towards his room. Or was it Cathleen?

She gave a long, weary sigh. Whoever it was must have settled down again. The house was quiet now.

Making her way along the landing, she wondered whether she really had heard a cry. I must have been dreaming, she thought. The first bad dream was some two years ago, the night after John had written to tell her he'd found somebody else. Since then, haunted by memories and regrets, she had forgotten what it was to sleep through the night.

As quickly and quietly as she could, Emily

checked the child. Satisfied that she was all right, she then went on to check her grandfather. Thomas Isaac too, was sound asleep, his contented snores reverberating through the house. No problem there. She smiled; that dear old man was never a problem.

Now, as she turned away, she caught sight of something out of the corner of her eye. Moving nearer to the landing window, she peeped out.

There was a light on in what used to be the brick-built storeroom, but which Clem Jackson had recently claimed as his own private place. Unwanted and cramped in the farmhouse, and needing somewhere to take his long procession of women, he had turned the storeroom into his own little kingdom.

Emily was relieved that he'd put a distance between them. What she and the family really wanted, though, was for him to go away and never come back. He was a hated man. But that didn't seem to bother him at all.

Sickened by thoughts of her uncle, she hurried back to her bedroom, climbed into bed and closed her eyes. But sleep was impossible. Her mind was too wide awake with troubled thoughts of John. In spite of him cruelly deserting her, she still loved and missed him.

Skewing to the edge of the bed, she reached over to the bedside cabinet, taking John's note from the drawer where she had kept it since that day when Lizzie brought it to her. She didn't open it immediately. Instead she held it tight to her breast, eyes closed and her heart beating fifteen to the dozen.

'Oh, John! How could you do it to us?' she asked softly. 'How could you forget everything we meant to each other?' Even now she found it almost impossible to believe that after all their dreams and plans, he could simply walk away, into another woman's arms.

Hesitantly, she unfolded the letter and read it for the umpteenth time, her heart breaking all over again.

After a while, she returned the letter to its place, put on her robe again and went softly down the stairs to the kitchen.

Behind her, pausing in the doorway of her bedroom, Aggie watched her leave. Every night was the same; her daughter would pace the floor restlessly, wander round the house. 'You've a lot to answer for, John Hanley!' she hissed. 'Leading her on, then dropping her wi'out the common decency to tell her to her face that you didn't want her any more.' Sending a letter was the coward's way out.

Suddenly the face of her own husband came into her mind. For a moment the tears swam in her sorry eyes, and then they were gone, blinked away in anger. He and John Hanley were a right pair o' cowards!

Yet, in the same way that Emily still loved John in spite of everything, she herself loved Michael.

Not a day went by when she didn't look over the hills, expecting to see his lean, homely figure heading for Potts End. The prospect had warmed her many a night, but there was no doubt in her heart that if he walked through that door, at any time, she would welcome him with open arms.

For now though, Emily needed her.

With that in mind, she followed in her daughter's footsteps, down the stairs and into the kitchen.

Unaware that her mother had entered the room, Emily was standing by the window, arms folded, her gaze reaching across to Clem Jackson's crude habitat.

'All right, are you, love?' Aggie's concerned voice gentled across the room.

Startled, Emily swung round and for one revealing moment, her hatred of that man, the father of her own daughter, burned bright in her eyes.

Aggie saw it, and not for the first time, she was afraid. There was a certain look in her daughter's eyes that went far beyond pure hatred, and it frightened her.

Quickly now, she crossed the room to see what it was that had disturbed Emily to such an extent. When she saw the light in Clem's place, she grabbed the curtains and flung them together. Her brother had probably got one of his trollops in there. Lately, entertaining streetwomen was a regular thing.

Aggie looked at Emily; at the raw emotion still etched into her face. 'What is it, love? What's wrong?'

The girl grew nervous. 'What do you mean?' Just now when she'd been looking across at her uncle's place, she was thinking about the day in the barn, when he had brutally possessed her. She hadn't realised how, in that moment, the murderous intent she felt for him had been alive in her face.

Aggie took her by the shoulders. 'I know you hate him,' she said softly. 'We all do. Only, it seems something more with you.' She had to ask. 'Did he ever hurt *you*, child? Has he ever made improper suggestions to you?'

Emily felt the blood rush to her face. 'No!' Shock and disbelief that her mother could ask such a thing made her lies all the more convincing to Aggie. 'I blame him for coming between me and John. It was him who warned John off!'

She wriggled out of her mother's grip and went to stand with her back to the wall, her voice breaking with emotion as she said, 'I'll never forgive him. Yes, I hate him! I hate the way he rules this family like the bully he is. I hate how he carries on his filthy ways in front of us all . . . in front of little Cathleen! And the pity of it is that there isn't a thing we can do to stop him.'

'All right, lass, I understand.' Aggie was more settled in her mind now about the suspicions she'd harboured. But she had little reason to be content. 'Come and sit down. I'll put the kettle on, and we can talk awhile. But then you've to go back to bed and try to get some sleep. We've a deal of work to do on the morrow, and we'll neither of us be capable of anything, if we don't take care of ourselves.'

Good as her word, Aggie put the kettle on, made the tea and cut two small helpings of her best fruit-cake. 'There y'are, lass.' She set the tray between them. 'Now then, what woke you out of your bed, eh?'

Emily shook her head. 'I'm not sure,' she answered, taking up her tea and slowly sipping it.

Aggie did the same. 'One of your bad dreams, was it?'

'I think it must have been.'

'Dreaming about John Hanley, were you?'

Emily smiled up at her. 'I can't forget him, Mam. I still can't understand why he did what he did.'

Aggie was straightforward as ever. 'It's like he said in his letter, lass. He just fell out of love with you and in love with someone else.'

Emily still could not accept it. 'I find it so hard to believe. We loved each other too much. I could never love anyone else the way I love John.' Her gaze fell away. 'How could he do it, Mam? How could he just turn his back on me, after what we meant to each other?'

Aggie sighed. 'I know it's hard, lass, but it wouldn't be the first time it's happened and I'm sure it won't be the last.'

Emily paused before asking, 'Is that what's happened with Dad, d'you think?' She didn't want to hurt her mother by raising painful issues, but her father had been gone so long, it was like he was never coming home.

Aggie was visibly surprised at her daughter's pointed question. 'I think he just gave way under the weight of debt and troubles,' she answered simply.

Emily valued her conversations with Aggie, and never more than now. 'If it had been another woman, would you be badly hurt by it?'

'Aye, lass, I would.'

'Enough to shut him out of your life for ever?'

'Aw, love.' Aggie smiled knowingly. 'I'm not saying you should shut John out of your life. What I'm saying is this: he was the one who did the shutting out. You mustn't spend your life waiting for him to walk in the door. He might never come back, and one day it'll be too late for you to start again. You've had no word from him in years.'

Every minute of every day, Emily was looking

for reasons as to why John had not come back to her. 'One day he may realise that the other woman isn't for him,' she said hopefully.

'If you're waiting for that to happen, you'll be wasting precious time.' Like any mother, Aggie wanted happiness for her child. She needed to see her settled and content before the years caught up with her. 'You're still young,' she said encouragingly. 'You should be looking for a fresh start, with a new man. And what about Cathleen? She's over four years old now. It won't be long afore she starts at the village school. What will she think, when the other children start talking about their daddies? An' how long will it be afore she starts asking questions about *her* daddy?'

Emily, too, had been troubled about that very thing. 'I don't know,' she answered truthfully.

'Will you tell her how her daddy ran out on you, and that you've no idea where he is?' Aggie asked innocently.

'Right now, I've no idea what I might tell her.' Emily had never argued with the rumours that circulated, about John being the father of her child. At the time it had seemed easier that way. Yet if he ever did come back, she knew she would be bound to tell him what had happened that day in the barn. She would have no choice but to confess that little Cathleen had been the result, and that though she herself would regret the making of her till the day she was gone from this earth, she would never regret knowing and raising that lovely-natured little girl.

'You must tell the child the truth,' Aggie said firmly. 'That her father went away and never came back. You can tell her all about him if you choose, or make up any story you like. But the child has a right to know who her father is.'

Emily's heart sank. 'That's for me to decide, Mam! You mustn't worry your head about it.' The prospect of telling Cathleen who her father was had caused her many a sleepless night.

'I'm not saying it isn't your decision, lass. All I want is for you to think about it and be ready, for when she starts asking the questions.'

For a moment Aggie discreetly observed her daughter deep in thought. There was a troubled look on Emily's face that prompted her to ask worriedly, 'Cathleen *is* John's child, isn't she?'

Emily looked up. 'Well, that's what they're all saying, so it must be right.'

'Yes, lass. It's what *they* say, and we all thought the same. But *you've* never said. You've never confirmed or denied it. Not so as I recall, anyway.'

Pushing the chair away, Emily excused herself. 'I'm feeling tired now, Mam,' she apologised. 'I'd best be away to my bed.' She kissed her mother on the forehead and was soon on her way upstairs.

Left alone, Aggie began to wonder. A dark suspicion crept in. If she wasn't John's child, then who was Cathleen's father? Emily had only ever had eyes for John Hanley. The lass never kept company with any other young men – not so far as she knew, anyway.

A shocking thought entered her head then; so terrible that she thrust it to the back of her mind. 'You mustn't think bad things, Aggie!' she told herself. *What happened with you was a long time ago. You mustn't let it colour your thinking, or it'll send you out of your mind!*

Afraid of her own rampaging thoughts, she took herself off to bed. But it was a long time before she could get to sleep, and even then, it was a sleep full of restless dreams.

~

In the morning it was as though the conversation between Emily and her mother had never taken place.

When Emily came into the kitchen with Cathleen beside her, Aggie was already cooking breakfast. 'Look what I found, Mam.' Emily sat the tousled-haired child at the table. 'One half-asleep, starving-hungry little girl.' She stooped to give her daughter a hug.

'Dolly Dora wants a hug too.' Cathleen held out her rag-doll. 'I think she wants some porridge as well.'

Aggie turned from the stove to give her a smile. 'Well now, we'd best feed you both, eh?' she chuckled. 'Afore you start eating the table!'

The child found that very droll. 'We won't eat the table, Grandma,' she said. 'Anyway, Dolly Dora hasn't got any teeth.'

While Aggie spooned out the child's porridge, Emily poured her a glass of milk. In a matter of minutes the child was settled, but no sooner had the two women sat down than there came a familiar tap on the door. 'Any chance of a brew for a weary, hardworking milkman?' Grinning from ear to ear, Danny poked his head round the door.

At once, Cathleen scrambled down from the table and threw herself into his arms. 'Danny! Danny! Dolly's having porridge,' she said, leading him to the table. 'You can have some too, if you like – can't he, Grandma?' Her face shone up at Aggie. 'If there's none left, he can share mine.'

'Oh, there's plenty left,' she answered readily. 'Only I've a feeling Danny might rather have eggs and bacon – and mebbe a sausage and a morsel o' black-pudding too?' She looked at Danny, who nodded emphatically.

'That sounds just the ticket,' he said, and sat himself at the table. 'Morning, Emily.' As always, his face lit up when he looked at her.

Emily bade him good morning. She brought his tea and served his meal, and the four of them sat together at the table, talking and laughing, and exchanging tales, just like a real family. For Danny it was a wonderful feeling. One he intended making permanent, soonever he got the chance.

When the meal was over, the dishes were carried to the sink. 'I'll give you ladies a hand washing up.' Danny sank his hands into a pot-sink full of soda and hot water from the kettle, but that was as far as he got. 'Take Cathleen up to see her grandad,' Emily suggested, 'while me and Mam wash up.'

'That suits me.' Danny drew his hands out of the water, and pretended to examine them. 'All this hot, greasy water is doing terrible damage to my skin.'

'Go on with you!' He always made Aggie smile. 'Get off upstairs, the pair of youse. Oh, and will you tell Dad I'll be along shortly to change his bedlinen?'

'I'll do that,' Danny answered with a cheerful grin. 'And will you be all right, Emily?' He always came back to her.

Emily gave him a grateful glance. 'I'm fine, thank you, Danny,' she answered. 'Give me a few minutes, and I'll be right behind you. Tell Grandad that for me, will you?'

Danny assured her he would. 'So now, Cathleen me little darling, shall we go and say hello to your grandad, eh?'

'Come on then!' The child slid her hand into his. 'Grandad's waiting.'

Beaming, he allowed her to lead him away.

'That man aches with love for you.' Aggie never lost an opportunity to sing Danny's praises.

'I wish he wouldn't,' Emily answered. 'I could never promise him anything.'

'He'd wed you tomorrow, given the chance.'

'I know that, and I'm flattered.' Emily had a soft spot for Danny, but it wasn't love and never could be.

Aggie, though, refused to give up. 'He's a good man.'

'I know that too, Mam. But it doesn't mean I have to marry him.'

Keeping her face to the window, Aggie dipped a plate into the hot water. 'Love isn't everything, lass,' she said, scrubbing the plate until it shone.

Emily took the clean plate and wiped it over with her cloth. 'Why do you say that?'

'Because it's true.'

'You and Dad loved each other.'

'Yes, and look what happened!' There was anger in her now.

Keeping her voice down so as not to let anyone else hear, Aggie turned to her. 'I gave him years of pampering. I worked alongside him, out there in all weathers. By! There were times when I were so tired and weary I thought I'd fall down on the spot, but I kept going, and when the day's work was done, I'd wash his clothes and cook his meal, and give him all the loving a woman normally gives her husband.'

Turning away, she shook the water from her hands and wiped them dry. 'After all that, he ran off and left me, when I needed him most.' Looking Emily in the eye, she warned her, 'You should never set too much store by love. There are more important things in life, such as security and contentment.' Wagging an angry finger she finished, 'You'd do well to remember that, my girl.'

She would have walked away, but Emily blocked her path. 'You still love Dad though.'

'Who says so?'

'I do. Don't deny it, Mam. You'd have him back tomorrow, wouldn't you?'

'Aye, lass, I would.' The whisper of a smile touched Aggie's mouth. 'But that's only because I'm a silly old fool who should know better.'

'I must be a silly fool too, because that's how I feel about John. I don't love Danny in that way, Mam.'

Aggie was humbled, but hopeful for the child's sake. 'Aw, lass. Are you absolutely certain you and he couldn't make a go of it?'

Emily gave an honest reply. 'If I really thought John was never coming back, I dare say we could. But it wouldn't be fair on him.'

'And you've told him that, have you?'

'Time and again. He knows how I feel, but he still wants to wed me.'

'For the child's sake if not your own, why don't you just say yes?'

'Is that what you want, Mam?'

'Oh, lass! It doesn't matter what I want. It's your life and as far as I can see, you've got two choices.'

Emily gave a sorry little smile. She knew the choices only too well, for hadn't she agonised these past years, and didn't she always come up with the same empty hope; that there was still time for John to realise he'd made a mistake and come home. The trouble was, time had run out so quickly, and with every day that passed, she dreaded the questions Cathleen was soon bound to ask.

Aggie went on, 'You can wait for John, and drive Danny away, so then you'll be on your own. The years will pass and you'll get lonelier and lonelier, and you might still not see hide nor hair of John Hanley. You'll have denied Cathleen the opportunity of having a father, and mebbe brothers and sisters, and as for yourself – well, it'll be awful hard, lass, because you'll need to be both parents at once. There'll be no companion, and no man there for you, not if you keep saving yourself for something that may never happen.'

Emily stopped her. 'I know all this, Mam,' she told her. 'I've thought of nothing else.'

Aggie persisted. 'The second choice and by my reckoning far the best option, is to accept Danny's offer of marriage. Think of it, lass. You'll have a home, and a husband who'll cherish you.'

She then gave Emily a deliberate shock.

'There's summat else you need to think of, lass, and it's this.' Holding Emily's questioning gaze, she informed her quietly, 'There will come a time when me and your grandad are no longer here for you, lass.'

Emily's heart turned over. She had never envisaged a life without her mother and it shook her to the core. 'Please, Mam. Don't talk like that.'

Aggie continued regardless. 'I'm only saying what's true. Hard though it may be, these things need to be considered. Besides, you owe it to yourself and the child to marry a good man, to make a home that will last. Be grateful and content that somebody loves you enough to keep pestering you, even though time and again you tell him no. There's a good chance that if you keep turning him away, he might just meet a young woman who values him enough to say yes – and then where will you be, eh? I'll tell yer.'

She was in full swing now. 'You'll be all on yer own, with a child to raise, with all the worries and decisions that go with it, and you won't be able to sit down of an evening and talk it over with your husband because there'll only be you. Is that what you really want, lass, and all because you can't put John out of your mind – a man who cared so little for you, he went away and set up with some other woman?'

In her heart of hearts, Emily knew that everything her mother said was true. She had known it all along, yet had pushed it from her mind. Instead of listening to her head she had been listening to her heart.

Now though, in the wake of her mother's outburst, she was forced to ask herself some harsh questions. Was she being selfish? Should she forget about John and settle for Danny? As a mother, shouldn't she be putting Cathleen first? But no less important: could she bear to live with a man who she couldn't really love? When he put his arms round her in bed of a night, how would she feel?

She considered all these things, and what came out as being most important was the child. After all, just like her mam said, Cathleen needed a father, and she already loved Danny in that way. But wasn't it ironic, that the same man who to her mind had driven John away and defiled her that day in the barn, was now ruling her life as never before, through that same innocent child?

On top of all that, Emily now forced herself to consider what John had done to her. How could he ever have really loved her, to do a thing like that?

'You keep thinking on it, lass.' Aggie saw how deep in thought her daughter was, and it gave her little pleasure to have pointed out what was necessary. 'I'm sorry if I've been brutal in what I said, but I only want you to do what's right, for both you and the child.'

Having said her piece, Aggie busied herself,

making the old man a brew. She then wiped down the pot-sink and put away the crockery. 'You'd best go up and see Grandad now,' she suggested. 'Like as not he'll be waiting for this.'

She gave the filled cup with saucer to Emily, together with a fond word or two. 'Look, lass, I don't hate John for what he did, though I wish it hadn't happened. But it did. And it seems to me, whatever dreams you and he had together are over now. He's carved out a life for himself, and to my mind, you need to do the same.'

'I'm not ready yet, Mam.' She sighed from deep down. 'Maybe I never will be.'

'Time will tell.' Aggie's heart dipped. She knew how turning your back on the man you cherished was not an easy thing for any woman. 'You know I love you, don't you, lass?'

Emily nodded. That much she had never doubted.

Aggie gave her a gentle nudge. 'Go on then. Take that up to Grandad.'

~

Upstairs, while Cathleen played at the window with her rag-doll, the old man and Danny were catching up on events. 'He strides round this place as if he owns it!' The old man had fire in his eyes. 'By! If I were a younger, fitter man, I'd have him down yon lane so fast his feet wouldn't touch the ground!'

'Don't get yourself worked up, old-timer.' Danny knew how frustrated the old man was, and how desperately he wanted rid of Clem Jackson – as they all did.

' 'Course I'm worked up!' Keeping his voice low so the child couldn't hear, the old fella hitched himself up in the bed. 'He's a thorn in my side, that's what he is.' Leaning closer, he imparted intimately, '*There's summat bad happening in this house. I don't know what it is, but I can sense it.*'

Startled by the old man's comment, Danny asked worriedly, 'Whatever d'you mean by that?'

Lying back on his pillow the old man sniffed and coughed and for a while he tried hard to think what it might be that played so heavy on his mind. 'I don't know exactly what it is,' he said finally. 'All I know is there's summat secretive goin' on. I can feel it in me bones.' He looked at Danny. 'Did you know he's fetching women of a certain sort back to the farm? I've seen the randy buggers from me window, an' it don't need no brains to guess what *they're* here for.'

Danny had suspected as much. 'What do Aggie and Emily have to say about it?'

'They haven't said owt, and they wouldn't.' He grinned from ear to ear. 'I know more than they think.'

Though he was not one for gossip, Danny was intrigued. 'In what way?'

Implying a secret, the old man tapped his nose.

'Folks often talk to theirselves,' he said. 'Sometimes in their sleep and sometimes when they're
on their own and think nobody's listening. If
there's bad things playing on their minds, they say
'em out loud. I know, 'cause I've 'eard it all with
me own ears.' His bushy eyebrows merged in a
frown. 'Secrets! Things like that!'

Hearing a door close somewhere downstairs, he
dropped his voice to a whisper. 'I know about
things that went on a long time ago. I've never
said, and I never will. But I don't like it. One o'
these days, I intend doing summat about it an'
all!'

Growing anxious, he began struggling to sit up,
angered when he fell back against the pillow.
'Damn it! I'm useless. Bloody useless!'

Danny helped him. 'You're getting too excited,'
he told him. 'Lie still and stop your worrying.' He
didn't know what the old man meant by the things
he'd said but, having been warned that Mr
Ramsden's mind was beginning to wander, he put
it all down to that. 'Emily will be along any
minute,' he said comfortingly. 'Aggie too. She said
to tell you she'd be up to change the bedlinen.'

The old man chuckled. 'Fuss, fuss! Why is it
women allus have to be doing summat?'

'They love you, that's why.' Danny was grateful
that, for the time being, Emily's grandfather
appeared to have forgotten what had got him so
agitated.

'Oh, I know they love me all right.' Thomas Isaac gave him a naughty wink. 'I know summat else too.'

'And what's that?'

'I know you love my Emily.' He had a twinkle in his eye. 'I'm right, aren't I?'

Danny laughed. 'Yes, you're right.'

'And do you love her enough to wed her?'

'If she'd have me, which she won't.'

'Keep on trying,' the old man urged. 'Don't take no for an answer. Wear the lass down! She'll soon get fed up saying no.'

Outside, balancing the cup and saucer while she opened the door, Emily caught the gist of that last conversation.

Not you an' all, Grandad, she tutted to herself. It seemed the world and his friend were trying to match her to Danny. But there was a stirring of guilt in her heart. If both her mam and her grandad thought it best for her and Danny to be wed, happen she ought to seriously consider what they were saying.

When she opened the door the two men fell silent. 'There you are!' Addressing Grandad, she told him, 'Mam's sent a fresh cup of tea for you.'

Hoping she hadn't heard what was said, Danny got out of the chair. 'Sit here,' he suggested. 'I'd best make tracks anyway, or the customers will be stringing me up, along with the horse!'

While Emily served his tea, the old fella gave

Danny a crafty wink. 'Don't forget what I told you,' he said connivingly.

Danny returned his smile. 'I won't.'

Emily didn't let on how she'd overheard the last part of their conversation. 'What's all the secrecy?'

'Nothing for you to worry your head about!' Grandad retorted, and realising she was being told to mind her own business, Emily said no more.

After a hug from Cathleen and a warm smile from Emily, Danny prepared to leave. 'Thank you for sitting with Gramps.' Emily saw him to the top of the landing.

'I always enjoy talking to Tom,' Danny said. 'Though he's a force to be reckoned with, that's for sure. Strong-willed and strong-minded, and a temper to go with it.'

'He's all of that,' Emily answered with a chuckle. 'So – we'll see you tomorrow morning, will we?'

'Try and keep me away,' was his reply.

'You'd best go now,' she suggested. 'We can't have the customers lynching you, can we?'

'Am I to understand it would bother you if they did?' Danny asked hopefully.

Emily didn't answer. Instead she smiled shyly and turned to leave him there. But then she was taken by surprise when he took hold of her and swung her round. 'I love you, Emily Ramsden. No! Don't say anything. I just wanted you to know that. So, now I've told you, I'll be on my way.'

Before she could open her mouth, he was down

the stairs and out the door like a scalded cat, leaving her feeling warm and content inside. It was a peculiar, if unsettling feeling.

CHAPTER ELEVEN

As always, the day was long and the work was hard, and on this particular August evening, the daylight lingered and the skies retained their clear blue lustre. Having drawn the horse and cart to a halt, Danny hurried across to the orchard, where Emily and her child were playing peek-a-boo round the apple trees.

'By! It were that hot in Blackburn town today, you could fry an egg on the pavement, so you could!' he told them.

They came to greet him, Cathleen at full tilt in front, and Emily sauntering on behind. 'It's a wonder your milk didn't go sour,' she said.

'I got rid of it all in good time,' he explained, 'though the churns do keep the milk cold, up to a point anyway.'

The child wasn't interested in whether the milk had gone sour or not. She had bigger problems than that. 'My swing's broke,' she told Danny. 'Mam says she can mend it, but she can't.' She gave Emily a forgiving look. 'It's all right though,' she promised, ''cause Danny will mend it now, won't you, Danny? Please?'

Danny followed the two of them to the biggest, oldest apple tree in the orchard, where Cathleen's broken swing hung down. 'Let's see now.' Lifting the seat he examined the underneath.

'Three times I've threaded the rope through the holes and tied the knot nice and big,' Emily explained, 'and it still keeps slipping through. It's dangerous. I think the timber's rotten.'

'Aye.' Danny slipped the seat off altogether. 'You're absolutely right. This wood is as soft as muck.' He poked his finger through the holes. 'That's why the holes keep breaking open.' He swung the child into his arms. 'It can't be mended. It's not safe,' he told her. 'It needs a new seat.'

'Can you make me one – can you?' The little girl's lips wobbled.

Danny chucked her under the chin. 'Hey! We'll have no tears, if you don't mind. Tears make me sad, and I don't like being sad.'

Cathleen smiled through her big wet eyes. 'Will you make me a new seat, please, Danny?'

He laughed out loud. 'I'll make you the finest seat in the whole of Lancashire. I'll even find a new length of rope in case that's going rotten too. Now then, Cathleen, what d'you say to that?'

'I say yes!' And she planted a grateful smacker on his face.

'While I'm doing that, you might go and ask your grandma if there's a drink going for the workman.'

'Do you want tea?'

He made a face. 'I'd rather have a cool drink.'

'Sarsaparilla?'

He shook his head. 'Not if I can help it.' It was too sweet a taste for his liking.

Cathleen's eyes lit up. 'I know what Grandma's got, and she gives it to Grandad too. He likes it a lot, only she won't let him have too much, because it makes him dizzy and he starts talking rubbish, that's what Grandma says.'

Danny laughed so heartily at her having got it all out in one breath, Emily couldn't help but laugh with him. 'And what drink is that then, eh?' he asked.

'It's called Ederber wine.'

'Is that so?' He tried hard not to smile. 'Well, it sounds good to me, so you be a darling and tell your grandma that Danny would like a taste of her "Ederber wine".'

At that, Cathleen ran off to the farmhouse.

'You're a terrible tease,' Emily told him.

Danny was always happiest when in Emily's company, but he was particularly happy when the two of them were alone, which to his mind, was not often enough.

'I hope I'm right in thinking she meant elder-berry wine?' He feigned innocence. 'Because if it's not, I'm beginning to wonder what I've let myself in for. Y'see, if I get dizzy I won't be able to mend her swing. And if I start talking rubbish, you won't like me any more.'

'If you started talking rubbish, I don't suppose anybody would even notice,' she joked. 'You know very well what she meant, so behave yourself,' she chided. 'As for Grandad, it's just that when he has his weekly measure of elderberry wine, it makes him a bit merry, that's all.'

'Quite right too!' Danny exclaimed. 'And why shouldn't a man be merry from time to time, that's what I'd like to know?'

The two of them sat on the bench. 'Where will you get the rope for the swing?' Emily wanted to know.

Danny had it all worked out. 'I'll borrow it from the horse's haybag,' he declared. 'I've got plenty more at home.'

'There's some rope in the barn.'

'We'll take a look and see if it's strong enough.'

Emily grew wary. 'Let's wait for Cathleen,' she said.

Feigning indignation, Danny turned to regard her. 'Well, o' course we'll wait for the child. What else did you think I was suggesting?'

Embarrassed, Emily was lost for an answer, except to say with a quick smile, 'I'm sorry. I didn't mean to offend!'

With smiling eyes, he enquired cautiously,

'Dare I ask you to show me where the timber is?'

Emily pointed to the smaller of the two barns. 'You'll find some pieces piled up in there, behind the manger.'

He nodded his thanks. 'Oh, and don't go taking great gulps outta my wine when it comes, because I'll know!'

At ease again, Emily grinned. 'You'll find a big coil of rope in there,' she told him. 'It's lying right beside the timber.'

While he was gone, Emily sat, contentedly waiting. It was a quiet time when she could sit and think, and remember. Any time of night or day, John was never far away. He was close to her now, in her heart and mind, and every sense in her body.

I still love you, John Hanley, she thought. Danny is a good man – a kind man. He wants to wed me and raise Cathleen as his own. He has a business, and money enough to help us be rid of Clem Jackson, and yet he asks for little in return. And still I can't bring myself to say yes, because all I can think of is you.

It was odd, that she could still love him as much as ever, while he could go off with nary a qualm. I ought to hate you, but I can't, and I never will.

Trying hard to shut him out of her thoughts, she listened to the familiar sounds of nature all around her. She could hear the birds singing, and not too far away the squirrels chased each other round the fields; the fruit trees were resting after giving up a wonderful harvest, and the skies were so clear you could almost see heaven.

'It's so beautiful here,' she murmured. Through the overhanging branches, the sunlight dappled on her face, and just there on the log-pile she could see a jay, its bright eyes looking straight at her, its many colours made vivid by the sunlight. 'What are you after?' she asked, holding out her hand. 'Hungry, are you?'

Nervous, the bird hopped away and was soon gone from sight.

Suddenly, and for no reason she could think of, Emily began to cry; soft, wet tears trickling down her face and her heart aching with memories of John and the way it used to be. *Why did you leave me?* Caught by the breeze, her words were soon gentled away.

Even now, after all this time, she could not bring herself to believe he had thrown her over for another woman, yet there it had been in black and white, in John's own handwriting. *We had it all, you and me.*

Opening her arms to encompass the landscape, she said aloud: 'We could have spent our lives together right here, in a place we both love. We had the chance of real happiness. What went wrong? Why didn't you come back? Why couldn't you have told me to my face how you'd fallen out of love with me? I might be able to understand, if only you'd had the courage to tell me yourself.'

Just then she saw Cathleen coming from one direction and Danny from the other; one going carefully with a small tray in her hands, the other covering the ground in long, easy strides, a bundle of timber under one arm, and a coil of rope in the other.

Quickly, before they could see, she wiped away the tears, put on a smile and ran to help Cathleen. 'Let Mammy carry that, sweetheart?' She held out her hands to take the tray, but the child was adamant. 'I can do it.' Balancing the tray, she picked her way over the ground. 'It's for Danny. Grandma sent him a piece of cake.' And right there on the tray was a huge slice of Aggie's best sponge-cake, with lashings of cream and jam oozing from each end.

Having reached the bench she set the tray down, at the same time telling Danny, 'Grandma says you're not to go just yet, 'cause she's making us all a picnic.'

'I'd best go and help.' Knowing how her mother would do everything herself, given the chance, Emily went at a run to the farmhouse. Behind her, Danny enjoyed Aggie's delicious cake, while Cathleen explained how she would like the swing to be a bit higher this time. ' 'Cause I'm older now, aren't I, Danny?'

'Old as the hills,' he said, rolling his eyes to make her laugh.

Inside the farmhouse, Aggie was putting the finishing touches to the picnic. 'Oh, Mam!' Emily was amazed at the spread. 'When did you plan all this?' she asked.

'When Danny told me he was hoping to get back this evening.'

'Well, you've done him proud,' Emily said warmly. 'You've done us *all* proud!' There were ham sandwiches, pork-pie chunks and small crispy apple-slices round the edge of the plate, hard-boiled eggs and potato salad, and in a small wicker basket were any number of little fairy cakes, some with chocolate icing, and others with dollops of cream on top.

A large, round apple pie twinkled with sugared pastry, next to a jug of cream for pouring. 'You should have called me!' Emily chided. 'I would have helped.'

'I didn't call you because you were busy enough with other things, and besides, there was only a small amount of baking to do. Most of it was already in the larder from yesterday.'

Collecting the wooden apple-crate from the pantry, Aggie turned to pack the food. 'Let me do that, Mam.' And before her mam could argue, Emily lined the crate with the green picnic-rug and filled it with the good things. 'I know what this is all about,' she said.

'Do you now?' Aggie had her motive, and Emily knew it. 'And what might that be then, eh?'

'You think Danny will ask me to wed him again, and this time, you're hoping I'll say yes – is that it?'

'Something like that.' Bringing the two jugs of cold drink from the larder, Aggie packed them into the crate; the sarsaparilla at one end; lemon-barley water at the other. 'That'll balance the crate as we carry it. Now then, where did I put the nap-kins?' She glanced round the room, relieved when her searching gaze fell on the pile of newly washed squares, folded on the sideboard.

In no time at all, Emily and Aggie were ready to carry the crate out, but first her mother had an errand for Emily. 'Run upstairs and ask Grandad if he'd like to sit out in the sunshine for a bit.' Aggie thought Emily would be able to persuade him where she couldn't. 'I asked him before, but he said no. If you recall, the doctor said he could sit out when the weather was warm, only the old devil's being obstinate. Do what you can,' she pleaded. 'It'll do him a power of good to feel the sun on his face.'

Thinking the very same, Emily started up the stairs. 'And don't you go trying to manage that crate all on your own!' she warned.

Aggie laughed. 'I might be able to do a lot o' things,' she answered, 'but I know my limits. I'll wait for you to come down. Don't you worry.'

She watched Emily go, and raised her eyes to heaven. 'Dear Good Lord, will You try and get her to say yes to Danny?' She could see a future for Emily and the child in Danny's loving care.

Taking Aggie by surprise, Emily was back in no time. 'I knew it!' Aggie stood with hands on hips and a look of consternation on her face. 'He won't budge, will he?'

'At first he was stubborn as a mule, but when I told him Danny was waiting downstairs, he wanted to know why we'd neglected him, and why he hadn't been asked before.'

Aggie smiled. 'He's a canny old bugger, that's what he is.'

Emily laughed at the pair of them. 'A bit like you then – eh, Mam?'

A few moments later, she and Aggie carried the box out to the garden, and laid it on the ground. Danny was horrified. 'You shouldn't be carrying that weight! Why didn't you call me?'

'We've a bigger job for you, son,' Aggie informed him. 'There's a cantankerous old devil upstairs, who's waiting to be helped down. The poor thing's been that badly neglected, we thought we might give him a little treat by way of an apology.'

Danny saw the look on her face and knew her father-in-law had been up to his old tricks. 'That'll be the day, when I see you and Emily neglect him. What! You spoil him rotten, the pair of you.'

Aggie thanked him. 'Happen you'd best tell him that,' she said. 'He seems to think he's hard done by. Or he *pretends* to think it, so he can put us through hoops, that's more like it.'

'He's entitled to,' Emily chuckled. 'I might do the same when I'm his age.'

While Danny and her mother went after Grandad, Emily and Cathleen returned to the house. 'I'll take the plates,' she told the girl. 'You can carry the salt and pepper.' Handing her the two condiments, Emily gave her a cuddle. 'You always want to help, don't you, eh?'

That done, the two of them laid out the picnic rug. 'You wait here, sweetheart.' Emily sat her daughter on the rug. 'I'll go and get the cutlery.' She was looking forward to the picnic, especially now Grandad was coming down.

Upstairs, Danny helped Thomas Isaac out of bed and held him upright while Aggie put on his robe and slippers. 'Stand still!' She almost toppled over, when he began his way towards the door. 'Your slippers are not properly on yet.'

'Hurry up, woman!' he retaliated. 'I'm hungry. It's hours since I were fed.'

'You ate soup and bread only half an hour since.' By now she was puffing and panting. 'Dad! Will you stand still? Or have I to ask Danny to put you back to bed?'

'You're a wicked woman, Aggie Ramsden.'

'Not as wicked as I'll be if you don't keep still for a minute.'

'You're tekking too damned long!'

Sighing and groaning, Aggie straightened her back. 'You're an awkward old sod, that's what you are.'

At which he gave her a smacker on the forehead. 'And you're lovely when you're angry.'

Danny laughed. 'Do I get a kiss too, then?'

'What!' The old man gave him a warning glare. 'You'll get a kick up the arse if you don't get me down them stairs and into that garden sharpish, afore the sun goes down.'

Danny redoubled his efforts. 'Come on, Aggie, me old darling,' he said. 'We'd best get this bundle o' trouble out of here.'

It was no easy task. The stairs were narrow and winding and the old man cursed each and every step. 'Damned things are too steep, they mek me dizzy. An' why can't they mek 'em wider, eh? I'm squashed agin the wall like a chop atween a bap.'

'I hope you're not blaming me?' Danny remarked good-naturedly. 'It wasn't me that built the stairs, so do us a favour; stop your meithering and hold on.' Inching the old man down the stairs was taking longer than he'd anticipated.

Thomas Isaac took not a blind bit of notice. 'Yer not doing very well, are yer?' he complained. 'If we keep going at this rate, we'll be here a month on Sunday.'

Panting from the burden of easing his legs one after the other down the steps, Aggie chided, 'You're not doing much to help yourself, are you?'

'I'm doing me best, woman!'

'You'll do even better if you save your breath for the effort, instead of having a go at me and Danny.'

'Danny's not complaining.'

'That's because he has respect for old folks.'

'I'm not old!'

'No. Just cantankerous.' Winking at Danny she bent her back and carried on regardless.

'If I'm such a nuisance, tek me back to me bed then.'

'I'll do no such thing. We'll get you down these stairs and outside if it kills us.'

Danny had an idea. 'Stand aside,' he told Aggie. 'He's right. We're getting nowhere fast like this.'

In a minute, much to the old man's horror, Danny had him in his arms and was carrying him bodily down the stairs. 'Put me down, you great ox!' The old man objected to being carried like a baby. 'You'll do me a damage!'

Ignoring the shouts and abuse, Danny took him all the way down the stairs, and out to the bench, where he gently sat him down. 'Now, behave yourself,' he said with a grin.

'Or he'll have to carry you all the way back again,' Aggie chipped in. 'Now then, Dad, do you want lemon-barley or sarsaparilla?'

'I'll 'ave a drop o' the good stuff.'

'If you mean elderberry wine, you've had your ration already.'

'Well! It's a picnic, in't it? What good's a picnic
if yer can't 'ave a drop o' the good stuff, that's
what I'd like to know?'

Emily agreed. 'It won't hurt just this once, will
it, Mam?'

Aggie gave a long, noisy sigh. 'Aw, go on then.
But only this once,' she warned her father-in-law.
'And don't think you can try it on again, 'cause
you can't.'

Aside to Danny, she explained, 'If he has too
much, he'll be singing and shouting and thinking
he can dance the night away. Then he'll get dizzy
and fall over. A small measure is good for him,
but I have to be careful, y'see? Like the doctor
says, he's just not well enough to take a full glass.'
She saw how, even now, the old fella looked pale
and drawn, and her voice grew soft with affection.
'He might swear and groan and make me want to
pull my hair out, but deep down he's a darling,
and I love him.'

Danny understood that. 'Well, who couldn't
help but love him, eh?'

While Emily went to fetch the elderberry wine,
Aggie gave out the pork pie and sandwiches. 'Eat
up. There's plenty more where that lot came
from,' she said, tucking into her own helping.

When Emily returned with the wine, the old
man was given a reasonable enough measure.
'That's only a quarter of a glass!' He thrust it back
at Aggie.

'Sip it slowly and it'll last all the longer,' Aggie answered. 'And it's no good you moaning and complaining. Just remember what the doctor said.'

'I don't reckon he knows what he's talking about.' Mimicking the whining voice of his ageing doctor, he went on, '"Don't let him have too much; a small measure once or twice a week, that's quite enough in his condition".'

'Aye, and so it is.' Aggie was taking no nonsense.

'Anyway, I don't know what condition he's talking about,' Thomas Isaac grumbled. 'Me poor old bones are weary, that's all what's wrong wi' me.'

'Don't try it on, Dad.' Aggie wagged a finger. 'You've got all the wine you're getting.'

He gave her a beckoning wink. 'Aw, come on, lass.' He held out his glass yet again. 'Fill it up t'top. It'll help me sleep well tonight.'

'The answer is still no,' she replied firmly. 'You shouldn't even be having *that* much, and besides, the fresh air will help you sleep far better.'

'You're a mean woman.'

'That's right, and I've got my eye on you.'

'I love you all the same.' Reaching out, he patted her on the shoulder. 'Even if you are a bossy bugger.'

'I love you too, Dad. So now eat up and enjoy the evening, eh?'

While all this good-natured bantering was going on, Danny thought how wonderful it was, to be in

the midst of this family and feeling such contentment. Now, as he glanced at Emily, his heart was
brimful of love for her.

As for Emily, she gave him a quiet smile that
said, 'Don't expect too much.' And knowing how
she felt, he merely nodded and looked away.

Just then, Cathleen tugged at his hand. 'Here's
a cake for you, Danny.' She held up the fairy cake
with its melting chocolate on top, and he took it
graciously. Already he felt he belonged. All it
needed now was for Emily to say she was willing
to wed him, and he would be the happiest man
on God's earth.

~

Inside the converted outhouse some distance
away, Clem Jackson was blissfully unaware of the
family gathering. Busy entertaining, he had his
arms full of a woman, and his belly full of ale.
Lying naked on the bed alongside her, he had
been pleased and satisfied and now he was ready
for more.

Turning his head he saw that she was sleeping.
She wasn't bad for somebody who sold her body
to any Tom, Dick and Harry, he thought, his eyes
roving the ample curves. As his gaze fell to where
the mass of dark hair curled in between her thighs,
a thrill ran through him and he became aroused.

In a minute he was on her, the force of his
weight startling her awake. 'For God's sake, we've

been at it all night,' the woman complained. 'Don't tell me you're still not satisfied.'

He laughed – a rough, raw laugh that betrayed the animal in him. 'It'll tek more than you to satisfy the likes o' me.'

Trying her best to throw him off, she pleaded with him, 'I never thought I'd say this to any man, but you've worn me out. I'm bone-tired.'

Struggling to get from underneath him, she found herself trapped by the sheer mass of his body. 'Get off!' Punching at him with her fists, she continued to struggle, until he slapped her hard on the mouth.

'Keep still, damn it! You should be used to men taking what they want, and why should you complain, eh? You get well paid at the end, don't you?'

The hard slap on the mouth sent her into a sulk. Knowing how he was strong and nasty enough to hurt her if he wanted to, she lay there while he satisfied himself. The fact that she didn't respond to his amorous advances was of no concern to him at all. In fact, it excited him all the more.

He was right in what he said, she told herself bitterly. She did sell her body to the highest bidder and in the past he had paid her well. But there was something about him that frightened her, and this time, she had come to loathe him more with every passing minute.

Now as he finished and rolled away, she

snatched the opportunity to scramble out from beneath him. 'I'd best get dressed,' she said, grabbing her clothes. 'Me and my sister are travelling to Manchester tonight.' It was a lie, but all she could think of. 'Dad's not been well, and we need to be there.'

'Liar!' She was halfway dressed with her blouse on and her skirt round her ankles, when he was on her again. 'Wherever you're off to, it can wait,' he grunted. 'I ain't had my money's worth yet.' With that he pushed her against the wall and pinning her arms out wide, he took her again, this time more brutally, and with deliberate cruelty.

Even now, in the middle of pleasuring himself, he couldn't resist adding insult to injury.

Wiping his wet lips over hers, he whispered spitefully, 'You're a bit jaded for my taste, so I won't be after you again, you can be sure o' that.' He took her quick and afterwards threw her aside.

Lying on the floor where he'd thrown her, she cried openly, while he continued to insult and degrade her. 'Get dressed and get gone. I don't want to see you again.'

'I need my money.' She had never been used like he'd used her, and she felt ashamed and angry. 'I'm not leaving without my money.'

'Oh, you'll get your money all right. I won't have it said that Clem Jackson doesn't pay his doxies.' Quickly dressing, he then flung open the door and stepped outside.

'Where are you going?' Frantic, she fell over herself trying to get dressed before he disappeared.

'To check on my animals. They're better company than you are.' He spat on the ground. 'Whore!'

Now he was out of the door, she couldn't get dressed fast enough. 'Wait!' She ran after him. 'WAIT!'

'Look, Grandad.' Seeing the woman running towards the field, one shoe on and the other in her hand, the child was curious. 'There's a lady, and she's only got one shoe on.'

The old man turned his head to see. He had already noticed Clem striding away and suspected the woman wouldn't be far behind. 'Don't worry about it,' he told young Cathleen. 'I dare say she'll be gone soon.'

As with all children her attention soon wavered. Looking to where Danny and Emily were working on the swing, she asked hopefully, 'Do you think Danny's finished my swing yet?'

'Go and see, why don't yer?'

'I can't – Danny told me not to go near until he called.'

Welcoming the idea, he answered with a hug. 'Quite right too, lass. You could likely get caught with one o' them timbers and we wouldn't want that now, would we, eh?'

He glanced across to where Danny was putting

the final touches to the swing. 'I reckon it might be all right now, though,' he observed. 'Why don't yer go and see? I'm sure it would be safe.'

She slid her tiny hand in his and, tugging hard, entreated him to go with her.

'No, lass. You go. I'll just sit here and wait for your grandma to come back.'

'Are you merry?'

He laughed at that. 'Why d'you ask?'

''Cause Grandma said when you drink that Ederber wine, you get too merry and then you fall over.'

'It's true enough,' he admitted. 'I might well fall over if only she'd give me a big enough measure to mek me merry, but there's no fear o' that. So no, I'm not all that merry at the minute.' He winked. 'It's grand to be out in the fresh air though, and I'm very grateful for that.'

'Did Danny carry you all the way down?'

'Almost.'

'Did it hurt?'

'Only my dignity.'

'He's nice, isn't he?'

'Yer right, lass, he is.'

'I'd like him for a daddy.'

'Would you now?'

'Will you ask him, Grandad? Will you ask him if he'll be my daddy?'

'No, lass. It's not for me or you to interfere, sweetheart. It's for your mammy and Danny to decide.' Thomas gave her a knowing wink. 'I've a feeling they'll work it out, lass.'

Leaping up, she threw her arms round his neck. 'I love you, Grandad.'

Tears filled his old eyes. 'Oh, an' I love you, child. You're a joy to be with.' With great difficulty he lifted her down. 'Go on then. See if your swing's ready.'

'If it is, you can have a go on it, Grandad. It won't break. Danny says it'll be strong enough to take an elephant.'

'Are you saying I'm heavy as an elephant?'

'No, but you can have a swing if you like.'

The old man chuckled aloud. 'I'd best not, but thank you all the same. Now go on. Be off with yer.'

Just then Danny called her name. 'Cathleen! Your swing's ready if you want it.'

Thomas Isaac smiled as she chased over to try out her new swing. 'By! You're a lovely, bonny lass.' Like everyone else, he had come to cherish the child. 'I can't even begin to remember what life was like afore you came.'

Wearied by the sun and his long conversation with Cathleen, he closed his eyes and let his mind drift.

When a moment later Aggie arrived from the kitchen with a brew of tea for him, he was dropping off to sleep. 'Dad, here's your tea.' Her kindly voice gentled into his dreams.

'Thank you, lass.' Wide awake now, he sat up and took his tea.

'Nodding off, were you?' She sat beside him and leaned back, sighing. 'I feel a bit like that myself.'

'Aye well, it's been a busy day for you and Emily, putting on the picnic besides all your other chores. You did us proud, lass. Everybody seemed to enjoy theirselves.'

Aggie thanked him. 'It were worth it, just to see Emily and Danny in each other's company. I'm hoping things might happen there, aren't you?'

'Aye, and so is young Cathleen from what she said.'

'What did she say?' Aggie sat upright.

'She said as how she wanted him for a daddy, and would I ask him, please.'

'Aw, bless her heart. She thinks the world of him. Danny and Emily getting wed would be by far the best thing for that little mite.'

'I agree, but what about John Hanley? Emily still cares deeply for him, as you well know.'

Aggie did know, only too well. 'It's been too long,' she replied thoughtfully. 'If he were coming back, he'd have done so afore now.' She turned to look at him. 'Don't you think so, Dad?'

He nodded. 'You're right, it has been too long. I reckon our Emily would do well to forget him. There's the child to consider now.' He smiled. 'By! She's a knowing little thing. Never misses a trick.'

He pointed to the field-gate. 'Just now she saw one o' Clem's ladyfriends running across the field. She had one shoe on an' one shoe off. I didn't see her at all, until Cathleen told me.'

Aggie's expression darkened. 'I wish to God he'd go away and leave us alone. He's a bad influence. Cathleen's of an age now where she watches everything. It worries me, Dad. I want shut of him.' Her voice dipped. 'I hate him. I've allus hated him!'

Sensing her darkening mood, he said pacifyingly, 'He'll be gone soon enough, I expect. A man like that doesn't put down roots and he knows he's not wanted here. Nobody wants to stay for ever, where they're not wanted.'

Aggie didn't believe that, although it would be wonderful if one morning she woke up and he was gone. 'He won't leave without his blood-money, and we'll never have enough to pay him off, so I shouldn't count on him going if I were you.'

For a moment they lapsed into silence, quietly watching the girl as she swung high underneath the apple tree. After a while their moods lightened. 'She's a bonny lass, don't you think, Dad?'

Grandad was already smiling at her antics. 'Bonny and loving. And I'll tell you another thing, lass. John Hanley caused an upset when he went away like that, but we can be grateful for what he left behind. God only knows we've had our troubles, and still have.'

His voice broke with emotion. 'That little lass is like sunshine after rain. She's the best thing that's happened to this family in many a day.'

Aggie saw how emotional he was, and placing her hand over his, she told him softly, 'You're thinking of your own son, aren't you?'

The old fella wiped away a tear. 'Aye, lass. More to my shame. After what Michael did, I should wipe him outta my mind for ever.'

'He'll be back,' she promised. 'He'll be back, and we'll all be glad to see him.'

'Not me! You'll never see the day when I forgive him for what he did. He left you when you had nobody else to carry the burden. He's a coward through and through, and I want no truck with him. Not ever!'

The sound of Cathleen's laughter caused them to turn and look. 'She's happy enough,' he said. 'None of the troubles have touched her, thank God.'

'No, and if I have my way they never will.'

'Then you must pray that Emily puts aside her fondness for John, and takes Danny as a husband. That way they'll both be safer.'

~

Some small distance away, Clem and his woman were also alerted by Cathleen's laughter. In the middle of an argument about the money, he paused to look across to where Cathleen was sending herself higher and higher on the new swing. 'She's a pretty little thing, don't yer think?' he said proudly.

Lately he had enjoyed taking more notice of his bastard child. He took notice of her now; of the way her baby legs were now longer and finer, and how her skirt rose provocatively above her knees every time she swung downwards. He saw the sweet, laughing face and the long hair, and was moved to say out loud, 'She's a damned good-looking kid.'

The woman thought the same, and said so. 'One of these days there'll be men crawling all over this place, wanting to be with her, and showering her with presents.'

Watching Cathleen now, he was riddled with jealousy. 'Over my dead body!'

'It's not up to you,' she jibed. 'It's up to her father.'

'Shut your mouth, bitch.' He raised his fist. 'Or d'yer want me to shut it for yer?'

Curious at his reaction, and realising she had touched a nerve, she laughed. 'Got you on the raw, have I?' she taunted. 'Sorry you never had a child yourself, is that it?'

Enraged, he took her by the shoulders, his eyes boring into hers. 'If you know what's good for you, you'll get on your way right now – afore I help you along with the toe of me boot.'

'I'll gladly be on my way!' She held out her hand. 'Just give me my money.'

Throwing her aside, he paused, his eyes drawn to the necklace round her throat. 'Looks to me like you don't need any money.'

'What do you mean?' His mood unnerved her. 'I've earned every penny of what you owe me, and I want it. *Now,* if you please!'

'If you're so desperate for money, why don't you sell that!' His wicked gaze focused on the necklace; a sparkling thing with a single hanging jewel. 'Looks to me like it's worth a bob or two.'

Beginning to think he was entirely mad, she put her hand over her necklace. 'It was a gift. I'm not selling it. I want the money you owe me. Just hand it over and let me go.'

Eager to be gone, she was half-tempted to leave without her money, but her pride kept her there a moment too long, because suddenly he snatched at the necklace and ripped it from her neck.

'If you value this trinket so much, you'll have to go fishing for it.' And to her horror, he threw it as far into the field as he could, laughing when it landed face-up in a boggy dip. 'You'll need to get your feet wet, though.'

'You bastard!' Pummelling him with her fists she was taken by surprise when he merely smiled and walked off.

For a moment she stood there, her attention divided between him and the necklace. 'GET IT

BACK, YOU BASTARD!' When he took no notice but kept right on walking, she made to go through the gate, but finding it locked had to scramble over, unaware that he had stopped only a few feet away, hidden behind the trees, out of sight yet able to see everything.

The bulls were lazing not too far away. Now, sensing that their territory was being invaded, the larger of the two rolled over and up, to emerge agitated, from the thicket. The other looked on, but made no immediate move.

The woman was only a short distance from the gate when she saw the beast regarding her with its bright, angry eyes. 'Oh, dear God!' The bull held her gaze for that split second before she turned to run, and then it was after her, its long strides covering the ground with amazing speed.

She had managed to make it to the gate when its thick short horns jabbed at her body, mangling her dress and slicing her leg from knee to ankle. Terrified and bleeding badly, she forced herself upwards, loudly yelling for help, and fearing for her life as the bull prepared to come at her again.

As she clung on, her senses beginning to slip away, she saw Clem looking across. 'Help me!' Sobbing, more afraid than she had ever been in her life, she implored him: 'Please help me!'

With a hostile stare, he coldly abandoned her. Only feet away now, the maddened creature pawed at the ground for a second or two before charging towards her, intent on finishing her off. Weakening by the minute, she summoned every ounce of strength, trying to pull herself over the top of the gate. It was too late. She felt the butt of the bull's head against her leg, the sharp sear of pain, and a feeling that it was all over for her.

'Hang on to me!'

Hearing her cries, Danny reached down and snatched her away. 'It's all right,' he told her. 'You're safe now, miss.'

~

In the farmhouse, Aggie set Cathleen a task in the bedroom. 'You fold the towels and put them in a neat pile,' she instructed, 'while I find the lady a suitable dress to wear. It won't be as fine as her own, but it'll get her home with dignity.'

'What's dignity?'

Aggie thought on that for a moment. 'It's when you feel right, and you know others feel the same about you.' That was as far as she could explain it.

'Who hurt the lady?' All Cathleen knew was that when they heard the cries, Danny had run to help. 'Was it the bull? Did she go in the field?'

'Yes, she did!' Aggie wagged a finger. 'It was a foolish thing to do, and now you know why I'm allus telling you never to go anywhere near that place.'

'I don't, Grandma.' The child's eyes grew big with fright. 'I don't want the bulls to get me.'

'That's right, lass. So you think on. Stay well away from there.'

~

Downstairs, Emily washed and cleaned the wound. 'It could have been worse,' she observed. 'If you hadn't been so near to the gate, that bull would likely have finished you off in minutes.' Going carefully, she dabbed at the wound and staunched the bleeding. 'Whatever possessed you to go into that field?'

'It was *him*.' Grateful for all they had done for her, the woman, whose name was Ruby, couldn't help but wonder why decent folks like these allowed a man like Clem Jackson to live anywhere near. 'He deliberately threw my necklace into the field, then watched while I tried to get it back.' It was hard to believe, even of him, but, 'He hid behind the trees and watched while that beast tried to kill me.' She started to cry.

Emily and Danny exchanged glances. It was a hard way for this woman to find out what Clem was really like, Emily thought. God forgive her, but she herself still harboured murder in her heart for what he had done to her.

On hearing what had happened, Danny went out looking for Clem. He searched the outhouse and the barn, and walked the whole way round the perimeter of the farmyard. But there was no sign of him.

Passing the field for the second time, he saw the necklace glittering in the mud; not too far away, the bull was keeping watch. 'Hmh! I'm certainly not going in there to rattle him again,' Danny said aloud. He knew if he did, he would be taking his life in his hands.

He thought it out, noticing two things in the meantime. Firstly there was a tree whose branches overhung a small area close to the bog. And secondly, the overhanging branches appeared stout enough to hold his weight.

Convinced he had found the answer, he made his way over there, collected a fallen, sturdy branch, climbed the tree and going as far out as he dared to the edge of the thicker branch, he reached down and hooked up the necklace. He managed to get it halfway up to him, when it slipped off again.

Cursing, he hooked it again and this time he had it in his grasp. 'Gotcha!' Climbing down from the tree, he saw Aggie coming towards him. 'I've managed to get the necklace,' he told her. 'It needs a bit of a wipe, mind.' Handing it to her, he said, 'I've been round here God knows how many times and I can't catch sight of him. I'll have another look. I shan't let him get away with this.'

'No. Leave it, Danny! I don't want you messing with him.'

Though he respected her wishes, Danny found it hard to understand. 'The man wants telling,' he replied, his eyes burning with anger. 'What he did was shocking! That poor woman might have been killed.'

'All the same, I'd rather you didn't go after him.'

By nature Aggie was a private person. Although Emily had probably told him all about it, she could not bring herself to explain the way it was with Clem – the huge amount of money they owed him; the terrible hold he had on all of them; the fear of eviction they lived under day after day.

Then there was the other thing. The thing that gave her nightmares. The thing she could never talk about to anyone.

All she could say was, 'I know how you feel, Danny, but it's best to leave him be. I want no trouble. None of us do.'

He was surprised at her stand, but the last thing he wanted to do was to go against her. 'If that's what you really want,' he said. 'Only remember I'm here for you if you need me.'

'I know, and I thank you for that.' Danny had long been like a son to her.

He gave a reluctant nod. 'How's the woman?'

'Yon Ruby will have a pretty scar for some long time, but she'll be all right, thanks to you.'

They walked back to the farmhouse together, talking more easily now – about Emily mostly. 'She's a grand lass.' Aggie never lost an opportunity to sing Emily's praises to him. 'I'm hoping to see the day you and her get wed.'

'You know how I feel about that, Mrs Ramsden.'

'Aggie!' she corrected. 'Haven't I allus told you to call me Aggie?' Lightening the mood, she told him, 'I think I might just manage to find a new hat for the occasion. The last time I treated meself was for me own wedding – and Queen Victoria still ruled over us all then, God bless her. I should think the moth's got to it by now and it'll be riddled with holes. Would be handy to stick me feathers an' hatpins in, though, wouldn't it?'

They were still laughing when they arrived back at the house.

Emily was putting the finishing touches to Ruby's bandage. 'I'm about finished,' she said as the others came into the room. 'I've done as much as I can.'

Grey-faced and still shaken by her experience, the unfortunate woman was sipping tea, while Cathleen dutifully stood by with the dress which Aggie told her to look after.

'You're welcome to use my bedroom to get changed,' Emily told her, and that was what Ruby did, emerging some short time later looking far more splendid than Aggie ever did in the blue flowered dress. 'By! It's been years since I wore that dress,' Aggie sighed. 'I were younger and slimmer then, but even at that I never looked like you do now. You're a pretty thing, Ruby, an' no mistake. So what in God's name are you doing messing with a scoundrel like my brother?'

'I didn't know he was such a scoundrel,' the woman replied in self-defence. 'If I had, I'd never have gone with him.'

Aggie had been showing the necklace to Emily and now, as Emily fastened it round the woman's neck, she said, 'It's a beautiful thing. I don't blame you for trying to get it back.'

'Take it,' the older woman said. 'You've been so kind, it's the least I can do.'

Emily graciously refused. 'What!' she smiled. 'After you've very nearly been killed trying to rescue it? No. It's kind of you, but I couldn't accept. I'm just relieved you came to no real harm.' She had told no one that, ever since losing her small gold locket containing a lock of John's hair, she would never wear a necklace again.

She was startled when Ruby threw her arms round her neck. 'I won't forget your kindness,' she said, and there were tears in her eyes. 'I'd best go now.' She hadn't got her money, but she still had her life – and that was thanks to all of these lovely people.

They walked with her towards the horse and cart, for Danny had insisted on taking her back to Blackburn town himself. 'You're very lucky,' Ruby told Emily, her gaze shifting to Danny. 'I can see how much he loves you. Few women ever know such devotion.'

With that they set off, with Ruby waving to them all the way.

'She's a fortunate woman,' Aggie said soberly. 'Another minute and that bull would have had her off that fence and trampled under his feet.' She had a hankering to go after that bastard Clem with a shotgun, and make him pay for what he had done.

～

Later, when Danny had returned, and he and Cathleen were trying out the swing again, Emily sat on the grass nearby and watched. The woman's words echoed in her mind, and she thought: You are right, Ruby. I *am* lucky to have the love of a good man.

Dropping her gaze to the wild flowers at her feet, she plucked one and lightly brushed it against her lips. The sensation was wonderful, reminding her as it did of the day John had picked a flower and traced the contours of her mouth with it, before kissing her for the very first time.

Closing her eyes, she asked silently, 'What shall I do, John? I can never stop loving you, but now I have Cathleen to consider. Should I do what Mam and Grandad want? Should I wed Danny for my daughter's sake, and make his life a contented one in return? Or should I wait a while longer, in case you decide to come home?'

It was the most difficult decision, and as always she was torn two ways.

Just then, when Cathleen came to throw her arms round her neck, it almost broke her heart. 'I love you, Mammy,' the little girl said.

Emily held her so tight. 'I love you too, sweetheart,' she murmured. But did she love her enough to make that one great sacrifice?

From where he stood, Danny saw the love between those two, and he was deeply moved. 'Aw, Emily, the child needs me, you know she does,' he murmured lovingly. 'Let that make up your mind, my darling. I swear, neither of you will ever want for anything while I'm alive on this earth. If only you could find it in your heart to put your trust in me.'

CHAPTER TWELVE

Two weeks before Christmas 1908, Emily and Danny were married in St Michael's Church in Salmesbury, and in spite of Emily's misgivings, it turned out to be a wonderful, joy-filled occasion, and one which – especially in the events that were to follow – no one would ever forget.

~

On her wedding day, Emily was out of her bed on the stroke of six. By half-past, she was washed, dressed in her everyday clothes and out of the house. Tired after another fitful night, she wandered the winter fields, talking to John in her mind, telling him all her thoughts. 'I'm getting married today,' she whispered into the chill, dark morning. 'Like you, I've settled for someone else. Danny is a good man and I'm lucky to have him.'

But though she was fond of Danny, and would not hurt him for the world, her heart wasn't in it. Oh, she put on a show and smiled and laughed and let them think she was content enough, but she wasn't, and never would be.

Now, having wandered until she was weary, she returned to the farm and sat for a while in the orchard. Huddled in her big, warm cloak, she closed her eyes and allowed her thoughts to drift back to the dear past, to those happier days with John. Even though their plans had fallen apart, just thinking of how it could have been was a bittersweet pleasure . . .

~

Unaware that her daughter was even out of her bed, Aggie entered Grandad's room. 'Wake up, sleepy head!' Placing his cup of tea on the bedside cabinet, she went over and riddled the small fire that had been barely smouldering through the night, and added a couple of lumps of coal. The flames sizzled and licked at the dust. She put back the big brass guard and laid her father-in-law's clean long-johns and long-sleeved singlet to warm on the top.

'What's up with yer, woman?' Regarding the clock through one half-open eye, the old fella groaned. 'Bloody hell! What d'yer want, waking me at seven o'clock of a mornin'? Can't a man get no sleep round 'ere?'

'It's a special day today,' Aggie told him. 'Drink your tea and stop moaning.'

Thomas Isaac dragged himself up in the bed.

'Special day?' He followed her with bloodshot eyes as she went to fully open the curtains. 'What's all that about, then?'

Aggie swung round. 'Don't tell me you've forgotten?'

Taking a deep breath he asked on the crest of a sigh, 'Forgotten what? Aw, Aggie, have a heart. Bugger off and let me drink me tea in peace.'

Aggie swished the curtains back on their pole and let the watery sunshine filter in. 'I'm surprised you could forget,' she chided. 'It's your granddaughter's wedding day!'

'Oh, my good God!' He laughed out loud. 'So it is! Why didn't yer wake me? There's things to do! I've to get washed and shaved, and 'ave yer wrapped me present? Good Lord, woman, what the devil are yer playing at, leaving me in bed till this time?' He got so excited he gulped down his tea and nearly choked. 'Now see what you've done! Yer trying to kill me off, that's what yer up to, yer bugger!'

'I'll kill yer off with me bare hands if you don't stop your antics!' Though she couldn't help but laugh.

Frantically wiping at his nightshirt, he then spilled the rest of his tea all over the bedclothes. 'Aw, just look at that!' Shaking a fist at her he yelled out with surprising gusto, 'Yer mekking me nervous, woman! Just look what yer made me do now.'

When she didn't answer he glanced up, to see her still standing at the window, a troubled look on her face. 'Aggie – what's to do, lass?'

But Aggie wasn't listening. Instead she was gazing down into the orchard, where Emily sat alone and forlorn on the bench by the apple tree.

'What are yer looking at?' the old man asked curiously.

Aggie half turned. 'Come and see for yourself.'

So, with a groan and a sigh at every step, Thomas Isaac made his slow, painful way over to the window. 'By, it's brass monkeys!' he grumbled. Poking his head over her shoulder he stared out. 'Why! It's our Emily. What's she doing out there at this time of a morning, on her wedding day an' all?'

Aggie smiled, but it was a sad little smile. 'She's thinking, Dad, that's what she's doing.'

'What's she thinking about?'

'Oh, just thinking. It's what women do just afore they get wed,' Aggie explained. 'There's allus them few, lingering doubts. You can't help but wonder if you're doing the right thing.'

Like all men, he didn't fully understand. 'I've never heard owt so bloody daft in all me life. If you've made up yer mind to get wed, what's to wonder, tell me that, eh?'

So Aggie told him. 'You wonder if it'll all turn out the way you want it to, and most of all, you ask yourself if you love the man enough to wed him in the first place.' Her voice faltered. 'That's what she's doing, bless her heart.'

The old man began to understand and for a moment he fell silent. Then, because Aggie was the only one he could talk to about it, he asked quietly, 'D'yer really think the lass is regretting what she's about to do?'

'Mebbe,' Aggie replied. 'Mebbe not.'

'D'yer reckon she's learned to love him?'

'Who knows?'

'Or d'yer think she's only marrying Danny for the sake o' the child?'

'I don't suppose we'll ever really know the answer to any of that,' Aggie sighed.

Thomas paused, wondering how he could help Emily, yet knowing there was nothing he could do to persuade her one way or the other. It was all beyond him, and that was the truth of it. He'd loved his Clare every day of their married life, and still missed her so much. 'Aye well. Today's the day, so she'd best get it right, or spend the rest of her life suffering the consequences.' Like his daughter-in-law Aggie, he was torn two ways.

When he gave a long, telling shiver, Aggie was alarmed. 'You'd best get back into bed, Dad.'

'I can't. The bed's all wet.'

'Oh, Dad! You didn't –'

He gave her a withering look. 'No, I bloody didn't. I'll remind you that I have never once wet the bed, and I'll thank you to apologise for what you said.'

'I'm sorry.'

'I should think so an' all.' Taking hold of her arm he instructed, 'You've worn me out, fetching me to this winder. Help me to the chair, and get me a blanket. Oh, and I'd like another cuppa tea. The last one got spilled all o'er the bed, thanks to you!'

Aggie was visibly taken aback. 'For somebody who's worn out, you're very forceful with your orders, aren't you?'

'It's up to you,' he said weakly. 'Either yer do as I ask, or you'll 'ave me down with pneumonia, then what will yer do?' For good effect he gave another dramatic shiver.

Aggie lost no time in getting him to the chair next to the fire. When he seemed more comfortable, she rushed to take a blanket from the cupboard and tuck it round him. 'There – is that better?'

'Where's me tea?'

'I'm not your slave, you know.' She thought he'd made a remarkable recovery. 'I've only got one pair of hands, and I'd be thankful if you'd kindly stop your blessed grumbling and groaning.'

As she went at the trot out the door, he called after her. 'Aggie!'

'What now?'

He gave her one of his cheekiest winks. 'You

like me having a go at yer, don't yer, eh? Life wouldn't be the same if we didn't 'ave a bit of a banter now and then, would it?'

First giving him a warm smile, she hurried down the stairs. 'You're right, Dad,' she chuckled heartily, putting the kettle on to make him a fresh brew. 'Life just wouldn't be the same.'

Glancing out of the kitchen window, she saw how Emily was still there, huddled against the sharp winter morning, her old shawl drawn tight about her head, which was bent, deep in thought. Aw, lass, her mother thought tenderly. What are we going to do with you, eh? But there was nothing at all she or anyone else could do. Except John, and he was not here.

On an impulse, she put on her coat and boots and prepared to go out to Emily. Then she took them off again. She'd best leave the lass be. Emily would have to work it out herself.

Aggie would have turned the world upside down to help her daughter but she knew that, when it came down to it, Emily was the only one who could decide what was best for her and Cathleen. And Danny as well, come to that.

A short time later she carried the old man's tea up, changed the bed, and decided to let him finish his tea in peace. 'I'll be back in a while,' she promised. 'Keep that blanket round you though, Dad. It's too cold to be wandering about in your undies.' She glanced out the window. 'I reckon it'll snow afore the day's out,' she observed. 'The skies are full of it.'

From where he sat, he too was able to see out the window. 'It'll not snow today,' he remarked in a matter-of-fact voice.

Aggie smiled. 'Oh, and who are you all of a sudden, then? The man in charge of the weather?'

'I'm an old farmer,' he replied confidently. 'And we know a thing or two about the weather.'

She wagged a finger at him. 'Aye, an' so do old farmers' wives,' she retorted. 'An' I say it will snow heaven's hardest. We ought to be good and ready for it, that's what I say.'

'Yer wrong, woman!' He looked her in the eye. 'It will *not* snow today, I'm telling yer.' He took a casual sip of his tea, and nearly leaped out of his chair. 'Bloody hell! This tea's scalding hot.'

'Oh, I'm sorry, Dad,' she answered meekly. 'Did you want it cold?'

'Don't talk daft! What use is a cold cuppa tea?'

He took another sip, this time relishing it, but as always he had to have the last word. 'One way or another I reckon yer mean to finish me off.'

Aggie went out of the room, laughing to herself. 'I'll not be long afore I'm back!' she called behind her, laughing louder when he retorted, 'If yer gonna mek fun o' me, you can bloody well stay away! An' yer can stop talking about summat you know nowt about, too, 'cause it *won't* snow today! You think on that.'

~

The old man couldn't have been more wrong, because it *did* snow. It began a couple of hours later and continued well into the afternoon.

On the stroke of one, Emily came down the stairs, wearing her wedding outfit and looking pale but very lovely.

'Aw, lass. You do us proud.' Aggie was close to tears as she looked on her daughter.

'Do I look all right then, Mam?' Like all brides, in the short time before she took her vows, Emily was trembling inside. 'You don't think folks will tut and talk about me, do you?'

Aggie was shocked. 'Whatever d'you mean?'

'Because of Cathleen. I've had a child out of wedlock, Mam. That in itself is bad enough, but dressing up to be wed and the child as bridesmaid . . . well, it's wrong, don't you think?'

'Having a child out of wedlock *is* a terrible thing – and nobody's going to deny that, lass,' Aggie said truthfully. 'But the child came out of love between you and John Hanley. Everybody knows that. They also know it wasn't your fault that he left you stranded.'

Emily listened to what her mother had to say and shame engulfed her. It was all a lie – a shocking lie that she had allowed everyone to believe.

But the truth was even more shocking – that her own uncle had taken her by force, and Cathleen was the result.

'Put it all out of your mind, love,' Aggie urged. 'This is your wedding day. You and Danny will be man and wife and afterwards, you'll be respectable in everyone's eyes. You'll have somebody to take care of you, and Cathleen will have a daddy. When you say the words and sign your name as Danny's wife, it's a new life, a new start. So you must put all the bad stuff behind you, sweetheart. It'll be all right, you'll see.'

'Thank you, Mam.' Emily threw her arms round that dear, familiar figure, holding so tight and for so long that Aggie herself had to break the hold.

'We'll be there for you,' she told Emily softly. 'Me an' Grandad, and Cathleen. When you get nervous and need some reassurance, just turn around and we'll all be there.'

Pushing her away, she said grandly, 'Now then, let's have a look at you.' She observed the smart cream-coloured suit with its fitted jacket, leg of mutton sleeves and flowing ankle-length skirt, and the pale blue hat with its smart cream feather and tiny veil above Emily's mop of shining brown hair, and she was moved to tears. 'By! You'll have their eyes popping out, that you will!' Taking out her hankie she shook it open and blew her nose loud and hard.

When Cathleen came running into the room,

dressed prettily in a suit to match her own and both made by Aggie herself, Emily took her into her arms and gave her a mother's kiss. 'Are we ready then, sweetheart?' However doubtful she felt, she must stay strong for the child's sake.

Suddenly the carriage had arrived and there followed a few minutes of pandemonium. 'Where's your grandad?' Aggie asked the child. 'Was he ready when you came down just now?'

' 'Course I'm ready, woman!' His voice sailed down from the upper regions. 'All I need is a helping hand to get me down these blessed stairs!'

A moment or two later, Emily and Aggie had the carriage-driver in to help the old fella down the stairs and out the door. 'We'll have you settled and tucked into your seat in no time at all,' the carriage-driver pronounced assuredly.

'Don't walk so damned fast, you silly arse!' To his horror, Grandad found himself being pro-pelled down the path at an extraordinary pace. 'We're not in no bloody race, as far as I'm aware.'

Inside the farmhouse the chaos continued. 'Where did I put my hat?' Aggie panicked. She wore a plain burgundy two-piece costume with a lemon-coloured blouse and a twiggy flower in her buttonhole that Grandad called 'half a bloody tree!'. But she looked wonderful, and felt it. 'Oh, look. There it is!' Grabbing the hat from the dresser she plonked it on her head at a peculiar angle.

'That's not right, Mam,' Emily told her. 'It makes you look as if you've had one too many.' She straightened the hat and looking in the mirror, Aggie was pleased to see how smart it was. 'Money well spent,' she said. 'And the Lord knows we have to count every penny.'

Gathering her daughter and granddaughter, she ushered them across the room. 'We'd best get a move on,' she said, 'or Grandad will be giving that poor man nightmares out there.'

'We forgot the flowers!' Almost at the door, Emily ran back to retrieve the flowers; a posy for Cathleen, and her own pretty, discreet bouquet. Being December there was a small choice of flowers, but thankfully the florist had managed to inject a measure of colour and greenery, all tied up with a pretty pink bow.

In a moment, to Grandad's relief, they were climbing into the carriage.

'There y'are, Dad – I told you it would snow.' Aggie couldn't resist saying I told you so.

'It won't last,' he answered sulkily. 'It's nobbut a little shower.'

' 'Fraid not, sir.' The carriage-driver folded the step-stool behind Cathleen, and prepared to close the door. 'I reckon it's in for the day, if not longer.'

'Who the devil asked for *your* opinion?' The old man gave him one of his probing glares. 'Just get on and do the work you're being paid for and mind your own damned business.'

As the disgruntled man slammed shut the door, Grandad added under his breath, 'It's a bloody shower, an' I should know!'

~

As it happened, the snow tumbled relentlessly from the heavens for some considerable time. St Michael's Church looked beautiful, although the path through the wych-gate and up to the big old oak door was treacherous.

Looking smart and dapper in his dark suit and tie, Danny welcomed his bride at the altar of the dear old church where they would be made man and wife. The snow continued to fall all through the service which, according to the locals who attended was, 'Not bad, considering the circumstances, an' wi' the bairn bein' there an' all.' And it carried on snowing all the way back to the farmhouse, where Aggie and Emily had earlier prepared a celebratory meal.

While the smell of roasting chicken filled the farmhouse and everyone enjoyed a glass of best sherry, Emily and Danny opened their wedding presents. There was a lovely timepiece from Grandad and Aggie, a pretty vase from Danny's father, Bob, and from Cathleen an embroidered sampler with their names and the date stitched carefully in pastel colours. Aggie had found the right-sized frame in a Blackburn junk shop, and the little girl and her gran had cleaned the glass and frame with vinegar and beeswax until they both shone. She also gave them each a hug and a kiss, while she in turn received a small, silk-figured Bible from her mammy and her new daddy.

Danny gave his wife a beautiful bracelet of marcasite and sapphire, and she loved it so much she asked him to put it on her wrist there and then. Afterwards, to his delight, she kissed him, hoping with all her heart she could learn to be the wife he wanted.

Cathleen showed everyone the small Bible she had been given as bridesmaid, and Grandad told them all how proud he was of his beautiful young women. He then gave a formal little speech, in which he thanked Danny and his father for contributing to the festivities. 'And we're delighted to receive you into the family fold,' he said affectionately. For a split second he thought of Michael, whose sacred duty it would have been to give away his daughter's hand in marriage, but then he brushed the thought aside.

Everyone clapped and it was time to eat.

They sat round the table – Danny's kind-natured father, Bob, a lean-looking man with soft eyes and a ginger moustache; then came Cathleen, pink-cheeked and over-excited, and Aggie bursting with pride.

Danny was so content he couldn't stop smiling, his fond gaze never leaving Emily's face and his hand constantly seeking hers under the table.

Then came Emily herself, feeling vulnerable and afraid, and not too certain what to expect from this new life she had embarked on. She tried hard to concentrate on Danny, but somehow John kept filling her mind and heart, and it was all she could do to smile at Danny with the look of a wife. But smile she did – as her mother noticed with approval.

As for Grandad, he greedily tucked into the delicious chicken, served with their own farm-grown vegetables, and loudly complained about the fact that there had been very few local people present at the ceremony.

'You'd have thought more of 'em might 'ave turned out to see one of their own get wed,' he said, in between scraping the last of the food off his plate and into his mouth. 'Miserable buggers, so they are.' He gave Aggie a knowing look. 'O' course, I don't suppose yer can blame 'em,' he remarked, sipping at his ale and getting more inebriated by the minute. He glanced at Cathleen. 'Folks don't forget in a hurry, do they?'

'That's enough, Dad!' Aggie cast a glance at Cathleen, who thankfully was so engrossed in counting the raspberries in her pie, she appeared not to have heard. 'Aren't you forgetting summat?' She drew his attention to the child. 'I reckon you should mind your tongue, don't you?'

'Oh, I'm sorry, lass!' Realising he was out of his depth, the old man leaned over and gave

Cathleen's hand a fond squeeze. 'Yer old Grandad talks rubbish sometimes.'

When, without looking up, Cathleen replied innocently, 'I know, Grandad, but it's all right,' everyone laughed and the atmosphere was good.

'If your mammy will fetch my accordion we can have us-selves a bit o' music,' Grandad suggested.

Without hesitation, and thankful that Cathleen was unaware of what had been said, Emily ran upstairs and found his cherished accordion.

'By! I've not played this for a while,' the old man said, making it screech and howl before he finally got to grips with it. 'Come on, then. If you've all finished feeding yer faces, let's see youse dancing till yer drop!'

On Aggie's insistence, Danny and Emily pushed the table back to make room while, also made merry by the plentiful ale, Danny's father Bob clambered to his feet and began shaking about in a frighteningly weird manner. 'My dancing's not what it used to be,' he apologised, and hoping they wouldn't have to endure it for long, everyone assured him he was doing just grand and encouraged him, by clapping to the rhythm.

After a while, Aggie got up to join him; more to stop him from falling over than anything else.

It wasn't long before the two of them had to sit down. 'I'm bone-weary,' Bob groaned, red in the face and fighting for breath.

Laughing, Aggie told him, 'We're a pair of old

crocks, you an' me.' Moreover, her feet felt like two raw pieces of meat where he had trampled them once too often.

When a moment later Grandad slowed the music to a waltz, Danny took Emily by the hand and led her to the centre of the floor. 'You look beautiful, Mrs Williams,' he whispered in her ear, and not for the first time made her feel humbled.

They danced to the music and he held her tight and she smiled up at him. To the onlookers it was a lovely thing to see.

Only Aggie knew the truth of how Emily must be feeling. Yet, like Emily, she had faith that everything would turn out for the best, and she clung to that with all her might.

When Cathleen decided to join them, the bridal couple enfolded her to them and the picture was complete. 'They look a proper family,' Danny's father declared. And Aggie wholeheartedly agreed.

~

Outside, made curious by the music, Clem Jackson peered in through the window. He saw Emily in the arms of her new man, and the child – *his* child – glad to be a part of that close family unit, and the more he saw, the more livid he became. 'I paid out all me hard-earned brass to help my fool of a sister and her gang o' hangers-on, an' I don't even get invited to me own niece's wedding!' he growled. 'Happen it's time I started claiming back what's mine!'

He watched a moment longer, so eaten up with jealousy he could bear it no longer. Cursing and threatening, he strode away, viciously kicking his dog, which whined and opened its huge mouth wide. He was a man rejected. A man who, when riled, was capable of anything.

~

At ten-thirty, Cathleen fell asleep on the sofa. Danny carried her upstairs where Emily put the child to bed and before he followed his new wife back down, he took the moment to kiss her long and hard. 'I love you,' he said passionately, and when Emily went to make a reply, he put his fingers to her lips. 'It's all right,' he promised. 'You don't have to say anything.'

He knew how she still harboured feelings for John Hanley and he had reluctantly come to accept that; though every day, he prayed it was a temporary thing.

Some time later, feeling the need to leave them alone, Aggie made her excuses. 'I've to be up at first light,' she explained. 'There's a whole crop of Brussels to be got ready for market.' When both Danny and Emily offered to help, she swiftly refused. 'You'll do no such thing!'

'By! I should think not.' Grandad as usual had to have the last word. 'It's your wedding night and

I should think you've got better things to do than get out of yer bed at four in the morning to pack Brussels sprouts.' His meaningful chuckle left nothing to the imagination.

'Hey!' Aggie gave him one of her warning stares. 'I reckon it's more than time you were in bed, old fella. It's been a long day for all of us.'

Meanwhile, blushing deep pink, Emily made her excuses to go into the kitchen, where she was filled with dread at the thought of what was to come, not least because the memory of what had happened in the barn was still vivid in her mind.

But Danny knew nothing of that, nor did she want him to. So, when he entered the kitchen to find her, she laughed the old man's comments off as best she could. 'Grandad has a habit of saying what's on his mind,' she apologised. 'I hope he didn't embarrass you?'

Danny took her into his arms. 'No, but he embarrassed you, didn't he?'

She nodded. 'How could you tell?'

'Because you went redder than a cockerel in full shout.'

She laughed at that. 'You're such a nice man, Danny. I really don't deserve you.'

'Oh, so I'm just "nice", am I?'

Now, when he kissed her on the neck in that same way John used to, she pulled away. 'I'd best make a start on these pots.'

In minutes she had the boiling water poured and the washing soda sprinkled, and her arms were up to the elbows in dirty crockery. 'You can help if you like?' she invited. Anything to delay the inevitable, she thought guiltily.

In the parlour, Aggie was persuading Grandad to call it a day. 'You look all in.'

'Aye, lass.' He had the good sense to see it. 'I am a bit weary.' He pointed to where Danny's father was fast asleep in the armchair, mouth wide open and out to the world. 'Look at that fella there,' he laughed. 'Not a care in the world an' snoring like a good 'un. Meks me feel tired just looking at him.'

He handed her the accordion. 'Yer right. Lead on, lass. I'd best do as yer say an' get a good night's sleep.' He chuckled. 'Who knows? I might just turn out of me bed at first light, and give yer a hand with them Brussels sprouts.'

Escorting him across the room, she declined his half-hearted offer with a groan. 'I'm best on my own, thanks all the same, Dad.'

When they were going up the stairs, he in front and she behind and helping him the best she could, Aggie chided, 'Honestly, Dad! What were you thinking of, to embarrass the young 'uns like that?'

'Why?' He could act the innocent when he wanted. 'What did I do?'

Aggie tutted. 'Sometimes, the way you blunder

in with your careless remarks, it's like you've got two left feet.'

He grinned naughtily. 'You know me, Aggie, lass. I can't help meself, that's the trouble.'

In the kitchen, Danny was telling Emily, 'When we're done here, I'd best get my father home.'

'I'll come with you,' she offered. 'We'll put him between us. One of us can drive the cart while the other makes sure he doesn't fall out.'

Danny feigned indignation. 'Are you saying my father's drunk?'

Emily laughed. 'Drunk as my grandad,' she answered with a twinkle in her eye. 'So, do I come with you or what?'

When they told Aggie, she wasn't at all sure it was a good idea. 'He can stay the night here,' she said. 'The snow's been falling most of the day, and the lanes might well be choked.' She didn't know how she would manage it though. 'We've no spare bedrooms, so we'll need to make him comfortable down here. I've plenty of blankets and a bolster, so he should be warm enough.'

'That's very kind,' Danny said, and they settled for that.

Half an hour later, with the makeshift bed on the floor and Aggie insisting they leave the pots and pans to her in the morning, they woke Bob Williams and explained how he was to stay the night. 'That's really good of you,' he said sleepily, and while he proceeded to take off his shoes,

Aggie went to her bed, followed by Danny and his new wife, whose nervousness was heightened with every step she took.

In the bedroom, she sat on the chair for a time, while Danny, also nervous but ready to die rather than admit it, went to the window and looked out at the endless expanse of fields, magically white and sparkling under the moonlight.

'There's two ways it can go.' He glanced at the skies. 'It'll either freeze over by morning, or disappear like a will-o'-the-wisp, as though it were never here.'

Emily said she hoped it would all be gone by morning. 'It makes our work outside a lot easier.'

An awkward silence followed, when each of them was momentarily lost in the enormity of the day's events.

After a while, Danny addressed her quietly. 'What have I done, love?' he asked worriedly. 'What have I said to hurt you?'

'Nothing.'

'There must be something, or you wouldn't be so quiet.'

'I'm quiet because I'm thinking, that's all.' And to put his mind at rest she stood up and gave him a kiss on the mouth. Not a long passionate kiss, but a kiss that told him she was fond of him.

Encouraged, he drew her into his arms, returning the kiss tenfold, his mouth covering hers and the need in him rising. 'I love you so much,' he whispered. 'I'll make you love me too, Mrs Williams.'

Slowly and ever so gently, he undressed her, taking off her pretty bridal garments, one by one.

Emily made no protest. Danny was her husband. She had taken his ring and his name and now she was his wife, with all the duties that came with it.

The lovemaking was hesitant and tender. He didn't hurt or frighten her as she had feared. Nor did he excite her.

Instead, her heart was with John. In her mind's eye she saw him as plainly as if he was there with her. During the half-hour that Danny was on top of her, she pretended it was John who held her in his arms, and so the ordeal was easier to bear.

Long after Danny had fallen asleep, his arm still round her shoulders, Emily lay awake.

This is my life now, she thought. Giving myself to Danny, and pretending it is all right. Only of course it wasn't, and never would be.

'*Where are you, John?*' she asked the darkness. '*Why did you never come back for me?*'

There was no answer. Outside, the snow fell thickly on her wedding night, covering all in a blanket of silence.

CHAPTER THIRTEEN

AGGIE WAS SHOPPING in Blackburn town, when she saw a familiar little figure just ahead of her. Recognising the woman at once as John Hanley's Aunt Lizzie, she called out: 'Lizzie! Wait on!'

The other woman had already quickened her steps, and darted inside the ironmonger's to escape her.

Unaware that Lizzie was trying her best to dodge her, Aggie persisted. 'Hey, Lizzie! Hold on a minute!' she shouted as she hurried down the street after her.

'Right, missus. What can I get you?' The man behind the big counter had seen his customer rush in and was eager not to let her rush out again without buying something.

'I'm just looking, thank you.' Hiding herself behind the nearest rack of shelves, Lizzie bent her head to examine the row of paint-brushes.

Undeterred, the man was out from behind his counter and beside her in a trice. 'What kind d'you want?' he asked. 'I've got all types and sizes, aye, and all prices to suit.' Hovering close by, he kept her trapped in that spot. 'There's your good-quality brush, then there's your cheap brush. It all depends on what you want it for, and how much you intend paying.'

Believing she had been there long enough for Aggie to have gone her own way, Lizzie pushed by him. 'I've changed my mind,' she said. 'I'll have to think on it.'

'You'll not find a better brush anywhere else.' Hands on hips, he blocked her way.

'I'm sure I won't,' she said sweetly. 'But if you don't move outta my road, the fish in my bag will begin to stink your shop out. Once the smell greets them at the door, you'll not get another customer this side o' Christmas.'

On that he swiftly moved aside and let her go. 'Don't forget,' he called after her. 'You'll not get cheaper or better, however far you look.'

When Lizzie came out, Aggie was waiting for her. 'I didn't follow you inside,' she explained. 'The man who serves in there is a nightmare. You can't look at anything without he's breathing over your shoulder.' Now, as he recognised her and waved eagerly from inside the shop, Aggie gave him a wave back and began to move away. 'I allus go into Preston if I need owt like that,' she confided out of his earshot.

As she had no real option, Lizzie accompanied

her back up the street. 'I threatened to stink his shop out wi' fish if he didn't let me go,' she laughed.

Aggie glanced suspiciously at the older woman's shopping bag. 'If you've got fish in there, you'd best tek it home a bit smartish,' she advised. 'It's early yet, but this July sun will fry it for sure, if you're not careful.'

Lizzie grinned. 'I were fibbing. I ain't got no fish at all,' she confessed. 'Only I had to tell him summat. The bugger had me trapped against the paint-brushes, so I told him a fishy story, if yer like.'

Aggie chuckled at that. Lizzie had always been easy to talk to, but since her nephew John had gone off and left their Emily with child, the woman had been keeping out of everyone's way. Aggie thought that was a real shame. After all, it wasn't Lizzie's fault any more than it was Aggie's.

'It's so good to see you,' she said warmly. 'It's been a long while since we've had a natter. I did call round a few times, only you were never in.'

'Oh, well y'see, I often go for long rambles now I live on me own,' Lizzie answered. 'Happen that's why you couldn't get me.' She hated lying. It made her feel uncomfortable, as it did now.

Since Emily had cheated on John, and she herself had lied to both him and to her because of it, Lizzie's attitude towards the Ramsdens had changed. In fact, she had decided it might be wiser to keep her distance. So, whenever she saw them coming up the lane to visit, she had locked the door and hidden herself away. Both Aggie and Emily had called on her many a time, until in the end they appeared to have given up, and that was fine by her.

'All right are you, lass?' Aggie had a sneaking feeling that Lizzie wasn't telling the truth. Moreover, the old dear looked a little under the weather.

'I'm very well, thank you,' Lizzie replied confidently. 'And yourself?'

'Can't grumble,' Aggie shrugged. 'I don't get time to be ill, what with the farm and everything.'

'No, I don't expect you do.' Through it all, Lizzie had always respected Aggie for the way she seemed to cope. 'I do admire you, lass, the way you soldiered on after your husband ... well, I mean ...' Having blurted out more than she intended, she now felt like crawling under a stone.

Aggie nodded resignedly. 'I know what you mean, and it's all right,' she assured her. 'Michael left us well and truly in the lurch. It's no secret hereabouts.'

'But you've kept it all going, and I think that's grand.' Relieved that Aggie had taken it so well, Lizzie added, 'And how's Emily?'

'Oh, she's fine.' Aggie's pride showed in her face. 'The lass is a treasure. Honest to God, Lizzie, I don't know what I'd do without her.'

It was on the tip of Lizzie's tongue to ask after the child, but she thought better of it. 'Is your father-in-law well?'

Aggie chuckled. 'As daft as ever,' she said. 'He drives me mad with his antics, but we're good for each other. He makes me laugh.'

'Give him my regards, won't you?'

'Aye, but you could do that yerself, if ever you chose to visit?'

Lizzie nodded. 'We'll see.' But she knew she wouldn't. To go down to Potts End and pretend that nothing had happened between the two families was all too daunting.

Even though Lizzie had not asked after Cathleen, Aggie was determined to mention her, if only to remind Lizzie of how her nephew had left Emily a shamed woman. 'The child is well,' she told Lizzie guardedly. 'A more darling lass you could never hope to meet.'

Lizzie nodded. 'I'm glad.' That was all she could say on the subject, because now her mind went back to the conversation with Emily, who had assured her that John was *not* the father of her child.

To Lizzie's thinking, that had cleared him of all blame – though lately, somewhere at the back of her mind, she felt things weren't quite what they seemed.

Emily and John had been so much in love, she had always known that. When it seemed that Emily had cheated on John, Lizzie had been shaken to her roots. She had been angry and disgusted, wanting to hit back.

All along, John had been her main priority. Believing she needed to save him from a woman who had betrayed him the minute his back was turned, she had sent him away, saddened and broken by her lies. Had she been right, she fretted, in telling John that Emily was happily wed, with a child by Danny Williams? Though it didn't matter now, she told herself, because now Emily really was wed. Danny had taken on the role of Cathleen's father, so Emily was made respectable and everything was fine. *Or was it?*

Day by day, Lizzie was becoming more and more unsettled and worried.

Unaware of the torture that Lizzie was going through, Aggie chatted away. 'By! It must be what – Christmas Eve when I last saw you out and about.' She chuckled. 'If you recall, me and Cathleen were out collecting a tree for the parlour – a huge great thing it was. We wanted it to be a surprise for Emily, so we chose the biggest one in the market. We got halfway across the street and couldn't carry it an inch further. If it hadn't been for you and that passer-by, I don't know what we'd have done.'

Lizzie found herself laughing, and she relaxed a little. 'Oh, I'm sure you'd have managed somehow,' she said encouragingly. 'But I'll tell you what. I couldn't help but notice how like Emily your granddaughter is, and what a fine young lady she's making.'

'Aye, she is that,' Aggie readily agreed. 'What's more, she's got a lovely nature to go with her good manners.' She paused. 'Mind you, she can be strong-minded when the mood takes her.'

Lizzie was curious. 'Really?'

'Oh, I'm telling you, when her and her great-grandad get started, it's a case of who might outwit the other. They're so alike it's unnerving.'

'How old is she now?' Lizzie asked. 'Five . . . six? She must be getting on that way by now.' Suddenly she was hungry for information.

Grateful that, at long last, Lizzie appeared to be taking an interest in Cathleen, Aggie happily enlightened her. 'She's six year old . . . and a few months.'

'She's at school then?'

'Oh, aye! Loves it, an' all. She's been attending the village school for some time now.' Aggie beamed with pride. 'She's especially good at drawing and painting pictures. But o' course they don't care much for teaching that sort o' stuff. They like to concentrate on reading and writing and learning 'em their times tables. Still, I can't say it bothers me, 'cause I'm a firm believer in a child learning its three Rs.'

Lizzie wanted to know more, like had they told the child who her father was yet, and had she

become aware of the lies about John being label-
led the villain? But she kept all that to herself, and
instead she asked after Emily. 'And you say your
daughter's fine?'

'She's well, yes. Thank you.'

'Enjoying married life, is she?'

Aggie was a little more coy. 'Seems to be.'

Lizzie smiled. 'Good.' She owed the family an
apology. 'Look, Aggie, thank you again for inviting
me to the wedding, but like I said, I wasn't feeling
too clever that day.' It was a downright lie, and
they both knew it.

In truth, it was shame and guilt that had kept
her away. Shame because she had lied, and guilt
because she was the one who had split John and
Emily up and driven her into marrying another
man – possibly Cathleen's father, although she
might never know the truth about that.

Since Danny had taken her as his wife, Lizzie
had deliberately avoided Emily, which was such a
shame, because at one time, she and the young
woman had been the best of friends.

'And is everything fine with you, Lizzie? I was
concerned when I couldn't seem to get hold of
you. But at least you got my notes.' Never able to
catch her at home, Aggie had taken to sending
her notes by way of Danny, and she always received
one in return. It was a pleasing thing.

'I can't complain,' Lizzie answered. 'Oh, and
thank you for your notes. Young Danny delivered

them along with the milk. All in all, he seems a very nice young man.'

'He is,' Aggie retorted. All of a sudden, her good humour left her, and the truth of her feelings began to spill over. She had kept them locked away for so long. 'Danny is a good husband and a good father to Cathleen, which is just as well because as we both know, the child's own father doesn't care enough about her to even ask after her!' Aggie was outraged by the way Lizzie had seemed to skilfully move away from the subject of her own great-grandniece. Lizzie's refusal to acknowledge Cathleen as part of her own family rankled deeply. It was a wicked thing, to Aggie's mind.

Taken aback by the ferocity of Aggie's remarks, Lizzie retaliated. 'John is *not* Cathleen's father!' she retorted. 'How many times do you need to be told, before you see the truth of it?'

'Oh, and what *is* the truth, pray tell?'

'You had better ask your daughter that.' Not wanting the conversation to degenerate into a shouting match, Lizzie stiffly bade her a polite good day and went about her shopping. The other woman let her go and this time, did not call after her.

~

An hour later, Lizzie paused to take refreshment in the pretty little café on the boulevard.

'Morning, love. I haven't seen you in a while.' Bessie, the woman behind the counter was a jolly sort with rolled-up greying hair and a wide, gap-toothed smile. 'Been poorly, have you?'

'No, just taking things easy,' Lizzie answered cagily. In truth she *had* been feeling unwell on and off for some weeks now, during which time she had only ventured out whenever she needed something for the larder. Even then she was always quick to hurry back home.

'What'll it be then?' Bessie asked kindly. 'Tea and a bun as usual?'

Gasping for a drink, Lizzie was thankful. 'That sounds like a good idea, yes, thank you.'

'Would you mind if I joined you?' Bessie asked. 'Only we've been that busy I'm fair worn out.' She glanced about at the empty room. 'Being as we're quiet now, I thought I'd stop for a few minutes while I've got the chance. I could just do wi' a cup o' tea an' a sit-down.'

Though she would have preferred to be on her own, Lizzie told her she'd be glad of the company, and so the dear woman hurried away, happily bustling about and singing to herself as she went.

While she was gone, Lizzie delved into her bag and took out a small, square envelope. Opening it up, she removed the letter inside, and read it through for the umpteenth time:

Dear Aunt Lizzie,

I hope this letter finds you well.

I'm writing again, because I have some important news to tell you. You remember I told you in my last letter, of how I had joined forces with a young lady called Rosie Taylor, and how together we have gradually brought her dad's business back to full swing?

Well, we've got on so well, and found so much pleasure in each other's company, that we've decided to make our vows as man and wife. It will happen in spring next year.

I know you'll be wondering if I truly love her, and in all honesty I can say that I could never love anyone as much as I loved Emily, and still do. But Rosie is a good, kind soul. We're both very lonely, and since I've got to know her so well, I really believe we can make each other happy. We already do.

Please come to our wedding if you can. I want you to be here. It's been five long years since we saw each other. I really need you beside me when I get wed, and there is so much to show you, as well as so much for us to talk about.

I'll be eagerly awaiting your reply. Please say you'll come. PLEASE.

All my love, as always,

John

There was an address along with a suggestion as to the best route to take once she reached Liverpool. At the bottom of the letter, a postscript: *I've enclosed a sum of money to put away for the time being. It will cover train and carriage, with enough left over for refreshments and such along the way.*

Lizzie sighed. You shouldn't be getting wed to no stranger, she thought, for that was how she saw this Rosie Taylor. You should be here, son – here, wi' me, and Emily.

Disheartened, she folded the letter and putting it back in her bag she withdrew a second one.

Taking it from its envelope, she read:

My dear,

I'm glad you've found a measure of happiness with this young lady called Rosie, though I must say, I hadn't realised it had gone so far as you and she planning to be wed. All the same, if that's what you want, then it makes me happy too.

As you already know, I'm not good at travelling. But I'll be there for you on the day.

God bless. See you in a few short months.

Lots of love,

Auntie Lizzie

The letter was duly signed and now she slid it back into its envelope and sealed it.

'There you are, luv.' Bessie returned with a tray

of tea and two buns. 'My poor feet feel like two raw chops,' she groaned, dropping herself into a chair. 'I don't mind telling you, I'm ready for this break.'

Oblivious to the fact that Lizzie would much rather be left alone with her thoughts, she launched into a harrowing account of how bad feet had always run right through her family. 'My poor old mam was a martyr to them!' she exclaimed. 'A martyr!'

Some time later, with her ears ringing about bad-smelling feet and relatives who suffered from wind, Lizzie made good her escape. Dropping her letter into the post-box, she had to smile. 'Poor Bessie,' she murmured as she went for the tram. 'I think *she's* the martyr, working all day on her own in that café.'

A short time later, seated on the tram, she took out John's letter and read it again, hoping with all her heart that he wasn't leaping out of the frying pan and into the fire.

In spite of the hope and assurances in John's letter, the stark truth was unsettling. Here was a man, in love with one woman and about to wed another. What good could come of it? Lizzie wondered.

PART FIVE

~

February, 1910

Hidden Truths

CHAPTER FOURTEEN

'WHERE ARE WE going?'
Half-asleep, his hair standing on end, and with two small squares of paper stuck over the areas where he'd sliced himself with the razor, old Archie was none too pleased to have been dragged out of his warm bed.

'For Gawd's sake, it's seven o'clock on a February morning!' he grumbled as they boarded the early tram. 'It's freezing cold and what's more it's Sunday – my only day for a lie-in. You work me like a dog from Monday to Sat'day. You'd think I'd be entitled to a lie-in!'

The three nights under Harriet's roof that Archie had been grudgingly allowed had long since extended themselves to several years spent as the new lodger in the cosy back room – an arrangement that suited the little man down to the ground. Spruce and well-fed, he was more fond of his formidable landlady, and she of him, than either of them would ever admit.

Ushering him to a seat, John slid in beside him. 'I don't know what all the fuss is about. If Harriet and me can get out of bed on a Sunday morning, why can't you?'

'Because I'm a poor old man, that's why.' Archie folded his arms sulkily and slunk deeper into the seat. 'Wake me when we get there.'

John let him sleep. He needed this quiet time anyway, to think about his future with Rosie. He had doubts – of course he did – but it had been years now, since he and Emily had made plans together.

His love for Emily was as strong as ever and always would be. But he knew now that in spite of everything, Emily had never felt the same way, or she could not have turned her back on him the way she did. It had taken years for him to accept the truth of that. Years when he had hoped and prayed there might be a way in which he could turn back the clock, but that wasn't to be, he knew that now. And painful though it was, he had to look forward, or live a lonely, empty life till the end of his days.

Putting Emily behind him would not be easy, but he could no longer spend precious time yearning for something that could never be. Lizzie was right. It was time to accept that Emily had gone her way, and he must go his, for it was plain that they were never meant to be together.

'Albert Docks!' The conductor's voice rang

through the tram. 'Last stop before we turn round. All off that's getting off.'

John gave Archie a nudge. 'Time to go.'

The old man didn't hear. Instead, with mouth hanging open, he remained seemingly unconscious, his robust snores shaking the tram while John tried frantically to wake him, but with no success.

'Here. Let me.' Impatient to be on his way, the conductor leaned forward and, taking the end of Archie's nose between finger and thumb, he held on tight and squeezed hard. At once the snoring stopped and Archie was fighting for air. 'Gerroff!' With arms flailing and feet kicking, he lashed out at all and sundry.

'There you are!' Giving John a triumphant wink, the conductor moved on. 'Pinch the nose till they can't breathe. It'll do the trick every time.'

As they got off the tram, Archie gave the conductor a hard stare. 'I won't forget *you* in hurry, matey.'

'And a good morning to you, sir.' The conductor tipped his hat and walked away grinning.

'I've a good mind to smack him one!' Archie rubbed his nose. 'He could 'ave broken it!'

Glancing at Archie's bright red nose, John couldn't help but chuckle. 'It's a good job the rozzers aren't after you,' he said. 'See you coming a mile off, they would.'

That tickled Archie's funny bone, and at once

his mood was lighter. 'Where are we off to then, eh?'

'Be patient,' John answered. 'You'll know soon enough.'

As soon as they turned the corner to the boat-yard, Archie guessed. 'You've finished the house, haven't you?'

'I might have.'

Archie was excited. *You have!* He gave John a nudge that nearly sent him hurtling into the canal. 'What's it like?'

John told him to wait and see.

They launched the narrowboat and were soon under way. On workdays it was a good half-hour to the site, but this Sunday morning, with fewer barges chugging about, the waterway was quieter.

Twenty minutes later they had moored the boat and were on their way across the site. 'I still can't believe what you've achieved here.' Not for the first time, Archie looked at the place where they worked and was amazed. Where the site had been unusable and derelict, it was now a thriving business, with large, well-designed buildings, a small office, and dozens of watercraft lined up in different stages of repair or construction.

Instead of rubble and grass underfoot, it was all neatly paved, with areas of concrete and a slipway second to none, complete with winches and machinery to lift the craft out of the water like a child might lift a toy.

'You've done yourself proud,' Archie told him. 'And thanks to you, we've all got work, so's we can hold up our heads in anybody's company.'

That meant a lot to Archie. There was a time back there when he thought he'd end up a tramp like Michael. And now, even Michael was respectable, thanks to John.

He mentioned the man now. 'Funny that, you knowing Michael from before.' Archie had asked about him many a time, but had always been given the same old brush-off. Now he tried again. 'What did he do before? How did you know him? What made him turn out the way he did? Was it to do with a woman? It usually is.'

Taken off-guard by Archie's barrage of questions, John tried to make little of it.

When, some time back, after Michael had cleaned himself up and John had recognised him, the man had pleaded to be left to sort out his own problems. He asked if John would mind not telling the others about his past and the shocking manner in which he had deserted his family.

John had readily done as he asked, for he knew that the man had suffered a complete breakdown, and he was sympathetic, as well as respectful to Emily's father for her sake as well as for Michael's. He did, however, inform Michael of Emily being happily wed, with child and all. It was cheering news to Michael, who was unaware of John's heartbreak. He knew of the friendship between Emily and John, yet had left Potts End before it had developed into love.

'Michael was a neighbour.' John gave Archie the same answer as always. 'As for his private business, I don't reckon it's anything to do with us.'

'You know more than you're letting on.'

'D'you want to see what I've done to the cottage or not?'

Archie good-naturedly took the hint. 'Go on then,' he said, and gave him a push forward.

Beyond the working area was the site of the cottage. With a screen constructed all round it, the building was hidden from view and no one – not Rosie, Archie or anyone else – was allowed inside – apart from the delivery men, who were too tired and preoccupied with their jobs to notice what was going on right under their nose.

'Mind you don't walk that muck into the cottage,' John warned as he led Archie over the rubble. 'And don't say a word until you've seen everything,' he ordered, 'upstairs *and* down. I want you to look properly, and then tell me what you think after we're done.'

'I should have thought Rosie would be the one to see it before me,' Archie pointed out. 'I mean, it's her who'll live here with you.' He smiled mischievously. 'Or am I invited into the happy home as well?'

John was horrified. 'Good God, man! Don't you think I've suffered your company long enough? Harriet and I have put up with your snoring, sleep-walking and smelly feet, and now she and the other lodgers can have you all to themselves. So, no! You're definitely *not* invited to share the cottage with me and Rosie.'

'Ah, go on. You'll miss me really,' Archie said fondly.

'Yes, I will, even though you're a crafty old bugger. Now then, shipmate – inside with you, and like I say, don't utter a word until we've gone all over. After that, I'll want your honest opinion.'

'What if I don't like it?'

'You will.'

'Mebbe, but what if I don't? Have I to say so, or would you rather I pretend?'

'I want the truth, Archie. Whether you like it or not, I need you to tell me the truth.'

'All right. Lead on.'

John entered the cottage first, with Archie treading carefully behind. As John had instructed, he took note of everything as they went from room to room.

'Good Lord above!' The old chap was flabbergasted. 'However did you do all this by yourself? I can't believe it. Since when were you a builder and decorator?'

'Since I set my mind to it,' John replied. 'Once you get started, it all seems to fall into place.'

Pointing to the sitting-room floor, Archie was about to speak, when John stopped him. 'Not a word, remember?' he warned. 'Until you've seen it all.'

Archie duly clamped his mouth shut and followed John upstairs, growing more and more amazed as he went. The last time he had been in this place, it was shabby and neglected, complete with crumbling walls, dipping floors you tripped over, and ceilings that sagged to a dangerous low. But now it was as pretty as a picture. Every wall and floor was straight as a die and made good; the floors had new floorboards and colourful rugs; the walls were finished in soft, subtle colours, and at each and every window were hung curtains of dainty floral fabric.

There were four fireplaces throughout the cottage; small, beautifully tiled ones in each of the three bedrooms, and a larger one in the sitting room. As with the other three, this one was newly fitted; blackleaded to a bright shine, and with a marble hearth surrounded by a smart brass fender – though unlike the other three, this one had a slipper-box at each end of the fender. The fireplace itself was a grander feature as this was the room where they would do their living and entertaining, if any.

The furniture had been chosen to complement the warm, homely character of the place: a deep brown horsehair sofa, matching armchairs and a delightful, honey-coloured deep-drawered dresser beneath the sitting-room window.

In front of the fireplace was the loveliest peg-rug of browns and greens, with a splash of cream round the edges. Hung on the wall above the hearth was a picture of a ship in full sail, and covering the mantelpiece, a tasselled cream-coloured velvet runner set the whole thing off to perfection.

The bedrooms, too, were furnished in the same simple but attractive manner.

'Well? What do you think?' Eager to know what somebody else made of his handiwork, John could hardly wait for the verdict.

As they came out, Archie closed the freshly painted front door behind him. 'I can't believe what I've just seen,' he answered quietly, shaking his head.

'What?' John's disappointment was etched on his face. 'You don't like it, do you? Rosie will hate it – that's what you're saying?'

Smiling, the old man put him out of his misery. 'I think it's the prettiest little palace I've ever seen,' he said proudly. 'You've done wonders!'

John laughed out loud. 'So, you think Rosie will like it, do you?'

Archie had no doubts whatsoever. 'She'll love it!' A thought occurred to him, though. 'How did you know what colours she liked? And what about the furniture – did she tell you what she wanted? Is that how you went about choosing it all?'

'I haven't even asked her.' John was made to think at Archie's observation. 'I just listened and watched and made mental notes when we were out and about. I saw how she'd furnished her father's cottage, and I got a sense of what she might like.'

'Hmh!' Archie thought he was a brave man. 'Women can be funny about such things.'

John was really worried now. 'I should have asked her, shouldn't I?' he groaned. 'I should never have done it without talking to her first.'

'Don't be daft!' Archie snorted. 'Rosie knew all along that you were doing the cottage up.'

'Yes, but she didn't know I was furnishing it and everything.'

'Oh, don't start worriting, man! Any woman would give her right arm to have that cottage. Trust me, she'll be over the moon.'

What Archie had said touched John deeply. 'Any woman'? And John couldn't help but wonder if Emily would have liked this place, too.

As though he had read his thoughts, Archie said gently, 'Don't go upsetting yourself about things you can't change, lad. The past is the past and this is your future – yours and Rosie's. You remember that, and you'll be all right.'

John nodded. 'You're right. The past is the past, and there's no going back.' He slapped Archie on the shoulder. 'You're the best mate I've ever had, did you know that?'

Archie made light of it. 'Does that mean you might still let me come an' live here too?'

John laughed out loud. 'Nice try, but no. And think how poor Harriet would miss you!'

Archie had noticed something else as he went through that delightful little cottage, and he told John now. 'You put an awful lot o' work into that place. For somebody who claims not to be getting wed for the love of it, there seems to have been a lot of time and care in the choosing of things.'

Taken aback, John swiftly put him right. 'That's because I was spending good money and I wanted it to be right for Rosie. She's a good woman, as you well know. What! If it hadn't been for her, I doubt we'd have a business at all.'

Archie had his own thoughts on that but he brushed them aside, as he asked hopefully, 'I know it's early, and I know it's Sunday, but there's a friendly landlord who might just serve us with a pint of good ale, to celebrate the forthcoming nuptials. What d'you say to that?'

John liked the idea. 'I say we should pay this friendly landlord a visit.' And that was exactly what they did.

~

The wedding took place on 1 March, at St Peter's Church in Liverpool. It was a cold day, but with a welcome smattering of sunshine. The church was packed, and it seemed that everyone the couple knew had turned out to wish them well.

There was Archie as best man, all done up 'like a penguin', as he aptly put it. Then Rosie's family: her father, Lonnie, a large-boned man who hid the pain of his physical disabilities behind a warm, proud smile, and her older sister, Rachel, who with her long fair hair and brown eyes looked uncannily like Rosie, but without the smiling eyes and sense of mischief.

Harriet Witherington was a guest of honour, looking grand and very overcome, her hankie at the ready for when the emotion of the occasion became too much.

Michael Ramsden lingered at the back of the church, his mind on his own wife and family, and the need to go home becoming stronger with every passing day.

The congregation kept arriving: the eight men who had been given work by John and who had come to admire and respect both him and Rosie for the honest and good people they were; and with them they brought their families, who also felt a need to wish the happy couple well on their special day. Two public-house landlords turned up, expressly to witness Archie in his unlikely role as 'best man'. They were followed by many other townsfolk, who packed the church. Everyone loved a good wedding, and they all knew of John

Hanley's story – how he beat the big boys and bought the derelict site at auction, then turned it into a thriving place of work.

The bride looked very fetching in her long white gown, with its high buttoned neck, tiny waist and swirling hem, and pretty tight sleeves culminating in an extravagant lace frill at the wrist. Her long fair hair was piled on top of her head and loosely draped in a veil of silk, cascading from a mother-of-pearl headdress.

Everyone agreed that Rosie looked beautiful. But the most beautiful part of all was her smile, for she had come to love John very deeply, and this was the day when, in the eyes of God and the world, he would take her as his wife: 'To love and to cherish from this day forth, till Death us do part.' Strong words, for a strong love. She knew John had loved before, and she had long suspected that he still felt great affection for Emily Ramsden.

When they first became good friends, before the friendship turned to love – at least on her part – John had begun to confide in her; not all of it, but enough for Rosie to realise that for whatever reason, he had walked away from the girl he adored. Once he and Rosie had decided to get married, he would not be drawn on the subject. So because she needed to, Rosie came to believe that he had finally got over that first, special love. She didn't ask. She didn't want to know what the answer might be.

Keeping her gaze on the man who was about to become her husband, Rosie walked slowly down the aisle, pacing herself with the man who walked arm-in-arm with her – her father, of whom she felt so proud. Her hero.

Leaning ever so slightly against her as he took each careful step up the aisle, Lonnie Taylor was determined to walk his daughter right up to the altar where her future husband waited. Situated at the top pew to reassure him was his bath-chair, where he would sit during the service.

Behind them came the older sister, Rachel, dressed as maid of honour in a pale blue gown and carrying a pretty posy of pink and white tulips, to match those of the bride.

And right there in pride of place next to Harriet, was Lizzie.

Having travelled up from Salmesbury and spent a couple of nights at Harriet's, getting to know her, and rejoicing in John's company, she was refreshed and smart in her new outfit of long coat and matching hobble skirt that finished at the ankles and allowed the merest sighting of her brand new, black boots. The only problem was, the left one pinched so badly that she had to keep wiggling her toes to keep the blood flowing. 'Take it off!' Harriet whispered. 'I'll bend it about a bit. It'll be all right then.'

Hoping no one could see, Lizzie unhooked the half-dozen buttons with the button-hook hidden in her little reticule, slipped it off and, true as her word, Harriet 'bent it about a bit'. When Lizzie surreptitiously eased it back on again, it was much more comfortable, and she was able to watch the service in relative comfort, though she secretly vowed that the minute she got back to Harriet's, she would exchange the boots for the comfy old shoes she had travelled up in.

Harriet herself was looking neat and tidy in an oyster-grey skirt, the wide belt with its silver buckle emphasising her considerable bosom. The bushy iron-grey hair was scooped up and rammed out of sight beneath a straw boater with an oyster-grey silk band and huge jet hatpin. Archie's eyes had gone out on stalks at the magnificent sight of her!

The service was conducted by a frocked priest who, when it was over, blessed the newlyweds and led them to the vestry, where they signed the register as man and wife.

Afterwards, when they emerged into the bright March daylight, everyone shouted and laughed and threw rice, before setting off on foot or climbing into their carriages to be whisked off to the grand inn on King Street, where the celebrations were soon under way, with the invited and the uninvited mingling to drink to the couple's happiness, and dancing until late.

In the ornamental garden at the back of the inn, hung with Japanese lanterns for the occasion,

Rosie told John how happy she was. 'You do love me, don't you?' she asked nervously. The feeling that he would rather be somewhere else was haunting her.

John thought she looked lovely and told her so. He took her in his arms and kissed her softly, and whispered in her ear, 'Of course I love you.' And he did. But not in the same way he had loved Emily – though he didn't tell Rosie that much. He was too fond of her ever to hurt her. That would be too cruel. She was his wife now, and he would care for her and look after her.

Yet for him, there would always be something missing.

'I know you can't love me in the way you want to,' she told him with understanding, 'but it won't matter. We have all the time in the world.'

Sliding his arm about her slim waist, he walked her to the pond. 'I do love you,' he said honestly. 'There are things I want to tell you, but I can't, not yet. Though like you said, we have all the time in the world and we'll use it to get to know each other, as well as any man and wife can know each other. The kind of love you deserve will follow, I'm sure.'

'We'll make it happen!' she murmured, nibbling his ear. For now she was content to know he loved her enough to take her as his wife.

'We will,' he said. 'With the help of God, we'll make it happen.' He kissed her tenderly. 'Meanwhile, Mrs Hanley, we have guests to tend, and Harriet's beautiful cake to cut.'

As they walked back to the guests, John could not deny there was a certain sadness in his heart. But when he walked through the door and everyone turned their heads to look at them, his handsome, ready smile gave nothing away. Instead, when the music started, he took his wife by the waist and waltzed her across the floor.

Before they, too, paired up and joined the dance, the guests allowed the bridal couple a few minutes on their own, during which time they held each other and seemed for all the world like two people deeply in love.

Lizzie knew the truth. She watched them for a long time, praying that her anger and lies had not ruined four young lives.

'We'll have to leave soon,' John told Rosie, taking her aside. 'We need to get moving before it grows dark.'

Rosie was intrigued. 'Leave for where?' Then she groaned. 'Oh John, don't tell me you forgot to book us in here for the weekend?'

'I didn't forget,' he said. 'I just didn't book it.'

'So where are we spending our honeymoon?'

'It's a surprise.'

'I knew something was going on,' she said with a knowing smile. 'Though I didn't like to mention it, we haven't had any wedding presents. Is everyone in on this surprise of yours, whatever it is?'

'Don't ask questions, Mrs Hanley,' he gave her a wink, '. . . and you'll get told no lies.'

Half an hour later, while Rosie was thanking the guests, John went to the landlord and collected the portmanteau he had brought here the day before. 'We need to get changed,' he explained. 'Is it still all right for us to use that back room?'

'Whenever you're ready,' the landlord confirmed. 'There you are, son.' Handing the portmanteau over, he wished John well. 'You found a good 'un there,' he commented, gesturing to where Rosie was laughing at Archie's little joke.

Catching Rosie's eye, John held up the portmanteau and she understood. While she drew the conversation with Archie to an end, John made his way to the back room. By the time Rosie arrived, he was changed and ready to leave. 'I just need to have a word with Lizzie,' he told her. 'Harriet says to leave our wedding clothes here, and she'll take care of them.'

Rosie was impressed. 'You seem to have organised everything,' she said suspiciously. 'I wish you'd tell me what you're up to.'

'You'll soon find out. Be as quick as you can. I've put your clothes on the chair.' He had the portmanteau with him. 'I'll take this.' It held all their necessities for the night.

First stop was Archie. 'I hope she likes what I've done to the cottage,' John said to his old mate.

'She'll love it!' Archie had no doubts on that score.

Going quickly round the guests, John thanked them all, and they wished him well, and then it was Lizzie. 'Are you happy, son?' She was concerned for him, and Rosie too. Ever since she had received his invitation, Lizzie had wondered if her nephew was making the biggest mistake of his life. 'Now I've met her, your Rosie seems a nice enough lass – a lot like Emily, I think. But I'm so worried you might have got wed for the wrong reasons.'

'Don't be,' he said cheerfully. 'I'm doing what you told me. I'm getting on with my life the best way I know how.'

Lizzie looked at him through tearful eyes. 'I so much want you to be happy.'

'How can I not be happy,' he said, holding her hand, 'when I've got you?'

Just as he'd hoped, she smiled through her tears. 'Go on with yer!'

'That's my Lizzie!' He held her in his arms awhile. 'We'll talk tomorrow,' he promised, and as he walked away, she seemed a little more content.

By the time he'd organised a carriage, Rosie was ready to leave.

Outside, everyone waved them off. 'What are you up to, John Hanley?' Rosie was loving every minute.

'Just you sit back and relax,' he told her. And she did, mainly because her feet were aching from all the dancing after the wedding, and her new shoes didn't help either.

When they reached the boatyard, they boarded the waiting barge, and were soon on their way. 'Now I really am worried!' she said, only half-joking. 'You're surely not making for the site, are you?'

'I am.'

'Do you intend setting me to work, is that it?' she laughed.

'I might.'

'My God! I've married a bully-boy.'

Negotiating the barge through the waters, he smiled at her from the tiller. 'I hope you like your wedding present.'

'What if I don't?' She knew now it must be to do with the cottage. It was common knowledge how he had busied himself behind the screen for months on end, not even allowing herself to enter.

'Archie says you'll love it.'

'Oh, I see!' She feigned indignation. 'So Archie's seen it, has he?'

'Apart from myself he's the only one.'

'Well, hurry up, then, husband. Get me there quick, before I faint from curiosity.'

~

On arriving at the cottage, John carried her over the threshold. 'I can't believe it!' Rosie could hardly trust her own eyes. Running from room to room, she was overwhelmed. 'It's beautiful!' She flung her arms round him. 'Oh, John! It's just perfect. Thank you. Thank you!'

A couple of the men had been in to lay and light the fires, keeping an eye on them until the hour John had said he'd be back. Rosie threw off her warm, outer clothes and danced jubilantly around the small house, exclaiming with delight at each new treat, while John lit the lamps and put the brand new kettle on the range for a wel- come pot of tea – their first in the new home. He was tired but very pleased with Rosie's – *his wife's* – unfeigned pleasure. He wanted her to be happy.

Later, when the first rush of excitement had settled to a feeling of contentment, they opened their presents together.

There was a flat-iron; a blue and cream china tea-set; a pair of cushion-cases; a pretty lamp; lav- ender bags that scented the air and other useful items that were made to suit different rooms in the house. 'You asked them to buy things for the cottage, didn't you?' she said, and this time, when she threw her arms round him, she didn't let go. Guiding his hands, she helped him to unbutton her pretty lilac blouse and to slide it off her shoul- ders. The single strand of pearls he had given her as a present gleamed in the soft light and he gazed at the fullness of her breasts beneath the virginal chemise.

'Make love to me,' she whispered naughtily. 'I'm your wife and I demand it.'

'You're a hussy!' He smiled at her boldness. 'But you're so pretty, how can a man refuse?'

There and then on the peg-rug in front of the fire he took her to himself, with reluctant passion at first. Inevitably, and much because of Rosie's unbridled enthusiasm, the passion deepened and in spite of his misgivings, he could not hold back. To Rosie, and to John, the lovemaking was both satisfying and beautiful.

Afterwards they sat together on the rug, looking into the fire. 'Got another little surprise.' John opened the lid of the portmanteau and reaching inside, extracted a bottle of best wine. 'Compliments of the landlord,' he quipped. There were two glasses, a bottle-opener and a large pork-pie as well.

Filling the glasses, John handed Rosie one and holding his glass to hers, he said quietly, 'Here's to happiness and contentment.' *Though without Emily, he couldn't help but wonder if he would ever find either.*

'I'll make you a good wife, John, I promise.' It was as though Rosie had read his thoughts.

'I know,' he answered. 'And I'll do my best to make you a good husband.'

'And we'll build our business up to be even bigger and better.'

'The best in Liverpool, if not the world,' he teased her.

'And later, we'll have children, won't we?'

'Dozens,' he laughed. 'All pretty and hard-working, like you.'

'Oh, so that's why you married me, is it?' she demanded with a playful dig in the ribs. 'Because I'm a work-horse?'

'Of course. Why else would I marry somebody who can't fry an egg without burning it to a cinder?'

She laughed out loud. 'I wish I hadn't told you about that now.'

Their laughter rippled across the room, before in a more sober mood she reminded him, 'I know we didn't marry altogether out of love ... and I know it was my idea to merge the businesses and make our relationship more permanent.'

John recalled the very conversation. 'It was a good idea,' he confirmed. 'It secured two of our best contracts. Merging the businesses was the best thing we ever did.'

'I agree,' she said. 'Only I didn't mean to fall in love with you. But I did, and to tell you the truth, I couldn't be happier.'

He smiled at that. 'I'm glad, Rosie,' he said sincerely. 'You deserve to be happy.' And so she did, he thought. Rosie was a delightful person, with a heart as big and kind as he had ever known, and though he didn't feel the same kind of joy with Rosie as he used to when he was with Emily, he thought a great deal of her, in his own quiet way.

Touching her hand to his face, she stroked it gently. 'My happiness would be complete if only you could feel the same way,' she whispered.

Draping an arm round her shoulders, he drew her closer. He didn't speak, because just then Emily came into his mind and subdued him.

Rosie sensed his sadness, and curling into the crook of his arm, she let him know she was there for him. No matter whatever else might happen in the future, she would always be there for him.

~

That night Lizzie's conscience would not let her rest. Long after she had said good night to Harriet, she paced the bedroom floor, thinking and worrying, and realising, not for the first time, how she had been wrong all along. Wrong to turn her back on Emily; wrong to have jumped to conclusions when what she should have done was talk with the lass, try and help, instead of damning her from the outset.

And she was even more wrong to have sent John away, believing the shocking lie that Emily was already wed. Maybe if she hadn't interfered in such a high-handed manner, John and Emily might have salvaged something good from a bad situation, and neither of them would now be wed to someone else. They belonged together. They had always belonged together, and it was she who had driven them apart.

It was striking two o'clock when Lizzie finally fell into bed, but even then she didn't sleep. Instead she lay awake fidgeting and fretting, and wondering how she could put things right. She heard the hallway clock strike three, then four, but heard no more until Harriet tapped on the door at half-past seven.

'I thought you might like a cup of tea,' the big woman said, poking her face round the door. 'For breakfast there's toast, bacon and egg, muffins and porridge. Which do you fancy?' Entering the room, she placed the cup and saucer on the bedside cabinet, surprised to see Lizzie making no effort to sit up. 'Just tell me what you want and I'll have it up here quick as a wink.'

'Oh, I couldn't face breakfast,' Lizzie answered faintly. 'Thank you for the tea though. It's just what I need to get me going.'

Having opened the curtains wider, Harriet seated herself on the bed. She noticed how slow Lizzie was in sitting up, and how, when she took hold of the cup, it rattled against the saucer. 'Are you all right?' she asked worriedly. 'Did you not sleep well?'

'I'm a bit woozy.' Lizzie laughed it off. 'I must have drunk too much wine last night.'

'No, you didn't.' Harriet chided. 'You had one glass, same as me, and you hardly ate anything, so it can't be the food that's upset you.'

Lizzie brushed aside the other woman's concern. 'I'm allus slow to wake,' she lied. 'I'll be right as rain, once I've had this cuppa tea.' In truth she didn't feel at all well, though she couldn't quite put her finger on why.

'If you're sure?' Harriet had no choice but to take her at her word, though she thought the old dear looked pale and worn. 'I'll leave you to get washed and dressed.'

It was an hour later when Lizzie came down. Harriet had served breakfast to her one remaining guest, apart from Archie, and was just saying goodbye to him. 'See you next month,' she said, closing the front door and fishing out her tin of snuff for a welcome pinch or two.

On seeing Lizzie, she explained, 'He's one of these unfortunate men who go round the shops trying to sell merchandise . . . He arrives here once a month and stays for two nights. Always seems worn out, poor thing. It must be hard making a living trying to sell things to them as don't want them.'

Eager for a womanly natter, Harriet soon had Lizzie and herself seated at the kitchen table, with a fresh brew in front of them. 'Your nephew is a real credit to you,' she said.

'John is my pride and joy,' Lizzie answered, her eyes shining. 'He came to me as a little lad, and I took him in as my own son. It wasn't easy, mind. We didn't have much money and there were times when I thought I'd never manage. But we got through, and I've never regretted one single minute of it.'

'And what do you think of Rosie?' Dipping a shop-bought biscuit in her hot tea, Harriet tutted when it got sodden and fell in.

Lizzie didn't hesitate in her answer. 'She's a very pleasant young thing. I liked her.' No one had been more surprised than Lizzie, when she took to Rosie straight off. 'I do, yes,' she affirmed. 'I like the lass.'

'She loves your John, that's for sure.' Fishing the melted biscuit out, Harriet licked it off the spoon. 'Head over heels, she is.' Swigging a gulp of her tea, she was confronted by another mouthful of biscuit, which she quickly swallowed. 'You've only to see her with John, to know how much she dotes on him.'

'I can tell that, yes.'

For a long moment, while Lizzie sipped at her tea, deep in thought, Harriet discreetly regarded her. She thought Lizzie to be well past her sixtieth birthday, though she would never ask a lady her true age; it was too personal.

In the same way Lizzie had taken to Rosie, Harriet had taken to her. She could see by the workworn face and the leathery hands that Lizzie had had a hard life. In many ways she wished she had met her earlier. They could have been good friends from the outset, but never mind, she told herself, we've met now, and we'll meet again many a time, no doubt.

Just then Lizzie glanced up. 'Sorry!' She was mortified to have been so rude. 'I was miles away.'

'Oh, that's all right,' Harriet assured her. She suspected Lizzie might be of the same mind as herself, with regard to John and Rosie so, daring to voice her opinion, she said warily, 'I'm not so sure he loves Rosie – in the same way, I mean.'

Lizzie was astonished. It was almost as though Harriet had seen into her mind. 'What makes you say that?'

Harriet explained, but with some reservations. 'When John first came here we made friends straight off. There were times when we talked a lot, about life and stuff like that. He said something to me, about someone he loved . . . Emily, was it?'

Lizzie felt relieved. At least John had spoken about her to someone. 'What did he say?'

'Not much – though you could see he desperately missed her.'

Lizzie didn't want to get into too deep a conversation about John and Emily, but she did tell Harriet, 'Emily was his first love. They planned to wed, but things sort of got in the way. He went away to sea, and she found comfort in somebody else.' She choked on the words. 'She's wed now, with a child – a delightful little girl called Cathleen, and –'

Harriet finished the sentence for her. 'And

John returned home, learned the truth and started a new life here, in Liverpool.'

Lizzie nodded. 'He was heartbroken.' She let slip a glimpse of what bothered her. 'I was that surprised when I learned he was about to be wed. I worried he might be doing it for all the wrong reasons.'

Harriet could understand Lizzie's concern but, 'Rosie is good for him. They look out for each other. He helped her and got her more work by repairing a badly damaged narrowboat.'

She went on to explain how the two of them had got closer. 'Later on, John bought the site he has now.' The fact that it had belonged to her would remain a secret for ever. 'Rosie ran the barges, and John built and repaired them. It was a natural thing that they should join forces. During the time they worked together they became friends, and I think the friendship gradually turned into something else.'

Lizzie was beginning to see the way of it. 'So, during that time, Rosie fell in love with him, and now they're wed. I can see how it all came about, but what of John? What was *his* reason for getting wed?'

'Who knows?' Harriet took another swig of tea. 'He might have thought they'd do better business-wise to be man and wife. Think about it, love. They're both very clever people when it comes to making things happen.'

Lizzie shook her head. 'You're saying that John got wed because he wanted to expand his business?'

'That's the way I see it.' As a businesswoman herself, Harriet admired him for it.

'But that's not my John's way of thinking,' Lizzie objected. 'It's too cold and empty a reason for him to take such a big step as marriage.'

'Well, maybe when Rosie told him she loved him, he married her because he liked her enough. Emily was lost to him and Rosie needed him. The business needed him, too, and to my mind that's a very suitable arrangement.'

Turning Harriet's words over in her mind, Lizzie lapsed into silence. It was possible Harriet was right in her assumption, but Lizzie wasn't satisfied with that. She needed to know that John was content in his marriage. It was true, the couple seemed well suited. But was it enough?

'Are you sure you're all right, dear?' Seeing how Lizzie had paled, Harriet was concerned. 'And you haven't eaten a thing.'

'I'm weary, that's all.' Getting out of her chair, Lizzie thanked her for the tea. 'I think I'll leave on an earlier train. I know John said he'd come back this afternoon and show me his site and everything, but I'm just too tired. I can always visit another time, can't I?'

'He'll be so disappointed.'

Lizzie was stood, her two hands gripping the

back of her chair as though without the support she might fall over.

'He'll understand – and besides, I'm sure he's got more important things to do than fuss over an old woman like me.'

Harriet wagged a finger at her. 'You'd best not let him hear you say a thing like that!' she chided. 'He thinks the world of you. What! When he gets started on the subject of "my Auntie Lizzie", you can't stop him.' She paused. 'Aw, Lizzie, are you sure you can't wait a while longer? Maybe go home tomorrow?'

Lizzie shook her head. 'He and I found time to have a good long chat,' she revealed, 'though there's never enough time, is there?'

Harriet gave a wry smile. 'Not in my experience,' she answered knowingly.

'I wanted to see him wed, and I've done that. I needed to know if he was all right in himself, and he seems fit and well enough, and doing good in business, just like he said.' She smiled. 'I feel a bit more settled now I've seen him. But I'm fair worn out, so I'll start my journey home on the next train. If I write him a note and explain,' Lizzie took hold of Harriet's hand, a look of gratitude on her face, 'you will make sure he gets it, won't you?'

'Of course I will,' Harriet assured her. 'The minute he comes through that door to see you and collect the rest of his things.'

'You've been so kind, Harriet. It's been a joy to meet you, but I really do need to get home now. The journey to Blackburn is a fair old way.'

Lizzie's one thought was to see Aggie. It was time that dear woman knew the truth of it. Moreover, it would be a burden off Lizzie's mind, to confess what a terrible thing she had done.

Harriet could see how determined she was. 'There you are.' Going to the drawer she handed Lizzie pencil and paper. 'When you've done that, prop it behind the clock on the mantelpiece.' Collecting her coat from the door she shrugged it on. 'While you're fetching your bag, I'll pop down to the inn to order a carriage to take us to the station.'

Growing more weary with every step, Lizzie climbed the narrow stairs to her room. In a surprisingly short time, she had packed and returned with her hand-made tapestry bag, to find Harriet back already. 'I'm ready for off,' Lizzie told her.

'And I've got the carriage waiting outside,' Harriet informed her proudly. 'My treat.'

Lizzie was horrified. 'I can't allow you to pay out for a carriage!'

Harriet was adamant. 'You're John's aunt and my guest, so don't argue!'

A few minutes later, wearing her outdoor clothes and carrying her precious handbag, Harriet led her to the door. 'If it's all right with you, I'm coming to the station,' she said. 'John would be happier to know I'd seen you board the train.'

'That would be nice, thank you.' Lizzie valued her company.

The carriage-driver took Lizzie's carpet-bag and helped her aboard, though when he came to give Harriet a hand, she cast him such a wicked glare, he scurried away and almost lost his footing as he clambered onto his lofty seat. 'All right for off, are we?' he shouted, and before Harriet had fitted her backside into the seat, he started forward.

'Hold your horses, you mad bugger!' she screamed. 'Are you trying to kill us or what!'

At the station, she ordered him to wait while she saw Lizzie on to the train. 'I can take myself onto the platform,' Lizzie pointed out, 'if you're in a hurry to get back.'

Harriet would hear none of it. 'I came to see you off, and that's what I mean to do,' she answered in her sergeant-major fashion.

Once Lizzie was aboard, Harriet waved until the train was out of sight. Poor little devil, I hope she'll be all right, she thought. She crossed to the waiting carriage. Something had upset the woman, that was for sure. Poor Lizzie didn't look at all well.

Before she climbed back into the carriage, Harriet gave the driver another of her warning glares. 'If you want paying, you'd best make sure I'm good and seated, before you go flying off up the street!'

'Certainly, missus.' He tipped his cap. 'I'll be as gentle as a babby.'

'Hmh!' The carriage tipped dangerously to one side as she hoisted her sizeable weight into the seat. Slamming the door shut behind her, she bawled out, 'You'd better be, if you know what's good for you!'

Up front, manoeuvring his carriage down the narrow cobbled street, the driver made faces as he chatted to himself. 'Yes, miss, no, miss. Think yourself lucky I let you in my cab at all, you lard-arse!'

When they reached the lodging-house, he smiled sweetly at Harriet, took her money and went away at the double. 'And good shuts to you an' all, madam!'

~

A few hours later, John arrived to see Lizzie. 'She's gone, lad,' Harriet informed him. 'She went some time ago. Said she were dog-tired and needed to get home. She's left you a letter, mind.'

Surprised and disappointed, John took the envelope she handed him, and opened it. The contents soothed him, for Lizzie had written a bright and happy letter:

My dear John,

Please forgive me for taking my leave, but I need to get back. Your Rosie seems a really nice young woman, and I'm so glad I came to see the two of you wed. Thank you both.

I'm sorry not to have waited for you this morning, but I know you will understand, son. In all the years I've lived, I've never once been this far from Salmesbury and Blackburn town. It just goes to show what an old stick in the mud I am, doesn't it? I know you'll be bringing your new wife to see me, and I really look forward to that.

I'll write when I'm home, and maybe you will do the same? For now, God bless you, son.

Give Rosie my love, won't you?

Lizzie XX

P.S. John, I'm so glad things appear to have worked out for you. You deserve all the happiness and all the luck in the world.

John read the postscript at the end and knew what Lizzie meant.

She was thinking of Emily, and wondering if he had got over her. Funny that, he thought, because he had spent many a sleepless night asking himself the very same question.

CHAPTER FIFTEEN

For lizzie, feeling poorly as she did, the journey from Liverpool to Blackburn seemed to take a lifetime.

Twice the passenger opposite had tried to engage her in conversation. Each time she smiled and listened but didn't feel able to do more than that. In the end he gave up and when he got off the train at the first station, she was relieved to be left on her own.

As the train drew away again, great billows of steam crept up to envelop the carriages and everyone inside. In the midst of that huge, grey cloud, it seemed to Lizzie that she was the only person left in the whole wide world. It was an eerie feeling; though the steam soon evaporated and glimpses of the outside world crept in.

A moment later she heard the muffled tap of footsteps going along the corridor. Fearing that people might come in if she smiled at them, Lizzie looked away when curious passengers peeped inside, their faces pressed to the window of her compartment. When they walked on by, she settled back in her seat and, closing her eyes, began to relax. The gentle rhythm of the train and the distant, soothing clatter of iron against iron, soon lulled her to sleep.

~

Many hours later, the weary soul finally arrived in Blackburn town.

The station was always busy, and this morning was no exception. With porters scurrying about, frantic people rushing in all directions, some passengers queuing for tickets and others reading papers or merely chatting to colleagues, it was all Lizzie could do to forge a way through.

'Need any help? Want a carriage, do yer?' The ruddy-faced little porter came tripping forward with his trolley.

Too fagged to answer him, Lizzie shook her head and moved on. She only had the one bag, and had no intention of travelling to Salmesbury in a carriage, not when there was a perfectly reliable tram service at half the price. 'Thank you all the same.'

She had tried to press on John the money he had left with her when he had first come back from sea, bursting with health and optimism, ready to marry his Emily. John had made her bring it home again: she must save it for her old age, he said – not that she would ever be old to him. But he and Rosie, and all who saw it, admired the beautiful patchwork bedspread she had painstakingly made for them over the months leading up to their marriage. It was a wonderful gift.

The symptoms she had experienced earlier still lingered. So now, as she wended her way towards the exit, Lizzie's footsteps got slower and slower, until she felt the need to lean against a pillar where she took long, gasping breaths.

'Are you all right, my dear?' A kindly old gent came up alongside. 'Do you need help?'

Embarrassed, Lizzie shook her head. 'No, thank you. I'm feeling better now.' Mustering all her strength, she moved on. Behind her, the gent watched her for a moment before hurrying for his train.

Outside in the fresh air, with the keen March breeze in her face, Lizzie took a few invigorating breaths and set off in search of the tram to Salmesbury.

'That's right, luv. We're about to leave for Salmesbury now. If you're coming along, you'd best get on board.' The conductor was a lanky sort, with a mop of wild ginger hair.

When Lizzie arrived, he had been lolling against the tram and puffing away at his pipe. Now though, he tapped out the bowl against a street-lamp. Helping Lizzie aboard he continued to chat. 'Been on holiday, have you?' He pointed to the big tapestry bag, which he had collected from Lizzie by way of his common duty. 'Somewhere nice, was it?'

As Lizzie climbed the two steps, it felt like she was climbing a mountain. 'I haven't been on no holiday,' she informed him. 'I've been to a wedding.'

'A wedding, eh?' Remaining on the platform while she made her way to a seat, he called after her, 'Now I see. It's late nights and too much booze that's wrong with you. A face the colour of chalk and not hardly able to put one foot afore the other – it gets me the very same way.'

Lizzie thought it best not to put him right. Instead she merely smiled at him. 'Mind you tek care o' my bag.' She was beginning to wish she hadn't let the cheeky monkey take it from her.

'Don't you worry about your bag, missus,' he called back. 'I'll put it here, under the stairs. Don't forget to ask for it as you get off.' He didn't hear Lizzie thank him, because now he had to contend with a woman and three boisterous infants, and not too far behind them came a miserable round, balding runt of a man, accompanied by his shrew-faced wife who went at him like a pecking hen. 'I told you we should 'ave caught the earlier tram!' she crowed. 'Now we'll be late and it's all thanks to you!'

'Yes, dear,' he answered meekly. 'It won't happen again.'

'You're right, it won't,' she replied sharply. 'Because next time, I intend going shopping on my own.' It was just as well she didn't see the look of pure joy on his face at such a promise.

Thankful that her queasy stomach was beginning to settle, Lizzie dropped into her seat. With home in sight, she was feeling more like her old self, well enough now to chat with the woman who was desperately trying to control her three offspring. 'I never had children of my own,' Lizzie confided.

'Well, I've got five . . . these three lasses and two big lads!' The poor woman was haggard and frantic. 'The boys are away at board-school, thank Gawd.' Loaded down with bags, which she had refused to leave under the stairs and, not wanting to cause a riot, the conductor had wisely allowed her to take them inside.

'I want a toffee!' The oldest girl looked to be about three. 'Sally 'ad a toffee, an' now I want one.'

Sighing from the bottom of her boots, the beleaguered woman dipped into her bag and, taking out a wrapped paper cone of sweeties, gave one to each child. 'That's all you're getting for today,' she warned.

Sitting back in their seats, the children were astonishingly quiet, until the toffees were sucked away and the arguments began. 'If you don't behave yerselves, I'll tell yer dad when we get home,' she threatened. 'He won't take no non-sense. He'll tan yer arses good an' proper!' That did the trick. Peace was restored, at least until Lizzie reached her stop.

As she climbed off the tram, she heard them starting up again. 'I'll not have arguing and fight-ing aboard my tram!' The conductor's voice sailed down the street. 'Any more hanky-panky and you'll be thrown off, the lot of yer!'

There then came the sound of the woman's voice, raised in anger. 'Don't you dare threaten to throw my kids off this tram!' she screamed. 'My husband's a big man!'

At that, Lizzie went away chuckling.

Instead of walking the whole distance along the winding Potts End Lane, she decided to take the short-cut across the fields; that way her cottage was only half a mile as the crow flies.

It wasn't the easiest of journeys, though – not with the weather suddenly turning and the drizzle beginning to trickle down the collar of her coat. Before long, the soil underfoot became boggy, and the going got harder.

When the drizzle thickened to a torrent, Lizzie found shelter under an aged oak tree, its out-stretched branches protecting her from the weather like a giant umbrella.

She looked across the valley and thought how beautiful it was. The rain poured down, and right there before her eyes, the grass began to sparkle clean and bright, glinting under the darkening skies, like an endless carpet of shining emeralds.

As quickly as it had started, the rain stopped and the skies cleared. The air smelled fresh and everywhere was newly cleansed and sharper to the eye.

Lizzie continued her journey along the valley's edge and up towards the brow of the hill. In the far distance she could see the sheep grazing, their heads bent and their bellies swollen with the weight of new life. Seemingly content with their lot, they relentlessly moved along, a white mass of munching machines.

At the top of the hill, Lizzie paused for breath; the sense of weakness was creeping back. 'Tek your time, Lizzie!' she chided herself. 'You might wish you were a young lass, but you're not. You're a silly old fool, with no right to be tackling this long trip across the fields.' She wished now that she had gone down the lane. At least that would have been firm underfoot, and there were no hills to climb. It was high time she learned that she couldn't do what she used to. Like it or not, them days were long gone.

Taking a moment or two to regain her composure, she roved her quiet gaze over the landscape. She was a fortunate woman to be living amidst such beauty. There were many folk who would give a lot for just a glimpse of this little piece of God's Heaven.

From where she stood, the view went on for miles. She could see her own little cottage tucked into the ring of trees like an egg in a bird's nest, and beyond that she located Potts End farmhouse, with its smoking chimney and pretty orchard – and oh, look there! Surely that was Danny the milkman, striding out across the fields.

She walked on a little way and stopped again, her legs feeling like a ton weight; although she was without the patchwork counterpane, the bag was beginning to weigh heavier at every step. She wondered if she should leave it behind and fetch it later, when she felt more able. Or maybe that nice young man Danny would pick it up tomorrow, when out on his morning rounds.

Her thoughts switched to Emily. First thing tomorrow, she must go and see Aggie. There were things the other woman needed to know. With that in mind she struggled on, pausing every now and then to rest awhile.

Her cottage lay away to the right, across Aggie's top field then over the little bridge. Thrilled at the prospect of being back in her own home, Lizzie quickened her pace.

~

Coming up from the farm, Danny saw her – a small figure in the distance, wending her way across the fields, and seeming to find it hard work. Concerned as to what Lizzie was doing out there in

411

the middle of nowhere, he set off towards her.

He didn't see Clem Jackson until he'd gone across the bottom field, but then he straightaway recognised the burly, upright figure pushing across the hills, with his fearful dog Badger walking obediently by his side. Whenever the animal began to trot off on its own, it was soon brought back under control by a whack of the thick birchstick in its master's iron fist.

'Somebody should put that stick across his own damned back!' Danny said aloud. Angered by Jackson's cruelty, and seeing how Lizzie was not too far from crossing that madman's path, Danny broke into a run. 'LIZZIE!'

She didn't hear him. Too far away and intent on her journey, Lizzie pushed on, eager to be home and in her own cosy parlour.

'LIZZIE, WAIT ON!' Danny's voice was carried by the heightening breeze, but still she didn't hear him. Nor did she see Clem Jackson coming up behind her.

Skirting the spinney, Danny was unable to see exactly what was happening, though when he emerged, he was horrified to see the dog bounding towards Lizzie. He saw how she cowered, her arms across her face, and Jackson running up, waving the stick and shouting, though Danny could not make out what was being said.

His first instinct was that Jackson had set the dog on Lizzie. 'JACKSON, YOU BASTARD!'

This time his voice *was* heard, and as he came on them, Jackson was dragging his dog off Lizzie, who by now was on the ground.

Danny's first instinct was to help Lizzie. Thrusting the other man aside, he fell to his knees, greatly relieved to see she was not badly mauled. All the same, she was frighteningly pale and shaking uncontrollably. Sliding his arms round her, he sat her up, his face turned now to the other man. Enraged, he demanded, 'What the hell were you thinking of, you mad bugger, setting your dog on a helpless woman! What kind of monster are you?'

He would have gone for Jackson, but Lizzie put her hand across his arm. 'No! He didn't set the dog on me,' she lied. 'The dog saw me stumble and he wanted to play. I just fell over.' She managed a smile. 'It was nobody's fault. Look, I'm all right. I just need to get home. Please. Get me home.'

Falling back into his arms, she closed her eyes. 'I'm tired, that's all . . . so tired.' She had been terrified out of her wits when Jackson sent the dog after her. She heard: 'Look 'ere, boy, we've a trespasser. Mekking for my field, are you, old woman? It seems to me you need teaching a lesson.' With one, swift command he had sent the dog hurtling towards her.

In the moment she was knocked to the ground, Jackson heard Danny's voice, and quickly called the dog to heel. 'Keep your trap shut, you stupid old fool,' he warned her. 'Unless you want more trouble than you can handle.'

The last thing Lizzie wanted was trouble, either for herself, or for Aggie's family. Besides, she was so relieved to see Danny, the attack didn't seem important. She wasn't hurt, and apart from a few bruises and a quickening heart, there was no harm done that she could see.

Danny wasn't convinced by Lizzie's explanation, but he could see she was ill. 'I'll get you home,' he promised.

Collecting her bag from where it had fallen, he then gently lifted her into his arms, at the same time giving the other man a stark warning. 'If I thought you *had* set the dog on her, you'd be a sorry man, Jackson!'

Jackson merely grinned in that unbearable, sly manner he had. 'You'd best mind yer mouth, Williams,' he said. 'You heard what the old woman said. Nobody touched her. She fell over . . . the dog thought she wanted to play – didn't yer, Badge? – and he ran across. There's nowt more to it than that.'

He watched them leave; Danny holding Lizzie close, and Lizzie glancing warily backwards. He deliberately winked at her, laughing when she wearily turned away. 'You're a wise old owl,' he muttered under his breath. 'You'll keep your trap shut all right.'

By the time Danny had got to the door of the

cottage, Lizzie seemed to have revived a little. 'Put mc down, please, son.'

With the same tenderness with which he'd picked her up, Danny put her down, noting how unsteady she was on her feet. 'If you tell me where the key is, I'll unlock the door for you.'

Lizzie pointed to the bag. 'Look in the purse at the side,' she instructed. 'You'll find it in there.'

Danny found the key and, opening the door, led her inside. As they entered the parlour, the cold air struck damp. 'I'll have a fire going in no time,' he said. 'Then I'll make you a hot drink before I fetch the doctor.' Leading her to the armchair he sat her down.

'I don't want no doctor.' Lizzie had no time for that sort of thing.

'You're proper poorly, my love. Even I can see that.'

Being as Lizzie had already set the fire for when she returned home, Danny soon had it lit and crackling away. 'By!' He rubbed his hands together and held them up against the flames. 'That'll soon warm your bones,' he told her.

Next he went to the scullery and, on Lizzie's instructions, located everything he needed to make her a brew of cocoa. There was no fresh milk, so he used boiling water and a grating of nutmeg to pep it up. He found a tiny bottle of old-looking brandy and added a teaspoon of that, too. 'Sip it gently,' he urged, 'but drink it all down.' Which she did.

'Now then, where will I find a blanket? You need something to keep out the cold until the room warms up.'

Lizzie didn't argue. 'Upstairs in the chest of drawers – front bedroom, bottom drawer,' she said, her teeth chattering.

He was up the stairs and back down in a matter of minutes. Tucking the blanket tightly about her, he asked worriedly, 'Wouldn't it be better if we got you up to your bed?'

'No. I'll be fine where I am, thank you all the same, Danny.'

He sighed through his smile. 'Are you always this stubborn?'

'Some might say so.'

'Right! Well, you sit tight while I fetch the doctor.'

'Didn't I already tell you, I don't want no doctor!'

'Now look here, Lizzie.' He tried to reason with her. 'You're not well. Let him look you over, that's all I'm asking.'

'No.' She spelled out her words slowly and deliberately. 'NO DOCTOR.'

'Oh, what am I going to do with you, eh?'

'Fetch Aggie.'

'Is that what you really want?'

'It's what I said, isn't it?'

He was relieved that at least she was admitting she needed somebody, if not the doctor. 'And will you be all right while I'm gone?'

Reaching out, Lizzie placed her hand in his. 'You're a lovely man,' she said gratefully. 'You've brought me home just as you promised, and you've made me warm and comfortable. I thank you for that, but now, I'd be obliged if you'd please fetch Aggie.'

Lizzie was fond of Danny. In her heart she believed she had done him a terrible wrong, just as she had wronged Emily, John and Rosie, for they were all caught up in a mess of her making.

That was what she truly believed. And that was what she must confess, God help her! For some reason, it seemed vitally important that she did it this day – this minute, even.

Before he left, Danny made her promise that she would not move, or try to do anything, until Aggie got there. Once he had secured that promise, he was on his way, running across the fields as though his own life depended on it. Stubborn as a mule, she was. Didn't want a doctor . . . wanted Aggie instead. He chuckled to himself. The old dear certainly knew her own mind.

When he burst in through the kitchen door, Aggie almost leaped out of her shoes; as it was she dropped the cabbage she was slicing, and the knife with it. 'Danny! What's wrong, lad?'

'It's Lizzie,' he answered breathlessly. 'She

collapsed near the top field. I carried her home and made her comfortable.' For the moment he said nothing about Clem Jackson and the dog. 'She really ought to see a doctor, but she won't. It's you she wants. "Fetch Aggie", that's what she said, and if I were you I'd get up there a bit sharpish. The poor old dear doesn't look at all well.'

Running to the door, Aggie took her coat from the hook and, throwing it on, began doing up the buttons as she went. 'I'll make my way up there now,' she said. 'You'll find Emily in the barn sorting out the cabbages. Ask her to put the stew on, and I'll be back soonever I can.' She gave a swift look around, then grabbed a can of milk, a pan of stewed apples, a couple of eggs and a small loaf of freshly-baked bread. 'Happen she's got no food in.' She quickly stowed them in her brown basket and set off.

Danny followed her out. 'I'll see Emily, then I'll come up to Lizzie's. You might need me.'

'That's a good idea,' she said, 'but give us a minute or two. Lizzie's a very private person. I don't know why she's asked for me, unless it's to stay with her until she feels better, but it might be best when you get back, if you don't come into the cottage straight away.'

Danny nodded. 'I understand. But I'll not be far away, you can be sure of that. If you need me, just yell and I'll be there in the wink of an eye.'

While Aggie hurried to the cottage, Danny

went in search of Emily and Cathleen. He looked in the barn and they weren't there. He peered into the other buildings and there was still no sign of them, not even when he called their names across the yard.

Growing anxious, he went in search of them further afield. And there they were, the two of them, playing in the orchard. Little Cathleen was running round the trees, screeching with delight, while her mammy came after her, making animal noises. Just then, Emily swept Cathleen into her arms, pretending to bite her. 'No, Mammy! NO!' Cathleen was in fits of laughter.

On seeing Danny she squirmed out of Emily's grasp and ran to him. 'Don't let Mammy get me!' She clung to his leg. 'She wants to eat me all up!'

'You'd best run then!' Dropping her carefully to the ground he watched her run and hide behind a stack of straw, her little face peeking out and her eyes shining with merriment.

While she hid, Danny told Emily what had happened. 'I'd best go up there,' Emily said. 'It might be that we'll need to get the doctor after all.'

Danny persuaded her otherwise. 'No. Your mam said to give her a few minutes then I was to go after her. I'll go up there with Cathleen, my love. We'll be back soon enough. Don't worry.'

For the sake of the child, Emily agreed. 'All right, but if you need me, come and get me.' She felt guilty about Lizzie. It was rumoured in the village that she had not been too well of late, and yet she had still gone to visit John, though no one was sure where John was these days.

'She's had letters postmarked Liverpool,' the postmaster had gossiped, but that was all anyone knew. Apart from something Lizzie had let slip to the man. 'She said as how John had sent her the money to go and see him – some special event, from what I can make out, but she wouldn't say no more than that. She only told me that much because she wanted me to take care of the stray cats while she was away, and she gave me a key to open the windows so the cottage wouldn't get too damp.'

Emily had thought about John ever since. In the long, lonely years since he'd been gone, Lizzie had made her so unwelcome, that in the end she had given up trying to visit. But now the old woman was poorly, and she wanted to help if she could.

Apart from that, she needed so much to talk with Lizzie. In the morning, if all was well, she would go and see her, and maybe this time, John's aunt would give her news of him at dear last. Emily hoped so, because for a long time now, she had been desperate to know how he was.

~

By the time Aggie arrived at the cottage, Lizzie was sound asleep. At first when there was no answer to her knocking, Aggie feared the worst, and when she inched open the door to find Lizzie slumped in the chair her heart sank to her boots. 'Lizzie?' She gently shook her. 'It's Aggie, come to see you.' She shook her again. 'Lizzie!'

Startled out of a deep sleep, Lizzie opened her eyes. 'About time an' all!' To Aggie's great relief, she sat up straight. 'You took an age getting here, lass.'

'I rushed over as quick as I could,' Aggie told her. 'But never mind that, I'm here now. So what have you been up to, eh? Travelling to God knows where and wearing yourself out. And why won't you let the doctor come and see you?' She was pleased to see how Lizzie had some colour in her cheeks and her eyes were bright enough, she thought. But there was something about Lizzie that worried her. 'Where do you feel ill, love? Do you hurt?' Waiting for an answer, she held Lizzie's hand.

The other woman shook her head. 'I'm just tired. Me every bone aches.' Her old eyes twinkled. 'And me feet are terrible sore. By! It was a long hard trek to get home.'

'You shouldn't have walked across the fields,' Aggie chided. 'Old Tom only lives a stride from the tram-stop. He'd gladly have brought you home on his cart. All you had to do was ask.'

Lizzie managed a laugh. 'I've seen his old cart, and I wouldn't fancy being jolted down the lane on that. It wouldn't have been me feet that hurt, it would have been my poor backside. And you know how he likes to josh with the women. No, lass. I'm too old for all that.' She pointed to her empty cup. 'Is that milk you've got there, Aggie love? Ooh, I'd love a cup of tea! Get yourself one, while you're at it.'

Aggie was puzzled. 'Is that all you wanted me for, to sit and drink tea with you?' she asked. 'I ran all the way here when Danny told me you were badly. Lizzie, are you sure it's me you need, and not a doctor?'

Lizzie nodded. 'I told Danny I didn't need no doctor, and I don't. It's you I need. Now then, do as you're told, lass. Get the two of us a nice cuppa tea and sit yerself down. Yer'll find biscuits in the tin wi' the late Queen on the front, God bless her. That's right, it's in the pantry . . . Then come right back in, Aggie. There's summat I have to tell you, and it can't wait no longer.'

Intrigued, Aggie quickly did as she was bid.

Bringing the tea, Aggie gave Lizzie her cup and sat herself on the chair beside her. 'No, lass. Go an' sit on the sofa where I can see you,' Lizzie instructed.

When Aggie moved to seat herself on the sofa opposite, Lizzie asked outright, 'Do you think your Emily is happy, wed to Danny?'

Momentarily taken aback, Aggie thought for a minute. There had been many a time when she had asked herself that same thing. 'She *seems* happy enough,' she said guardedly.

'Does she ever mention John?'

'Sometimes, when the two of us are on our own. Though I'm sure he's on her mind all the time.'

'Do you think she and John would have been happy together?' Lizzie needed to find out the answers to what was plaguing her.

Taking a deep breath, Aggie sighed. 'She still loves him, I'm sure of that. But it's no good speculating as to what might have happened, is it, Lizzie? If this . . . if that. What's the use of it? John's not here. Emily's married to Danny, and they're raising Cathleen as his daughter. Things would have been different, of course, if only John hadn't done what he did. It was a great shock to Emily and I truly don't think she's ever got over it. But as far as I'm concerned, it's all water under the bridge.'

Lizzie paused before embarking on the truth. 'It could 'ave been different, lass,' she murmured, 'if only I hadn't interfered.'

'Now that's silly talk, Lizzie. You mustn't blame yourself.' Aggie thought it a strange thing for the other woman to have said. 'I don't see how you could have changed anything,' she said forthrightly. 'Your John did a bad thing. He got my Emily with child, then went off and set up with some other woman. That wasn't your fault. You couldn't have foreseen that, any more than I could.'

Lizzie thought there was only one way to say it, and she did. 'He did come back for his Emily. He loved her, y'see ... still does, I reckon.' She paused, knowing she would shock Emily's mam with what she was about to divulge. 'He didn't go away on his own accord,' she blurted out. 'The letter I delivered to Emily was all a lie ... there *was* no other woman. Y'see, it were *me* as sent him away.'

'What?' Aggie was suddenly bolt upright on the sofa. 'What are you saying? I don't understand. Why would he write that he'd found some other woman, if he hadn't? And why did you send him away?'

'It wasn't easy, but he was shocked and hurt when he saw Emily with Danny and Cathleen. I lied to him. I told him they were happily married, that Cathleen was Danny's child. I convinced him that going away was the only thing to do. I did it, because I didn't want him taking on the responsibility of another man's child.' There! It was said and there was no going back.

Aggie almost leaped out of her chair. 'That's nonsense and well you know it!' Bearing in mind that the old woman was poorly, Aggie tried to keep calm. 'Everybody knows the child was John's.'

Lizzie shook her head. 'Gossip,' she said. 'Vicious gossip.'

'Did John tell you that?' Aggie asked angrily. 'Did *he* claim he wasn't the father?'

'He thought the child was Danny's.'

Aggie was trying hard to keep control. 'But why in God's name would he think that?'

'Because I told him so.'

It was all too much for Aggie. Dropping back on the sofa, she said in a quiet voice, 'Lizzie, tell me something, will you?'

'That's what I'm trying to do, lass.'

'You're saying that Cathleen is *not* John's child, and that John believed *Danny* was the father. Have I got that right?'

Lizzie nodded.

'So John denied being the father, did he?'

'He didn't need to. I already knew he wasn't.'

'How could you possibly know that?'

'Because Emily . . .' Remembering her promise to the girl, she hesitated. Then: 'Because your lass told me so herself. She made me promise I would never tell, but I reckon it's time you knew the truth.'

For a long, shocked moment, Aggie fell silent. Then she asked: 'Is that the God's honest truth? Emily told you herself *that John was not the father*?'

'As God is my judge.'

There was another long silence. Aggie simply could not understand why Emily should con-fess that to Lizzie, while all the time letting her own mother and family believe that John was Cathleen's father. It was too upsetting. Moreover, it posed yet another question, which she had to ask. 'So who *is* Cathleen's father? Did she tell you that?'

Lizzie shook her head. 'No, lass. I did ask, but she wouldn't tell me.' Lizzie remembered the very day when Emily had cleared John of having got her with child. 'All I know is, she stood in this very room and told me that John was not to blame. When I asked her who was the father, she sort of panicked.' Lizzie recalled how Emily had rushed off, unwilling to stay and talk. 'She seemed frightened – refused to be drawn on the matter, other than to clear John's name.'

Aggie leaped at the chance. 'She could have been lying to protect him!'

'No, lass. She was telling the truth. Besides, you know as well as I do that Emily is not given to lying.'

Aggie was mortified. 'You're right. I've never known her to lie – about anything.' She had another, more burning question. 'You said she seemed frightened to talk. Are you sure about that?'

'As sure as I can be, yes.'

Now Aggie was out of her chair and pacing the room. Something had come into her mind and it was a terrifying thing. 'God Almighty!' She put her hand to her throat. 'Oh, dear God Almighty!'

Lizzie looked up to see an expression of sheer horror on Aggie's face. 'What's wrong?' she asked.

Though her heart was beating too fast for her

to breathe easily, Aggie tried to conceal her fear. 'It's nothing, Lizzie.' She smiled, but it didn't reach her eyes; instead it froze on her face like a mask. 'It's just that this whole thing has got me worried. Why didn't Emily tell *me*? Why would she come to you instead of me? What reason would she have, and why did John desert her the way he did?' The frantic questions tumbled out.

'I already told you . . . it were me as persuaded him to go.'

Aggie resumed her seat. 'Look, Lizzie, I think you'd best tell me what happened, right from the minute she came through the door. I need you to tell me *everything*!' she instructed. 'Don't leave out a single thing.'

So Lizzie told her. She explained how John had saved almost every penny he'd earned while he was at sea. She revealed how he had come home that particular day. 'Full of joy at being back and wanting to ask Emily if she would be his wife. Y'see, he had every intention of buying the debt from Clem Jackson and giving you back your farm.'

'So why didn't he stay?'

Lizzie went on, more slowly now. Tears of remorse were gathering in her eyes. 'As I recall, it was the child's birthday. John was making his way across to your farm to see Emily, when he saw her . . . with Cathleen and Danny. They were laughing together, seemingly very happy in each other's company. From the way the child ran to

Emily, John could tell straight off that she was Emily's. He didn't know what to think, so he came to me, and I told him that Emily had cheated on him, and that Cathleen was the result.'

She held nothing back, even though her voice shook with the shame of her confession. 'I made him believe that Danny was the father, and that he was now wed to Emily, and they were very happy together.'

'Oh no, Lizzie,' Aggie breathed. She was heartbroken for her poor daughter. 'You should never have done that. You should have let them talk.'

'I know that now.' As she spoke, the tears poured down Lizzie's face. 'I didn't want him saddled with another man's bairn. I was trying to protect him, you see? I was so angry with Emily. I thought she'd waited till his back was turned and let another man bed her. I thought she was little more than a trollop. Oh Aggie! What an old fool I am! It's too late now. All too late.'

Seeing her distressed like that, was deeply upsetting to Aggie.

'No, Lizzie.' She went and put her arms round the other woman's shoulders. 'You did right under the circumstances. Any other mother would have done the same. All you knew was what you could see with your own eyes, and John the same. Emily had a child and it was not John's responsibility. What else could you think of her, but that she had cheated on him?'

She could see now, how Lizzie might have sent John away with a lie. 'Yes, you did right to send him away. I would have done the very same.'

Lizzie brightened at Aggie's brave words. 'Would you, lass? Would you honestly?'

'Yes. If it had been the other way round, I wouldn't have thought twice.' She gave Lizzie a hug. 'Now then, stop your worriting. Let's go through it all again, and we'll see what we can come up with, eh?'

At the back of her mind was the other thing.

After what Lizzie had just told her, it tormented her now, like never before.

Thankful for Aggie's comforting words, Lizzie asked her to make another brew. 'The tea's gone cold, lass.'

Later, they went through the story again, comparing notes.

And the more she learned about Emily's predicament, the stronger grew Aggie's terrible suspicions.

CHAPTER SIXTEEN

'I'D BEST GIVE you a hand before we set off for the cottage.' Having come into the barn to give Emily a kiss, Danny was concerned to see her lifting the heavy crates of vegetables. 'You and Cathleen sort the cabbages while I stack these up against the wall.'

Emily was grateful for the help, but said, 'I thought you were in a hurry to get to the cottage?'

'And so I am, but Lizzie's in good hands with your mam.' While he stacked the crates, he carried on talking. 'This job won't take but a few minutes. Besides, I wouldn't be much of a man if I left my wife to stack these heavy crates.'

'All right.' Emily knew him well enough by now to realise that once Danny made up his mind, there was no changing it. 'I suppose you're right – two pairs of hands are better than one. Between us we'll soon have it done.'

And so they did.

When the last crate was stacked, Danny grabbed

Emily into his arms and looking into her brown eyes, whispered of how much he loved her.

'You're the best thing that ever happened to me,' he said. 'I know we got off to a shaky start, but now I can never imagine being without you.'

When Emily gave no reply, he kissed her tenderly and holding her at arm's length, told her how pretty she was.

Emily smiled at that. 'What? Covered in muck and looking like a scarecrow?'

'All of that,' he laughed, kissing her again. 'Look, sweetheart, I'd best be off. Cathleen and I will be there in minutes. Though I'm sure, with your mam in charge, everything is fine and dandy up at the cottage.'

'I hope so.' Emily had never forgotten the time she had gone to Lizzie with the truth about John not being the father of her child. She hoped Lizzie would keep her promise and not say anything, because if her mam ever found out – well, she just didn't dare think about the consequences.

A moment later, Danny was walking across the fields towards the cottage, with Cathleen dancing along beside him, while Emily stood at the barn door watching them go. You're a good man, Danny Williams, she thought. I don't deserve you.

∼

Having passed the barn on his way to the bull-field, where he loved to admire the great beasts, Clem

Jackson had seen Danny take Emily into his arms, and he was greatly excited by it. He still had fond memories of that day in the barn, when he had possessed the girl against her will.

Now, leaning on the gate, his huge dog sitting obediently at his feet, he watched Danny leave. There seemed to be a lot happening this morning, he thought, with all this coming and going.

'I expect it's that damned old woman again!' he said to the dog, which instinctively curved its back in fear. 'You should have finished her off while you had the chance.'

Prodding the cur with his cane, he snapped, 'I'm going to find out what all the fuss is about. You just stay where you are!' When he took a step away and the dog seemed about to follow him, he held the cane to its nose. 'Badger – *Stay*!' The animal immediately whined and skulked to the ground, its big frightened eyes uplifted to him.

Grinning triumphantly, he stomped off and left it there.

~

With Danny and Cathleen gone, Emily got on with her chores. She had swept the floor of the barn and was bagging the last of the cabbages when Clem's hands gripped her shoulders. With a cry, she tried to turn but he held her there, one fist clutching both her hands behind her back, and the other squeezing her neck from the front, holding her in such a way that she couldn't move. She couldn't even kick out, because his legs were tight against hers, effectively pinning her to the wall.

'Well, here we are again, my beauty,' he growled. It was so good to touch her soft skin. 'Been missing me, 'ave yer?'

'Get your filthy hands off me!' Momentarily frozen with shock, Emily hadn't been sure who had taken hold of her. But she was sure now, and she was terrified.

Clem swung her round and smacked the back of his hand hard across her mouth. 'Careful how yer talk to me, lady,' he warned, 'unless you want a taste o' my fist.' As the blood trickled from the corners of her mouth, he leaned forward and licked at it with the tip of his tongue. Forcibly restraining her, he pushed his face close to hers, his mouth lolling open in a sinister kind of grin. 'I'm sorry to have neglected yer, lass, only I've been that busy with my other women, I ain't had much time for you. This past week or so, they seem to have deserted me – fickle creatures, women, don't yer think? But I'm 'ere now, so you'll be glad to know we can tek up where we left off.'

Emily began desperately struggling. 'ENOUGH, YOU BITCH!' He raised his hand and slapped her round the head; chuckling when she fell at his feet, dazed and bleeding. 'That's better.' Getting to his knees, he straddled her and began undoing his trouser-buttons. 'Don't go unconscious on me,' he told her, breathing heavily, 'I like my women to have a bit of life in 'em.'

It was when she felt her skirt being lifted and his whole weight bearing down on her, that Emily seized her chance. Taking him by surprise, she kicked out and managed to clamber free from under him. By the time he realised what was happening and chased after her, drawing up his trousers as he went, Emily had got hold of the pitchfork and was ready for him. 'Come on then!' She was like a wild thing. 'I'm ready for you now. *Come on*!' Pointing the sturdy steel-pronged fork at his stomach, Emily would not have hesitated to use it.

Unfortunately she did not allow for his cunning. In a swift movement, Clem stooped to grab a handful of dust from the heap she had swept on the barn floor and threw it into Emily's face. As she reeled away, he darted forward.

Half-blinded and still dazed from the beating he had given her, Emily ran. She couldn't make for the door because he was blocking the way, so she scrambled upwards, into the hayloft, where she planned to drop down the outside shaft to the ground. She was halfway up the ladder when he seized her by the ankle. 'Thought you could get away from me, did you?' he panted.

With superhuman effort, Emily managed to kick him away and jump down to the ground. Racing for the door, she thought she was safe. She even managed to get outside, but Clem was right behind her. 'Oh no, yer don't!' Grabbing her round the waist, he carried her back inside, punching her in the face when she started shouting for help.

'There's no help,' he snarled. 'So you might as well keep still.'

~

Having woken from his afternoon nap, Grandad had gone to the window in time to see Emily run from the barn. He saw Jackson come after her and he saw how bravely the lass tried to fight him off.

Frantic with fear, he knew only too well what Clem had in mind. 'Dear God Almighty!' He began shouting, 'AGGIE!' When there was no response, he went to the door and opening it, yelled again: 'AGGIE, FOR CHRISSAKE!'

Taking the thick woolly jumper from the chairback he pulled it on over his nightshirt, then sliding his feet into his slippers, he started his awkward way down the stairs, calling as he went, 'AGGIE! DANNY!' He soon began to realise that he was the only one who could help. With that thought in mind he gathered a superhuman strength.

He knew well enough where the shotgun was kept, for wasn't he the one who some years before had built the cupboard to keep it safe?

~

While this scene from Hell was being enacted in the dark cathedral of Potts End barn, another man, walking steadily towards the farm, believed himself to be approaching Heaven.

Some distance away, oblivious to what was going on, Michael Ramsden covered the tracks to the farmhouse. 'Home at last,' he breathed. Pausing to view the familiar, beloved landscape he was filled with awe, wondering how he could ever have walked away from such a beautiful place and his precious family.

Over the past ten years, he had known deprivation and despair; he had rummaged in filth for a bite to eat and thought many a time to end it all. But now, with John Hanley's help he had regained his health and his self-respect; he had something to live for. I've some making up to do now, he thought ashamedly, moving on. A terrible wrong to put right. There was no guarantee that they'd have him back. He dreaded meeting his father's eye: was the dear old man still alive? And his young daughter was now a mother herself; he, a grandfather. As for Aggie, his wife . . . mere words were no good to explain the way he felt about her, and about what he had put her through.

For a moment, Michael was tempted to sit and weep, but the strange peace of the place, and the hope within him, dried his tears. It was time for action. He needed his family. He needed to let them know how much he loved and missed them. As for Clem Jackson, it was more than time he faced him head to head, man to man . . . time it was all thrashed out, one way or another! He had never been so determined to rid himself and his family of the plague that was Jackson and now, thanks to John, he had the means to do it.

As he pushed along, head bent and his heart alive with determination, Michael did not spot Aggie at first. But then, as he raised his head he saw her – and emotion clogged his throat. 'Oh, my God . . . AGGIE!' he cried, but no sound came out.

She was closer to the farm than he was, and now as he called her name again, this time in a quivering cry, she went out of earshot, an urgent purpose in her gait as she pelted towards the back of the farmhouse and out of sight.

His heart lifting at the sight of his precious woman, Michael also took to his heels and ran after her.

~

In the barn, Jackson had Emily at his mercy. 'Now then, my pretty, let's 'ave no more trouble from yer.' He knelt once again, rolled up her skirt, and revelled at the sight of her soft white thighs.

'Don't seem right that yon fool of a milkman should 'ave this all to himself, let alone striding around *my* farm as if he owns the bloody place. I'll set the dog on him, I will,' he said viciously, and reached forward to fondle her. His mood changed.

'We made a good 'un in that daughter o' yourn, didn't we, eh? Growing up fast, she is – looks the image of her mammy. By! I wouldn't be surprised if one dark night, I didn't mistake her for you . . . *if you know what I mean?*'

The more Emily struggled, the more he goaded her. Try as she might, she was no match for his brute strength.

But there was another who was, and that was Aggie who, after talking with Lizzie, had finally seen the truth about Emily, about Cathleen and Clem. Some terrible instinct had made her run back here, had made her run all the way . . . At that moment, she was standing behind him with the pitchfork at his neck.

'I could so easily run you through from back to front,' she said in a low, harsh whisper. 'Mek no mistake, I won't even hesitate.' And to prove her intention, she gave her brother a taste of the steel when she jabbed it and pierced his skin. 'Get up from there!'

The sound of his sister's voice put the fear of God in his cowardly heart. His face etched in terror, he slowly got to his feet.

'Over there!' Another sharp jab in his neck sent him stumbling towards the wall. When he hesitated, he was sent forward with another painful jab of the prongs.

When flat to the wall he turned round. Emily had clambered up and was crying but nodding to her mam to show that she was all right. Aggie for her part, was again advancing towards him. At the look of murder on her face, he shrank back, cowering like a baby. 'She wanted me to. She was ready for it,' he said lamely. 'Same as before.'

Standing only inches from him now, with the pitchfork pressed so hard against his bare belly it would have taken only one sharp push to skewer his guts, Aggie knew real cold hatred. Killing him was what she intended. But first, she wanted him to suffer.

'You never learn, do you?' Aggie's voice was as hard and unforgiving as her expression. *She had never forgotten how he took her against her will, when she was younger even than Emily had been.*

Fuelled with loathing, her eyes bored into his. 'I was just a girl . . . your own sister! That night all them years ago, when you crept into my room, drunk as the devil and out of your mind, you took my maidenhead and now I've just learned you did the same to my daughter, you evil man, and what's more, you've got our Cathleen lined up too – that innocent young lass. You mean to ruin that same child – your own daughter, damn you! Damn you to Hell!'

The deep disgust she had borne all these years

was etched on her face. 'Your own sister!' She shuddered. For what seemed a lifetime she had lived with her own shame and said nothing, because the horror of what her brother had done to her was too awful to speak about. Because of him she had felt tainted and dirty, unfit to share the lives of ordinary, decent people, until she had met her Michael, who had restored her belief in life and in herself. *Oh Michael, if only you were here . . .*

'I mean to kill you, Clem,' Aggie said, and he knew he was lost. His one hope, the dog, was too scared of him to move from the gate where he had ordered it to stay. For the first time in his wasted life, Clem Jackson tried to pray.

Thankfully, Emily did not hear her mother speak of her own traumatic rape because, having seen Danny striding over the fields, she had limped out of the barn towards him, blood pouring down her face.

Grandad heard, though. As he entered the barn, shotgun at the ready, he was stunned by what Aggie was saying. And yet he found he already knew! He had always been aware of some tension between his daughter-in-law and that bully-boy brother of hers, ever since the foul creature had bought his way into their lives and taken over the farm. This terrible scene confirmed an old suspicion.

Shuffling closer, he levelled his gun at Jackson.

'Move away, Aggie.' His voice was flat. Lifeless.

'Dad, no!' Shocked to see her father-in-law there, Aggie stood her ground. 'Go back to the house. This is between him and me.'

Seeing his chance, Jackson kicked the pitchfork away, sent Aggie flying across the barn, and made his escape.

Behind him, the old man fired off a shot. But Jackson was already out of range.

～

Hearing the gunshot, Danny told Emily to stay with Cathleen. 'You'll be all right now,' he promised. 'Don't move from here, my darlings. I'll be back for you both.'

Then he went off at a run, following Jackson, who was headed away from the barn and down, towards the back field.

In a matter of minutes, Danny was on him. 'You filthy bastard!' Enraged by what Emily had told him, Danny swung him round and with a clenched fist gave him a mighty punch that sent the big man reeling backwards. He went after him again, and again, until Jackson was once more in fear for his life. Finally, hitting out with bunched fist, he managed to send Danny sprawling.

While Danny was down, Clem scrambled over the gate and into the field – but Danny was right behind him.

Leaping on Jackson from behind, he forced

Clem down. The fight was fierce, with first Jackson being floored, then Danny – and now Jackson was running again. But Danny was determined. Going after him, he fetched him such a hard upper-cut that the older man reeled back and fell in a crumpled heap, bloodied and beaten. 'Get up!' Gasping and panting, Danny hauled him to his feet. 'I'm not finished with you yet!' he spat.

The blows were exchanged with murderous ferocity; first Danny, then the other man, and now Danny again.

From the far end of the field where they had been dozing, the bulls were alerted by the disturbance. Curious at first, they ambled over to where they could see the two men locked in battle, their own wicked bloodlust slowly rising. The bulls stood awhile, scraping the ground with one front hoof, and then, heads down, at full speed, they thundered across the field. This was their territory, and they tolerated no intruders.

The old man saw them charging, as did Aggie and Emily, who had gathered at the gate to see Jackson take the beating he deserved. Emily hid her daughter against her skirts. '*Danny, watch out!*' they screamed in unison.

Emily started to climb over the gate to rescue him, but Aggie pulled her back. 'No! You'll be killed!' Then all three were roaring out to warn him. 'DANNY! THE BULLS! GET OUT OF THERE!'

What followed happened so quickly there was little anyone could have done. For whatever reason, the bulls made straight for Jackson. Slicing his flesh with their short thick horns, they threw him in the air, and when he fell again, they went in for the kill.

As much as he hated the other man, Danny could not stand by and see another human being trampled and gored to death. Instinct set in. Oblivious to the shouts of his family, he snatched off his jacket and ran at the bulls, waving his coat and attracting their attention away from Jackson.

Incensed, they turned their tiny red eyes on him. When in that moment they came at him, he dropped the coat and took to his heels, making for the gate and safety.

He was almost there when one of the bulls stabbed him in the side with its horn. He stumbled, straightened and clung to the fence, gasping from pain and a terrible fatigue, but by then the same bull had charged again, and gored him in the leg. As he lay there, helpless and in shock, all Danny could do was pray.

Suddenly, the air was shattered by the *crack!* of a gunshot. The bulls paused in their attack and then ambled away, as if nothing had happened.

Slipping in and out of consciousness, Danny heard the old man yelling, 'For God's sake . . . get him out of there!' Then came another voice he did not recognise. He saw Michael's face looking down on him. 'You'll be all right, son,' the man who was his father-in-law said, lifting him effortlessly into his arms. 'I've got you now.'

PART SIX

~

March, 1910

What Goes Around

CHAPTER SEVENTEEN

J ust as she had done every afternoon for the past week, Emily climbed the stairs to the first floor of the infirmary. At the top she turned left and continued down the corridor, quickening her steps as she went.

In a matter of minutes she approached the ward. Weakened by the loss of blood but, thankfully, free from the dreaded septicaemia, which would have cost him his life, Danny was well on the way to recovery. During the first few days following his brutal fight with Clem Jackson, he had drifted in and out of consciousness, but now, thanks to good care and tending, he was regaining his strength.

As she thanked the nurse who was greeting the families at visiting time, Danny saw her and his face lit up. 'Hello, sweetheart.' He held out his arms for a kiss. 'Home tomorrow, God willing.' He beamed at his wife.

'Don't get your hopes up too high,' Emily

warned. 'Wait until the doctor tells you himself.'

'He already has.' Danny explained how the doctor had been called away for some emergency or other. 'He dropped in to see me . . . said he was so pleased with my progress, he might let me go home tomorrow. Matron should be round any minute to confirm it.'

Emily was delighted. 'Oh, love! That's such good news.'

His face was wreathed in smiles. 'You'd best get the fatted calf out,' he joshed. 'They only feed you on carrots in here.'

Holding him for a moment, Emily kissed him with real affection. 'I'll go and find a vase for these daffs and sticky buds,' she said. 'I picked them from up Potts End Lane. Your dad helped me – and he sends his love. Cathleen can't wait to have you back, nor can the rest of us, neither. See you in a minute, love. I want to be here when the matron comes.'

Without further ado she hurried away to search for a vase, but by the time she'd found one and got back to Danny, he was smiling all over his face. 'I've missed her, haven't I?' Emily groaned. 'All right, so what did she say? As if I couldn't guess.' His jubilant face told its own story.

'I shall need my clothes tomorrow, 'cause I'm coming home,' he said excitedly.

Emily was relieved but, 'Don't go getting all worked up and putting yourself back,' she said.

'And what about the stitches?' He had twenty-one stitches in his side, and twelve in his leg. Apparently the gashes had been so deep there had been damage to the muscles. 'Will you be able to get about all right?'

'They've already made me walk slowly round the ward a few times,' he told her, 'but when I come home, I'm to use crutches. When I come back to have the stitches out, I should be off the crutches and walking unaided – that's what I intend.'

'You'll do it. I know you will,' Emily replied fondly. 'As long as you take things easy and don't damage the muscles any more than they are already.'

While he chatted, asking after the family and Michael in particular, Emily told him how good it was to have her father home again. 'At first Mam gave him the tongue-wagging he deserved, and even Grandad had a lot to say . . . after he refused to talk to him for a whole day! It was so much for us all to take in, what with him walking in like a ghost and nearly giving Mam a heart attack, and then the fight with Uncle Clem,' she shuddered, 'and meeting his granddaughter and son-in-law for the very first time . . .'

She took a long, long breath. 'They're all right together now. Oh, Danny! Everything's so wonderful. Once you're home, it'll be just perfect. I feel sure everything will go like clockwork now.'

In that moment, John came into her mind and she felt a pang of regret. Her father had told her of John's part in his rehabilitation, getting him back to work and giving him the chance to regain his mental balance and his self-respect. 'He's wed now – a lovely lass named Rosie – an' he's building a good life for her and their bairns when they come.'

When Michael had come out with this, for a time Emily could think of nothing else, even though she had known about the other woman for years – ever since his letter. Emily still believed he had left her for someone else, all those years ago. She had cried bitter tears in secret, back up in the hayloft, and wondered how it could all have gone so wrong between her and John. But then she put it to the back of her mind, for it was too painful. And now, seeing her brave Danny so well, and knowing her mam and dad were reunited, thanks be to God, her heart was uplifted.

~

The following morning, there were celebrations to prepare. Cathleen and Emily had already hung fancy decorations in the barn, and Aggie was rolling up her sleeves to get the food started. The meat had been cooked last night and the jelly moulds put to set in the cold larder. Now it was time to get the cakes mixed and put in the oven.

Aggie had been up since early light, and now

she was resting in the rocking-chair, a cup of tea in one hand and Mrs Beeton's famous recipe book in the other. 'I were thinking to make some of these fluffy pastry things,' she said to her husband.

'If you want my opinion, I'd stick to what you know best, lass.'

That was Michael, who had got out of bed soon after her and now, tousle-haired and more content than he had been in an age, was pouring himself a brew. 'If I were you, my love, I'd throw that Beeton book in the oven and bake it. Nobody makes cakes like you,' he told her loyally. 'You're the best cook around.'

Aggie laughed. 'You allus were an old flatterer, Michael Ramsden,' she said. 'But you're right. Happen I'll stick to what I know best.'

'That's my woman,' he murmured, coming to nibble her ear. 'Listen to them as knows.'

She looked up at him then, and she thought of how he had gone away and left her to pick up the pieces. But she had never stopped loving him, and never would. Smiling back at him now, she held out her empty cup. 'Make yerself useful and fill that up,' she said with a wink.

Having done that he sat down with her and they talked of events just gone; mainly the demise of Clem Jackson. 'He brought it on himself, but it's a terrible way to go . . . being mauled to death by his own beasts.' It would take Michael many a long year to forgive himself for leaving his elderly father and his womenfolk to the mercies of that warped and evil man.

'He deserved every inch of what he got!' Aggie had sworn her father-in-law to secrecy about her having been molested by Clem. But the bitterness and the loathing of that man, who had deflowered both her and Emily in their tender years, and then turned his eyes on the child ... would live with her for ever. She thanked God for sparing young Cathleen any trace of a physical resemblance to that devil, and her heart ached for the lonely torment and public censure her poor daughter Emily had endured.

Michael saw the dark loathing on her face but mistook the reason for it. 'He's gone now, lass,' he said, holding her hand tight. 'Thanks to you, our Emily was kept safe. What's more, it's only a matter of time afore we get the farm back, you see if we don't.'

'Why does it all have to be so legal-like?' Aggie wanted to know. 'Clem's dead, so we don't owe him owt any more, seeing as he'd got no family but us. Why can't we just take the farm back? It's *our* farm, after all.'

For the umpteenth time, Michael explained. 'When your brother first came here he did pay off all the debts, and so he had a hold on the farm. But then, as it turns out – and none of us knew this – he got into serious gambling. The debts piled up again. He then forged papers of ownership and such, and borrowed money against this place. It all has to be rectified, and it's such a mess, the solicitor says it will take some considerable time.'

Aggie was not given to understanding legal stuff, and right from the first, there was one thing that played on her mind. 'Will we lose Potts End, Michael? Tell me the truth.'

At the request of his aged father, Michael had taken on the responsibility of going through it all with the solicitor. 'I have faith,' he answered thoughtfully, 'but we need to go about it in the right and proper way. In the end though, when rightful ownership is proved and the money's paid back, thanks to the generous loan John Hanley has offered us, it should all come out right.'

Aggie nodded. 'Please, God!' she murmured, hands in prayer. 'This farm is all we've got.'

Michael continued the conversation. 'I only wish John's loan was enough, but that evil bastard borrowed so much against this farm, we've had to take Danny's offer of money as well. I know you've always refused it before.' Ever an honest man, Michael was prepared to work his fingers to the bone to repay both men and with interest. 'Both John and Danny say we're to see their money as a gift, but I can't do that.'

Aggie knew what he was saying and she was proud of him. In spite of that, she harboured reservations. 'It'll take years to pay back.'

'I know – but I'll do it. First Danny, because he and Emily will need a place of their own one day. Then John. Oh, I know he insists he doesn't want or need the money, but my pride's at stake here. I need to pay my dues.'

Aggie saw it differently. 'Pride comes before a fall, or so they say.'

Michael picked up on her doubt. 'What – you want me to take their money and never give it back?'

'No. All I'm saying is, there's no point in breaking yourself to pay it back. If John and Danny say it's a gift, then it's a gift because they love you and want to help you.'

'Yes, lass, I know that. But like I say, I have my pride to think of. God knows I haven't had much to be proud of so far.'

'Listen to me, husband. They each have a business and neither of 'em are short of a bob or two. All I'm saying is, you have your pride I know that, and it's good. But to my mind, the gift of friendship is more important.'

'In what way?'

'Well. If someone thinks enough of you to give you a gift, what might they think, if you can't wait to give that gift back?'

Satisfied that her words had got Michael thinking, she deliberately changed the subject. 'Come on!' She clambered out of her chair. 'I'll get on with the baking while you get washed and changed. You look like the scarecrow outta the field. Besides, you've Danny to fetch home soon, don't forget that.'

'As if I could.' He kissed her and went away, deep in thought. She had touched something in him, with her wise words about friendship and how Danny and John would feel if he threw it all back in their faces. 'Happen she's right,' he murmured. 'Happen pride doesn't come before friendship, after all.'

~

When Danny limped through the door, early that afternoon, the cry went up. 'Welcome home!'

Standing tall and straight, albeit throwing some of his weight onto the crutches, he beamed from ear to ear, his cheeks a slight shade of pink and a look of acute embarrassment on his face. 'It's good to be home,' he said.

Aggie hugged him; Grandad shook him by the hand. 'By! Yer a sight for sore eyes, so yer are,' he exclaimed happily.

Cathleen held his hand and walked with him as he went to the armchair, and Emily watched the two of them with a strangeness in her heart. In her mind's eye she could see John in her husband's place and, for a little while, her thoughts were as muddled and painful as they'd ever been.

That afternoon, while the celebration tea was being set out, Grandad fussed about, wanting to wear this shirt, now that one. Then: 'Why do I need to wear a smart shirt anyway – strangling mesel' when I'd much rather be comfy? It's only a party, after all.'

Aggie insisted he look his best. 'We have company coming, Dad,' she reminded him, 'and I don't want you showing me up.' Throwing the clean shirt and trousers on the bed, she urged him to, 'Get yourself washed and changed and make your way down the stairs. If you need any help getting ready, just give me or Emily a shout.'

'I'll do no such thing!' he replied proudly. 'When the day comes that I can't swill my own face and put on a shirt, I'd sooner it was over.' And so she left him to it.

Danny, too, was of the same mind. Having been set up a bed in the back room until his leg was easier to carry him upstairs, he graciously refused Emily's help. 'It's my leg that is paining,' he told her. 'There's nowt wrong with my arms.' And she, too, was sent out of the room.

'Let the buggers get on with it!' Aggie laughed. 'Michael an' all. I've lost patience with him. The trouble is, none of his clothes seem to fit. He's never put back the weight he lost when he were away, so I've had to nip and tuck his trousers and move a button or two on his shirts, and they still don't seem to fit right. But I keep telling him, he'll look right dandy, if only he'd stop his moaning and groaning!'

Emily sighed. 'Men!'

'But we couldn't do without 'em, that's for sure.' Aggie had gone a whole ten years without her husband and she knew the loneliness in that. 'Oh Lord. There'll be your grandad an' all, upstairs not washing behind his ears and wi' a tidemark round his neck,' she laughed. 'He'll have his shirt done up wrong, and his hair standing on end like he's had some sort o' terrible fright.'

Emily laughed at the image of Grandad, just as her mam described. 'And there'll be Danny hobbling about on one leg, trying to get the other leg into his trousers and falling over in the event. But he'll not ask for help. He'll roll in two hours late rather than do that.'

'Never you mind.' Aggie took a tray of cakes out of the range. 'We're here if they need us, so let's get on with what we've got to do, and leave them to do the same.' Turning the cakes onto a wire-rack to cool, she put the tin in the potsink and set about slicing the meat. 'Where's Cathleen?'

'I left her upstairs getting ready. She's been washed, had her hair brushed till it shines like new-spun silk, and now she's trying on her dressing-up things to see which she might wear.'

'I thought you bought her that nice pink dress with the big sash?'

'I did.'

'So, what's wrong with it?'

457

'Nowt. She'll end up wearing it. When she shows her face downstairs, you see if I'm not right.'

While she was speaking, Emily was busy making the custard for the trifles. When that was done, she cooled it by placing the pan in enough cold water to cover the base. She stirred and stirred with a wooden spoon, keeping the custard free of lumps, and while it continued to cool, she thinly sliced the apples and taking the two cut-glass bowls of set jelly out of the larder, she arranged the slices all over the top.

Next came the helping of drained, bottled raspberries, and a layer of fresh-made sponge cake, and now, when the custard was cold enough, she poured it all over the two trifles, helping it to settle evenly with the back of the wooden spoon. Lastly she sprinkled grated chocolate all over the top, then popped a glacé cherry in the middle; a ring of half-cherries on the outside and they were finished.

'There!' Placing them on the pine-dresser, next to the other dessert of Aggie's butterfly cakes, she stepped back to view the goodies already lined up. There were various platters of sliced cold meats and sausages, home-made savoury herb scones and bread rolls straight out of the oven, little pots of butter, wedges of cheese, and pickles of every kind, and a dish full of succulent, home-boiled beetroot.

The attractive-looking buffet was finished off

with a selection of dressings made by Emily herself. The plates were neatly piled and the cutlery, all wrapped in white linen napkins, lay alongside. There were bowls of seasonal fruit and lashes of cream in large milk jugs, and now, as Aggie placed the sliced lamb next to the bread rolls, the feast was ready and fit for a king.

'That's a grand trifle,' Aggie told Emily. 'You allus were good at trifles.'

Dressed as Emily had predicted, in her flouncy dress of pink and white, Cathleen came running down from her bedroom. 'What about my cake?' she asked. 'Do you think they'll like it?'

Her cake had pride of place on a china cake-stand with a big paper doily beneath it. A mis-shapen thing with a sag in the middle and the ugliest marzipan-man uneasily straddling it, sup-posed to represent her daddy, the cake was an eyesore, and heartily amused all who looked on it.

'It's the best thing there,' Emily told her lov-ingly. 'You did well, sweetheart.'

'You did wonderful!' Aggie exclaimed. 'They'll be fighting over it, you mark my words, lass.' She and Emily exchanged a smile and a wink.

'I saw that!' A canny child, Cathleen didn't miss a thing, but she saw the humour of it and laughed with them. 'I don't think I'll let them cut it,' she said, 'I think I'll take it to school for the teachers to share.'

'Oh, I'm sure they'd be delighted,' Aggie told her, stifling a smirk.

'You'll close the school for a month if you give 'em that,' Emily remarked tongue-in-cheek, and they all burst out laughing again.

The family were soon ready: Grandad looking smart in a new muffler, Danny seeming comfortable enough in his good brown cord trousers and green shirt, Cathleen in her party frock, and Aggie looking years younger in a slim-fitting brown skirt, wide belt and white blouse of her own making. Even Michael, who still complained that his shirt was too big and his trousers were falling down, looked 'a real dandy!' Aggie was pleased with her handiwork.

To greet her husband on his return from the infirmary, Emily had chosen a dark blue, ankle-length skirt with flouncy hem and dainty belted waist. With it she wore a rich blue blouse with boat-neckline and pearl-buttons at the cuff. Her marcasite bracelet completed the ensemble.

'By! Yer look a treat, lass.' Thomas Isaac had always appreciated a pretty girl.

'I've allus liked that blouse on you,' Aggie told her, 'but we've no time to stand here admiring each other. There's a table to set. Come on, our Cathleen. You do that, while me and your mammy make sure we've not missed anything. Grandad can wind up the gramophone, and Danny can sit himself down and rest his legs.'

'I'll do no such thing,' he replied. 'I'll pour us

all a drink – elderberry wine for us and a glass o' sarsaparilla for our Cathleen. We deserve a fortifying drink, before the others start arriving.' And he would not take no for an answer.

An hour later everyone was there and the celebrations were under way with a burst of accordion music from Grandad, and drinks all round. 'Here's to Danny!' Thomas Isaac had got his second wind and was leading the cheers, while Danny blushed and fidgeted until they were over, then he thanked them and sat down.

It was a good party, with enough people to make it a happy one. There was the Ramsden family, the neighbouring farmer with his buxom wife and entire clan, and Danny's father Bob and his new woman-friend Elspeth. Lizzie, seemingly over her bout of illness, had promised to come later, and two of Cathleen's schoolfriends were there with their parents.

'By! Our little farmhouse is bursting at the seams,' Aggie remarked when she and Emily returned to the kitchen for more dessert plates.

'Aye – an' there's four more to come yet.'

Both women turned, to see Michael standing at the door looking sheepish.

'Four more – and who might they be?' Aggie asked, all at sea.

But Emily had already guessed. 'It's John, isn't it?' she asked, her heart beating so unevenly she thought she might faint.

'Well, yes it is, lass. He and his wife Rosie, and their pal Archie are coming, along with Lizzie. I thought he should be here, as he's been such a good friend to me. The lad was coming to see his Aunt Lizzie, and I couldn't miss the chance to ask him over.' Looking from one to the other, he couldn't understand why their mood had suddenly changed. 'It is all right, isn't it? I mean, we know him well enough, don't we?'

Aggie had seen no reason to enlighten him yet about what had taken place between John and Emily. In fact, because it served best, she had deliberately said nothing. Now, she was quick to reassure him. 'Of course it's all right, love. Why shouldn't it be?'

'Tell him, Mam.' Emily had been worried about the truth being kept from her father.

Michael frowned. 'Tell me what?'

So while Emily left the room, Aggie told him most of the story, finishing, 'So now you see how it could be a bit awkward?' Whatever happened, she would never tell the truth of Cathleen's parentage, not even to her own husband. Danny and John would each go on believing that the other was her father.

Michael nodded. 'I suspected there might be a woman somewhere,' he admitted, 'from the way John spoke sometimes. But I never dreamed it was our Emily.'

'It's all right, Dad.' Emily had returned. 'I'm

married to Danny now. He's part of our family and I love him. All that with John – it happened years ago and it's all water under the bridge.' So why did her heart dance at the thought of seeing him again?

Michael had seen the look on her face and was unconvinced.

'It will be *good* to meet up with John again.' Emily put on a bright but shaky smile as she passed him. 'We owe him a lot. Right – I'd best go and make sure Danny's not overdoing it.'

With Emily gone, Michael asked his wife, 'So was it really serious between them? I mean, had it gone as far as them planning to be wed and all that?'

'It were just young love,' Aggie answered lightly.

'I see. But it fizzled out – is that what you're saying? After she met Danny, and had his child, John was left out in the cold?' After his own behaviour, Michael had never felt able to ask his son-in-law why he had waited so long before making an honest woman of their Emily. They were married now, and that was all that mattered. He himself was looking forward to seeing John and young Rosie again. They had been the saving of him.

As she walked about, seeing to the guests and making sure the wine and food kept flowing, Emily was as nervous as a kitten. When John walked through that door, how was she going to feel?

How could she look at him and not show her true emotion?

~

During the course of the afternoon, Aggie managed to take Grandad aside. 'Sit here with me awhile,' she invited. 'You look like I feel – worn out.'

'I am,' he confessed. 'I'm an old dog trying new tricks, and I should have known better.' He had been dancing with the farmer's wife and now he could hardly walk. 'Me back hurts, me arms ache and I need the lavvy.'

'You'd best go down the garden then.' The Ramsdens had an outside water-closet, like everyone else in Salmesbury, and made do with chamber-pots at night. Thomas Isaac had his very own armchair commode – the subject of many jokes, but an absolute godsend.

'Not yet,' he answered in a whisper, his gaze going to the farmer's buxom wife. 'If I so much as move, she'll be on me like a ferret after a bunny rabbit.'

Aggie hid a smile. 'What – you mean she's been making up to you, is that it?'

'Aye, summat like that.' When he saw the red-cheeked buxom wench eyeing him again, he confided from out of the corner of his mouth, 'She med a point o' telling me how the old man doesn't keep her satisfied . . . if yer know what I mean?

What's more, she calls me "Tommy-Izzie" an' it's drivin' me potty.'

Aggie couldn't hide her smile any longer, especially when at that moment she got a dark glare from the woman herself. 'By! She's a big 'un, isn't she? I reckon she'd be too much of a handful for you, Dad,' she said and, made merry from the elderberry wine, they broke into fits of laughter, which had the woman turning away in disgust and everyone else smiling, though they didn't know the reason for it.

'I'd best hobble down t'path now,' the old man tee-heed. 'It wouldn't do to wet me pants in front of all and sundry,' he cast a wary glance at the farmer's wife, 'especially not in front of *her*.' Hoisting himself upright, he leaned on the wall for support. 'She thinks I'm a virile, active fella, so she does.'

'You'd best behave yourself,' Aggie cautioned. 'You're not as young as you were.'

'No, and I'm not so agile neither,' he said, falling against the wall. 'Me old pins don't seem to carry me where I want to go.'

'D'you want me to take you to the lavvy?'

'What!' Horrified at such a prospect, he straightened his shoulders and looked her in the eye. 'I keep tellin' yer, woman, I may be a bit wobbly on me pins, but I'm not a flippin' babby!'

When Aggie looked at the woman and caught her winking at Grandad, she chuckled under her breath. 'I don't know how you've done it, lass,' she muttered, 'but you seem to have tekken years off our Dad. By! I've not seen him so frisky in an age.'

She told him the same the minute he ambled back. 'Whatever you say about her, yon farmer's wife seems to have given you a new lease o' life,' she joshed. 'You're very full of yerself, all of a sudden.'

Making much of it with his groaning and grunting, he sat himself down. 'Aye well, yer know I have good days and bad days. Today seems to be one o' the good 'uns.'

'Sez you!' Slipping off her shoes with a sigh of relief, Aggie gave him a wink. 'I reckon there's life in the old dog yet.'

He actually blushed. 'Gerraway with yer, woman!'

Later, when the joshing was over, they sat talking about this and that. 'Look at our Emily,' he said. 'Do yer think she'll be happy enough with Danny?'

'I hope so.' Since Danny's father had taken up his turn on the accordion, Aggie had seen Emily chatting non-stop with her husband. Worried as she was, it did her heart good to see them together like that.

'Danny's a good husband,' Grandad interrupted her thoughts. 'An' he's a wonderful daddy to the lass.'

'D'you want another drink?' Aggie asked. 'Or will it be safe?'

'Whatever d'yer mean?'

Aggie chuckled. 'I mean, will it send you wild after the farmer's wife?'

He laughed at that. 'Yer a tormenting bugger, so you are. And yes, I'd like a drink. A cuppa tea would go down nicely, lass, thank you.'

Aggie went off to the kitchen.

On her return with two cups of freshly brewed tea, she spoke to Thomas in a serious manner. 'You must never talk about what you overheard,' she said solemnly. 'About what that fiendish devil did to me all them years ago, and then to our Emily – his own niece, God bless her! If it ever got out that Clem Jackson was Cathleen's father, I don't dare think what it would do to the family. Cathleen herself would be so upset!' She rubbed her hands over her eyes as if to shut it out. 'It would be a terrible thing if it ever became common knowledge. Even our Michael doesn't know. I just can't bring meself to tell him. God knows what it would do to him, Dad.' Her eyes were full of tears.

'Don't you worry, lass,' he told her firmly. 'My lips are forever sealed.'

And thankfully, Aggie knew she could trust him above all others.

It was getting late. 'I'm feeling the weight of the day on me shoulders,' he said. 'I'll not be long afore I go to my bed.'

Aggie was tired as well, but she was more than

content to sit there, watching the folks dancing and enjoying the food she and Emily had put out. Now, as Emily smiled at her from beside Danny, she nodded back.

When she turned to look at her father-in-law, she realised he'd been kidnapped by one old dear, who was leading him onto the floor. 'Ah! Look at 'em, bless their old hearts!' she chuckled at the sight. 'Where there's a will there's a way.'

Beginning to feel lonely, she was delighted when Michael came in from the cold and asked her to, 'Give us a twirl on the carpet, lass.' In a minute she had been whisked away, and the two of them were soon dancing to the jolly music of the accordion.

Soon the party got its second breath and was in full swing, though Grandad and his new friend had fallen by the wayside to rest their sore feet and commiserate with each other about how old and feeble they'd become.

Cathleen sat at their knees, eating one cake after another. 'You'll be sick as a pig!' Thomas Isaac warned her.

'No, I won't, Grandad.' Jumping up, she gave him a sticky kiss. 'I've only had three.'

By the dance floor, Danny stood with Emily in his arms, loath to let her go. 'You look so lovely,' he said, and held her even tighter.

Some movement at the door made her turn, and when she saw him there, her heart almost stopped. 'John!' Instinctively, Danny held on to her, as though not to let her loose.

Pausing in the doorway, John's eyes were immediately drawn to hers. There was a poignant moment when their gazes held and there seemed no one in the room but the two of them. They drank in the sight of each other.

Seeing it and fearing that everyone else might sense that same magnetism, Aggie got out of her chair and bade the accordionist to keep on playing. 'Something bright and cheerful, Bob!' she urged, and going to John, she warmly shook his hand. 'Come on in! It's so good to see you, lad,' she said, 'after all these long years. Michael told me he'd invited you. I can't thank you enough for everything you've done. I reckon my Michael owes you his life, and for that we'll never stop being grateful. Come away in, all of you, and welcome to Potts End!'

Drawing his gaze from Emily, who he thought to be even more lovely than he remembered, John thanked her in return. Then, bringing Rosie forward, he introduced her. 'This is Rosie, my wife.'

Rosie gave her a kiss. 'Thank you so much for inviting us, Mrs Ramsden.'

'Nay!' Aggie protested. 'The name is Aggie. You call me that and I'll call you Rosie, if I may.' And so it was settled, and the two women liked each other straight off.

'And this rogue here is Archie!' Propelling the

old chap forward, John explained, 'He was my mate at sea, and he's been my good mate ever since. In fact, I don't know what I'd do without the old rascal.'

'Well now, my dear, I never expected to see such a fine-looking woman, no I never!'

Charming as ever, Archie bent to give her a kiss, and was jokingly chided by Michael, who had just approached. 'Steady on, Archie! Mind how you handle my wife,' he mocked, and the friendship between them all was sealed for ever. Archie gallantly escorted Lizzie to a chair and set about fetching her some of the buffet.

Considering it to be his duty, Danny limped over with Emily to greet the Hanleys. 'Of course I know of you,' he said, 'but I don't recall ever having made the acquaintance.' He shook hands with John and Rosie. 'I'm pleased to meet you.'

'Likewise,' answered John.

Rosie and Emily also shook hands politely, both thinking that the other was attractive, and had a certain aura. When Emily briefly shook hands with John, she was dazzled by his good looks and his confidence as a self-made businessman. He and Rosie made a lovely couple, she realised, and the knowledge stabbed at her.

In spite of their outward politeness, there was a certain wariness between the two men, that had not gone unnoticed by Lizzie, who was quietly watching from her seat by the fireplace, where

Archie was plying her with a glass of elderberry wine.

'Come and have some food.' Aggie broke the mood. 'You must be famished.'

'Thank you, Aggie, yes, I am.' That was Rosie.

'Me too!' Archie chipped in as he rejoined them. 'Me stomach's playing a tune to set all our feet a-tapping,' he joked – with a hearty laugh that had them all smiling.

As they walked away, Rosie saw the possessive way in which Danny was holding Emily, with his arm round her waist and one foot before hers. She knew well enough what had happened here, because John had told Archie everything, and Archie, being the good friend he was, had told her – though John had already let her know enough for her to realise that there was still a measure of love in his heart for Emily.

'Danny!' Rosie called him away. 'I wonder if you wouldn't mind helping me to choose something to eat, and afterwards we might even dance?' She was bold because she knew he was on the verge of breaking up the talk that John and Emily so desperately needed.

Being the gentleman he was, Danny could hardly refuse. 'Will you be all right?' he asked Emily. 'I'll be back soon as I can.'

'You go and keep Rosie company,' she said warmly. 'I need to talk with John . . . if that's all right with you?'

He looked into her face and he saw the love there; love for him – yes, but love for John also, and it was that love which bothered him. Yet he was sensible enough to know that if he took her away now, he might live to regret it for the rest of his life.

'Danny!' Rosie called him again. He looked round and in her eyes he saw a warning. She knows, he thought. She knows how it is between these two, and she's telling me to give them the time they need.

'All right.' He gave Emily a kiss on the lips. 'Talk with John if you must.' He had no choice – he knew that. 'It's all right by me.' Addressing John now, he told him kindly, 'I'm sure there are things to be ironed out.' His meaning was clear enough: *Say your piece and be gone . . . leave Emily to me.* That was what he had in mind, but he didn't say it. How could he?

As he walked away he glanced back to see the couple walking out of the door, and his heart was broken.

'Right then!' Aggie was off in search of her own wandering husband. 'Danny will take care of you,' she said. 'If you need me, I'll be around.' Her first stop was the barn. It was where Michael always went whenever he felt nostalgic, and lately, he was deeply regretting every minute he had spent away from his beloved family.

Aggie understood. There were times when even

she needed to get away on her own, where she might peaceably contemplate past and future.

~

When John led Emily out to the garden, it was all Danny could do not to hobble after them. 'Leave it be,' Rosie warned him kindly. 'I know how you feel, but they knew and loved each other long before we came on the scene. If we interfere now, we'll only drive them away. Anyway, I hear you've only just come out of hospital. Let's have a bite together, and I'll tell you all about me barges.'

For the next half-hour, Danny stayed with Rosie. They ate and drank, and all the while their glances kept going to the door. Though she wouldn't say as much, Rosie felt every bit as apprehensive as Danny. 'I don't know what I'd do if he left me,' she confided when they were seated away from the others. 'John didn't really marry me for love. We were both lonely and working long hours together. We just drifted together.'

Her smile said it all. 'I love him, though. We'd only been married a few weeks when I realised I could never imagine being without him.'

'It's the same with me and Emily,' Danny replied softly. 'She was honest enough with me. She told me she still loved John and was only waiting for him to come back. I've loved her for ever,' he imparted shyly. 'It were me as persuaded her that John wasn't ever coming back. I talked her into marrying me, and o' course there was little Cathleen to be considered. I love that darling little lass.'

'But she's yours, isn't she?'

He smiled. 'She is now!'

At his remark Rosie was made curious, but sensing there was more to it than met the eye, she wisely said nothing.

~

Walking in the twilit orchard, strangely shy and awkward in his company, Emily listened to what John had to say.

'I came back for you that day,' he told her softly. 'I had the money in my pocket and the dream in my heart, and then I saw you with the child, and Danny, and I knew I'd lost you.' He bowed his head. 'It was the worst day of my life.'

Close to tears, Emily slid her hand into his, warmed and content when he curled his strong fingers about hers. 'If only you hadn't gone away,' she told him. 'Things may have been so very different.'

A yearning came into his expression. Suddenly she was in his arms and he was holding her so close she could hardly breathe. *'She should have been my child . . . not Danny's!'*

For a while, Emily made no reply. She was

relieved for him to believe the child was Danny's. Now though, she felt his fleeting rage and it was a frightening thing. As she felt his grip loosen she looked up to see him gazing down on her, his eyes dark with emotion. 'I never stopped loving you,' he told her fiercely. 'There were times when I thought I'd go crazy without you.'

Bending his head he cupped her face and for a long, wonderful moment he just looked on her; seeing those familiar features and gazing into those wonderful eyes, feeling that he was home at long last.

Emily saw he wanted to kiss her and she raised herself to him. Locking her arms round his neck, she softly pressed her lips to his, thrilled when he drew her closer.

It was a passionate, hungry kiss – the kind of kiss that neither of them would ever forget, and yet there was something else. Some other emotion that neither of them had ever experienced before.

Peering out of the window with trepidation, Danny and Rosie saw it happen and they were afraid. When Danny stepped forward to end it, Rosie pulled him back. 'No!' she whispered, and held onto him.

He stayed, gaining strength and comfort from her, some deep instinct telling him she was right and he was wrong. 'Let's leave them, Danny.' Older and wiser than her years, Rosie ushered him back to the kitchen, where she got him a hot drink and sat chatting quietly with him.

～

Taking her by the hand, John led Emily to the bench, where they sat for a long time, she curled into him, and he with his arm round her, holding her close, as he had yearned to do all these years. 'Are you happy, sweetheart, with Danny?'

Emily took a moment to think about it. 'I believe so.' She didn't look up, nor did she move. There was that special closeness between them that allowed her to stay in his arms the way they were. 'And what about you, John?' she murmured. 'Are you happy with Rosie?'

He smiled. 'She's kind of grown on me, I suppose.'

Emily smiled at that. 'They've been watching us from inside.'

'I know.'

'They're both good people.'

'I know that, too.'

She drew away. In the quietness of evening with the skies above and the stars twinkling down on them, it was as though they were the only two souls in the whole world. 'John?'

He looked at her then, his eyes roving her face and thinking how deeply he loved her. 'Yes, sweetheart?'

'I'll always love you.' A single tear ran down her cheek.

'I know that.' He wiped it away. 'And I'll always love *you.*'

They kissed again, only this time it was more gentle, more of a binding, lasting thing. 'Are you ready to go back now?' he asked gently.

She nodded, but didn't speak. Her heart was too full.

They walked back arm-in-arm, easy and content in each other's company. This was the night they would carry with them for all time. This night, this love, and the knowledge that the love would always be there, drawing them together, yet keeping them apart. It was how it should be.

As they approached the farmhouse door, Danny was there, with Rosie by his side. They saw Emily and John, and for a moment were afraid again. But then they saw the easy smiles, and realised how it was; and the joy in their hearts was almost too much to bear.

When Emily came towards him, Danny clasped her close. 'I thought I'd lost you,' he said brokenly. 'Oh Emily, I wouldn't want to live without you.'

Rosie said nothing. She just walked to John and, looking at him with tears glittering in her eyes, she smiled knowingly.

'It's all right,' he murmured. Then he slid his arm round her shoulders, and took her inside.

As Emily and Danny came up the path, Aggie

was rushing out of the door. 'Have you seen Lizzie?' She seemed frantic. 'She's not been seen for a while, and we can't find her anywhere!'

A search got under way. The entire party went out into the farm, hunting in every nook and cranny; even Grandad hobbled about, pausing every now and then to hold on to something or to sit down while he got his breath back. *'Lizzie!'* His voice sailed on the night air. 'Where the devil are you, woman?'

It was Bob who found her, sprawled out in the orchard. She seemed lifeless. 'She's 'ere! For God's sake, hurry!'

Once they got her inside, it was Aggie who discovered what the problem was. 'She's drunk!'

'Never.' Leaning down, Archie took a sniff of her breath. 'Well, the old bugger,' he laughed. 'She smells like a brewery!' Everyone laughed at that, until Emily reminded them, 'She's been lying out there half-unconscious and she feels cold. We'd best get a doctor all the same.'

At which point Lizzie opened her eyes. 'Don't want no doctor! Why does everybody allus want me to see a ruddy doctor? I'd be better off wi' another measure o' that elderberry wine.'

When the laughter was over and everyone had drifted away, Grandad leaned down to give her a telling-off. 'How much 'ave yer drunk, you devious little bugger? And what the devil were you doing out there?'

Reaching up, she took hold of his coat collar and drew him down. 'It's all right,' she hissed. 'I saw them together, and it's all right.'

He realised what she was saying, and his old heart was thrilled. 'Oh Lizzie,' he kept his voice low, 'is that what you were doing – so worried that you were knocking back the good stuff? An' then yer follered 'em outside to see how it might all turn out?'

She nodded, but then groaned suddenly. 'I don't feel well now.'

Thomas Isaac laughed. 'What am I gonna do with yer, eh?' he said out loud, and people's heads turned to listen. They were highly entertained when he answered his own question. 'I shall 'ave to marry yer, I can see that.'

Smiling, Lizzie nodded again, and everyone cheered. 'Go to it, Grandad!' somebody called out.

When he gave Lizzie a kiss, they clapped until the little farmhouse shook.

~

Two weeks later, Grandad and Lizzie were wed. 'We're too old and decrepit to have a long court-ship,' Grandad joshed, and hugging him tight, Lizzie agreed. She had always got on well with Tom and his wife, Clare, and she knew he was a good man.

At their own request, there was just the family

present: Michael and Aggie, Emily and Danny, and little Cathleen – the intelligent and loving child who had sprung like a miracle from a brutal and incestuous rape. The name of Clem Jackson was never spoken. His remains had been interred in a churchyard on the far side of Blackburn, and the very air in Potts End Farm seemed the purer for his absence.

Lizzie's beloved nephew John was there too, of course, back down from Liverpool with his wife.

Rosie had been feeling proper peaky ever since the night of Danny's welcome-home party. It was worse in the early mornings, and she'd gone right off the taste of tea . . . She hadn't told John yet, but in her heart she knew their first bairn was growing inside her and in her wisdom, she also knew that it was the completion he needed.

Archie and Harriet were there too, both considered members of the extended family. Many unsubtle jokes were made about marriage, and when John saw Harriet looking coy, he slapped Archie on the back and sprinkled bridal rice on his old shipmate's shrivelled pate.

The ceremony took place in the same church where Danny had married Emily. It was a quick service, given with a blessing, and afterwards a little tea in the local inn, at Grandad's expense. 'It's not every day I tek a bride,' he announced. 'Besides, I've allus 'ad a bit put by for a rainy day.'

'You'd best save a bit more if you're coming to live at my cottage,' Lizzie quipped. 'I need new curtains, and the sofa's started sagging in the middle, and –'

'Stop right there!' Grandad told her, and when she went quiet, he put his arm round her. 'You can 'ave yer curtains,' he said, 'but the sofa can wait, 'cause I mean to tek you away.' Brandishing two tickets, he told her proudly, 'We're off to Blackpool for a couple o' nights. I've booked us into a little guest-house on the front. The journey'll probably kill me, with me arthritis an' all, but what a lovely way to go.' He laughed naughtily and ducked when Lizzie turned to swipe him.

~

Several months after the wedding, Michael and Aggie received news that ownership of the farm had been rightfully restored to them. Once the paperwork was safely completed, Michael told Danny and Emily that he and Aggie had drawn up plans to build a cottage for them in the orchard. 'We know how much you love this place, and we want you to have your own home, near us,' Aggie said.

'Oh, Dad! That's wonderful!' Emily cried with joy. She and Danny and Cathleen immediately went outside to look at 'their spot'. While the child danced on ahead, Emily went more slowly, leaning on her husband who was now her support, as she was seven months pregnant.

The orchard had always held some special magic for her.

~

When a year later the cottage was ready, Emily and Danny moved in with Cathleen and their ten-month-old son, George Isaac – 'Georgie'. 'A little brother for you,' Emily had told Cathleen after the baby's birth upstairs at Potts End. Her daughter held the child in her arms. 'He's lovely, Mammy,' she said.

And so are you, Emily thought.

Now, as she looked out of the window of Orchard Cottage, Georgie on her shoulder having his back gently rubbed, in her mind's eye she could see herself and John, young and carefree, running across the fields and swimming in the brook. She could see the place where they had shared their very first kiss, and the place in the orchard where, on the night of their reunion, they had shared their very last one.

At that moment, down in the meadow, where the lambs chased each other, watched by a curious hare, the sun caught on a gold locket that had lain hidden in a path of flowering clover through many seasons, and for a second, the glow was dazzling. And then the sun's rays encompassed the whole field, and the farm – and the entire vale.

And up in the cottage bedroom, a baby cried, and the woman dreaming at the window turned to comfort him.

She would never forget her first love. They had been two young people setting out on life's journey. Two lovers who had shared a dream and lost it, but in the losing had found something else. The love that had grown between them was still there, but it was a different love now. It was a strong, binding love that would go on for as long as they lived.

The love of friendship.

Λ precious thing, after all.

If you have enjoyed *Lovers and Liars*,
read on for an exclusive extract from
Josephine Cox's new novel

Live the Dream

OUT NOW

PART ONE

~

February 1932

The Way It Was

CHAPTER ONE

For a long, regretful moment he stood observing, his tall, strong figure merging into the shadows, his heart aching, and his dark gaze intent on the house. It was such a beautiful house, he thought . . . so warm and inviting. *Like she used to be.*

His thoughts shifted to the woman inside. She was still beautiful, and sometimes, when she was afraid, her warm hand would slip into his. But that was all. There was rarely any passion in her gesture. Seldom a smile or welcome in her eyes.

She neither loved nor wanted him. But it wasn't her fault – he knew that. He still loved her, but he didn't know her any more, not in the way he used to.

He felt such deep regret, and yet, in a strange way, he was also relieved, as though he no longer needed to prove anything. There was no need. *There was no one to care.*

He had loved this house since that first day,

seven years ago, when he had carried his wife through the wide, oaken doors and swung her round while she held on to him, laughing and happy, her beautiful face glowing with love for him and, oh, how he had adored her in return. Now all he had left were the memories.

His heart ached for things to be how they once were. But however much he wished it, there could be no going back.

With a deep sigh he made his way across the delightful garden, with its pretty, meandering paths and multitude of shrubs and trees. It was early February now, and here and there the buds were already forming. In another month or so, they would open and the garden would be filled with colour. Walking through it, you could imagine yourself to be in paradise.

Sometimes, when the symptoms of her illness became too much for him, he would come out here, and walk and think until his spirit was refreshed. Then he would go back inside, ready to deal with whatever came his way.

Today was Tuesday, and Tuesdays were very special. For a time he was free to follow his heart, to do what he wanted, to be whoever he wanted to be. Tuesday was *his* day. *His sanctuary.*

He quickened his steps towards the outbuilding. Here, he took out a bunch of keys, unlocked the door and let himself in. He threw back the makeshift curtain at the window, and a shaft of sunlight fell on the cloth-covered easel at the back of the room.

Sliding away the cloth, he revealed the painting of a beautiful, slender woman with chestnut-coloured hair flowing to her waist, and dark, sultry eyes. For a while he stood there, thoughtfully observing the face, with its exquisite features and soft, smiling mouth. Reaching out, he traced the tip of his finger around her inviting, sensuous mouth. A great sadness took hold of him.

'I'm so sorry,' he murmured. 'If I could only change things, you know I would.'

A moment longer, then he covered the painting and strode to a large wooden chest; opened the lid. From where it was hidden beneath layers of paint-trays and brushes, he took out a heavy iron key. It was his passport to another world.

He slid the key into his jacket pocket and left, securing the door behind him. Then he quickly made his way through the gardens and out of the side gate.

~

From the bedroom window she watched him leave ... that same woman he had painted so lovingly and whose portrait was hidden in the outhouse. She saw him carefully close the gate; she heard the familiar turning over of the engine, and in her mind's eye she imagined him driving the long black saloon he had bought only a few months ago. She knew the smart new car was in part a compensation. He'd bought it after everything had changed. She heard the engine swell as it was driven away, and through the beech trees that lined the road she caught a fleeting glimpse of the car as it went from the house.

Even when she could no longer hear the engine, she remained, thinking and wishing, until, startling her, a voice from the door called her name.

'Sylvia! I've been looking for you everywhere.'

With a smile, she turned from the window. 'It's such a lovely day, don't you think, Edna?' But the smile was forced, because now he was gone and already she was lonely.

She often felt alone now – detached from her husband, from Edna, and from her sister. No one came to visit. Too scared of her moods. She couldn't help the violent eruption of temper – it was as if she became another person. The medication helped suppress the anger, of course, but it also made her feel sleepy and stupid, as if looking at life from within a glass box, unable to join in, and not really wanting to. Sometimes the anger was better than the semi-death of the drugs, and so on occasion she would hide the medicine and only pretend to take it. It was better to be alive, wasn't it – even living this life? On the really bad days, though, she wondered if this were true.

Though his thoughts remained with her, the further he got from the house, the more he felt as though a great weight were being lifted from his shoulders. The frowns eased and his face softened; his dark eyes began to twinkle and his whole body relaxed into the seat. It was Tuesday, he was heading away, and a sense of freedom flooded his soul.

Today he would drive out to the coast, twenty-odd miles away. He liked the open sea and sky after the neat residential street in Blackburn, and the noise and sootiness of the factory on other weekdays. Then he would turn inland, to enjoy the special pleasures and freedom of his precious day off.

A flock of seagulls swept up from the beach. Drawing on the handbrake, he climbed out of the car and watched the birds as they flew away. 'Free as a bird' – they made the perfect symbol for a Tuesday. When they were mere specks in the far-away sky he momentarily closed his eyes, wishing he was up there with them.

His gaze flowed across the beach to the horizon. The sea was unusually quiet.

In the far distance, on the beach, tall and easy, a woman strolled with her two Labradors, one running ahead, the other trailing behind. She was a regular walker here. He had seen her many times before.

His gaze travelled: to his left the man at the tea

stall was already opening up, and beyond him the flower shop was ablaze with spring flowers. Life goes on, he thought. *If only they knew.*

Getting back into his car he reminded himself that it was Tuesday. Put the dark thoughts out of your mind, he thought. He'd best get going, or the day would be gone before he knew it.

At the end of the seafront road, he headed inland towards the fells and the Ribble Valley, every familiar curve and landmark a comfort to him.

The lanes became narrower and more meandering, until at length they disappeared altogether and he was bumping along a mere track that carried him deeper and deeper into the woods, beyond civilisation . . . beyond the burden of his duty and responsibility.

~

Almost a full hour after leaving the house, he arrived at his destination, where thick woodland hid him from the world and high trees almost blocked the skies above.

The winding, babbling stream glittered in the morning light, and look there! Excited, he inched forward to see two small deer drinking at the water's edge. This was what he needed. Through the week when he was driven by work and duties, *this* was the magic his soul craved.

He made his way towards the little log cabin,

built by his own hand over two long, wonderful years. Afterwards, when it was finished he would sit on the covered veranda for many an hour, lazing and thinking, and though his troubles were heavy, he always found time to thank the Lord for his many blessings. The land had been owned by his family for generations, and he had spent happy childhood summer holidays riding, fishing and picnicking here, when visiting his grandparents nearby.

Taking the key from his pocket he slid it into the keyhole and opened the door. As always, when he came back after a week away, the clammy, damp air instantly wrapped itself around him. Impatiently he threw back the wooden shutters and opened the windows to let the fresh air in. When that was done, he took a box of matches from his pocket and set light to the carefully laid pyramid of paper and wood in the grate.

Soon, the fire was cheerily blazing, airing and warming the whole cabin.

He felt a sense of pride in his achievement. The place was strong, built to last, with a tiny bedroom, makeshift bathroom, and a large centre area providing a sitting room and kitchen. Serviceable and attractive, the cabin was ideal for his own modest needs.

The furniture itself had been hewn from the trees outside, before being lovingly shaped by his own hand, to provide all that was needed: a small, square table and two chairs; a strong, deep chest of drawers; a long settle against the fireplace, where he would sit of an evening and dream of a life he would never have.

Then there was the bed. Square and sturdy enough to take a man's weight, it was a handsome thing. Covered in wine-coloured eiderdown, it was roomy enough for two. After all, he could dream . . .

Beside the bed stood a narrow wardrobe, not spacious by any standards, but enough to hold his most cherished possessions.

The bath and washbasin used water that was carried in a bucket from the stream, and there was an earth closet in a separate little shack.

If he got hungry there was always a supply of tinned food in the larder, and titbits to be gathered in the woods, depending on the time of year. Running wild in those idyllic childhood holidays had been excellent training for cabin life.

Having placed the guard before the now crackling fire, he went to the wardrobe. He took out the canvas and easel and carried them to the corner of the room. He did not uncover the painting. Instead he held it for a moment, his thoughts going to a cozy little café in the centre of Blackburn. That was another part of his secret life. Then he set the frame on the easel.

From the chest he took out a pile of clothes and draped them over the wire cage of the fire guard to warm and air, while he stripped off his suit, shirt and tie.

When he was dressed again the businessman was gone and in his place was an ordinary workman, dressed casually in brown cords, green check shirt and heavy black boots. The uniform of duty was discarded, and he was now a man at ease with himself.

Now was the moment he'd anticipated with pleasure since his last visit. With great care he slipped the cover from the painting.

When it was laid bare he gazed at it for a long, wondrous moment, his dark, smiling eyes roving its every feature.

Smiling back at him, the young woman with the tumble of hazel hair seemed almost alive. Her laughing eyes, blue as the darkest sapphire, were painted in such a way as to be looking at him wherever he went in the room. Her pretty, slightly parted lips seemed so real he felt she would suddenly talk to him. But she never did, except in his dreams. She probably never would.

Yet he knew her well, that small, vibrant woman who had invaded his thoughts. A special part of his Tuesday life, she hardly knew of his existence.

Returning to the wardrobe he collected his paints and brushes. A few moments later he was stroking the tip of the brush over the curling ends of her brown hair, 'You don't know me,' he murmured fondly, 'but I feel I know you. I've seen how you light up a room when you walk into it . . .' Images of her came into his mind – going about her own Tuesday life, laughing with her friend – making him smile. 'And I know you have a wonderful sense of humour.'

Changing his brush, he worked on her cheekbones. 'You can't imagine how much I've been looking forward to seeing you.'

He paused, his thoughts going back to the house and the woman who waited there. 'Maybe it's just as well you don't even notice me,' he sighed. 'You see, Amy . . . a man might dream and hope, but dreams are not real, and life can drag you down. I do my best, but I'm hopelessly trapped. If only I can find a way to change how things are.'

~

That night as he sat on his veranda watching the stars twinkle and dance, a great loneliness in his heart, he had no way of knowing how Amy was watching those same stars, and that in her heart were the same impossible dreams, and sense of awful loneliness.

Leaning on the windowsill, arms folded, her gaze raised to the skies, she wondered where Don was, and whether he ever thought of her. She did not wonder whether he might come back, because his parting words had been that she would never see him again. And although for many months after he'd gone, she had prayed he might change his mind and come back, he never had. Now the pain had settled to a sense of loss or disappointment about her broken heart with the acceptance that what he had said was true. Unlike when he had asked her to marry him. There had followed weeks of planning and excitement when the date was set and the church booked. The bridesmaids were chosen, the bridal gown ordered and even the honeymoon arranged, before he confessed to her that he had never really wanted family or responsibilities.

Sometimes she wondered if that had been a kind excuse – a way of letting her down gently. He had been so handsome and such fun. Maybe she hadn't been good enough for him . . .

Amy had been devastated when he left, and even now the love she had felt for him still lingered.

Pressing her nose to the window she recalled the happy times they had shared.

'I don't hate you, Don,' she murmured. 'I could never hate you.'

She remembered his smile and the way he would hold her in his arms, and her heart was heavy. But she no longer fooled herself. It was over.

'Goodnight, Amy.' That was her mammy on the landing.

'Goodnight, Mam.'

'Don't forget we've an early start in the morning.'

'I won't.'

The sound of passing footsteps, then the closing of a door, and the house was quiet again.

Leaving the curtains open so she could see the stars, Amy went softly across the room and slid into bed.

She closed her eyes, shut out the memories and sank into a deep sleep in which her dreams were wistful rather than sorrowful.

THE JOSEPHINE COX NEWSLETTER

If you would like to know more about Josephine Cox, and receive regular updates about her novels, just send a postcard with your name and address to the address below to receive a brand new newsletter. The newsletter is also packed with competitions and exclusive Josephine Cox gifts, plus news and views from other fans.

Chatterbox
Freepost
PAM 6429
HarperCollins Publishers
77–85 Fulham Palace Road
Hammersmith
London
W6 8BR

LOVERS AND LIARS

Josephine Cox was born in Blackburn, one of ten children. At the age of sixteen, Josephine met and married her husband Ken, and had two sons. When the boys started school, she decided to go to college and eventually gained a place at Cambridge University. She was unable to take this up as it would have meant living away from home, but she went into teaching – and started to write her first full-length novel. She won the 'Superwoman of Great Britain' Award, for which her family had secretly entered her, at the same time as her novel was accepted for publication.

Josephine says, 'I love writing, both recreating scenes and characters from my past, together with new storylines which mingle naturally with the old. I could never imagine a single day without writing, and it's been that way since as far back as I can remember.'

For information about the Josephine Cox news-letter, please see page 501.

Also by Josephine Cox